Tara Pammi can' ... wasn't lost in a bo ... was much more e: ... at school. Years later, ... imagination and love for the written wor... revealed what she really wanted to do. Now she pairs alpha males who think they know everything with strong women who knock that theory *and* them off their feet!

Jackie Ashenden writes dark, emotional stories, with alpha heroes who've just got the world to their liking only to have it blown wide apart by their kick-ass heroines. She lives in Auckland, New Zealand, with her husband, the inimitable Dr Jax, two kids and two rats. When she's not torturing alpha males and their gutsy heroines she can be found drinking chocolate martinis, reading anything she can lay her hands on, wasting time on social media or being forced to go mountain biking with her husband. To keep up to date with Jackie's new releases and other news sign up to her newsletter at jackieashenden.com.

RETURNING FOR HIS UNKNOWN SON

TARA PAMMI

PREGNANT BY THE WRONG PRINCE

JACKIE ASHENDEN

MILLS & BOON

First Published in Great Britain 2021
by Mills & Boon, an imprint of HarperCollins*Publishers* Ltd,
1 London Bridge Street, London, SE1 9GF

www.harpercollins.co.uk

HarperCollins*Publishers*
1st Floor, Watermarque Building,
Ringsend Road, Dublin 4, Ireland

Returning for His Unknown Son © 2021 Tara Pammi

Pregnant by the Wrong Prince © 2021 Jackie Ashenden

ISBN: 978-0-263-28276-4

12/21

MIX
Paper from
responsible sources
FSC™ C007454

RETURNING FOR HIS UNKNOWN SON

TARA PAMMI

MILLS & BOON

CHAPTER ONE

"I THINK WE should get married."

Priya Pillai looked up from her desk to find Christian Mikkelsen, genius tech whiz, general mayhem-maker and absolute playboy, leaning against her desk and considering her with an intensity that she couldn't ignore. Her heart kicked in her chest at the ridiculous proposal he'd just thrown at her, as casually as he'd asked her yesterday if she'd accompany him to a conference in Switzerland. His blue eyes, usually alight with mischief, glinted with resolve.

Christian, other than being her boss and the CEO of Modi Mikkelsen Tech, was her dead fiancé's best friend and the man she'd come to count on the most in the last few months. Despite the fact that they'd never been close before Jai had died a year ago.

With his long legs stretched out in front of him, broad shoulders filling her vision, his physicality was becoming harder and harder to ignore, without counting the fact that he possessed a charming playfulness that was distracting at the best of times. He had the usual piece of wood and tiny chisel in his hand. His gaze flipped to her face and to the block of wood, back and forth, as he carved her face.

At first, she'd found it disconcerting to find his intent gaze on her. Jai had once mentioned that it helped Christian focus a lot of his unending energy with his hands occupied like that. Christian was a genius when it came to numbers and code, seeing patterns where no one else could. But it wasn't until Priya had seen the miniature he'd carved of Jai's face, the depth of character he captured, that she'd realized how much more there was to Christian.

How much more beyond the good looks, easy charm and razor-sharp mind.

Shaking her head, Priya shifted her focus back to her computer screen. She was so close to figuring out the bit of algorithm that had been blocking her for days. Taking a sip of her coffee, she hit Compile. Only then did she turn her attention back to him. "It's too early in the morning for your jokes, Christian," she said, keeping her tone casual. Warning herself to not betray her increasing fascination with…every nuance of his face, his gestures and the barely contained energetic vibe he gave out.

But she couldn't help noting that while he looked immaculate in a crisp gray suit with a blue tie that she'd bought him two Christmases ago, he hadn't shaved this morning. Dark blond bristle covered his jaw, and dark smudges brought out the blue of his eyes.

Whose bed have you rolled out of this morning? she wanted to ask. *The supermodel Stella or the soccer player Ellen?*

Really, if she thought about it—which she did far too much—Christian was at least an equal-opportunity playboy. He didn't seem to have a particular type—or rather any woman who interested him was his type—and he…

"Why are you looking at me like that?" he prompted, running a hand over his jaw. His brows drew together, forming that line between them that she wanted to trace with her finger, that she sometimes wanted to touch with…

She stifled a groan and looked away.

What the hell was wrong with her? Where were all these useless and inappropriate thoughts coming from? When had she started collating a database of Christian's likes and dislikes in a woman?

She'd thought she was solving the problem of an overly protective parent, at times stifling the breath out of her. Mama had always been a lioness because of Priya's poor health. Her heart condition, the numerous trips in and out of the ER as a child and adolescent…had made sure her mother was always in hyperdrive.

But with the period of depression that had followed Jai's death, she'd caged Priya, treating her like a precious vase rather than a living, breathing person.

Only Christian had recognized her grief. Only he had given her the space to mourn, instead of needing her to be okay for his own peace of mind. And when it had been time, he was the one who had dragged her, screaming and kicking, back to join the living.

She'd come to work for Modi & Mikkelsen Technologies as a solutions architect—something she'd planned to do after graduating when Jai had been alive. She'd moved out of her parents' house and into Christian's apartment with minimal fuss from Mama, because, of course, Christian's reassurances held more weight than Priya's own. She'd even gone to a couple of parties with Christian and his friends and, for the most part, enjoyed herself.

But this… This was a trap she hadn't ever imagined she'd fall into.

Not for a second had she foreseen that sharing a space with him would lead to the kind of intimacy she both craved and was terrified of. Or that she'd have front-row seats to Christian's love life. And no, she wasn't jealous.

To be jealous of his girlfriends meant she wanted Christian's attention in the first place—as fickle as it was. She *didn't.* Seeing him live his life with a revolving door of girlfriends only reminded her of what she'd lost when she'd lost Jai. This was loneliness, nothing else.

"It proves you aren't dead inside," her cousin had said when Priya had confided this sudden, inexplicable fascination with Christian. *"You're twenty-two and horny, that's all. Christian's a seriously hot guy. Your reaction is nothing but normal."*

"Go away, Christian," she said, rubbing a hand over her face. "Unlike you, I have a boss to answer to."

"Oh, didn't you hear? Grandpa and the board are looking for reasons to kick me out."

"What? That's preposterous. You and Jai breathed new life into this company."

He shrugged. "Apparently, I'm bringing a lot of bad publicity to their door, what with all my many and varied affairs. Really, it's just that old dog Chatsworth with a stick up his ass. He doesn't like the fact that I dumped his daughter."

He looked down to find Priya glaring at him. Eyes warm, he assumed this angelic air that made her grin, despite the state of near constant alertness she needed to adopt whenever she was with him. He'd always been good at making her laugh, despite her determination to keep him at a distance. To dislike him even, in those first two years after Jai had introduced them.

"Oh, come on, Pree, is it my fault if the woman thinks I'd have proposed to her after only a month of dating? While I agree that Samantha's both beautiful and brainy, did she forget my reputation? And for the record, she was the one who pursued me."

"Imagine that," Priya added dryly, but her mind was churning away.

While she'd isolated herself for months after Jai's accident, Christian, on the other hand, had hit the party circuit hard. Which was saying something since the man was already an inveterate playboy. It was as if without Jai's solid, unflappable presence to ground him, Christian became wilder and wilder. No wonder Mr. Mikkelsen had threatened to eject him from the company.

Because the one thing Christian did hold dear was MMT. The tech company that Jai and he'd built through high school and college. That had become the backbone of Mikkelsen Technologies in the last decade.

"While I agree with you that Ms. Chatsworth can do a lot better," Priya said, grinning, "it's possible she saw something worth loving even in you, Christian. Greater miracles have been known to happen."

"Now you're just kicking me when I'm down," he said, mock hurt in his voice. But the warmth in his blue eyes made her feel as if she'd won a prize. "The thing is I've got to beat the old man at his own game. And you're the only one who can save me, Pree."

This time, Priya didn't have to fake her disbelief. "Save you, Christian? I'm far too much of a realist for that."

"So you do agree that I need saving?"

There was something in his question that felt off to Priya. That held a depth, a hunger she didn't want to delve into.

She could feel his gaze sweeping over her face, as if he was waiting to see if she'd take the bait.

Ducking her gaze, she made a show of tidying her desk, searching for something to bring their conversation back to neutral ground. "If you want the truth, you've been a bit out of control recently. I can't blame Ben for trying to bring some—" she cleared her throat when he raised that devilish brow "—balance back into your life." And because she should have said it long before now, she added,

"I don't know what I'd have done without your support over the past year, Christian."

"You'd have survived."

"You have more faith in me than I do," she added. On an impulse, she took his hand. His fingers had a deliciously abrasive texture, thanks to how incessantly he played with pieces of wood and his chisel. Sensation coiled deep in her belly, a cavern yawning wide open for more. She let go immediately. "I'm sorry for not being a better friend to you. For not realizing sooner that you lost Jai, too."

He pushed a hand through his hair, not meeting her eyes.

She cleared her throat, wondering if she'd made him uncomfortable. No, grief wasn't something Christian shoved away. Then why? "You look a wreck, Christian. Ben has a good reason to worry about you."

"I'm not one of his precious horses for him to corral and be quietly led back into my stall."

"And if Jai were here to say you're spiraling out of control, Christian?"

He pressed the heels of his palms to his eyes and let out a breath. "I'm not interested in settling down, Pree. Not for anyone. Damn it, I'm only twenty-four years old." Those penetrating eyes pinned her. "But I wasn't joking when I suggested we get married. It solves more than one problem."

As if the very universe was helping him support his case, her cell phone chirped. Priya looked at the screen to find Mama's anxious face peering up at her. Priya slammed it facedown. It continued to chirp, the sound progressively getting on her nerves, until she thought she might scream.

It finally stopped. They both stared at the company phone on the desk. Right on cue, it started ringing.

Priya pushed her fingers through her hair, swallowing a growl of frustration.

"Don't tell me you aren't a little bit flattered to realize you're the first woman I've ever proposed to," Christian teased, putting himself between her desk and her.

And his distraction worked.

Her hand on her heart, Priya fluttered her lashes. And threw in a mock gasp for effect. "Oh, my! How cynical of me to not realize what an honor this is. The first woman that the unconquerable Christian Mikkelsen proposed marriage to. Maybe I'll get a sash which says that and wear it every day."

"It would certainly be an improvement," he said, his gaze doing a quick sweep of her beige pantsuit.

She craned her head toward him and lowered her voice into a theatrical whisper. "Your proposal needs a little work, Christian. Keep trying and the twentieth woman might just accept."

He pushed off from his position, making her solid wood desk shake.

The framed picture of Jai she had on a tiny wooden shelf shifted and fell forward. Priya reached for it and her fingers clashed with Christian's. The frame balanced there, in both their palms. Her heart ached, but she was used to that hole. What Priya wasn't expecting was how the glide of Christian's fingers on her wrist sent a spark of sensation down her spine.

She pulled away, her skin jumping at the contact. Her heart began thudding urgently. He'd straightened up but he was still there, close enough to touch. The scent of him filled her nostrils and the warmth of his body beckoned. Her skin tingled with an awareness that Priya couldn't ignore. She swallowed, wondering if she was slowly losing her mind.

"I'm serious, Priya."

His matter-of-fact tone sent relief crashing through her. Thank God he hadn't noticed her ridiculous reaction to him. Thank God that he was just as unaware of her as he'd always been. For years, she'd been his best friend's shy, geeky girlfriend and then fiancée.

This attraction was unwelcome. He was her fiancé's best friend—granted, the fiancé who'd been dead now for close to a year. When Jai had been alive, she'd always got the feeling that Christian thought of her as an annoying sister or cousin he had to put up with, for his best friend's sake.

But now Christian was her...*friend.*

Surprise hit her in the gut. Somehow, over the last few months, Christian had become a bigger and bigger presence in her life. From dragging her back to work, from feeding her mother lie after lie that she was too busy working, thereby saving her from Mama's stifling concern, to letting her stay at his penthouse apartment, challenging her mind by throwing unbelievably innovative problems at her... He'd been gradually guiding her out of her grief-stricken shell.

Beneath the arrogance and the ruthless charm he used so skillfully, Christian hid a heart of gold.

Maybe it wasn't that strange that their grief over Jai's loss had brought them closer together. After all, they'd both loved him, adored him. But this attraction for Christian that she'd begun to feel recently, this was *not* okay. If he got even a whiff of it, he was going to tease her endlessly—mock her like there was no tomorrow. Just the thought of it made her face burn.

"Come back to me, Starling. You're off in some other land again," Christian said, his voice unusually grave.

Priya bristled. "Stop calling me that," she said automatically. Just as he'd intended.

It was a game between them since the first time they'd met. The bird was native to the Pacific Northwest area. A small, frail thing that had a beauty of its own. The nickname had always grated on her—maybe because it suited her.

"Fine, I'll call you a crow, then," he countered, as he always did.

Her mouth tilting up at the edges, she met his gaze. Those sensuous lips stretched into a wide smile—a real one that touched his eyes. Turning him from a simply good-looking man into a strikingly gorgeous one. Something arched across the distance between them—something far too real, something full of an ache and longing. Chest tight, Priya looked away before he could realize all of that came from her.

Which meant it was time to answer him seriously. "I don't want to overcomplicate things, Christian."

"It won't." He sighed. "I'm sick and tired of the board using any and all means to control me. You know it was a problem even when Jai was here. For every new direction we wanted to take the company in, they came up with a million excuses. And you…"

"What about me?" Priya said, tilting her chin up. An expression in his eyes made her spine snap with steel. She could stand his mockery, his teasing, but not his pity. "You don't have to fight my battles, Christian. At least, not anymore."

"What if I just stand like a shield in front of you to give you breathing space?"

Something about the angle of his head when he said it

twisted her gut. Priya shot to her feet, frustration leeching away any calm she'd felt this morning. "Mama came to see you again?"

"Your parents came to see Ben. She—" Christian cleared his throat "—waylaid me on my way to work. She said they're canceling their trip to India, that she doesn't feel comfortable leaving you here by yourself. Your dad couldn't get in a single word."

Priya banged the table with her fist. "They've planned this reunion for the last decade. Her entire family's coming—her sister from the UK and her aunt from Australia… Damn it. How do I get it into her head that I'm fine? That I don't need a keeper?"

"You marry me," Christian said, swooping into the space. Blocking her agitated steps. "Look at me, Pree."

When she didn't, he tilted her chin up. She had no idea what he saw in her face, but it made him take a step back. He rubbed a finger on his temple. "You trust me, don't you?"

The thread of barely there hurt in his voice arrested all other concerns.

No, that wasn't possible. Of all the upside-down things in her world, there was no way Christian could be hurt by her opinion of him. And yet, the longer she remained quiet, the more something deepened in his eyes. "Of course I trust you." Then she laughed into the building silence because there was no way she could let him realize it was herself she didn't trust. "I'm not the one with a billion-dollar empire tied to his brain and his name."

He regarded her thoughtfully, that frown still in place.

"I see the logic in your plan," Priya added, shoving aside her own confusion. "I'm just…"

"What is it, Priya?"

She rubbed a hand over her belly, recognizing the knot

of fear there. "Okay, fine. We can do this...convenient-marriage thing. I'll sign whatever prenup you want me to."

"Please don't insult me and our relationship by using that as a shield. You and I both know I'd trust you with every single dollar to my name."

She nodded, knowing it was unfair. To them both. "At the end of it, I..." She looked into his eyes, and it felt like she was diving deep into something both terrifying and exhilarating, but she couldn't stop. "I don't want to lose you, Christian. As a friend, I mean. I couldn't bear it if we...messed this up."

He didn't laugh it off like she thought he would. Or mock her. Or tease her. Or tell her that she was needlessly worrying about a nonexistent issue. That there was nothing to blur the lines in their relationship.

He simply gathered her to him—like he'd done in the hospital when she'd fallen apart after Jai had died.

Priya buried her face in his neck and breathed in the scent of him. Instinct overrode common sense as she wrapped her arms around him. He was warm and solidly male. *His body around hers was both familiar and terribly exciting.*

Because this time, it wasn't simply solace she felt. Her belly rolled and every muscle in her urged her to get closer, to press harder against him. It was more, so much more. Something dangerously close to naked desire.

"I promise I won't let anything come between us," he said, breathing the words into her hair, and before she could blink, he put her away from him.

When he looked at her again, his expression was smooth, steady. Not an ounce of the emotion she'd heard in his voice or the need she'd imagined in the press of his arms around her. No sign of the tension she'd felt in his back and shoulders.

He was the Christian the world knew—smooth and shallow with a ruthless edge.

"I'll arrange for a license as soon as possible."

She nodded, still chasing that emotion in his face. It was like a roar in her head—this need for what she'd found in his voice just moments before. Even when it wasn't the quietly sensible thing she always did.

"Just remember why we're doing this, Pree. Your parents can go on that trip to India without feeling guilty. I can get the board off my back. And you can continue to live in the apartment. I won't even be in your hair once we land that collaboration with the Swiss team. The infrastructure itself will take six months to get set up and needs a lot of oversight."

"And your girlfriends?" The question burst out of her mouth before Priya even knew she was thinking it. She could feel the heat creeping up her cheeks. "Forget I said that. None of my business."

"Are you sure?" he asked in a soft, silky voice that sent a prickle of heat all along her skin.

Priya nodded, though she wasn't sure whom she was trying to convince. There was that demand in his eyes again. As if compelling her to ask him. As if he knew. "Of course I'm sure, Christian. Your love life is none of my business."

For the rest of the day, Priya wondered at how it was the strangest thing a woman could say to the man who'd just asked her to marry him.

CHAPTER TWO

Eight and a half years later

PRIYA MIKKELSEN PAID the cab driver with a swipe of her phone and stepped out into the pouring rain. She could feel his gaze on her back, wondering if she was a little cuckoo, walking out into a downpour with nothing but a cashmere wrap for protection. He might even wonder if she was deranged since she was marching up to one of the wealthiest estates in the Pacific Northwest looking like a woman on the edge.

She didn't care. Tonight, she was not a mother who had to put on a smiling face for her seven-year-old son.

She wasn't a granddaughter-in-law who had to bandy words with an eighty-nine-year-old man who doted on her son and put all his faith in Priya.

She wasn't a daughter who had to reassure an overanxious, overprotective mother who'd drown her in suffocating love if she didn't look perfectly happy at all times.

She wasn't the CEO of a major tech company battling with the vulture cousin of her dead husband and a board of directors who constantly tried to question her leadership.

She was simply Priya. The woman who was so lonely that the stench of it clung to her very pores. A thirty-one-year-old woman having a ridiculously juvenile tantrum even her small son would laugh at.

The smooth whir of the electronically manned gates after it scanned her thumbprint reassured the concerned cabbie that he wasn't dealing with a possible criminal.

Priya started up the incline, her four-inch stilettos making her thighs burn with each step. The raindrops soaking through the dress and the steep pathway forced her energy and thoughts into putting one step after the other.

If Mama was to see her now... Priya let out a bark of laughter.

She'd wonder if her calm, coolheaded daughter had gone completely bonkers. Then she'd watch over Priya day and night, drag her to a therapist and then a matchmaker. Not that going to a therapist was wrong.

It was just that no therapist in the world could solve Priya's problem.

Sharing her loneliness and its source with her mother would be nice. But Mama wouldn't simply listen to her vent.

No, the moment she heard Priya mention her unhappiness, she'd arrange a solution. Without exaggerating the matter, Priya knew she'd be married to within an inch of her life in no more than two months. Mama's will was something one should never provoke or invoke—a lesson she and her dad had learned a long time ago.

But Priya didn't want a husband. She didn't want a relationship and all the misery and heartache it could involve. She didn't want a man to dictate her life any more than she wanted Mama to.

She wanted flirting and long, heated glances. She wanted kisses and caresses and yes, sex, she admitted to herself, wiping rain from her lashes. But not the impersonal, hushed-up encounter she'd been propositioned with this evening. Definitely not the man who'd turned ugly within a minute of her retreat. She wanted to feel like a woman instead of a mother and a daughter and a great-granddaughter-in-law and the CEO who held the reins of so many people's livelihoods in her hand.

No, she wanted a long night of seduction and intimacy and warm, sleek male skin at her fingers and broad shoulders and hard thighs enveloping her.

Basically she wanted one man.

Laughing blue eyes and dark blond hair and a roguish grin. The face in her mind's eye shouldn't have surprised her. But it did. He'd been an astonishingly good-looking man. But more than that, Christian had had a presence. A magnetism that drew people to him. An energy and verve for life that had equally amazed her and terrified her.

It shouldn't be a complete shock then that her mind conjured up Christian again and again. Even though he'd largely avoided her when they were married, she'd surprised herself by discovering how much she'd enjoyed being his wife. Until suddenly she wasn't anymore.

So that's what she was trying to do again now—take baby steps toward feeling alive again.

Being the face of one of the biggest tech companies in the world meant dating was even more torturous than the painful twinges in her feet as she rounded the steep hill and the house came into sight. She'd already written off sleeping with any of these dates.

The chance of her finding a man she could trust enough to bare herself, to be that intimately vulnerable with…was very low. But God, was it too much to ask for a decent conversation for just one evening? Too much to hope that the men she met over an app didn't turn out to be either dull or so incredibly full of themselves?

Or did the fault lie with her?

Maybe she had too many expectations. Maybe what she wanted was irrational and ridiculous… Maybe that's what the universe was telling her by sending her foolish, dull-as-rocks men on these casual dates she'd tried. That she'd already had her share of good men—two in one life-time—and there were no more to spare for her. Even if she'd lost them both.

Laughter fell from her mouth at the crushing thought, with an edge of hysteria to it.

Grief was a strange thing. It had ravaged her and re-shaped her—not once but twice. When Christian's plane had crashed, she'd pushed the grief into a corner of her heart, locked it tight and moved on to what had needed to be done.

She'd inherited not just a tech empire but a grieving grandfather. And then the baby growing inside her had been born and needed her. Being a mother—a single mother at that—had been a challenge she'd never fore-seen but had grown into.

Now that grief crashed through Priya, threatening to take her down at the knees, demanding its due. Maybe it was the fact that Christian had been gone for eight years this week that was making it all raw and fresh again. Maybe it was the fact that her son was beginning to ask questions about his father. Maybe it was the fact that she'd never admitted what he'd meant to her. Not even to herself.

She was soaking and shivering, fresh tears pouring out and being washed away by the rain when she reached the house. Motion sensor lights flickered on, illuminating the fountain and the courtyard and wide, majestic steps with giant pillars straddling them.

Her chest burned with the exertion and she stilled to pull in a deep breath. The cold kiss of the rain was a sting against her skin. And then she saw him standing there, with the focus lights illuminating his face.

That sharp nose with a dent in it, the dark blond eyebrows, the glittering blue of his eyes, the wet hair that gleamed like burnished gold and that sensuous, sculpted mouth partly hidden by the thick beard... But it was definitely him.

It was Christian. Waiting for her. Staring at her.

She felt a feverish chill in her bones that had nothing to do with her soaked skin. How far gone was she in her madness that she was seeing a man long gone standing there within touching distance?

"Pree," the man said, her name a soft whisper on his lips.

He's real, came the frantic whisper inside her head. Only he called her that.

This Christian was not some mirage conjured up by her feverish imagination. This Christian looked as solid and real as he'd always been.

The man moved then, stepping out of the circle of light, from under the high-ceilinged porch into the rain. He stilled on the top step while Priya looked up at him, her heart running at a thousand beats per minute now.

Rain pelted his face, poured down that arrogant nose of his into his mouth, where it was swallowed up by his beard. His white linen shirt was soaked through to his skin, delineating a muscled chest and hard abdomen, but he didn't seem to care.

He stared at Priya with an energy that rivaled the storm raging around them. He stared at her as if he meant to inhale her whole. He stared at her as if...he'd walked out of a nightmare just to find her.

Priya laughed brokenly and wiped the water from her face. No doubt she was dreaming because Christian Mikkelsen—her convenient husband of a few short months—was not the kind of man who had ever pined after a woman. Would never have stared at any woman with such acute longing in his eyes as this illusion looked at her.

The breeze carried the scent of him to her and Priya shuddered afresh. She knew that scent well, better than she knew her own. She'd chased that warm scent of his for years since the crash, digging through rows and rows of his designer suits, walking through his closet like some kind of otherworldly specter. She'd even gone into labor while wearing one of his Armani shirts. But after a couple of years, the scent of him had vanished from those clothes. She'd lost even that part of him.

And the memory of that longing, of how she'd hardened her heart a second time... It loathed this weak part of her that ran after illusions. It wanted only truth.

She stretched out a hand, fear and hope making the simple movement exquisitely painful. Her palm landed on his chest—hard and defined. His head jerked, his chest rose and fell at her touch. His heartbeat matched the thunderous beat of hers.

Her stomach felt as if she'd just fallen from a great height, was still falling. Priya spread her fingers, seeking more and more of that hard flesh. Curling her fingers, she dug her nails into his abdomen, determined to hold him in place. Up and down, she touched him, waiting with a stifled sob, waiting for him to disappear.

A groan fell from his mouth as she raked a nail over the taut skin at his chest, bared by the V of his shirt. She wanted to do more. She wanted to bury her face in his throat, she wanted to nip that racing pulse with her teeth, she wanted to taste his skin with her tongue, and she wanted to...

He said nothing. Did nothing. He simply stood there, letting her ravage him with her fingers, his head almost bowed in supplication. The Christian she remembered never bowed to anyone, much less her. It had to be a dream, a dream so far from reality that Priya almost laughed again.

Raindrops clung to his lashes and his blue eyes glittered with an understanding that only made her angrier. When she'd have jerked her hand back, his fingers wrapped around her wrist, holding her hand there, over his chest. "No, Pree. Don't pull away," he whispered in a voice that had visited her a thousand times in her dreams.

I'm here, Pree, that voice had said when her fiancé and best friend had died.

Use me, Pree, that voice had said when she'd been flung this way and that by her mother's overbearing love.

If you want me, Pree, you'll have to come and take me, that voice had challenged her when they'd been stranded at a remote cabin in the Alps and she'd wanted him in her bed for the first time and had no idea what to do about it.

Her legs shook under her, her breath became shallow again, and her stomach roiled.

She stopped fighting the beckoning darkness and indulged herself one more time as she gave in to it.

Priya came to consciousness to find herself flat on the ridiculously elaborate chaise longue in her study. To be precise, she was lying down on Christian's chaise longue in what used to be Christian's study. Which she'd appropriated because he was supposed to be dead and had stayed dead for eight long years.

Reclining like some useless heroine from a gothic novel who fainted at the sight of a vigorous, virile man walking in from the rain was precisely who she'd been once.

Priya Version One. Basic. Fragile. Easily breakable.

It was exactly how Mama and Jai and Christian had always seen her. No, it had been her. While she'd had no control over her health and her heart, she'd let them coddle her, protect her, treat her like a fragile thing. She'd always played in the margins, taken the easy options, let everyone else drive her life.

But she wasn't that person now, not in mind, not in body. Not in her soul.

Now she was Priya Version Two—broken and rebuilt and patched over until she was near indestructible.

Christian sat sideways near her legs, a bunched-up towel in his hand, and was quite uselessly mopping her face and neck while he softly whispered her name. This, more than anything, told Priya that he really was Christian. The man was singularly useless at anything else other than writing code, making millions and chasing after women. And apparently staying dead for eight years and playing games with his family and friends.

He's alive. He's solid and real, a part of her brain kept shouting. The lizard brain, Priya was sure. The part that equated big, broad manly husband with security and safety and happiness.

Of all the ridiculous reactions her body could come up with… She'd never fainted in her life before.

This episode she knew was more about shock than physical health, but still. Pushing herself up into a sitting position, she swatted at his hand with all the force of her anger and hurt and something else she didn't want to examine right then.

Blue eyes met hers and held, in a silent battle of wills. His skin was tanned and weather-beaten, but he was unmistakably pale underneath it. Broad shoulders filled her field of vision, separating her from the world, from reality itself. The heat from his body stroked against hers in a welcoming wave.

She should be shivering, her damp dress sticking to her skin. Instead all she felt was a blazing heat claiming her skin, as if a switch had been turned on inside her.

"Move aside," she said, cutting her gaze away.

He stood up but continued to regard her with that tunnel focus that felt like a caress on her skin. The same focus that she'd always found incredibly unnerving when it shifted to her. She moved away from him and looked out into the storm that was still raging outside through the French doors, trying and discarding words.

What did you say to a man who'd abandoned you for eight years?

"You need to get out of those wet clothes."

His voice had always been deep. Now it bordered on a raspy whisper. Priya flushed, memories hitting her hard and in places she didn't want to think of. She'd heard it that husky only once. On that long-ago night when they'd been stranded at a ski cabin in the Alps and she'd finally given in to what she'd considered to be a forbidden desire for him. Technically, they'd been married for five months by then.

God, she'd been a naive, prudish fool. Chastising herself for days afterward about what it meant. Running away from her own desires as if they were somehow wrong.

The memory was a whiplash against her senses—vivid and evocative. He'd sounded like that when he'd been deep inside her, whispering filthy things in her ear, tipping her over into climax again and again.

"It's clear that you have lost the little common sense you ever possessed," he said, jerking her attention back to him in the now.

Priya looked at him over her shoulder, fisting her hands,

trying to find her equilibrium. Whatever sexual miasma clouded her head fizzed away instantly. "That's what you want to say to me right now?"

"I don't care what you want to hear from me. You need to change, Pree. Now, before you almost die again from pneumonia."

His harsh words tilted her world back on its axis. Hot, scalding anger filled her, washing away every fond, heated memory. Turning around, she poked him in the chest, which was still annoyingly hard.

"How dare you talk to me as though I'm a child. In case you've conveniently forgotten, you were gone for *eight years*. Doing God knows what while I held everything together—the company from all the vultures circling it, your grandfather and his grief and your..."

Christ, he didn't know about Jayden. He didn't know that they had a...son!

Tears gathered in her throat, and she took a deep breath to blink them away. No way in hell was she crying in front of Christian. No way in hell was she going to let him think she needed rescuing. That she was still that frail wisp of a girl.

Something almost like anguish crossed his face. And she realized she'd hurt him, somehow. "I didn't simply leave you. You know me better than that, Pree."

"No, I don't. It's been eight years, Christian. I know how to take care of myself, but you...you..."

One dark blond brow rose in that stunningly good-looking face. His arms folded at his abdomen, he towered over her. "It's good to see you're still that Goody Two-shoes who turns pink at the mere thought of a curse word." The flash of his white teeth against that dirty blond beard rendered him stunning.

"You," she poked him again, moving closer, "arrogant," another poke, "smug," once more even harder, "bastard."

The humor in his eyes deepened, turning them a dark gray blue. That glimmering, almost wicked challenge with which he'd always greeted her was back. And something more—a darker emotion she couldn't quite identify.

"I don't need to be rescued anymore."

"And yet you stand there in that soaking-wet dress, spitting mad at me," he said, the scent of him coiling around her, "when your first thought should be for yourself."

"It would serve you right if I did catch pneumonia again and died on you. Then you'd know how it feels to be left behind." She regretted the childish declaration the moment she made it.

Insult over injury came in the form of a sneeze. Then came one more and then another, until her head felt like it would explode. Her breathing turned shallow, and she shivered again.

How very like the universe to mess with her in this moment.

Christian's smile disappeared and a flurry of the filthiest curses she'd ever heard painted the air. The scent of him assaulted her nostrils. In the next blink— or was it the next sneeze?—Priya was suspended over his shoulder, hanging upside down.

For a few stunned seconds, she wondered if she was in one of those strangely feverish dreams she'd had of him so many times. If she was going to wake up and find herself scrabbling through the covers looking for that warm, male body, only to discover she was alone again.

But the dig of his hard shoulder into her belly was far too real to ignore. As were his back muscles against her chest and his abdomen at her thighs. The thin linen of his shirt had dried and his skin through the material was warm against her chin. Whatever outrage Priya could've mustered dissipated like morning mist as warmth from his body tingled all over her. Her sinuses were happy for the ride and her head cleared of the shock that had taken over ever since she'd spied his figure waiting for her.

She considered punching his broad back with her fists just to affect outrage. Instead she sighed and hung on.

Challenging Christian with her mortality had been at best a cheap shot and at worst, a cruel joke. Didn't matter if he deserved it or not. Death of the people he cared about—even as a joke—wasn't something he could ever tolerate.

With her slung over his shoulder, he walked up the wide staircase without breaking for a breath. Her eyes fell on the huge portrait of him hanging on the wall on the landing. Laughter burst out of her, cleansing the last remnants of grief, washing away the niggling doubt that all this was nothing but another dream she'd have to wake up from.

Her breath grunted out of her when he hitched her higher on the shoulder and then she did call him a thousand names. The curses came as if she'd stored them up for eight years. His laughter exploded around them, his chest rumbling against her belly, sending a quiver of sensation up and down her body.

He kicked the door of the master bedroom open—his room that was now hers—and walked past the huge king bed that had been custom made to accommodate his six-foot-three-inch frame, as he liked to sprawl out. Past the dresser with a framed picture of them on their wedding day eight and a half years ago.

Her in a simple off-white knee-length dress and Christian in his black leather jacket with a white shirt underneath and blue jeans. Standing outside the city hall. There wasn't the usual joy or laughter or love that was found in pictures of a newly married couple. They had married purely for convenience, after all. But there had at least been trust between them.

Despite never understanding her strange, unbearable attraction to him after losing Jai, Priya had always trusted him. Because Jai, the common thread that had bound them to each other, that had brought them together, had trusted him implicitly.

Of course, Christian hadn't simply abandoned her. That wasn't something he'd do. Was it?

She couldn't be sure, because they were little more than strangers now. And yet he was also her husband and, even more important, he was the father of her son.

Priya's feet hit the cold, solid black marble floor of the vast bathroom as Christian gently put her down. But she'd never felt less sure of the ground under her feet.

CHAPTER THREE

"Unzip me."

Christian's head jerked in the direction of that soft command so fast that it wouldn't be surprising if he'd permanently damaged his neck.

Her dark, damp hair pulled away from her neck, Priya looked at him over her shoulder. Her brown eyes glittered with a challenge that struck him, hard and deep. He held her gaze, not caring what she saw in his. Then because he was a greedy bastard parched for sustenance, he let it rove over her with a thoroughly possessive attitude he didn't even try to curb.

For so many years he'd wondered if she was the product of his imagination. Of some illusion his mind was weaving because of a deep-seated need to discover who he was. The intense quality of those dreams about her, his mindless obsession with her, had kept him going. As if she was the tugboat he needed to hold on to to eventually reach the shore.

Even when he hadn't been able to remember who he was, battling the blackness in his head year after year, her face had stood out in his mind, wreathed in shadows. Bits and pieces of her beckoning him closer. From the straight little nose and the wide mouth to the cascading silk of her jet-black hair.

Now that he was here, staring at her, that desperate need he'd felt then was multiplied a thousand times. He drank her in, noting little details that had remained hazy in those dreams. He had a feeling it would take him a decade or more to fill in the smudged picture of her he'd carried inside his damaged memory for so long. Another decade to note all the new facets of her.

His wife—Christian refused to think of her any other way—looked like a goddess. A siren he was ready to surrender to, with pleasure.

Her long neck arched as she considered him with a quiet boldness he'd always sensed beneath her surface shyness. His fingers itched to follow the deep dip of her small waist and the flare of her hips. He wanted to cup her buttocks and pull her to him until she was plastered against him. This need for the woman in his dreams had forced him to survive when all he'd wanted to do was surrender to the black void in his mind.

But now that she was in front of him, a thread of something he didn't understand filled his heart. It kept him still, even as desire filled his very veins, washing away all that aching emptiness that had driven him nearly insane.

"Have you forgotten how to take the clothes off a woman, Christian?" she said, her expression full of a haughty arrogance that was like tinder to the explosive desire coursing through him. "Have the last eight years changed you that much?"

Laughter barreled out of him, from deep within him, shaking him, purging the last remnants of the fear he'd carried within himself. Until he'd seen the shock and surprise in those beautiful brown eyes. Until he'd held her slender body in his arms and carried her into the house. Even his childhood home had felt like a stranger without her in it.

But beneath his laughter, there was discombobulation, too.

This wasn't the Priya he'd met when he'd been a cocky eighteen-year-old.

She wasn't the girl he'd been fascinated by when she'd been his best friend's shy yet whip-smart fiancée who'd found holes in his code and broken his app with one try. Not the girl with whom his obsession had tied him up in knots of guilt and self-loathing.

Because he was the man who'd always had everything in the world and still, he'd lusted after his best friend's girl. The very friend who'd been a brother and family to Christian from the moment they'd bonded in middle school.

She wasn't the girl he'd rescued from a fog of grief and gut-wrenching loneliness that had threatened to devour them both after they'd lost Jai in a freak road traffic accident. She wasn't the girl with a shy smile and wary words and unwavering loyalty who had been his only link to sanity when all he'd wanted was to howl at the universe and its cruelty in snatching away a person he'd loved yet again.

She wasn't the girl he'd married and tried his best to keep at arm's length, even then protecting her, this time from himself.

She wasn't the girl in whose eyes he'd seen desire for him and promised himself that he'd taste it once. Only once.

She wasn't a girl at all. This was a woman fierce and angry and sexy—a combination that sent his muscles curling with the kind of need that he was sure he'd never allowed to touch him.

The last eight years had left their mark on her. There was a fire in her eyes now and a cloak of armor she seemed to have wrapped herself up in. The hot pink dress clung to her curves—a sure departure from the mostly baggy clothes she'd worn then. The stilettos made her legs look longer.

Even the way she stood there and watched him over her shoulder was different. It was confident. Sexy as hell. It was also inexplicably bewildering.

With that hard-won patience he'd developed out of necessity, he examined his own confusion. He wanted the comfort of that shy, quiet girl she'd been. He wanted the comfort of knowing that she hadn't changed in eight years. That she hadn't moved on with her life without him. That she hadn't stopped...*needing* him.

Which was more than a little messed up but at least it was the truth.

He was Christian Mikkelsen, billionaire, one-half of the brilliant tech company Modi Mikkelsen Technologies and a philanthropist to boot. Although that last part had been mostly instilled in him by Jai. The one man he'd tried to emulate and whose standards he'd always tried to live up to, even after he'd died.

And this woman who stared at him with such undisguised anger and poorly hidden desire was his wife. A wife he'd acquired as a chess move against his grandfather and the MMT board's compulsive need to curb his *extracurricular* activities. More important, she'd been a friend he'd sworn to protect, even from himself.

As he reached her and breathed in the scent of her, Christian understood the most important thing in all the muddy disaster of blackness his life had been for the last eight years. The attraction between them was as fierce and as wild as he remembered.

His heart thudding, he moved closer to her. Because of her struggle, the zipper of her dress had gotten stuck in the fabric. It was still damp in places. That urge to rip it off her and envelop her in the thickest, warmest blanket was overwhelming.

Weird how his mind remembered so vividly the time when she'd almost died due to pneumonia. He and Jai had spent an agonizing forty-eight hours in the sterile hospital café waiting for news. He'd been on edge all night, and Jai, as always, had been the calm, solid presence. When Priya had finally been out of danger, the distasteful truth had dawned on him—he was madly in love with his best friend's fiancée.

At that time, he'd told himself that her appeal was that she was forbidden to him. God, what an idiot he'd been.

"It's stuck," he said, raising his hands but unable to drop them down onto her shoulders. His fingers shook slightly. It wasn't that he felt useless so much as he was awed by how desperately he wanted to touch her. Anything that made him this desperate, he usually resisted. That was a truth he knew of himself.

The tall mirrors all around them reflected them back, blurring the boundaries between their bodies. He met her gaze in one.

"Christian?"

"I haven't touched anyone in eight years." The words came easily.

Her eyes widened, the bones in her neck standing out in stark relief. "What?"

"I couldn't bear the thought of anyone touching me, either."

He wasn't sure why he was telling her this. He was also sure that this wasn't him—this man who simply said whatever was in his heart. The skin of his abdomen still stung a little after she'd raked her fingers over him, marking him when she'd thought he was nothing but a mirage. How desperately she'd wanted for him to be real.

A cacophony of emotions sang through him, not that he could make head or tail out of them. Only that he needed her to know. To understand.

Her chest rose and fell and the calm she cloaked herself with shattered.

Christian thought she'd bolt out of his reach, out of shock if nothing else. He hated the thought of her being scared of him. Despised it.

A fire he'd never seen before burned in her gaze as she held his in the mirror. "Why didn't you come back once you recovered from the plane crash? How *could* you stay away? After what happened with Jai, how could you be so cruel as to let me go on thinking, *even for one damned day more*, that I'd lost you, too?"

He touched her then, the anguish in her words pulling him along.

She was cold and shaking and he pressed his fingers deeper into her shoulders. It felt as if he'd touched a live wire. Her skin was soft and silky to touch. "I was in a coma for two years after I washed up ashore. Stuck in a corner bed in some hospital on Saint Martin, dependent on the charity and goodwill of strangers. This French nurse... She looked after me, I was told, with devotion I'm sure I didn't deserve. After I regained consciousness, I had no idea who I was." He leaned his forehead against the back of her head, his breaths coming shallow again. "My mind's been blank for so long, Pree—like a dark, long, stretch of the ocean I couldn't cross however hard I swam..."

He shuddered at the memory of how thick and biting that darkness had been.

The tips of her fingers reached his, barely touching, but reminding him he wasn't alone in that unblinking darkness anymore. Christian sensed her hesitation as clearly as the thud of his heartbeat. Her ache for him was written across her lovely features.

He continued, wanting to get it over with. "Two days ago, I saw your face on an old newspaper. Wrapped up around a piece of fried fish. It was from the tech convention in London two months ago. Your name was under it in big letters—Priya Mikkelsen. Everything fell into place, as if someone had suddenly played a reel of my entire life and forced me to watch. You and Grandpa and Jai and..." He swallowed, trying to keep emotion out of his tone. "It was as if a curtain had suddenly been pulled back. It took me this long to put enough funds together to buy the plane ticket home."

She didn't move or speak for a long time. For all the reflections of her face in the mirrors around him, he had no idea what she was thinking. The silence that surrounded them didn't feel uncomfortable or awkward though. Didn't feel like that unending quiet in his head that he had hated so much.

They stood like that for a long time, almost touching but not quite.

"Tear it off," she said suddenly, the words rupturing the quiet. "The dress, now. I think I've wasted enough time walking around in it like some hapless waif."

If he felt a sliver of disappointment in his gut, Christian shoved it away. Priya had never been one for elaborate words or expressing effusive sentiments. And he had no doubt today had taken a toll on her.

Damn it, he'd wanted to remember his life, himself. He'd wanted to be back with his family for eight long years. Still, watching her walk up to the house had shaken him, in more ways than one. He wasn't going to expect anything from her and definitely not some falsely sweet words. And yet, there was a part of him that wanted everything, whatever the hell that meant.

"It doesn't suit you anymore."

"What?" Her question zoomed out of her mouth like it had gossamer wings made of need and longing.

"The waif look. Like an ill-fitting dress one grows out of."

Her eyes flared wide. "So you're still in possession of your senses, then."

"Would you have tossed me out if I wasn't? If I'd shown up here, blank as a slate, not right in the head?"

"Don't inflict that self-indulgent drama on me, Christian. I'm not Jai to put up with it."

"There were days when I thought I'd lose my mind. When I thought hope might be the thing that would kill me."

Instant regret filled her eyes. "I'm so—"

"Don't," he said, shaking his head. "Don't apologize for things you didn't even know about."

"How did you… How did you stand it?"

"Will you look at me differently if I tell you?"

"Christian —"

"Don't… Don't hold your punches, Pree. Don't treat me differently now."

She held his gaze, stubbornly denying him. "How did you get by on those days?"

"There was this gut feeling all the time. That said there was someone waiting for me. That… I couldn't just give up." Some instinct of self-preservation made him stop there. "It told me I was too brilliant to be just a woodworker."

She scoffed gently, recognizing the dig he'd made at himself.

"That's what my nurse guessed. After studying my hands," he said, holding out his palms.

"Is that how you lived?" she asked.

He nodded. "I did general construction work, yes. In the beginning, I couldn't even manage that much. But then I started carving, even when I was still recuperating. It was one of the things that called to me, calmed me. When Marie put the wood and chisel in my hands... I felt less like a shadow for the first time in weeks. Or I might have gone out of my mind completely."

Priya turned to give him her back. He had a feeling she'd turned to hide her expression. That cloak of armor falling into place once more. It infuriated him and intrigued him, even more, if that was possible.

Still, he followed the line of her spine with his eyes like a greedy puppy eying its treat.

"Okay," he said, his voice gruff. "I'll have to jerk on the zipper hard."

Palms spread on the wall in front of her, she braced herself. The movement arched her back toward him. "Do your worst. I won't break."

Was she aware of how sensuously challenging that sounded? Or was eight years of slumbering libido making him hear things he'd only dreamed of?

Shaking his head, he covered the little gap left between them. The scent of her coiled through him instantly. This time, when his fingers landed on her shoulders, she shivered and for an infinitesimal second, her spine arched toward him again.

His mouth dried.

With a loud huff of breath, her shoulders squared, as if she was willing herself to shed that awareness. But Christian had no such self-control and he wasn't sure he'd employ it even if he had.

The soft hitch of her breath, the silky glide of her hair along his knuckles, the barely there graze of her backside against his front—awareness slammed into him like the punch of his pugilist friend back on Saint Martin.

Bracing one hand on one slim shoulder, he tugged at the lip of the stuck zipper. His fingers slipped on it, and Priya fell back against him with a jerk. Every time her curvy bottom grazed his groin, his muscles curled.

A groan ripped from his mouth.

"What?" she asked, facing ahead.

"This is…a special kind of torture," he whispered. "You won't understand."

"Because you assume I don't feel the same pull toward you? Because you think I didn't miss you as much as you did me? Because you think I don't find it extremely disconcerting to look at you and see the man I trusted above everyone else, only to have my mind whispering that you're a stranger to me now…" She pressed her cheek to the cold tile, her shoulders tense. "Believe me, Christian, I'm right there with you."

The barely banked anger in her tone —at this situation, the confusion and the pain—was like a cooling wind against his own fury.

"That I'm holding it together doesn't mean I'm not also falling apart," she murmured cryptically.

Head jerking up, Christian wondered how she knew what he'd needed to hear. He squeezed her shoulder, the pad of his thumb making mindless forays over her neck. His breath settled. For the first time in years, he felt like he wasn't alone.

On the next try, the zipper ripped open with a tearing sound. The fabric of the dress immediately flapped aside, revealing the line of her spine and a swath of silky brown flesh. He swallowed as his gaze dipped to the lush curves of her bottom barely covered by lacy white panties.

Longing coiled through him, heating up every limb and muscle.

She turned around and he jerked his gaze upward. Her long silky hair had dried and covered the slopes of her breasts revealed by the slipping dress. Her eyes held his, a steadiness in them. "I'm glad you're back, Christian," she said, with a tilt of her mouth that made his gut twist with want. "In here," she said with a hand on her chest, "beneath all the confusion and the anger and the ground being ripped away from under my feet." She cleared her throat. "I'll leave now so you can have your bedroom back."

"No," he said, raising his hands and stepping back. "No, stay. This is your room now. Your house. I'll take the guest room."

Her eyes big in her fine-boned face, she nodded.

He felt like that nine-year-old boy who'd suddenly lost his parents all over again. Damn it, he had to get a grip on himself. It wasn't fair to expect more from her tonight. Even though all he wanted was to talk to her. Or listen, rather. He had an overwhelming urge to hear about all that she'd done in the last eight years. He didn't want to miss a single bit of it.

"We have a lot to catch up on," she added, obviously thinking the same thing. "Why don't you get a good night's rest and we can talk tomorrow—"

"I'm too wired to sleep."

"So am I," she said, a sudden resolve entering her eyes. "If you're sure you aren't too tired, I'll meet you in the library for a drink."

He considered her with a smile. Neutral ground—that's what she was going for. Not quite strangers but not quite a husband and wife, either. Maybe not even friends, for all they had known each other intimately once. "I don't drink anymore."

When he'd have turned away, she called his name in a soft whisper.

"Yes?"

Fingers clutching her dress to her chest, shoulders bare, long, silky hair touching the upper curves of her breasts, she was the most beautiful thing Christian had ever seen. The one thing that had pulled him through the unrelenting nightmare of the last eight years. And yet, nothing was the same, not her, not him.

He felt like he finally had everything he'd wanted and yet... It didn't feel like he had it at all.

Chin tilted up, she said, "Will you hold me? Just for a moment?"

An avalanche of want opened up inside him as he took in her face. The flash of vulnerability she was allowing herself. The risk she was taking for both of them. The reward was his—because this need to hold her, to touch her was excruciatingly powerful.

It was a truth he'd always known—that she was the bravest one among all three of them, her, him and Jai. For all she'd been cocooned and cosseted most of her life.

Without another word, he walked to her and gathered her to him. She folded into his arms as if it was exactly what she'd needed all these years. Her face tucked into his neck, the bridge of her nose rubbing against his pulse. Her hands still clutched the dress between their chests, but her thighs leaned against his, trembling.

"I missed this," she said so softly that for a second he wondered if he was imagining it. "More than anything else in the world."

His throat closing, all he could manage was a grunt.

It felt like they stood together, shaking and trembling, falling apart but somehow holding on, for an eternity. Yet no more than a few seconds could've passed. He made himself let go of her, feeling an ache like nothing else the moment he released her.

He was almost out of the bathroom when it struck him. "Where were you coming back from tonight? When you walked up to the house in the rain? In that dress?" he added, unnecessarily. As if to make sure she didn't evade the truth.

He saw the realization land in her eyes. Saw the bold tilt of her chin. "A date. I went on a date," she said, her chin tipping up in pure provocation.

Patience built over eight long years helped him stare back at her, even as her reply landed like another punch. Even as something in him roared like a possessive savage, the savage he'd almost become cut off from everything he held dear. But he held his polite smile, his brow raised in tacit query.

In that moment, he knew himself better than he had in eight long years. In her eyes, in the way the challenge was written all over her body language, in the way every part of him roared to claim her, Christian found himself.

He left the room and closed the door behind him, his heart thundering in his chest, a wide smile curving his mouth. Feeling more alive than he'd felt for a long time. Even the quietly raging frustration in his veins that he might never be the man she'd missed, the man she deserved, was still better than the blankness he'd battled for so long.

"Where were you coming back from tonight? In that dress?"

Just remembering the combative look in Christian's eyes sent a shiver down Priya's spine. The spray of water from the shower felt too hot on her skin so she turned the knob off and reached for the towel.

Apparently, chemistry was a thing that roared back to life despite not seeing the other person for eight years. Despite the fact that Christian could've changed irrevocably.

And yet, she knew in her heart, that where it mattered he hadn't changed. She knew it in the irreverent curve of his lips, in the way he watched her, in the way he had... held her.

What she wasn't sure of yet was if that was a good thing or a bad thing for her heart.

She took forever getting dressed, even knowing that she couldn't simply escape the ground still rumbling beneath her feet, shoving her this way and that. Escape the six-foot-three-inch man who suddenly once again took center stage in her life.

At least, she'd owned up to the fact that she wouldn't be sleeping tonight. To not postpone the big truth she still had to tell him. But then, being brave hadn't been a choice ever since his plane had crashed. It had been a necessity.

She palmed the moisturizer into her skin and pulled on a matching silk top and shorts set. Excitement beat through her veins like an incessant siren. Gripping the marble vanity, she forced herself to pull in a few long breaths.

Not more than an hour ago, she'd been railing at the universe, loneliness an ache in her chest. And now that he was back, she couldn't stop shaking. Couldn't stop her mind from exploring and weighing a thousand different possibilities.

Yes, she was glad that Christian wasn't dead. Of course she was.

But she needed to remember that he might not even want this marriage, or her, anymore in his life. Not the woman she'd become. Not when he recovered from the emotional shock of being back in his home, around familiar faces once again.

That's what she had to be ready for.

CHAPTER FOUR

AFTER THROWING ON her robe, it took Priya ten minutes to find him. In Jayden's small bedroom. Surrounded by the dinosaur-covered walls that she'd hand-painted, the tiny bookshelf and the colorful buckets of Lego pieces, this big, broad man looked so incongruously lost that her heart ached.

His knees folded up, he was sitting on the race car bed, still in the same clothes. His dark blond hair looked like he'd ravaged it with his fingers, and his skin was pale under the tan. Grief was etched so deeply into those usually mobile features that she found her own eyes filling up.

A pang of pain rushed through her—for all the nights she'd wished him back, for all the moments when she'd have given anything to share the burden of parenthood with him. For all the moments of sheer joy he should've been a part of.

"Christian?" she said gently, walking farther into the room. She wanted to touch him. To lay her fingers on his shoulder, to hold him tight. To let him know that she was here to see him through this. That he could lean on her, like she'd done so many times.

But under the weight of his grief, she recognized anger and loss. The slight tilt of his head away from her when she called his name spoke volumes. So she kept her hands to herself and gave him space.

Seconds ticked by slowly, tension sucking the oxygen out of the room.

Finally, after what seemed like forever, he raised the framed picture of Jayden with his left hand. It was such a familiar gesture that her breath caught. "Who is he, Pree?"

She closed the distance between them, but he didn't look at her. "My son." She saw his head jerk back and blanched. "I'm sorry, that was automatic. I've never said this out loud before..." She swallowed and said, "He's *our* son."

His throat worked as Christian looked back at the picture. His thumb pressed into the sharp edge of the frame. "Our son?"

She sat down on the other side of the tiny bed. Despite her own need to be close to him in this moment. Despite everything in her aching to be held again.

"I found out I was pregnant two weeks after your plane crash. I'd been so shaken by the news of your accident that I... I didn't even realize my period was late." She looked at her tightly clasped fingers and then forced herself to release them. "That weekend at the cabin in the Alps—"

"I remember when he'd have been conceived," Christian said, in a low growl. "Believe me, when my memories came back, no parts were missing. Especially that weekend. Every single time I rolled over to find you warm, within reach and willing, every time I woke you up, every time I buried myself inside you, I remember it all."

The raw ferocity in his words made her stomach dip and roll. Molten heat pooled low in her belly. "Of course you do," she murmured, her voice husky.

And yet, the day after, he'd been anything but that passionate, insatiable lover. Anything but the man who'd so desperately and openly made love to her. Even the friend she'd come to cherish and depend on had disappeared. Within a day, she'd found herself on the flight home alone without Christian even saying goodbye. Without acknowledging what had happened between them.

And three weeks later his plane had crashed and he'd been gone.

Caught up in her own naive confusion, she'd been glad that he'd maintained that distance from her. Had been relieved that he'd regretted it so much that he couldn't even look at her.

In the last few years, however, it had eaten away at her. Why had he turned away from her after they'd made love? Had it been such a ghastly mistake?

"Where is he?" Christian said, pulling her back to the present.

"With Ben and my parents in Switzerland. I had a merger to see through and I didn't want him to miss out on the trip. He's very attached to Ben." She chanced a glance at him. Only to find his jaw set so tight that a vein pulsed in his temple. "They'll be back tomorrow afternoon."

She shifted on the bed, her knees pointed toward him, but still keeping her distance. "Christian, I can't even fathom what's going on in your mind," she said, reaching for his hand, but he shot up from the bed. Rejecting both the words and her touch.

"What's his name?"

"Jayden."

A stunned look entered his eyes. He looked at the picture and then back at her again. "You named him after Jai." There was something in his voice that she couldn't quite put her finger on.

"Jayden Mikkelsen," she said, reminding him that her son, no, *their son* had his last name.

He said nothing for so long that all her defensive hackles rose. If she was a predator like the ones on the walls, she could've touched the damn pokey things on her back. But she calmed herself, pushing aside her confusion. "You don't like it?"

He didn't deny it. Suddenly, she felt unsure of every decision she'd made as a parent. As if he was questioning her very worth. Which she knew was a knee-jerk reaction. Clearing her throat, she said, "Talk to me, Christian. Ask me something, anything about him."

He wielded his silence like a weapon against her.

When he still didn't say anything, she whispered, "I did my best with him, Christian. And with your company. And with your grandfather." She laced and unlaced her fingers. "I know that this is a lot to absorb, but I hope you'll understand that I held it all together to the best of my abilities."

His nostrils flared, and his shoulders were so tense that Priya wondered if he'd break if she touched him. He hadn't said anything about Jayden, but she'd seen something in his eyes. Or was it simply shock at the discovery of a son? Whatever it was, his silence had claws that neatly dug into her skin.

The realization made her chest burn with something like shame. God, did she still want his approval so desperately? Or was it that there was so much she wanted to share, so much she wanted to unburden on him, and he looked like he didn't want any piece of it—or them?

Just like that, she could feel whatever strength she'd built up over the years crumbling against his silence, leaving her painfully vulnerable to him.

She rubbed a hand over her temple. "Maybe this wasn't such a good idea." A dry laugh escaped her mouth. "I'll be in my...in the master bedroom. When you're ready, whenever it is, come find me, okay?"

He didn't even lift his head as he whispered, "Running away again, Pree?"

Priya stilled.

Hot anger pulsed in his question. But this, this she could take. She could handle anything but the awful silence from him. "Sometimes it's the best choice."

The impact of what she'd said struck her deeper as the words came out.

Maybe that's what she needed to be prepared to do at some point. To let him go. To walk away.

This wasn't the old Christian she'd gotten back. Every passing minute made that obvious. It was very possible she was never getting that man back. And maybe it was unfair—to herself *and* to him—to even want or expect that man back.

Instead of laughter and charm, this Christian was full of shadows and an intensity that made her skin zing.

"Good night," she said, walking by him.

"Don't go." His arm coiled around her waist in a move to stop her. It had always amazed her how gentle he could be for such a giant of a man. Even now, pressed against her abdomen, his grip somehow managed to be both gentle and firm. "Please."

She fell back against him, her hip hitting his, the guttural want in the last word swallowing her whole. Her breath quickened as the heat from his body enveloped her. Warm breath coated the rim of her ear and the arch of her neck. She trembled all over and his hold tightened. Bringing his corded arm precariously close to the swell of her breasts.

Every cell in her body seemed to coalesce there, waiting, wanting.

"I'm not passing judgment on how you carried out your responsibilities," he whispered, not touching her anywhere else. Not releasing her, either. "Or how you raised…our son. Not at all."

Leaning against him, letting him take her weight, Priya closed her eyes. They were locked against each other. Just like in their lives. She couldn't deny he still had a place in her life. But neither could she simply hand over the reins after everything that had happened.

It was clear, even after all these years, that she was like a hungry sponge around him. Desperate for anything he could give her. She'd had eight years to imagine all the things she'd do differently if she got one more chance with him. But it wasn't another chance when it wasn't the same man.

All her bright hopes and naive expectations she hadn't even realized she'd harbored, all the quiet whispers of her heart during the long, lonely nights, were clamoring to be given voice, shimmering under her skin. They would only lead to disappointment and frustration. And worse. If she let him… He could break her heart. Even if he didn't mean to. Her falling apart at the slightest hint of rejection from him wasn't going to help any of them—especially Jayden.

"Whatever you are feeling, it's valid," she said, thankful for her steady voice. "The fact is that we're…strangers to each other now. Accepting that is the only way forward."

His forehead touched the back of her head, and his thighs pressed against hers. She felt the strength in his large body—the slight shudder in it, even as he easily contained it. "And yet, my body knows yours."

There was such deep longing in his voice that she shivered.

"As mine knows yours," she acknowledged. "Or at least

the lizard brain part of us that recognizes a source of mindless pleasure." She smiled wryly, deliberately lightening the moment. "Apparently, I'm now into sexy lumberjacks who communicate through grunts and brooding silences and are into character-building celibacy bouts."

His laughter rumbled out of his chest, sending vibrations through her own body. "Sexy lumberjack, huh?" His nose was at her temple and she felt his deep breath in the way it ruffled her hair. And then, as if it had taken him this long to understand the gist of it, a strange sort of stillness went through him. "You admit that—"

"That I want to climb up all over you and jump your bones? Yes. What's the point of lying to myself? We have enough knotted past to wade through as it is."

His shock told her what a monumental thing she'd done by admitting it. It came easily to her now —this honesty— but all he knew, all he remembered was the girl who'd been frightened by her own needs.

"I'm not the Priya you used to know," she reminded him, wishing she could see his eyes. His mouth. Drink in his laughter.

Her pulse raced as she waited for him to pick up the gauntlet she hadn't meant to throw down. The old Christian would have. He'd have teased her, tormented her and laughed at her. And would've taken her up against the wall, maybe.

This new Christian didn't see it even as an invitation, she was sure.

"I'm sorry for not having the right words, for…hurting you," he murmured and just like that, the tension and uncertainty between them leached away.

This was the man she knew. The man she'd come to admire so much. Even when he'd been at his lowest, he'd never hurt her.

"You didn't hurt me," she said, a little too loudly, determined to convince herself more than him. "That's just your usual arrogance speaking, thinking everyone in your orbit is affected by your moods."

His mouth opened against her temple. She didn't have to see his face to know he'd smiled at her snarky comeback. It moved through her body, filling up all the lonely places.

"I meant it when I said I won't break, Christian. Not at your hands. Not at your words. Let's just focus on you and Jayden for now," she added, settling into a sensible voice, smothering her own confusion.

"You're definitely not the Starling I left behind."

He didn't it say it like it was a bad thing. Or a good thing, either. "I wouldn't have survived the last few years if I was still that person. Discovering I was pregnant after your plane crash… I don't have the words to describe the feeling to you. Perversely, it was the one thing that finally made me take stock. That made me decide I'd had enough of fate and Mama and everyone else running my life. You should've seen Mama and Ben when I started ordering them around. You'd have been proud of me."

"I've always been proud of you, Pree."

Priya touched him then. She couldn't not. Not after that. She moved her fingers over the corded forearm still wound around her midriff. The rasp of his hair felt delicious against her palm. And at her back, she could sense the change in his chest and thighs, packed with powerful muscles that one didn't acquire at a gym.

He was broader and wider and less…polished. So different from that suave, sophisticated Christian he'd once been. As if all the surface things had been stripped away from him, leaving only a core of steel behind.

But for all the changes in him—inside and out—everything in her still responded to him. Everything in her wanted to touch him and hold him and give him succor. Wanted to demand he give her what she needed, what she wanted only from him.

Slowly, he released her.

She turned, a strangely protective instinct rising up in her. There was no way she could even begin to imagine what he must have gone through. But what she could do, could give him—after everything he'd done for her—was to be here for him.

"Eight years is a long time to be on your own, Christian. Give yourself space and time to find your footing. Do the things that bring you peace and joy. Even the smallest things that might center you, things that you used to enjoy before."

Leaning against the opposite wall, he smiled. "I can see how MMT flourished under your leadership."

"Pinpoint the biggest problem first and then solve it. You and Jai taught me that."

"So I'm the problem now, huh?"

She grinned. "A six-foot-three-inch brooding man, suddenly taking up space in my bedroom and my life..." She swallowed the words *"and my heart."* He wasn't allowed there. "You can't say I'm wrong."

He dipped his chin in acknowledgment. "I will take it slow."

It was one of the things that had always made him stand out for her. Unlike so many men, Christian actually listened to good advice, no matter who gave it.

"What's the one thing you desperately missed all these years? A perfect cup of coffee at your favorite café? An Armani suit? Maybe a ride on your bike? What did you really want and couldn't have?"

"There was one thing I desperately wanted. Even when

I didn't know who I was." His gaze on her mouth was like a laser beam, his intent unmistakable. "Even when I didn't know who you were," he finished silkily, a challenge in his blue eyes. "I wanted to taste that mouth that teased and tormented me, even during waking hours."

Her chin hit her chest, shock blooming low in her belly. Her thighs trembled and she desperately wanted to clutch them together. "So you remembered my face?"

"Like a smudged picture," he admitted. "And that piece of music you incessantly practiced in our apartment, during those few months…"

"When we were married. When I waited at home, playing my sitar like a sad, neglected wife and you twisted yourself upside down to avoid me and never came home…" Some devil in her demanded its due. "Those few months? I wondered if you ever found…other company."

An expression flashed in his eyes so quickly she couldn't identify it. "Do you really want to get into it now, Pree?"

"What else? What else did you remember about me?" she said instead, backing down. This was too important. More important than those first thorny few months of their marriage.

"Mostly, I remembered that I'd made a promise to you that I wouldn't mess it up between us." His tone of voice clearly conveyed how badly he thought he'd failed to keep that promise.

"Oh." His gaze tracked her as she moved around the room, straightening things that didn't need to be straightened. Her mind whirred, every small thing he revealed tugging her closer and closer to him.

He had remembered her—smudged image or not. *He had remembered her.* Her hungry, greedy heart jumped over that little nugget.

This had been inevitable from the moment she'd run her hands all over his body in the rain to make sure he was real. But Priya didn't want it to be inevitable. She didn't want to be swept along by grief or guilt or rage or relief.

She wanted it to be a choice. Her choice.

And his choice. But he wasn't going to ask her. That was clear.

Slowly, she worked her way toward him, every nerve in her body on high alert.

"And now?" she asked, her hands itching to touch him, to hold him, to soothe the tension in his body.

He didn't exactly push off from the wall. But she heard the shift in his breathing, the energy beneath the tremendous stillness he seemed to be made of. "Now what, Starling?"

She stilled when there was just enough gap between their bodies to let air pass. So close that the heat radiating from him was like a whip, branding her flesh. "Do you still want to…kiss me? Or are you worried you'll find reality to be a poor imitation of your memory?"

CHAPTER FIVE

CHRISTIAN TOOK A deep breath. The scent of her skin greeted him like an old friend, something so inherently *her* that his lungs expanded, greedily taking it in. Silky tendrils fell away from the knot on top of her head, caressing that delicate jawline. Her skin shimmered silky soft. The deep V of her robe hinted at a cleavage he wanted to bury his face in. Her eyes…glittered with unhidden desire. With her makeup gone, he could see the dark shadows under her eyes, but there was still a glow to her face. There was vulnerability and strength in the set of her features as she looked up at him that was like a shot of liquid fire straight to his veins.

Damn, she was…bold. Bold and beautiful and better than any memory his messed-up mind could conjure. She was warmth and life and brightness that made him want to go down on his knees and give thanks.

He tugged the reins of his self-control tighter around himself. "I don't remember you being a tease."

She laughed, and he saw the pulse fluttering rapidly at her neck. She was just as agitated and nervous as he was and yet, she was here. She didn't back down. "I'm not bluffing, Christian."

He grunted, fisting his hands by his sides.

Her gaze trailed up his body, with that same boldness.

"Priya... This isn't a good idea," he said, his voice all hoarse and forbidding. God, what a coward he was...

"Can I come closer?" she whispered, apparently not at all intimidated. "Can I touch you, Christian?" Her tongue flicked out to lick her lower lip, her gaze drinking in his chest as if she was parched. "Please."

Something in Christian broke, some invisible wall he hadn't even known he was holding up. Protecting himself or her, he had no idea.

"Yes," he muttered, desperate to see what she'd dare to do. Curious to see how far she could push him.

Her arms came around his neck first, fingers clasping against the nape of his neck. The tips teased the edges of his hair, sending shivers down his spine. Slowly, she fell against him, until her breasts were flattened against his chest. Until her flat stomach pressed up against his abdomen. Her thighs were shaking against his, demanding to be straddled, until he widened his stance. And then she was fully leaning against him, pressed up so hard that he could hear her heart thumping away against his own. Every muscle in him clenched at the glorious, full-body contact, at how soft and warm and delicious she was against him. He uttered a hoarse, needy groan.

An echo of that same sound fell from her mouth as she settled herself against him to her satisfaction. Her face came to the open V of his shirt, her breath teasing the hair on his chest. "Put your arms around me," she demanded, her voice all deep and fluttery.

He raised a brow and refused to comply.

Her mouth made a pout. "You're no fun anymore."

"Is that what this is?" he demanded grumpily, every ounce of his willpower and energy going into staying still, into not devouring her whole like he wanted to.

Her lashes flicked down, her palms spread greedily on

his abdomen, stroking up and down, over and around, as if she was frantically mapping the terrain of his body and couldn't stop. "Maybe we both need a reminder."

"Of what?"

"That—" she leaned her cheek against his chest "—this is a good thing that I can hear your heart thudding in my ear. That you're here and I'm here."

When he was holding her like this, when his hands were full of her warmth and softness, it did feel like a good thing. His hands betrayed him first. They moved over her back, patting, smoothing, stroking, relearning her, and she arched into his touch, her breath coming in shallow strokes. "Then why does it feel like I've lost more than I've gained?" he said, angry with himself. So...furiously powerless. It was like a raging fire inside him that had no outlet.

Her throat bobbed up and down as she swallowed hard, her hands inching back over his shoulders to the nape of his neck. She pressed it, demanding he look at her. Her eyes shimmered with unshed tears. "I felt like that once. That day the doctor confirmed that I was pregnant, all I wanted was to crawl under the sheets and never come out. I wanted to simply let Mama and Ben take over. One moment, the baby felt like a gift, and the next... Memories of how we left things between us the last time we saw each other would eat through me. But then I thought of you and Jai and how you were both gone and I... I was disgusted by how I was wasting the chance at living that I'd been given. I was damned if I was going to let everyone else take over my child's upbringing. So I decided then and there it would be a new beginning. I would be a different Priya. *I* would dictate the direction my life and my child's life would take, not anyone or anything else. Make this choice too, Christian. Take the reins in your own hands and make this a new beginning."

Her words were a balm to his soul, her touch a benediction that filled up all the empty spaces inside him. He tugged at a strand of silky hair, marveling at the woman she'd become. "What shall I do with you, Pree?" he said, his voice gentle and needy. The question came from deep in his soul.

"Kiss me," she said, her teeth gently nipping his chin. Her smile was a prize. "I want to kiss you. I've wanted to kiss you for a long time. Actually, I've wanted to do a lot of things, but I'll settle for a kiss for now."

He grunted.

Her eyes shone like jewels in her face. "I think that's a grunt of assent, Mikkelsen. See, I'm beginning to understand this new language you communicate in."

His mouth dried, his synapses pretty much fried from all the contact.

"After everything you've been through to find your way back to us," she whispered, "after everything we've been through..." Her lashes flicked down and up again. "...we deserve a reward, don't you think?"

He grinned more confidently, cupping her hip with one palm. "Are you my reward, Pree?"

Jutting her hip out, she fell back onto one foot. The gesture was feminine and fierce. "Not good enough for you, Mikkelsen?"

"You're the most beautiful thing I've ever seen," he retorted huskily, finding an infinite joy in the return of that simple humor that had always colored their exchanges.

A blush darkened her cheeks. "Also, it might help us figure out one big thing."

His other hand found her hip now. He spread his fingers around, until the tips of his fingers touched the upper curve of her bottom. The more he touched her, the more he wanted her. "And what's that?"

"This tension between us… It's very possible that it's just an echo of the past. Of what we once meant to each other."

His hands lowered to cup the tight curves of her bottom, tugging her even closer while she peppered kisses soft as butterfly wings all over his jaw. Not a lover's kisses but something more. Something that unraveled him bit by bit.

"Who knows? Maybe this kiss will be so bad that we can happily settle into a pattern of co-parenting and friendship and—"

Christian slammed his mouth down on hers, desperate to swallow away any of the possibilities she'd just spouted off.

She met his kiss with a ferocity that rocked the ground under his feet. And that was saying something for a man who'd lived with a blank mind for eight years. She tasted like the crack of thunder, that charge of electricity in the air, hot like summer's breeze… And he gorged himself on her.

If he'd thought to call her bluff, to push this bold version of her until it fell away, then he'd have been disappointed.

Her fingers curled in his hair, pulling him closer, and her greediness amplified his own need. Like a harmonic, it zinged between their bodies, between their mouths, between their breaths, one's desire feeding the other's. For the first few seconds, their lips clashed in a tangle of teeth and tongues, all the emotions and tension from the last eight years exploding in their faces. They were too hungry for each other, too desperate from the first brush of their mouths for her theory to be true. The fire between them far too easily stoked with an accidental touch for this to be any less raw, less real than it was.

And yet she'd pushed him. Offered this up to break him out of the spiral of anger and grief he'd descended into when he'd realized what he'd missed out on. Reminded him that he had a gloriously abundant life waiting for him, a son, for God's sake. It was more than he'd dreamed of ever having again.

Stroking his palms over her arched body, he left her mouth to draw a line of kisses along her jaw, to her neck. He licked the pulse at her neck. And then back up again. This time, their kiss was soft, unhurried, brushing and licking and teasing and retreating, a lover's exploration after the first explosion.

"You provoked me into that, you manipulative minx," he whispered, tracing the bow shape of her lips with the tip of his tongue, over and over again. Her mouth was a silky whisper against his as he licked at her, her body somehow both leaner and curvier in his hands than he remembered.

Again and again, he brushed and nipped, licked and laved at her mouth, parched for sustenance. Parched for her.

"You know how fond I am of testing theories," she said, with a smug smile against his mouth.

The press of her lips, the way her tongue tangled with his, the way she'd swept it through his mouth, searching, seeking, as if she wasn't going to leave even a little bit untouched... She was surer in her caresses than before, audacious about what she wanted.

Everything about this new Priya—bold and assertive and so damned sexy—turned him on. As if she could hear his thoughts, she went up on her toes. He groaned as she notched her hips against his erection in a seeking thrust.

One hand in her hair, he tugged her lower lip with his

teeth. Her throaty moan reverberated through him, curling every muscle into readiness. Every thought to keep this under control, of boundaries, of possible consequences, evaporated as pleasure crawled up the back of his thighs. This wasn't an experiment, this was an explosion, and all he wanted was to burn with her.

Hand on one knee, Christian opened her up farther until she could feel his erection exactly where she needed it. She moaned in sensual delight and sweat coated every inch of his body, almost a fever in his blood. With his other hand, he pushed at her robe. A clinging, silky top bared a taut midriff, her nipples pebbling against the fabric.

Bending his head, Christian licked first one tight knot through the silk, then the other.

She arched into his touch, moaning, panting, her body bowed with tension. He licked, and laved, and nipped as he rolled his hips to give her the downward pressure she needed. Her fingers dipped into his hair again, pulling his head up, up until their lips met.

Pulling her leg up to wrap around his hip, Christian flipped them around until her back met the wall. She fell against it with a loud thud, her mouth still clinging to his. "It's been so long," she kept saying, a sob rising through her chest. Christian growled and swept his tongue into her mouth for another taste and she let him be the aggressor now. As if tuned into him and his needs. As if she knew exactly how and what he wanted. And now, he was the one chasing the thrust of her hips. Rolling and grinding his hips into her, her moans egging him on.

She followed his mouth with hers, her body undulating back and forth between him and the wall. He dived in again, locking her hands against the wall, chasing his own release, thrusting into the cradle of her thighs with a force that...

Suddenly she flinched, her body bucking under him. Her cry of pain had Christian jerking away from her. In the haze of lust, it took him a few seconds to realize that something had hit her on the head. Fat tears filled her eyes, as her chest rose and fell.

He looked down to see a heavy picture frame near her feet. They'd been writhing so frantically against the wall that it had fallen off.

Laughter replaced her tears until she was sliding to the floor in an elegant heap.

Breath rushing through him as if he'd gone a couple of rounds in the ring, Christian sank to his knees. Willing himself to be gentle when his heart was thumping away, he clasped her chin. He felt like a mountain man, his hunger uncontainable, too deep. And she was so…slender and delicate and… He shouldn't have touched her at all.

Sinking to his knees, Christian tipped her chin up. "Pree? Pree, look at me."

Slowly she opened her eyes, one hand gingerly inching up her forehead. "I'm still seeing stars," she whispered, her mouth twitching. "You haven't lost your technique, Mikkelsen."

Laughter burst through him and all he wanted to do was to pull her into his lap and stay there the entire night. Maybe the entire week and then a month and then a lifetime. "You're…hurt?" he demanded. Slowly, he pushed away her hair. His fingers met a nasty bump. She flinched. A curse exploded from his mouth. "What can I do?"

Something in his tone made her pin those eyes on him, her smile disappearing. "It's just a bump, Christian. I'm fine."

He joined her against the wall, dipping his head into his hands. "I'm sorry."

"For what? I did a sloppy job of hanging it up, clearly."

He took the picture from her hands. It was a photo of when he and Jai had found their first seed investor. Taken by Priya. They'd been coming off a twenty-hour-long coding session. They looked painfully young, full of dreams and ambition. He didn't even recognize himself in the face that looked back at him. He didn't remember the ambition, the drive, the future he'd wanted back then. The cocky arrogance, the ruthless charm he'd used effortlessly…the need for more, more and more.

Priya took the picture from his hands with a purposeful grip that pulled his attention back to the present. She crawled up to his front on her knees. Apparently, she still wasn't done.

Hanging wide open to her elbow, her robe parted to reveal the tight top with her nipples still pebbled against it. The strip of silky midriff and the shorts hanging low on her hips… He wondered if that was the new image that would haunt him in his dreams.

She pushed her hair away from her face in a gesture that was achingly familiar. "So our experiment is at an end?"

He grinned, despite everything else. There was something so fiercely alive about her that it was impossible to not smile, not be thankful. Reaching out, he straightened her robe, his fingers lingering far too long on her neck. She closed her eyes as he tied the knot of her robe. "I think we disproved your hypothesis very clearly."

"I've never been more excited about being wrong," she whispered, one side of her mouth hitching up. Color darkened her cheeks as she flicked a look at him from under her lashes. "I feel like I should apologize."

He leaned his head against the wall. "For what?"

"I didn't mean to push you into something you're not ready for."

He laughed then, and it came from his belly. It was

relief and exhaustion and so much more that he couldn't even identify. Tangling his fingers in her hair, he twisted it around. Wanting to touch her was like needing his next breath. Wanting to be inside her a craven longing in his belly. "I was this close to grinding us both toward a climax in our clothes, like a randy, out-of-control teenager. What about that says I'm not ready to you?"

"You looked relieved about stopping. The bump notwithstanding."

He thrust a hand through his own hair, still tasting her on his lips. He needed to say the words even if they hurt her. Needed to draw some kind of line around this, for both their sakes. "I don't want to complicate things between us right now."

"You used to say sex should never be a complication."

"I was clearly insufferable and arrogant. And between us, it was never that simple."

For a long time, she didn't say anything. Her hands stayed on his knees, as if to tell him she was still there for him. Christian felt each and every muscle relax. Something about this silence—shared with her—didn't weigh him down. Instead, his mind calmed—her touch, her scent, the warmth of her body anchoring him to her. It was the most peaceful he'd felt in a long time.

"Will you tell me a little about what it was like for you?" came her question, soft, tentative and oh-so-guarded.

For long seconds, Christian fought the words that rose. Tried to sterilize and sanitize the truth. His gaze roamed the colorful room and landed on the boy.

No, *his son*, in another picture, with light brown hair, and large, solemn brown eyes, his mouth kicked up on one side. A candid shot that had caught him at the end of a tantrum probably while his mother... She was on her knees, her arm around him, a wide smile curving her mouth. The pure joy and love in the frame melted away every feeble protest. Burned down the hesitation. If nothing else, she deserved truth from him, as much as he could spare.

And it hit him then. This tight band that had cramped his stomach from the moment he'd walked in here. It wasn't anger. Or even grief. It was fear.

Because, God, he wasn't ready. For that little boy who'd already changed his life irrevocably. He didn't feel remotely ready for Priya and Jayden and this life he'd desperately wanted to get back to, for the weight of this beautiful life.

The terrifying fact was that he wasn't sure if he'd ever feel ready. If he'd ever feel good enough.

His jaw tightened so hard that Priya braced for him to shut down, to shut her out. Had she pushed him too far today? Would he ever let her see him? That was the biggest difference she saw in him—how closed off he was now. How little he shared.

Even that kiss, she felt as if she'd stolen it from him. Taken it for herself. At least, in the beginning. Her first thought when he'd brushed his lips against hers was that he tasted the same.

From all those years ago, from the kisses and caresses he'd lavished upon her. But also different. Or was it her who was different?

The attraction between them, however—it seemed it had remained constant. Maybe even the only constant between them because they were clearly different people now. She didn't know if she could seek solace in that or not. Because it was clear he'd given in to her against his better judgment, even though it had been exactly what they'd both needed.

Even though, once they'd started, it had been a conflagration. While it felt like her body was still burning in the wake of it... He looked like he'd left it far behind already. Shadows wreathed his face now...carrying him away from her, from this moment. Far away, where she wasn't sure she could reach him.

Maybe she shouldn't want to reach him there, the sensible voice in her head pointed out. Maybe it was better to keep her distance from him, like she'd done all those years ago.

"I've been...a stranger to myself," he said, after what felt like an eternity, "for eight years. Once I'd recovered from the coma, I'd wake up every day with this hope in my chest that something would trigger all my memories back. I'd look at my face in the mirror and hate that blank stare of a stranger. Each hour, each day passed was excruciatingly slow. Each sunrise felt like a...curse.

"After the first couple of years of that, I used to wake up wishing for no hope at all. I thought that would be easier to bear. For the last two years, I... I think I was done. I didn't even know when I gave up. I wasn't happy but I'd made my peace. I was starting to let go of everything, I think.

"And then suddenly, there you were... When I saw your picture, it brought me to my knees. My hands wouldn't stop shaking as I went about my day, terrified that it was all going to disappear again. I've never been so scared in my life... Not even the day I woke up alone in the hospital do I remember feeling that fearful. I kept thinking what if..."

Priya pushed up between his legs. Her breath shuddered out in strangled relief when he didn't push her away. She laced her fingers through his and held on tightly. So many questions rose, and she swallowed them all away.

"On the flight here, I was on pins and needles, jacked up on excitement and hope. Now...to learn the sheer amount that I've lost, to learn that life has moved on so completely without me… It feels as if I still don't know myself. As if I'm walking through a stranger's life." He turned to the framed picture of Jayden, his eyes deep blue pools. "The uncertainty… I haven't gotten used to it even after all these years."

"Especially for a man who liked to lord it over everybody else with his whip-smart brain, his dazzling good looks and easy, seductive charm," she added, determined to pull him out of the murky depths of grief.

Her reward was a sudden wicked grin. "And yet, I don't remember making much of an impression on you."

Priya heard the undertone of dissatisfaction in it. As if he didn't like that he hadn't left an impression on her.

Intense Christian was…*intense*.

She let it go, for now. Because he wouldn't believe it even if she told him that the opposite was true. Did the past even matter anymore? Was it anything but a weight dragging them down?

She sat back on her folded legs, keeping their fingers clasped together. "So how about, between you and me," she said, adopting a casual tone she was far from feeling, "we only think of you as a work in progress?"

He communicated what he thought of that with a single, raised brow.

"Just hear me out, okay?"

"I can't wait," he said. The exaggerated roll of his eyes undercut the sarcasm. Not that anything would stop her.

"What if we agree…" She was the one to swallow now; a part of her felt as if she was losing him again already… "that you're not committing to a life with us?"

He flinched as if she'd punched him. Or called him half a man. Or whatever it was that this new Christian found insulting. "That's the most ridiculous thing I've

ever heard. Not forgetting that it's damned unfair to…
him." Another nod toward Jayden's pic. "What are we
going to do—not tell him that I'm his father? Ask him
to wait a couple of years before he could call me dad? Or
just don't tell him I'm alive?"

Hurt pinged in her belly that he didn't consider himself
returned to her, only to his son. Which was ridiculous because he was being sensible and considerate and cautious
about him and her. She had to acknowledge that. Reckless
Christian had always driven her nuts.

"I can't just ask…you to sit on the sidelines while I figure out myself. I can't."

"You aren't asking, Christian. I'm offering. At least
with me, you don't have to… There are no expectations
between us. No certainties I'm demanding of you."

He banged his head against the wall, tension bracketing his mouth. "This from the girl who always dealt in
absolutes, who saw the world in black and white, as right
and wrong?"

She cringed at his description of her. "If you were a
reckless, arrogant idiot, I was a self-righteous prude who
preferred to hide in the margins of life. No wonder we
drove each other up the wall."

His mouth twitched. "Did we?"

"Our marriage…" She looked down at her hands, pushing away all the little wishes and hopes of her heart into
one corner and locking it away. "…it's just a piece of paper,
Christian. It's always been just that. Nothing more than a
partnership—two friends saving each other. That's what
you called it, remember? All that's different now is that
we share an additional responsibility—Jayden."

He swept his fingers over his face. "And if I hurt him,
Pree?"

The pain in those words threatened to tear Priya apart.

"You won't. However you've changed, whoever you are now, I know, here—" she brought his hand to her chest to feel the steady rhythm of her heart "—that that will never happen. I'm here, Christian, to help. With everything."

Blue eyes held hers, inscrutable. Studying. Searching. He pulled his hand away from her. "Tell me about… Jayden."

Crawling on her knees, she pulled out an album she'd made of Jayden's photos by month ever since he'd been born. Midnight came and went as they pored over the pictures. As she described to him what a curious, sensitive boy their son was. How much she'd already told him about Christian and her and Jai. How very cunning and cute he could be, depending on his mood. How precocious he was on an emotional level.

Her legs were numb when Christian pulled her up after what felt like more than a few hours. "We won't make a big deal of who you are when he gets here. I mean, he already knows you from your pictures. He's a happy, well-adjusted child but it still might take him a little time to warm up to you. Just be…yourself."

He looked so concerned about that Priya immediately added, "Trust me, Christian. Even if you don't trust yourself right now." She plucked a stuffed toy—a triceratops—and ran her hand over the soft beak and frill jutting out of its head. "Do you… Do you need anything more for bed?"

Just as the silence began to inch into awkwardness, he said, "I have one more question for you. Since you seem to be the one with all the answers right now."

There was no rancor or resentment in his words. He was content to let her lead in this, for now. It was the Christian who easily gave others the spotlight when it was demanded. Without tripping over his own ego like so many powerful men she knew. "Yeah?" Priya said, noting his gaze take her in from head to toe.

"What do you get out of all this? What about your needs?"

"My needs are secondary to yours and Jayden's right now," she said, sudden tears in her throat.

"I don't—"

"Except maybe I can feel less guilty about one thing."

"About what?"

"About going on a date, like I did today. Now that you're here, I don't have to worry about Mama finding out about—"

He was on her then—all six feet three inches of him—before she could blink. Priya felt like the time she'd taken Jai to a zoo and they'd watched a group of teenagers make faces at a tiger. Here the cage was invisible, self-imposed by Christian, but still...if it broke through...

"No. No more dates for you. Not unless you want me to descend into insanity imagining you with another man..." A growl erupted from him, drenching her skin in goose bumps.

She raised a brow, loving the possessive edge in his voice. "But I have...needs that have to be met," she said innocently. Hand on his chest, she fluttered her lashes at him. "Unless you're offering to see to them?"

He pushed into her touch. His erection was a brand against her belly, singeing her where she stood. "I won't play nice anymore. I will swallow you whole."

She wished she hadn't been a naive, prudish fool that weekend in the Alps. That she'd met him as an equal. Then maybe he wouldn't have turned away from her afterward.

"And how do you know my tastes haven't changed? Maybe I like being devoured by an intense, sexy lumberjack who gets me all hot and bothered with one look."

She laughed when he rolled his eyes at her, and kissed his cheek one last time, the effort of pulling away from him taking every ounce of energy she had. "Good night, Christian," she said, and went to bed with the image of him looking at that old photo she'd once clicked of him and Jai.

CHAPTER SIX

CHRISTIAN HADN'T BEEN able to even imagine what or how he'd feel until a little boy whose head barely reached his thigh looked up at him out of a pair of thoughtful brown eyes. His heart jumped into his throat, cutting off his ability to form words. Nothing in all the misery and darkness he'd lived through had prepared him for this moment.

It had ended up being two more days before his grandfather and Priya's parents returned with Jayden. Two days that he'd spent in the guesthouse where he'd used to hang out with Jai and his friends during high school.

Then, he'd wanted to escape all the restrictions Ben had tried to place on him.

Now, he didn't know what he was running away from— himself or this new life. He'd even asked Priya not to tell anyone other than her parents, Ben and the estate employees that he was back.

If Priya thought it strange that he wasn't staying in any of the guest bedrooms, she didn't mention it. In fact, she'd mostly left him to his own devices after that first night, poking her head in only once in the evening to inquire if he needed anything. If he thought the silence in the guesthouse would provide him with a measure of peace, he was wrong. He felt just as unsettled here as he did in the house but at least she wasn't there to witness it.

Christian knew he was being a selfish beast, but he couldn't help himself. After such a long stretch of having no one and nothing in his head, that first evening had been intense. He needed to recover from it and since he barely slept these days, it meant working out most of his excess energy by running around the trails on the estate. He'd also shooed away the gardeners and gotten his hands dirty with the seasonal chopping and culling that the woods required.

His grandfather's estate—his now and Jayden's in the future—was full of untamed woodland from natural preservation areas to three ponds and it felt like the only time he could breathe was when he was out there.

The last thing he needed was for Priya to know how little he slept. Or how he was still struggling to get through most days without enough sleep and with too many headaches.

And now, here was his son.

Darker than him in coloring and lighter than Priya, Jayden had his mother's serious brown eyes and the straight little nose but his smile... It was full of mischief. Like his own had been once.

Jayden had run out into the backyard, where he'd been waiting, on tenterhooks. Within a few minutes of Priya talking to him after they'd arrived, Christian went to his knees on the grass.

He'd been so nervous, his skin so clammy, that he'd asked if they should wait for one more day. Wait until maybe Jayden got over his jet lag. If Priya had seen him fudging for his own sake, thankfully, she'd kept quiet.

Now, his son stared at Christian with a thoughtfulness that felt beyond his age.

"You're not dead."

"No," Christian replied, his throat full of emotion.

Jayden looked at his mother, who came to stand behind him.

Christian could feel Priya vibrating with her own nervous energy, felt her need to wrap her arms around Jayden in reassurance. But she kept her distance, letting Jayden explore this new development however he needed to.

Trusting Christian to do it right, too. His heart settled at the faith she showed in him.

"Then why didn't you come back?" Jayden said finally, eying Christian up and down. His gaze was very much like his mother's—far too intent for a little boy. "You don't like us?"

Christian put one hand on his son's shoulder. Emotion whipped at him how terrifyingly small he was and yet he could skewer Christian with one look. Words came to his lips and fell away. He sighed and decided to go with the truth. "I recovered from the accident but I was still sick in my head for a long time. I..."

"Here?" Jayden said, tapping Christian's temple with a small finger.

Christian nodded. "Exactly. It made me forget about your mama and your great-grandpa."

His eyes solemn, Jayden nodded. "Does it still hurt?"

Refusal sprang to his lips but Christian held it off. More than anything, he did want an honest relationship with his son. With Priya.

Eight years of being lost in your own head meant he was never going to take things for granted ever again. And definitely not this little boy who had already burrowed his way into Christian's heart. God, how had he doubted even for a second that he wouldn't feel this overwhelming love for his own child? "It does hurt once in a while. I have bad dreams, too," he added, wondering if he was overburdening a child with the truth.

But somehow it was easier to confide in Jayden than Priya. Which he knew would send her into a rage, justifiably so.

"I don't want you to worry about me, okay, Jayden? I'm getting better every day. Especially now that I've got you and Grandpa Ben and your mama back."

"Okay."

Sticky little fingers pressed into his temples on both sides. Christian drew in a rough breath, a quiet sob building in his chest. His brows drawing together in concentration, Jayden looked determined to help him. He forced himself to stay still, to keep his expression steady.

"I sometimes get a stomachache." Jayden cast a surreptitious glance at his mother. "Grandpa Ben lets me eat donuts for breakfast. And then the same day, Grandma gives me cake for evening snack. I eat them without telling the other. That's when I get sick."

Christian furrowed his brow. "Oh, I don't think you can be expected to say no to donuts or cake."

Jayden grinned a crooked smile. "That's when Mama talks about you. When I've been naughty. She says something about an apple and a tree."

Laughter burst out of Christian's belly.

Jayden leaned toward him and Christian was assaulted with the smells of soap and grass. His chest expanded to pull in more and he knew he'd just fallen in love with this beautiful boy of his. That in a matter of few seconds, the entire axis of his life had tilted.

He'd lost his parents when he'd been not much older than Jayden. Ben and he had always had a combative, contentious sort of relationship. In hindsight, Christian knew he'd been one hell of a troublemaker for a sixty-year-old man to look after.

It was only when he'd met Jai in middle school that he'd settled down. A bit.

"Don't tell Mama about the sweets, okay? She'll feel sad."

"Yeah?" Christian whispered back, his gaze flickering to Priya, whose hawk-like attention had been distracted by her mother. They were in a deep discussion, the older woman's face all animation while Priya's spoke of calm resolve.

This morning, she was dressed in a white dress shirt and black trousers, with her hair pulled back in a braid. Teal-colored pumps added a splash of brightness to her outfit. When he'd finally wandered into the main house both mornings long after noon, the staff had informed him that Mrs. Mikkelsen had left for work. Whenever it was that she'd returned, he'd been gone.

Even from the distance that separated them, Christian could appreciate the long line of her legs, the dip of her waist, the rounded curve of her breasts in the tight-fitting shirt. Any assumption he'd made that the impact of seeing her would lessen after forty-eight hours ground to dust.

"I know why she sometimes gets sad," Jayden said, tugging at Christian's attention.

"Would you like to tell me?" Christian said, in what he hoped was an encouraging tone.

"Mama's got an important job. She's a CEO. That she means she's like—" Jayden scrunched his brow "—the boss of all the bosses. I learned that when she did a show-and-tell for my class. And she says it's like…super important for her to do a good job. To make sure bad people don't steal the company. Especially now that Grandpa Ben's retired."

That his stubborn grandfather had retired from the company was news to Christian. As was everything else, of course. He'd hit his quota of shocks after learning about the existence of a seven-year-old son. After the kiss he and Priya had shared. Everything else had felt extraneous to his world.

It still did.

"She told me how you and your best friend worked really hard to build the company and she said she'd be damned if she handed over the reins to your evil cousin Bastien," Jayden finished in that near whisper.

Shocked, Christian stared at Jayden.

How on earth could he have forgotten about Bastien? He'd always been a thorn in Christian's side. He could just imagine what a giant headache he might have become for Priya, seeing that he'd always resented the place she and Jai had occupied in Christian's life.

His hand over his mouth, his son flushed. "Don't tell her I said that, okay? She doesn't know I heard it. Mama doesn't like it when I curse."

Christian pursed his mouth and nodded. It was more than clear what a wonderful boy his son was and what a stellar job Priya had done raising him.

There was so much to learn, so much he had to figure out. And the thought of doing that without Priya by his side made bile rise in his throat. The physical sensation was so strong that he frowned. It was a weakness, this constant need for her, to see her as his anchor, but God help him, he had no idea how to shed it.

Jayden's small hand moving over his head brought him back.

Just looking into his face made Christian breathe a little easier. Apparently, his son was a fount of all kinds of interesting information. "So why do you think your mama would be sad? About you eating all those sweets?"

Jayden tapped his forehead. "She says Grandpa Ben and Grandma spoil me rotten. But she's got to be a CEO, too. So she has two big jobs. She says being my mama's the best out of the two, though."

"I don't doubt that," Christian said with a smile. His mind was running over all the problematic scenarios Bastien would've created for Priya, all the challenges she'd have faced. All the different things she'd had to juggle over the years without any kind of emotional support. He also had no doubt that her mother and his grandfather—both with strong, dominating personalities—had often put her in the middle of their squabbles, too.

"I wouldn't have survived if I remained that weak waif, Christian. I had to grow up."

"Thank you for sharing your secrets with me, Jayden."

Jayden nodded but the thoughtful look was back in his eyes again. "So you're my dad, right? Can I call you that?"

Christian ruffled his hair, his throat full again. "Whatever you want to call me is okay, buddy."

With no warning, Jayden threw himself at Christian. Christian rocked onto his heels but caught him anyway. Less to do with his son's tiny body and more about the innocent affection. Again, he was hit by a sense of alarm and awe at how big a place this tiny boy had already carved in his heart. By that sense of loss that he'd missed so much of Jayden's life already.

"You want to play with me and Aiden later? Aiden's my best friend. Kinda like you and Uncle Jai used to be. Sheela might be there, too," he said, with less enthusiasm.

Christian pushed to his feet and took Jayden's hand. "Absolutely, I'd love to play with you and your friends. And this Sheela... You don't like her?"

"She's a lot of fun, for a girl," Jayden said and snuck a glance back at his mom. "Mama says I shouldn't say that. It's just that Sheela changes the rules. But I swore I'd be nice to her."

"Yeah?" Christian said, laughing.

"Yes. Mama said you and Uncle Jai were the bestest friends. That you were never mean to her just because she's a girl. She says that's how I should behave."

Christian's gaze shifted to Priya, who was almost upon them. There was that hum under his skin again, as if he was a magnet vibrating in her presence.

"What are you both talking about?" she asked.

"Just boy stuff," Christian explained, with a wink at his son.

Jayden beamed. "Boys have secrets, Mama. Now I won't tell you all those gross jokes."

Priya ruffled his hair. "I didn't mind, Jayden."

Jayden turned to Christian. "You should tell her when your head hurts again... Dad." He looked at his mother and she nodded. His brown eyes twinkled as his smile took over his entire face. "She'll cuddle you and give you the best kisses, and then your headache will disappear, like this," he said with a click of his fingers that wasn't quite a click.

Then he took off without a backward glance, his short legs bounding off.

Christian felt as if his son had established a direct line to his heart and was tugging it, this way and that. That he was going to do it for the rest of their lives and there was nothing to do but accept it. To count this as one of the blessings he'd never thought to receive.

Jayden ran to his grandparents and Ben. All three of them immediately joined his game of catch with undivided attention.

Priya stood leaning against the wall, her gaze landing on his face but not quite staying there. He felt a different kind of tug as his eyes rested on her. The V created by her dress shirt gave a glimpse of smooth brown skin. He still couldn't get over how fiercely different she looked. It was as if her resolve had etched itself into her features, becoming a part of her.

"Your cuddles and kisses come with the highest recommendations," he said, propping his shoulder against the opposite wall. The wall at his back felt good. The sun on his face felt divine. The sight of the evergreens that straddled the property... It finally felt like home. Yet the same contentment had escaped him when he wasn't around her. And that bothered him.

"You're welcome to give them a try yourself."

God, the minx had gotten so good at teasing. Damned good at poking him in exactly the right spot to provoke a real response. "I'll keep that in mind."

He felt her gaze move over his face, just as welcoming and warm as the sun. She might as well have traced every shadow and plane with those curious, greedy fingers. "You don't look so good, Christian."

"I thought you were into rugged mountain men."

He heard her gasp and felt desire curl through his belly. He was building up a database of all her sounds. All her reactions.

"How are you feeling this morning?" she pressed.

"Perfect. I'm perfect."

"The guesthouse... Do you need anything?"

"In case you forgot, I had it built more than a decade ago to be the perfect man cave," he teased, going for levity. "It's still perfect."

He waited for her to ask why he was avoiding the main house. Why he was putting so much distance—emotional and physical—between him and the rest of the family. Why he wasn't doing his level best to bridge the gap between him and his real life.

"Your seven-year-old son's much easier to manage than

you," she said dryly, surprising him again. "And that's saying something."

Laughter burst out of him.

Jayden's own whoop of laughter from the yard tugged their attention. Christian turned to watch his son. *His son*—he was never going to get over that. "I spent so many hours in his room before I met him, touching his things, smelling his clothes. And yet I didn't realize how real he is until he looked at me. Pinning me with those big brown eyes."

A moment of pure harmony arched between them. It was impossible to not look at that little boy and know that there were precious things in the world. "That's how I felt when the nurse handed him to me that first time. I'd made all these plans during the pregnancy and then there he was, tiny and beautiful and so very real."

"He's very…mature for his age."

Priya nodded. "He's extremely bright emotionally. Almost too tuned into others. Sometimes, I'm scared I won't be able to protect him, give him all he needs."

Christian reached for her hand and after a moment's hesitation, she gave it to him.

He laced their fingers and squeezed. Lifting their clasped hands, he pressed a kiss to the back of her hand. Rubbed his nose against the soft, silky skin, unable to let go. Then he gulped in a big breath and forced himself to release it. Every time he touched her, it was harder to let go.

"What was that for?"

"You've a done a wonderful job with him. I can't tell you how much I'll always regret not being here sooner."

"Thank you. I tried… I try hard every day." She laughed softly. "In all the literature you read about being a mother, they don't tell you about the guilt button."

"What's that?"

"It's like it gets embedded inside you. Every morning, every night, every word your child speaks, every hurt they get, your first response is, did I do it wrong? Was it my fault? Am I a bad mother? Should I have done something differently? And it just gets more intense as they grow older."

He heard the emotion in her tone and couldn't help but take her hand again and tug her toward him.

She came. Sliding his arm around her waist, he folded her to him. She clung to him, plastering her front to his side, burying her face in his upper arm. "So many nights... I wished you were here to hold him, to see him. To tell me I was doing okay, to hold me when I felt like crying in those early months. To share a laugh with when he started to walk, to marvel at him with when he said his first word."

It was the first time he'd heard that wobble in her voice, that insecurity. He'd been so deep inside his own head since he'd arrived, that he hadn't given a thought to how she'd survived, how she'd come through the other end so fierce. And he had a feeling the only reason she'd even admitted this much to him was the fact that it was about Jayden, about being a parent.

"You're doing spectacularly." He squeezed her hard, hoping he could convey the right message. "I'll do my best to share the responsibility. I don't know the first thing about being a parent, so you'll just have to tell me what you need. Where you need my help."

"I don't..." Whatever she saw in his eyes, she sighed. "I've gotten used to doing things my way. Don't expect me to just give in to everything like I used to."

"I don't remember you giving in to anything you

didn't want to," he said, a hard edge to his voice that he couldn't control.

Their one night together swirled in front of his eyes. Was that what she meant? Had she come to regret it in the years that followed?

Jayden shouted for them as the staff started serving lunch.

The last thing Christian wanted was to join Ben and Priya's parents. He suddenly wanted to burrow deep into the very hole he'd done everything in his power to crawl out from. That he'd once been such a party animal was unfathomable to him now.

But he recognized the need for the ritual, the place everyone had in Jayden's life. It was on him to fit into the existing landscape, not fragment it to suit himself. Ben needed him, too, even though the old goat would die before admitting it.

For now, he could only tolerate the presence of Jayden and Priya—that had become clear in two minutes. With Jayden, there was nothing but the freedom of being himself. Of being the best man he could be today, without worrying about expectations. It was, he was glad to discover, easy to love his son, easy to be himself with him.

And with Priya… It was a thorny knot of need and comfort and familiarity that he didn't have the energy to untangle right now. But despite the knots, there was a constant hum of desire between them, an awareness as potent as his own breath.

He made to move when Priya stopped him with her hand on his elbow.

"Just one more thing."

"Yeah?"

"Come back to the main house. Sleep in the master bedroom."

His head jerked up, every suppressed instinct in him reacting to that invitation like a hungry dog offered morsels of meat. "I told you I'm not throwing you out of your own bedroom."

"No, I'm not planning on leaving." She blushed when he narrowed his gaze. "I'm saying you should sleep in there, too. I spent all day yesterday reading up on your... condition."

"I see," Christian said, not wanting to have this conversation of all things. With her.

Which was messed up and unfair because she was the one dealing with the consequences of him pushing his way back into her life, the one who'd been acting like an adult from the very first moment. But the last thing he wanted was for her to see him as some kind of patient. As a feeble man she had to look after and care for.

"I couldn't concentrate at the board meeting. I couldn't... I kept wanting to call you just to see your face. To know that you were really here."

"I know it's hard for you to keep the knowledge that I'm back a secret for now. I'm sorry."

"No. I mean, yes, it's hard. But I like it. I like the idea of having you all to ourselves for now." Her smile wavered as she hurried on. "I got so restless thinking of you here alone and I realized I should've taken the day off, been here with you."

"No, I needed the space," he burst out before he could temper his tone.

"Of course, you're right," she said quickly, not a hint of hurt in her eyes. "Anyway... I did a lot of research into what this must be like for you. Living alone and having that long dissociative episode, then your memories hitting you all of a sudden..."

"What about it?" Christian demanded, all too aware of

the medical terms for his condition. And tired of names that did nothing to explain what the hell had happened inside his head. Or if it could even happen again. That was his biggest nightmare, one he faced every minute of every day.

"Everything I read said you…might need physical comfort, Christian. You need touch, the warmth of another human being. In whatever form that feels good and safe to you. I'm…" There was that Priya he'd once known so well—wary and blushing and all the good things of the world rolled into one cute little package. "—offering it to you. I want you to sleep next to me. Hold me, if you need to."

"I didn't realize you'd taken up nursing, too," he said in a low whisper, unable to keep the bitterness out of his words. Ashamed of himself for everything he was feeling and everything he couldn't control. "Or are you simply feeling sorry for me?"

She regarded him with those big eyes, as if he was a child like Jayden. Patiently waiting for him to get over his tantrum. "You must be really confused if you think I feel sorry for you after everything I demanded the other night."

Something in her tone assuaged the raw parts of him that were still chafing. At what, he had no idea.

"Why do you assume that it's only for you anyway? Consider me for a second. I've been lonely, too. You know what the hardest part of it all was for me, of being in the limelight all of a sudden, of being a single mom, of being the one who had to hold it all together? That there was no one to touch me at the end of the day. No one to hold me. No one to…" She swallowed and looked away. "It's not just sex that I missed, it's companionship. A friend's touch. A comforting hug. A reassuring palm on my back. It's such an instinctive need... I think it's why I can't seem to be able to keep my hands to myself around you."

He knew it wasn't easy for her to admit that to him. To bare her soul to a man who was little more than a stranger to her. And yet, he was like a wounded beast, striking if she dared to get close. "And if having sex with you made me feel better, would you offer that, too?"

"If that's what you need, happily," she said, not even batting an eyelid. Not at his blunt language, nor at the idea. "As we have clearly demonstrated with our little experiment, I wouldn't even have to call it my conjugal responsibility. No closing my eyes and thinking of England or whatever the saying is."

He choked with laughter. Damn but the woman was tying him up in knots.

Her brown gaze glittered with challenge and humor and it terrified him how much he...liked her like this. How much he didn't want to hurt her. How much he wanted to be the version of Christian she deserved.

"You wouldn't have hesitated if I was in the same position. No, in fact, if I look through our tangled past, you did do the same for me."

He turned to her, a possessive urge snaking through him. "I didn't have sex with you that weekend because I felt sorry for you, Pree. Whatever your own reasons were."

She blanched. For the first time in two days, she looked shaken. Unsure of herself. And still, she didn't back down. "Why are you being so stubborn about this? What's wrong if—"

"Anyway, I've never been a fan of all that cuddling and touching and emotional stuff in bed," he said, cutting her off. Going for a cheap shot that neither of them deserved. "That part of me hasn't changed."

He strolled into the garden and took the chair next to Jayden without waiting for her response.

Minutes later, Priya took the chair opposite, smiling at something Jayden said. For two hours, while he brooded and struggled to even smile, she smoothed over his silence, soothed his grandfather and his son, answered a hundred invasive questions from her mother and did it all without showing the strain of how much it might be costing her.

How complicated her life must have been.

And here he was, only adding to her troubles, despite his best efforts.

Because Priya was doing all the right things—giving him space, walking on eggshells around him, dealing with company headaches, not announcing his return to the world and acting as a shield between him and his grandfather. Him and his son.

He could almost see her thought processes—here was a friend who was struggling. A man she felt obligated to help. A man she shared a tangled history with. Her integrity would never let her walk away from him, never give less than 100 percent of herself.

And the desperately needy coward that he was, he could still taste the comfort and pleasure of touching her, of tucking her against him. Of her lean yet curvy body soothing the ache he felt right to his bones. But he couldn't keep using her like that.

He didn't want Priya's pity. He didn't want her obligation. And the very thought of pity sex made him angry, restless.

But even worse was the idea of how much more addicted he'd become to her if he took her to bed. If he gave himself everything he so desperately craved. The very intensity of it stayed his hand, and yet had made him lash out at the one person who was holding him together.

"I'm sorry," he said, wrapping his fingers around her wrist when she got up from the table. Everyone had retired to the house, along with Jayden, who'd been flagging in his seat, half-asleep. "I don't want to hurt you. You have no idea how much I appreciate your offer. I just didn't…"

She leaned her hip against his middle, not quite looking down at him. He pressed his face into her palm and she clasped it with such tenderness that he couldn't breathe. "I know that. I do, Christian. You might think everything about you is different, and to some extent that's true, but I still know you where it matters."

"You have more faith in me than I do."

"Like you had in me, once. That's what this…relationship has always been about, hasn't it?"

He released her and she walked away. And while it still bothered him on a level he didn't want to examine, at least her friendship was something he could accept. Something he would allow himself. But nothing else.

CHAPTER SEVEN

PRIYA TIPTOED THROUGH the hallway drenched in pitch-black toward Christian's bedroom in the guesthouse. If her heart wasn't thumping a thousand beats a minute about what state she'd find Christian in, the whole thing would've felt like a gothic comedy with her creeping around and spying on him.

The digital clock had said past midnight when something had woken her. She'd instantly looked for his tall, broad figure roaming the woodsy acreage through the curtains she'd kept open in her bedroom.

She'd spotted him in the middle of the night several times over the last few weeks, running through the trail in nothing but dark gray sweats. Moonlight had illuminated the hard planes and ridges of his bare abdomen. Molten heat had unspooled at her sex and she'd had to cross and uncross her legs to try to make it go away.

Even if she didn't know about his nighttime…adventures through the woods, his tightly drawn features when he greeted her and Jayden in the patio every morning would have alerted her to the problem.

He wasn't sleeping and it was the hardest thing to do to not intervene. To stifle the urge to help, in some way.

Pushing him to lean on her, she'd realized, was mostly selfish on her part. Because she wanted him to "get better" fast. Even that felt wrong in her head—that insidious implication that he was somehow "not enough" for her exactly as he was.

Amidst the tangle of confusion, she knew it wasn't even 100 percent true.

Because the very little he'd let her see of him, she admired far too much. Admired and respected and...liked. She couldn't help but adore how easily and effortlessly he'd learned to handle Jayden. How seamlessly he took up all the small things Jayden had been missing in his life.

And while he didn't confide in her, he was slowly knitting himself back into the fabric of her own life. For all they were keeping his return quiet, he'd started listening to her when she wanted to talk about work. He was there like the solid evergreens at the end of a long day.

Keeping her distance when she'd known him for so long—when he'd been the best friend she'd needed once upon a time—was hard. And the worst part was missing him—like an ache in her belly, even when he was right in front of her. Because except for the kiss that first night that she still thought she'd stolen, he'd kept her at a distance.

Tonight the gardens had been empty, but now she was awake, she couldn't fall asleep again until she'd reassured herself that he was okay. Just one quick peek, she told herself. He wasn't going to like it, but she didn't give a damn.

Finding him in his bed asleep was good enough for her. She was almost out the door when the guttural moan stopped her.

Another moan came, wrenched from the depths of his being.

Priya rushed to his side. His covers were tangled around his lower body. His naked chest gleamed with perspiration. Her body lit up like some kind of sensory panel as the musky, heated scent of him filled her nostrils. Everything about him, even the pain etched into his tightly drawn features, called to her.

But for her own sanity's sake, Priya considered walking away. Leaving him to what was clearly a nightmare. He'd made it clear he didn't want her help or comfort. And yet, how could she let him suffer like this?

Brow furrowed, the soft duvet twisted in his fists, he was writhing on the bed. Dark shadows hung beneath his closed eyes. His thick hair, badly in need of a cut, stuck to his damp forehead.

Heart racing, Priya sat down on the bed. Her hip nudged up against a solid rope of thigh muscle, sending awareness prickling through her. Smoothing away the damp hair from his forehead, she touched him. He was hot and damp.

A throaty murmur left his lips as he thrashed again. His arms shot out suddenly, almost sending her flying off the bed. Thanks to fast reflexes, Priya managed to hang on by gripping onto the tight, tense muscles of his shoulders. His head shook from side to side with a force that scared her might damage the tendons standing out in his neck.

Bending forward, she clasped his jaw, the pads of her fingers holding the hard bone firmly so he couldn't shake her off. "Christian, it's okay, baby. Shh… You're okay," she whispered like she did with Jayden. "I'm here, I'm not going anywhere."

Behind his eyelids, his eyes moved rapidly, as his body continued to writhe. She wished she had the upper-body strength to hold him still. Her arms clenched painfully against the increasing pressure. Sculpted lips that used to be ready to smile parted with a hiss, murmuring unintelligible words between painful-sounding groans.

Priya shook him again, her fingers almost losing purchase on his damp skin. "Christian, wake up."

Whatever nightmare held him in thrall, it was tormenting him. Her eyes prickled with wet heat, but she arrested the tears with a deep breath. If it took the entire night to rouse him, she'd do it.

Bent low over his face, she continued with the litany of soothing words. Pressed a trail of soft kisses over his collarbone and farther down. She crooned to him, the same lullaby she'd used to sing to Jayden when he'd had a bad night.

Electric-blue eyes suddenly held hers, vacant and unseeing.

The blankness of his stare made her flinch, more than his rough thrashing had. Fear of losing him again, fear of being left behind, was a stroke of lightning, scorching every little spark of joy she felt in him being back. An abyss of grief welled in her chest and her words broke on a sob. "Christian, come back to me, baby, please, you've got to—"

That gaze that had mocked and laughed and teased flicked toward her again and this time, recognition danced in his eyes. He went from asleep and thrashing to alert and present in two breaths. And in between those two breaths was her biggest nightmare. That he'd forgotten who she was. Again.

His hands moved to her bare arms, his fingers gripping her tightly. "Pree, is it Jayden?"

"No." Unshed tears clogged her throat. "I'm scared, Christian. So scared."

He shot up into a sitting position. The remnants of his nightmare were there in his pinched features. "It's okay, Starling. I'm here. I'm not going anywhere, ever again," he whispered into her hair, repeating the same words she'd whispered to him moments ago. It was the infinite tenderness in an otherwise hoarse voice that did it.

That cloak of practical competence she wrapped around herself like armor splintered. With a soft cry, she buried her face in the sweat-damp hollow at his throat. Clung to him like a child, seeking reassurance. Crawled into the space between his thighs, half kneeling, half shaking. And completely undone.

He went utterly still. And then those steel band-like arms squeezed her so hard that her heartbeat happily rattled against his. After a few seconds, his hold became loose. As if she was some wild, tangled thing that might break if he held her too tightly.

Priya soaked it all in—the salty heat of his skin against her lips, the rapid beat of his pulse, the damp warmth of his body, the clenched tightness of his muscles. She reveled in the soothing words he whispered at her ear, in the tenderness in his tone, in the up-and-down motions of his fingers combing through her hair gently. She felt as breakable as she'd been once, as fragile as they'd all thought her.

"I'm here, Pree," he whispered again, and the vibrations of those words swept through her, lighting pathways through her nerves, to every limb, to her heart, to her lower belly. "Whatever you need, it's yours."

The words landed like a soft crooning her soul was desperate for. Her tremors subsided, the tears dried up and something new broke through. "Anything, Christian?"

"Yes, baby, anything," he said, laying the world at her feet. But she didn't want the world.

She wanted him. Not as her son's father, not as a friend, not as a partner, but as a lover. She wanted the man who'd once broken down all her barriers and dragged her screaming and kicking into living her life.

She grazed the skin at his throat with her teeth. His

broad, powerful shoulders stilled and his heart thumped. He was pure male on her tongue. She did it again. Pressed the tip of her tongue to that hollow. A little nip here and a quick lick there. And she felt the rumble of the groan building in his chest, the clench and release of his muscles around her.

Refusing to be chased off, she brought her mouth to his chin and he looked down. Their gazes held, bare and honest, for the first time since he'd returned, and something almost like gratitude filled the moment.

"Kiss me," she begged.

The first press and slide of his lips sent her heart thundering at a dangerous pace. His beard rasped against her lips, providing an alarmingly pleasurable contrast. His fingers slipped into the hair at her nape, holding her still as he ravaged her mouth.

His tongue tangled with hers, swept over every molten inch of her mouth, pouring his need into hers, taking her breath into him. Hands filled with the taut muscles of his shoulders, she pulled herself closer to him. The press and slide of her flimsy-lace-covered breasts against his chest had her groaning into his mouth.

She sank her teeth gently into his lower lip. "More, Christian," she demanded.

His mouth took hers in a rougher, deeper kiss. She tasted his hunger for her, his desperation, and returned it with her own—eight years' worth of want she'd been carrying around.

On the next dip of his lips, Priya chased his tongue and sucked at the tip. On and on, she devoured him. Urged by instinct and nothing else, she bowed back into the bed. He followed her, his body covering hers.

Groans ripped out of their mouths, an erotic symphony in the air.

He was a heavy, delicious weight, a taut, tense press of hard muscles, fitting around her curves perfectly. Her thighs fell away immediately, and the instinctual thrust of his hips knocked the breath out of her. He was hot and hard and everything she wanted.

"What do you want, Pree?" he whispered, his mouth at her neck, his hands petting her all over. "Now, Starling. Ask me before I come to my senses."

Priya looked up at him, even as a lone tear fell down her temple into her hair. If she lost him again... No, he was here, now. All over her. Around her. "I want... I want so much pleasure that all the fear and the loneliness and everything else is scrubbed from my mind. I want what you dared me to ask for, that night. What I shied away from because I was naive and a coward and..." She was half sobbing now.

His blue eyes widened, his swollen lips parting on a soft gasp.

"Do you remember?" she whispered, moving his palm from her neck to her breasts to her belly.

His fingers spread, staking his claim to every inch of her. Something wicked shone in his eyes. "Yes."

She brought his hand to her pelvis, where his palm covered her sex. Her hips jerked up at the contact. "I want your mouth here, Christian. I want so much pleasure that it will wreck me. In the very best way."

One knee planted on the bed, still out of reach, Christian loomed over her—a magnetic, dark presence that had always called to the dormant wildness in her. She felt his shock at her words in the stillness surrounding him.

He wasn't the Christian who had once mocked and teased and taunted until she was forced to strip away all the half-truths and white lies and layers of armor she usually hid behind.

But he was doing it again. Even if it wasn't on purpose. Making her face her worst fear. Stripping even a semblance of control from this situation. And Priya was going to take everything he'd give. Every last inch of him that was on offer. She needed it to sustain herself through the storm he'd brought back into her life.

"Whatever you want is yours," came his soft reply. A hoarse whisper wrapped in a dark promise. His other forearm came down on her belly, pushing her down. "Lie back down."

Gathering the thick mass of her hair with one hand, Priya obeyed. Her gaze saw the pristine white ceiling, her thoughts slowly untangling. "Are you doing this just because your poor neglected wife is demanding it?"

His mouth was on her belly, breathing the words into her skin. "I like it when you call yourself that."

She wanted to move, she wanted to thrust her hips up, but he locked her under the weight of his corded forearm. "What, neglected?"

"No, my wife." His smile was a tattoo against her warm skin. "As to why…to wake up and find you in my bed, desperate for me…to find you offering me a taste of you… demanding I give it to you, it's the stuff dreams are made of, Pree. Now shut up and hold on."

Eyes closed, Priya smiled. Let the night and the darkness and the intimacy take over. She lifted her hips as he stripped her shorts and then her little lacy top from her body. Reaching out again, she sank her fingers into that thick hair. She tugged, asking him to pay attention. "Christian?"

"Yes, Starling?" he whispered, nuzzling into the crease of her thigh.

A bolt of lust held her still under his lazy ministrations. "I don't want tender or soft. I don't want you to coddle me or cosset me or treat me like I'm still that fragile thing I was before. Because I'm not."

His breath turned shallow and deep at the same time. "I think I'm beginning to believe you, Pree."

His fingers wrapped around her ankle, and then she felt his mouth travel up her calf. A kiss at her knee. A whisper of silky breath at her thigh. Her skin tickled in some places, begged for more in others. He drew a pattern all over her legs with his mouth and fingers, as if he was more than content to just stay there.

And then it came—a drag of his lips at her inner thigh.

The rough scrape of his beard on the sensitive skin no one had ever kissed before.

The jagged coating of his exhale.

Another kiss over her hip bone.

The abrasive scrape of his finger pad against her most tender areas.

Her senses ran from place to place, pleasure centers pinging all over her body, wondering where he would land next. Kiss next. Touch next. Lick next.

Her breath stayed on a jagged edge, her hips writhing under his caresses, silently begging for more. Off came her panties. Priya shivered as the soft breeze—the little let in by his broad shoulders between her thighs—kissed her sex.

"What's this?" he whispered, the question loud in the aching silence.

His fingers rubbed the tattoo, the skin low on her pelvic bone warming up dangerously at the back-and-forth.

The tips of his other fingers feathered, oh, so carefully, over the strip of her hair left above her sex. Just grazing. Just barely touching. She had to swallow the need in her throat before she could say, "It's a tattoo of a bird, a starling."

She'd gotten it close to the crease at her thigh, not wanting to reveal it in a bikini. Not wanting to share it with anyone.

"I see that." Again, that roughness to his voice. A hesitation. As if it was coming from far away. One hand cupped her left hip roughly while his other hand traced mindless circles around the tattoo. The abrasive scrape from his fingertips and the proximity of his mouth there... Her senses flayed open. "You're terrified of needles. I remember that time when you were recovering from pneumonia. You screeched at the idea of having a shot of antibiotics."

The flick of his tongue over the tattoo, over the crease of her thigh, was a flash of lightning. She gasped. He didn't give her a second to process the delight and sensation that skittered from that point. He bit her there gently and then his tongue flicked over the spot, again and again. Until pain chased pleasure and pleasure chased pain and she was nothing but sizzling sensation and stuttering breath.

"Why would you get a tattoo of a starling when you're scared to death of needles?" he pressed.

"I..." she said, licking her lips, searching for breath. "It was an impulse. It wasn't as if I was ever going to forget you. Even if I didn't have Jayden as a daily reminder, you were... You meant something to me. But one of those nights when it felt like I couldn't go on for another day alone... I wanted to remember what you saw me as, Christian. I wanted a reminder, etched into my skin, that I could be more than that fragile, frightened girl hiding from life. That you saw the possibilities in me. And I needed to be that woman, at least for our son."

He kept rubbing at the tattoo, his fingers splayed possessively over her skin. Over her hip bone. Over her flesh. Over her heart. Over all of her.

Her pulse raced as her thighs were nudged farther apart by his shoulders.

She felt his face over her pelvis. Taking a deep, shuddering breath as if he meant to inhale her whole. And then his clever fingers were delving into her folds, and his tongue licked her in slow, soft, languorous strokes. His hand reached out and cupped her breast. Clever fingers flicked and stroked the tightening bud, sending direct shocks to her sex. His lips and tongue and fingers and shoulders, everything, moved in a strangely hypnotic symphony over her body, playing her, winding her up.

Her hips bucked off the bed when he gently pinched her nipple, but his forearm pressed her back down again. "More?" he growled.

"Yes, more."

Sensuous licks. Soft nips. Unhurried breaths. He built her up and then wound her down. Up and down.

"More," Priya demanded again, heart in her throat.

He upped the tempo of his tongue's caresses, gathering her wetness and drowning her in it. But still not enough. Never enough. She was never going to get enough of him. Spine arching off the bed, her hips chased his mouth shamelessly.

"More," she begged again. "Faster. Rougher. Deeper. I need everything, Christian."

And he gave her more. He gave her things she didn't ask for. As always. This man who had always been there for her. Who had helped her see who she could be, who she was. Without asking for anything in return. Never asking for anything.

Breath shuddering over peaks and valleys, Priya pushed herself onto her elbows. She saw his grin from between her thighs as he looked up at her. "You taste like heaven, Starling. Just as I imagined, so many times."

Something about his words split her open. But the errant thought flitted away, chased out by rippling sensation. Dipping his mouth down again, he took another lick of her. Then there were his fingers. First one and then two, carefully penetrating her, thrusting in and out, while his lips…oh, God, his lips…licked her and sucked her and nipped her.

"God, you'll swallow me whole," he whispered against her folds.

Priya was sobbing and begging and pleasure was pooling and pooling, spinning her away. He didn't let up for a second, his breath and fingers and lips, tuning her tighter and tighter, sending her higher and higher. And when he gently, oh, so gently, tugged at her most sensitive nub with his lips, her hips came away from the bed and she screamed aloud.

Release barreled down her spine, spreading in concentric circles from her pelvis, so acute that it was almost a lash of pain. He wrung wave after wave of it with his fingers and mouth until she was sobbing and moaning, her cheeks as damp as the rest of her skin. He'd wrecked her, just as she'd asked him to.

And when her tears wouldn't stop, when her chest felt tight and her breaths short and shallow, he crawled up her body and took her in his arms. Fear left her in fast rivulets, cleansing and releasing the hold on her, her body deliciously tender and satiated from his caresses.

"I've got you, Pree," he said, tucking her into his arms, his front against her back, one leg thrown over hers. He held her so tightly and yet somehow gently that the shivers subsided. He was rock hard against her buttocks, his heart a deafening thunder against her back. "I'm here, Pree. I've got you," he whispered over and over again.

For the first time since she'd seen him standing there outside the house in the rain, waiting for her, Priya fell into a deep sleep, finally letting go of that tight leash she bound all her desires and needs with. Letting go of the tight control she kept over her heart.

Christian knew the exact moment Priya's breathing changed and she gave herself over to sleep. Every rational voice in his head said he should untangle himself from her and maybe stand under an ice-cold shower. Yet again. He raised a hand to his hair and found it slightly shaking. His body screamed for release, his erection tenting the front of his sweatpants.

Instead he pushed himself up on an elbow and studied her to his heart's content. Something he hadn't been able to do till now, with her perceptive gaze stalking him anytime he was close.

She looked so...*right* in his bed. Like nothing else had since his return. The image he'd been running toward in reality and in his nightmares.

Damp strands framed her forehead. Her lips were dark reddish brown and swollen. At her jaw, he saw the faint pink marks his beard had left when he'd kissed her. The worn out T-shirt hugged her breasts. Then there was the enticing strip of her midriff and those loose, low-slung shorts. The way she was lying hid the sexy tattoo.

So many new things about her —it would take him a lifetime to know them all. The strange thing was that he didn't mind the idea. Nothing in him recoiled as it did over so many things in his newly discovered life.

He ran a finger over her jaw, his thoughts unraveling faster than he could keep track of. Her taste in his mouth...

was like magic that seeped through him, waking up deep desires he'd forgotten along with everything else. Wants he'd suppressed in order to survive. He trailed his finger over the rise and fall of her hips, loving the feel of her silky skin. Pushing damp tendrils from her forehead, he pressed a kiss to her temple.

It *was* a new beginning and he had to let the shadows of the past go. He had to let go of who he used to be. Being stuck in the past, searching for himself there, was useless. He had to look forward. And he would, too. He would be whoever he needed to be for Priya and his son. If all he could have of her was her friendship and this echo of their past relationship, he would make that enough. He had to. He didn't deserve anything more. He didn't dare even think of having more when he wasn't fully whole.

If only his mind would let him be, if only there were no fingers of doubt creeping inside his head every minute, if only he could somehow shed the visceral fear that he would wake up one morning and see nothing but strangers around him again...

Priya moaned in her sleep, as if tuned into the tension thrumming through his body again. He relaxed his fingers on her hips.

She sighed and tucked her feet between his calves, as if it were the most natural thing to do. As if they'd spent the last eight years learning each other's patterns and rhythms. So easily and effortlessly reaching for him. Trusting him.

Christian smiled, and it came from someplace deep inside him, making his chest expand like a sunbeam stretching and reaching every dusty, dark corner of him. All he wanted in that moment was to wake her up with his mouth, whisper filthy nothings into her ear and then beg to be inside her. To feel that tightness of hers surround him, clutch him, hold him deep inside her until he shattered...until he was nothing but pleasure and sensation. Until fear was nothing but a shadow.

She'd let him, he knew. And not just for comfort.

God, he understood now. Understood that she saw him for who he was. Accepted that in some way or other he was broken but it didn't matter. Not to her.

He understood that she wanted him—this version of him—as much as he wanted her. The truth settled deep into his pores, undoing the tight knot in his chest, releasing him from his previous assumptions.

His fingers moved from the arch of her neck to the jut of her collarbones to her bare arms to the flare of her hip. He wanted to see that tattoo again, his fingers itched to touch it, he wanted to kiss it again and again.

The tattoo she'd gotten despite the fact that she was terrified of needles...to remind herself of the strength she already possessed. She raised their son, she ran the company and she expertly managed demanding family members. Everything about this Priya was fierce and unapologetic. Even the kiss the night he'd returned. Teasing and taunting him to allow them what they'd desperately needed.

And tonight, the pleasure she'd demanded he give her, the vulnerability she'd let him see... Yet he... He'd been nothing but a coward ever since he'd returned. Buried so deep inside his own head that he hadn't believed half the things she'd told him. So angry and hurt about everything he'd lost that he couldn't see all the beautiful things he'd gained.

Because he had gained them. He had a wife and a son.

If she could not only survive losing Jai and him and raising a son alone and being true to herself... How could he do any less? How could he not give her anything less than all of him?

How could he deny her this…himself…after everything they'd both lost? After everything they'd gone through to face this day together again?

CHAPTER EIGHT

PRIYA CAME AWAKE GRADUALLY. For all of a second, she was thrown by the utter stillness of the darkness around her. A quick shuffle of her legs under the duvet sent a pleasurable ache between her thighs and just like that, she knew where she was. More important, she remembered what she'd asked of him.

She could feel Christian in the room, even with the curtains closed, nothing but inky darkness filling the space between them.

"How long did I sleep?" she asked, her voice still husky from all the screaming she'd done earlier.

"A couple of hours." His voice came from the armchair in the corner.

"You went for a run?"

"How'd you know?" She heard his smile in that question. "I showered."

She shrugged and then realized he couldn't see her. "You don't sleep. Or maybe you can't sleep. So you run around the estate until your body gives out from exhaustion. I've seen you." She licked her lips. "Christian?"

"Yes, Pree?"

"Is it easier for you to talk in the darkness?"

"For what I want to say, yes." He groaned and she blinked. Now she was able to see a faint outline of his face.

"It's very possible that what I'm about to say is very… messed up. So just bear with me, okay?"

"Are you leaving us?" The words shot out of her on a wave of piercingly sharp fear.

His head jerked up. "What?" He reached her in the next blink, his palm cradling her cheek. "Of course not. I'm—"

She pressed her palm against his mouth. "Don't…apologize. Don't…" She leaned into his clasp. "That was a stupid question. But the thing is I don't want to…shackle you here, Christian, if it's not where you want to be." She leaned forward, seeking more of him, and buried her face in the crook of his arm.

"What if I tell you that what you see as a shackle… you and Jayden… You're my anchors right now, Pree. I want to be here with you both. I'm sorry for making you doubt that."

"I believe you," she said softly. "I wish you'd give me the same benefit of the doubt."

"I'm getting there, Starling."

Priya nodded, relief warming her limbs. "I'm not expecting some imaginary perfect version of you, Christian. In fact, the reason you sometimes rubbed me the wrong way back then was because you thought you were all that and more."

He laughed and the weight on her chest lifted. "My point is neither of us is or ever has been perfect. And that's okay. I'd rather you be real with me."

His exhale coated her temple. "But you're the closest thing I've known to perfection, Pree. At least that's how you tasted to me."

Priya was blushing and groaning and yet the fact that he could joke and tease her like this made her chest expand on a bubble of pure joy. Like she was getting all the good parts of him back again. There was also a part of her that was gobsmacked that he thought her close to perfect. Some truth she didn't understand lingered in those words, but she didn't care to examine it just then.

He dipped his forehead to her shoulder. "I don't want you to treat me as if I'm an invalid you have to take care of. As another bullet point in your long to-do list of everyday tasks."

Scrambling back from him, Priya turned on the bed lamp. Just the little bit she'd scooted back on the bed made his head clearer. The planes of his face were still in shadow but his blue eyes... She could clearly see the shame and doubt in them, and something else there, too.

"Is that how you thought of me when we met all those years ago? Like an invalid you pitied? Like a girl that was somehow beneath you because I was half-broken?"

The sudden switch in the conversation, the assumption in her question, made Christian jerk back. "I know I was full of myself but God no, I never thought that."

But she wasn't listening. He watched as she leaned over and reached for something in the drawer of the nightstand. It was a fat envelope. She'd barely pulled it into her lap when prints of photographs spilled out. She gathered a few more and placed them around her on top of the duvet, a glorious smile he hadn't seen in so long curving her mouth.

"Do you remember the day we met?" she said, picking one up and handing it to him.

"Pree..." he said, refusing to take it, instinctively resisting the pull of the past, of her. There was enough he couldn't deal with in the present, without dragging in the past, too. He was beginning to feel more and more like a spider caught in her web. A web that she didn't even know she was spinning.

She scrunched her nose. "Just indulge me this once?"

"I just did, didn't I?" he said, raising a wicked brow, suddenly feeling more like himself in this one moment than he had in eight years. He licked his lower lip, searching for her taste again. But she was embedded deep in him already—her taste and her scent—and he was beginning to wonder if that's what he was running from. "Although I'll agree that it felt deliciously restorative for me, too."

Her cheeks reddened but she held his gaze. "I'm still terribly outdated when it comes to certain…etiquette. And I made it worse by falling asleep afterward. Should I thank you?"

He grunted.

She smirked. "So that's a no. I guess the nice thing to do, then, is to offer you the same in return?" Her gaze flipped to his lap and then back up.

He immediately felt himself harden just at that passing look. "Is that why you'd want to…do it? To be nice to me?"

"I think I'll let you answer that question for yourself."

"That mouth… It's going to get you into all kinds of trouble."

She bit her lower lip, pure feminine challenge in the movement. His blood roared. "This mouth wants to get into trouble with you."

They watched each other hungrily but there was laughter in that moment, too. A bridge beginning to be built between them again. Whatever he remembered about their chemistry before his plane had crashed, it was a live thing now. The most real thing.

She glanced down at the photo in her hands. "I think Jai clicked this one. The first time I met you." Her gaze shadowed as it did every time she mentioned her late fiancé. But a half smile lingered on her lips. "It was the summer after I turned seventeen. He brought me to see you after my last major surgery. He made me wait in the car, so that he could give you the spiel about my history, I think. He was so worried that you might be your usual 'ruthlessly focused snarly self,' as he called you, with me."

Christian smiled. "Making sure his precious princess was treated right."

Priya stuck her tongue out at him. "I'm sure you don't remember that day because you were in a foul mood just as he'd guessed and there were those two girls who'd been walking out just as we—"

"You were wearing a sleeveless pink blouse and denim shorts. With legs that went on for miles and that huge camera hanging around your neck…" Christian closed his eyes and the memory was there, as clear as if it had been yesterday. "Your ponytail bounced with every tilt of your head and you kept touching the heart pendant on your gold chain—the one Jai bought you for your birthday. You walked in," he continued, "and kept casting me surreptitious glances the entire time. As if I were some wild predator. And then you sat down at one of the computer stations and broke my program within two minutes."

The silence that followed made him search for her expression in the feeble light. Her eyes wide, her mouth open, she looked stunned.

But Christian was tired of all the tangled threads in his head. Tired of pretending, even with himself.

The past was a gift. Even if he forgot it again, it had brought him here, to this moment. It had given him Priya and Jayden and that meant he would never lose it completely again.

Ever. Not as long as he had them.

"And then when I asked you to sit down and help me figure out the hole, you said—without quite looking at me, in that prim voice—that it was six thirty already. And then you turned to Jai so sweetly and asked if he would please take you home before your mom started freaking out."

"You know she would have done that," Priya burst out, half outraged, half laughing.

He dipped his head, grinning. "I know that now, yes. But back then… In that moment, I thought you were the most brilliant and yet the most naive girl I'd ever met. You didn't add up."

"So you kept poking at me and that whole year you tormented me…" she joined in, shaking her head. "'Pree, do you want to get your mama's permission to go to the club with us? Pree, do you need a pity date for the prom? Pree, do you want a juice box? Pree, shall I be your babysitter this evening? Pree, you're such a chicken, a scaredy-cat, a Goody Two-shoes, a doll in a glass case…' Oh, my God, you used to drive me so…*mad*."

Christian groaned and rubbed a hand over his face. Even as his mouth curved up. "I was such a jerk. No wonder you hated me."

"I never truly hated you. I thought I did, yes, for a long time." She smiled now and shifted toward the edge of the bed, that girl he'd once known shimmering in that smile. Memories inked across her features, illuminating that gorgeous face. "But can you blame me? You were an insufferable, arrogant, privileged, puffed-up brat, so full of your invincibility that you made me want to draw blood sometimes. Especially those hours-long coding sessions you forced on the three of us…"

Christian barked out a laugh. "Hey, brilliant ideas were born during those sessions."

"At what cost? I wanted to punch you in your face so many times, mess up all that perfection just a little." She covered her face, laughing, shaking. Tears shone in her brown eyes and she wiped a hand roughly over her eyes.

"I didn't even know I had such a violent streak until I met you. God, if we didn't both love Jai so much, if he hadn't made us behave, and tolerate each other and work with each other... And you?"

Christian stilled. "What about me?"

"What would you have done if Jai hadn't been there to call you off? I have a feeling you'd have ripped into me."

He shook his head, wondering if she could hear the thundering roar of his heart. The words hovered on his lips, screaming to be let out. But whether she was ready to hear them or not, Christian suddenly knew that he wasn't. That he might never be ready to tell her.

Not now. Not when he still couldn't trust his own mind. Not when that guilt and grief remained as painful threads that vined around his chest.

It was his last layer of armor against her. His final thread of self-preservation.

"I used to find immense pleasure in getting a rise out of you, yes," he said hoarsely. It was all he could have of her back then—that anger, that dislike of him, that near-violent reaction to his poking—and he'd been okay with that. Her honesty, her outrage, the simmering temper beneath the shy facade—they had belonged to him. Only him. "In pushing you as far as I could. No one called me an arrogant jackass until you. At least not to my face."

"Nothing compared to my own naiveté... It took me some time to appreciate what you did for me," she said, pulling the ground from under him. She rubbed a hand over her face, her mouth bitter. "Too long, if you ask me."

Christian swallowed. "What I did for you?"

Her fingers twisted the duvet, her gaze flickering down to hide from him. "You made it so easy to dislike you, you provoked me so much that I didn't even realize until a long time later. Not until I lost you."

"What, Pree?" he demanded roughly, desperate for any little nugget.

"You treated me like you treated everyone else, Christian. You pushed me and annoyed me and you...bugged the hell out of me but beneath it all... You didn't treat me as less than anything I was."

The vulnerability in her tone made him angry on her behalf. Even as he still felt confused about where she was going with this. "Why the hell would I? You had a razor-sharp mind and a tongue that matched it if you were provoked enough, beneath all that shyness you wrapped around yourself."

"It was so unnerving in the beginning—not to be coddled and treated like I'd break at any slight pressure. I didn't know how to act toward you, so I pretended to dislike you to an extreme that wasn't possible. It was easy to convince myself of that because you hated me anyway."

"No, I didn't," he said, jerking his head up.

"Oh, just own it, Christian. You really didn't like that I was becoming a part of your life. I was there at work, and in your personal life, disrupting your relationship with Jai. An annoying third wheel... You were so possessive of him, I started showing up just to annoy you. Jai wouldn't agree with me, but I knew. And then when he and I got engaged, you made it clear I wasn't good enough for him. Let's count all the ways you made that crystal clear, shall we?"

"That's not true."

"It's okay to admit you were wrong about me," she said with a teasing laugh. "I wasn't this glorious back then," she said, gesturing to herself.

He grinned, even though he knew how wrong she was. How truly naive she had been about what he'd found attractive. "I asked you to come work for us."

"So? Your dislike of me had nothing to do with what you thought of me professionally. But the thing I'm trying to say, far too many years too late, is that... You were actually good for me back then, Christian."

"You've lost your mind," he bit out, her words falling on him like the first drops of rain on a parched earth. Like a benediction he hadn't known he needed for his soul.

She went on unfazed, refusing to let him fracture this. "Jai always encouraged me to step out of my comfort zone, but he'd also known me my entire life. It wasn't possible for him to see me differently—as a normal, healthy young woman with her own messiness and insecurities but also her strengths and dreams. But you could and you did, and you made sure I knew how I was limiting myself. And you made me see myself in a completely new way. I started doing things I'd have never imagined just to prove you wrong about me. Just to prove to myself that I could. Jai always used to say you have this knack of bringing out the best in people and he was spot-on. You changed me for the better, Christian, more than anyone else in my life did."

Christian buried his face in his hands, a roar of something rising fast in his chest. She was unraveling him, bit by bit, tugging at threads he didn't want to let go of. Undoing him, perversely, by baring her deepest secrets and vulnerabilities. And if he told her now, if he admitted the truth of why he'd treated her the way he had back then, the scales would fall from her eyes.

She'd see the truth of him.

He scoffed and the sound resonated in the silence. "You've got it all upside down."

"What do you mean?"

"Let's just say we remember two different realities."

Her brows tied together, she looked at him out of that steady gaze, drilling through him, searching his words for answers. His breath bated, Christian waited for her to ask. To demand an explanation.

"The point of that walk down memory lane," she said, backing down and he wasn't sure if he was relieved or angry or both right then, "is that I understand, more than you can imagine, how it feels to be unable to trust yourself."

He looked up and exhaled a rough breath. How had he forgotten that her life had constituted so many surgeries and hospital stays? That there was a reason for that sheltered naiveté—the absence of a normal childhood or even adolescence? She'd spent so much of it in hospitals and clinics and under the care of nurses before she'd finally been pronounced fit and healthy. "Pree…"

"I need you to listen, Christian. But I can say this only once. I know exactly what it's like to constantly worry about when your own body might betray you, wonder which step might be your last one, what might bring the darkness flooding back… That's not even the worst thing."

"What is?" he asked, desperate to be done with this conversation. Desperate for the shadows in her eyes to be gone.

"You start stretching out your moments and your days, as if that will make a difference, linger on the sidelines because you're so afraid you'll break… I lived like that for a long time. I was surrounded by people who loved me, but who also made me so afraid, who couldn't see me as anything but a patient. But in the end, my heart condition wasn't the thing that made me hide from life. It was fear. Jai and you… You helped me see that. You helped me shed that fear. Don't let that happen to you, Christian. Don't hide from Jayden and…me. And even worse, don't hide from life because you think you're not ready. Or because you're not enough."

He took her hand in his, his heart lodged so tightly in his throat that he couldn't say a word. She'd not only understood the root of his fear but she'd shared her own vulnerabilities, bared her own deepest fears. He was humbled by her strength. By her understanding. By her refusal to let him be anything less than he could be.

God, he didn't deserve her. He hadn't deserved her then and he didn't deserve her now.

He blinked, fighting the wet heat behind his eyes. "I want to protect you from this. From me. I want…"

"You're protecting only yourself. Not me." There was no hesitation in her voice. "You treated me better than this when I was fragile. Why would you treat me as anything less now? If you try that, then I'll—"

"You'll what?"

"I'll lecture you until your brains are leaking out of your ears." She buried her face in the fold of her arms on her knees, looking suddenly small. "When I walked in here and I saw you in the grip of a nightmare, I told myself I'd be here for as long as it took you to wake up. That I'd let you know that I'm here for you. I promised myself you'd never wake up alone again. Your nightmares and your grumpy moods and your noncommittal grunts and your brooding silences and your reluctance to touch me until I crawl into your bed and demand that you give yourself to me… I can handle all of those, Christian. What I can't take is you hiding the truth from me."

He flinched, but she hadn't finished.

"For a second there, when you woke up, you didn't see me. Maybe it was just a remnant of your nightmare. Maybe you were just half-asleep. But if that can happen again, if there's a possibility you might forget me again…"

She waited and Christian looked up and whatever she

saw in his face, she squared her shoulders. She was a lioness, this woman.

"Then I need to know. I need to be ready. And not for just your sake but for Jayden's and my own, too. I need to know what you're going through, Christian, if only for the fact that you shouldn't be alone with that knowledge. Not when you have me to talk to."

You have me...

The words lingered in the air, taking on their own life, morphing and amplifying until they splintered through the walls he'd built around himself. She was unraveling him, bringing him to his knees, and Christian wasn't sure he could fight this anymore.

He wanted to take everything she was offering and yet the hungry cavern inside him wanted even more.

"I just—" he thrust a hand through his hair "—don't want to be a burden to you."

She got off the bed, came to him and plunged her fingers into his hair. She tugged through the strands, her voice close to breaking but not breaking yet. "The Christian I knew, the Christian I admired and respected... He'd never have babied me like this. He'd have made me face the truth just so I knew what I was up against. He'd have respected me enough to share all the truths with me, even the painful ones. Why would you push me away now when we've been through so much together?"

And just like that, his decision was made. He had nothing left to fight her with.

"Ask me what you want to know."

Priya's breath left her in a long exhale.

"Why aren't you seeing a neurologist? Why aren't there a bunch of specialists here to help you transition back to your life? Why aren't you seeking therapy or medication for your headaches and insomnia? How frequently do you have those nightmares?"

He looked at her, a smile curving his lips. "I can imagine you like this in the boardroom, making all those crusty old men toe the line. Busting their asses, calling them on their greed. You must be quite the thing to see."

"Don't distract me from this."

His fingers pulled at his dark blond strands. "Just because I don't share everything with you doesn't mean I'm not addressing it. And for God's sake, stop looking at me as if I was a fixer-upper project you can't wait to sink your teeth into."

"That's the most ridiculous..." Priya trailed off then and raised a brow, giving it some thought. "Hmm. You're not completely wrong about me wanting to sink my teeth into you. Who knew I was into grouchy guys with tight asses?"

His curse rang around them, but when she looked at him, his blue eyes were warm.

Despite her frustration, she understood his reluctance to share everything with her. For a man who'd thrived on being a leader, on being the best at everything, not being able to trust his own mind, not knowing what tomorrow might bring would be nothing short of torture. Her annoyance—spurred on by fear mostly—left her as fast as it had come.

"You've lost almost a decade of your life. I should've recognized that you're in mourning even if you didn't. Because I... I did mourn you. And you should have that space, too."

"Did you? Mourn me? As more than a..."

Whatever he'd been about to ask, he cut it off with a growl. Priya watched him, confused. What was the piece of the puzzle from the past that she was still missing?

They remembered *"two different realities,"* he'd said before. But what exactly did that mean?

"I'm scared," he admitted then, and it almost felt like he was confiding that just to get away from the subject of their past. And it did that. It whipped her straight back into the painful present. "I'm scared of letting anyone look into my head. Of letting a psychologist or a hypnotist or a neurologist poke about in there and making things worse. I'm scared of losing what I've finally remembered after all these years. I just…"

His confusion was like a thorn under her own skin, digging in deeper the more one tried to get it out.

"The risks outweigh the benefits right now," he added, in a voice steadied through sheer will. "My head feels a little unstable, overwhelmed. In a good way but still. I need some time before I can shore myself up. I'd never willingly do anything to hurt Jayden." His fingers landed on her clasped ones at his midriff. "Or you. Never," he whispered again, imbuing the word with so much feeling that it lodged inside her heart.

"However, I have started talking to a therapist. The first session was pretty brutal."

She clasped his hand, loving the rough texture of it against her own. "Tell me if I can do anything else for you. Whatever you need."

His hands climbed to her hips, and he buried his face in her belly. Liquid heat gushed at her sex. "Anything?" His blue eyes were so full of charming naughtiness, that challenging, wicked gleam of old, that it was a punch to her heart.

She nodded, her mouth already dry.

His fingers stretched back until they reached the twin swells of her behind. "I love how your body has changed," he said then, and pure feminine power jolted through her. "Everything about you turns me on."

She gasped when he cupped her buttocks firmly and his mouth was at the seam of her panties again. "And yet you won't take what you want from me," she pointed out.

He looked up and color crested his cheeks. "I might not be that good anymore. In fact, it's been so long I have a feeling I'm going to embarrass myself pretty fast."

His grin was the most beautiful thing she'd ever seen. "Then we need to get the edge off. So that you can—" she licked her lips, tension thrumming through her "—last as long as I want you to last inside me." She dipped her fingers into his hair. "I want to do all kinds of wicked things with you. I want you to do all the wicked things you once promised me you'd do."

He groaned—it seemed to be ripped from inside him— and she laughed.

Joy was a giddy thing inside her chest. For the first time in weeks, she felt like they were making progress. She still wasn't sure why he'd held himself back from her. Why he didn't want to have sex with her when desire was etched into the planes of his face. But she didn't want to delve, didn't want to push him into a corner.

"I guess I should you tell, then, that I've made another decision, too. When you're in this mood where you'll grant me anything I wish."

"What?" she asked, every cell in her standing to attention.

"I want some time to myself. Being here, in my old life, I thought it would settle me. Instead it's been disconcerting, to say the least. I need a few weeks. Away from who I used to be."

Somehow, Priya kept her face from showing her shock, her distress.

How could it already be this hard to let him go? What was she going to do if he didn't return to her? He'd never abandon Jayden, she knew that. She'd seen the love in his eyes when he looked at their son, love and an ache. Fear, too.

But her... What if she couldn't have even the little of him she had now? What if, for all her talk that she was strong, that she had no expectations of him, she'd always be weak and vulnerable when it came to him? What if he walked away tomorrow from being her husband? What would she do then?

Could she survive the loss again? How could he have so much power over her heart already?

This was supposed to be about friendship, about being a source of strength for him. And yet it had become something so much more in just a few short weeks. The truth of that terrified her.

She nodded, somehow evading his eyes. Somehow breathing through it all. "Of course. That sounds like a very sensible idea. Where do you plan to go?"

One broad palm clasped her cheek with such infinite tenderness that she felt wet heat knocking behind her eyelids. "To the villa we own in the Caribbean. You're going to be flaming mad, but I've already made arrangements for us to be gone for at least a month."

Priya sprang from the bed. "You what? Us who?" She didn't wait for his answer, as much as it wrecked her. "Taking Jayden with you isn't a good idea, Christian. Not because I don't trust you but..."

"Not just Jayden," he said, pressing his fingers to her lips, "but you, too. I want you both with me. For as long as you can bear it."

Priya was so relieved that he'd included her that she

couldn't even muster an ounce of outrage that he'd made the decision without even consulting her.

"We'll leave in a few days."

With that arrogant command, he reminded Priya of who he used to be.

"There's a board meeting in three days. I know you'd prefer it if we kept your return quiet for a little longer, so I can't really afford a vacation at this point, Christian. There are a lot of things I want to make sure get done before I hand over the reins to you. Before you…" She shrugged, not wanting to elaborate.

If he was curious about it, Christian didn't let on. She still couldn't believe how casual and easy he'd been about the company since his return. The ambitious twenty-four-year-old who had once devoted days and nights to building new technology systems, the drive that had led him and Jai to make their first million right out of college, was nowhere to be seen since he'd returned.

Not that Priya begrudged him the break.

"I know about the board meeting. You can meet us at the airstrip after."

"How did you… Who did you talk to?"

"I called William Constantine. He was here yesterday, walking me through the company's details over the last few years." Ah, there was the man she'd just wondered about—the ambitious, brilliant CEO who'd taken the tech world by storm at such a young age. "I trust him to keep it quiet until I'm ready."

Priya tried to sound casual. "You've been busy."

"Did I step on your toes?"

She shrugged. "Of course not. I thought you'd ask me to go over everything with you when you were ready, but as chief financial officer, William was a good choice."

"You have enough on your plate." For once, Christian

seemed oblivious to her dismay. "My point is it won't be long before I take my share on again, okay?"

Priya nodded. "I'm ready whenever you are to do the transfer."

And before she could betray her confusion, before his hawk-eyed gaze zeroed in on her growing distress, she walked out of the room.

Christian's preferring to talk to the CFO instead of her didn't mean he didn't trust Priya or her handling of the company. Or that he wanted an outsider's opinion on her performance. Neither did she understand this sudden reluctance she felt about handing back the reins of the company to Christian.

For all Mama continued to gripe that her job left her little time to be a mother, Priya had enjoyed the challenges of leading the company. Of making decisions that affected thousands of livelihoods, of seeing the fruits of her labor when again and again MMT had been hailed as one of the best companies to work for in the last decade.

Maybe because managing MMT had been her rite of fire, the vehicle through which she'd found her strength and her endurance. And now it was time to say goodbye to that role. It made sense that she'd have mixed feelings about it.

She stared at the closed door to his bedroom.

Christian wasn't going to like some of the things she'd implemented as CEO since he'd been gone. In fact, he probably wasn't going to like most of them. But what was done was done. She'd done her best to lead MMT and she'd make the same decisions all over again if she had to.

CHAPTER NINE

IT TURNED OUT to be more than a week later when Christian carried a sleeping Jayden into the rear cabin of their private jet. Perching on the other side of the bed, Priya tucked him in carefully.

Christian watched as she pushed the hair off Jayden's forehead with the same tenderness she used with him. His heart lodged into his throat painfully at the picture she and Jayden made together.

The possibility that he might lose them again was never far from his thoughts. Even worse was the fear that he was only going to disappoint them.

Like with Jayden's behavior this morning.

Christian had no doubt Jayden was throwing a tantrum and yet, he also knew that it was something he'd done that had triggered it. He wasn't sure what, though.

In the month since he'd returned, he'd never seen his son so cranky and uncommunicative. Even after Priya had joined them, five minutes before takeoff, the little boy hadn't thawed. He'd retreated deep into his seat, with a book open in his lap, even as Priya spent ages trying to get him to come out of his shell. He'd refused to eat or talk and wouldn't make eye contact with Christian the entire morning. Finally, he'd fallen asleep, scrunched in the corner.

Christian rubbed a hand over his tight chest, feeling both powerless and exhausted.

For the past week, his sleep patterns had only gotten worse. At this point, he was in survival mode—he had no doubt of that. So he'd used all that restless energy to catch up on eight years of MMT's operations, had gone through document upon document. He'd hoped to have some things finalized before Priya and he left for this trip.

Instead, the more he'd delved into all the goings-on at MMT, the more dissatisfaction he'd felt. And of course, then he'd had to deal with his annoying-as-hell cousin Bastien. Leave it to him to spin the eight years that Christian had missed into some kind of bizarre conspiracy tale. With Priya at the center of it all, apparently attracting far too many unsuspecting men into her web with her womanly wiles.

He'd understood Bastien's dirty strategy within two minutes of his cousin opening his mouth. To drive a wedge between him and Priya and get Christian back as CEO. But suddenly drowning in stock numbers and board ultimatums, his cousin didn't know that that was the last thing Christian had discovered he wanted.

He took a relieved breath, knowing that another part of the puzzling piece of his future was falling into place.

Priya was sitting in the seat next to their son, head tilted back and slim fingers resting on Jayden's forehead.

With William Constantine and Bastien walking in and out of his study, they'd barely talked in the past week. Now he noted the tension that bracketed her mouth and the dark smudges that hugged her eyes.

She hadn't been exactly cool with him since the night he'd told her he wanted to take this trip. But now that they were away from the house and work, he realized she hadn't sought him out again. In fact, she'd been keeping a polite distance. Just like she used to do, before he'd disappeared.

He scowled. Almost as if he were an unknown to her again. As if they hadn't bared their innermost fears to each other. As if he hadn't tasted her and held her body after he'd brought her to screaming ecstasy.

And he missed it all. He missed her teasing, her touch, her hungry gaze and her warm concern for him. He missed her like a hole in his heart.

"You said routines were important to him. Is he unhappy because we took him out of school and away from his friends?" He was too tired, too grumpy to keep out the accusatory note in his tone.

If Priya noticed it, she was too damn nice for her own good to call him on it. Her shoulders drooped with the same exhaustion that Christian felt. Jayden's body was tucked against her thigh. On top of managing Christian and his moods and Jayden and his crankiness, she'd also worked an eighty-hour week.

"Give me your feet."

Eyes still closed, she raised a brow.

"Please," he said, almost choking on the word. "You're exhausted and I need to feel useful." And because he was a needy, grumpy bastard, he added, "I know that's the only relief you'll allow me to give you."

"You might be surprised at what I'll allow," she said, a soft smile curving her lips.

His body twitched in his jeans.

After a moment's beat, she turned so that her feet stretched across the small gap and landed in his lap. With slow movements, he undid the tiny buckles and pulled off her high heels. Gently, he pressed at her toes, drawing lines to her heel.

A soft moan left her mouth, and her chest rose and fell

on a deep breath. "You're spoiling me," she said in a low, hoarse voice.

"And that's bad why?"

Her eyes still closed, she sighed. "You're setting a dangerous precedent. I'm going to make all kinds of demands on you now."

"So?"

Those gorgeous brown eyes flicked open and held his. "Is this extra grumpiness because of Jayden? Or because no sleep and no sex is finally wearing on you as much as it's wearing on me?"

Continuing to massage her feet, he muttered, "I always thought of kids as running, screaming bundles of energy. At least that's what I thought in theory. I know now that Jayden's not quite like that. That he's more...mature. But he's been so withdrawn today. It's worse than any tantrum I could imagine."

"And you feel like the worst parent on the planet."

"Yes," he added, realizing now what she'd meant about sometimes being lonely and overwhelmed as a single parent. And yet, she'd done such a fantastic job. Notwithstanding today's episode, Jayden was usually a happy, well-adjusted child.

She ran her hand over Jayden's forehead, pushing away the silky light brown hair. Sitting still, Christian felt jealousy skewer through him at the open affection in the gesture, at the overpowering emotion in her eyes as she looked down at their son. It was only an echo of an old desire, a remnant of his past need, he told himself. Once, he'd wanted her to look at him like that.

Not anymore. Not now, he repeated like a mantra. He was happy with what he had now. With what they were. There was a certain peace in accepting that.

"I have no more answers than you do, Christian. Although if you'd like, I can make an educated guess."

"Guess, then," he growled, channeling some of the brooding energy that Jayden had been showing all day.

Her mouth twitched and again, his body did the same in his trousers.

She sighed and said, "You're not going to like it."

"Try me anyway."

She turned to face him. "He was fine when I left for work this morning. In fact, he was super excited about skipping school and going off on some treasure hunt in the Caribbean with his dad. He wouldn't stop going on and on about pirates. Good job on that."

If his chest puffed out anymore, it would rip through his shirt, like in one of Jayden's action hero movies. Priya's praise had always mattered to him but in the matter of parenthood, it made him feel ten feet tall. "All I'm hearing is you say what a wonderful dad I am," he said, running his fingers up over her shapely calf.

"Have patience, Christian. I'm feeling my way through this."

He remained silent.

"From what I gather from Mama, Bastien visited you this morning."

Christian grunted.

"You both closed yourselves off in your study for almost three hours. And when Bastien walked out, he had a bloody nose." She sighed again. This sound was so exaggerated that Christian smiled, his brooding mood falling off him like water off a rock. As if she had to contend with not one but two boys with no impulse control. "My guess is that Jayden saw Bastien walk out of the house. For all I want to tar Bastien with a mustache-twirling villain's brush, he's always been good to Jayden. I think seeing you and Bastien fall out upset him. And then when he asked you about what happened, you told him it was none of his business."

Christian put her feet back on the floor and got up to pace around the cabin. "I never said it like that."

"I'm not blaming you. I told you Jayden's extra sensitive." When he'd have interrupted her again, defensively no less, she stood up and walked toward him and stopped his pacing by placing her palm on his chest. His heart kicked hard in there, as if it wanted to reach out to her. "I don't mean that his feelings get hurt by everything. But he knew something was bothering you—you've been like a wounded dog since this morning, admit it, Christian. And when he tried to find out why, you promptly shut him down."

"He's just a boy. I don't want to fill his head with tales of irritating, spiteful cousins."

"But since your return, you've been astonishingly honest with him. About your headaches, your mental health... And you've settled into a dynamic together, one of growing closeness. Today, he thinks he's done something to upset you, to change that dialogue."

"That's convoluted."

"He's a boy who can't process all the things he's feeling. Just like his dad."

"You've been waiting to throw that in, haven't you?" he said, wondering at how easily they fell into this routine of worrying over their child.

A smile split her mouth. "Like I said, we're all having to make a lot of adjustments and we're all struggling in one way or another."

"What are you struggling with?" he asked with a frown.

She didn't deny it and he felt overwhelming relief that he'd gotten that right at least. "I'll tell you but not just yet."

Christian covered her hand with his, trapping it against his chest. He loved touching her. And not just sexually. "What do you suggest I do to fix this with Jayden?"

"Tell him some version of what happened between Bastien and you. Also, in future, show him by example that we don't solve our problems or disagreements—" she pulled her hand away and traced the punctured skin over his knuckles with her fingers "—with our fists. If not, be prepared for a host of complaints about your son and school fights."

"Bastien deserved it. It's better Jayden learns that bullies never change."

"Christian, I…"

"After losing so much for so long, I thought I'd be all Zen about everyone and everything. That I'd appreciate all the things I do have and remember when I didn't. But not that worm. I can't forgive him for what he put you through for eight years. I can barely forgive myself. Why didn't you tell me how badly he behaved?"

"I dealt with him as best as I could, Christian. Can you at least give me credit for that?"

"Yes."

"What did he tell you that has you this angry?"

"Other than the fact that he tried to undermine you on the board for years? That he opposed you at every single turn?"

Priya tried to turn away but he didn't let her. The tightness around her mouth, the wariness in her eyes… Suddenly he had a clue. "You've been acting weird ever since Constantine showed up at the house."

"What does that even mean?" she said, trying to bluff her way out of it.

"This wariness creeps into your eyes every time I mention the company. It reminds me of all those years ago." He ran a hand over his nape. "I don't like it."

"Why?"

"You used to look at me as if I was the last man you'd ever trust. As if you were constantly wondering what Jai saw in me. Somehow, you always managed to make me feel about two feet tall."

"Was this your *I'll sleep with every woman in the Northern Hemisphere* phase?"

Smiling, he tapped a finger over her temple. "What's going in that head of yours, Pree?"

"I've just been waiting for the other shoe to drop."

"Which shoe is that?"

"You've seen the numbers. You know by now that not everything Bastien complains about is untrue."

"Are you talking about MMT?"

"What else? I had the R&D division dismantled. I increased the yearly bonuses across all the tiers. I cut the perks for the board members. I implemented a new program to bring in a bigger workforce from community colleges, not just Ivy League universities. I fought tooth and nail to increase the proportion of women and minorities, too. We're renowned for being a great place to work, but there's more than one financial report that says MMT has stagnated financially under my leadership. Our stock prices never really fully recovered after your…crash and disappearance. It's not the future you, or even Jai, envisaged for MMT."

Christian frowned. This was what had been bothering her? "Even if you'd run the company into the ground, I still wouldn't blame you."

She stepped away from him, agitation written into every line in her body. "But I didn't. Can you at least appreciate that?"

"Of course I appreciate it. Hell, Pree, the minute you took the reins, the minute you sat in the chair, it became your company. The last thing I'm going to do after letting you down for eight years is criticize you for not making us another hundred million. MMT became something else with your vision at the helm. I'm proud of your accomplishments and I have no intention of mucking about with things that are already working perfectly."

She was wearing such a stunned expression that her eyes went wide. "You're not?"

"No. And since we're on the topic, shall I drop another piece of big news in your lap?"

His expression made her swallow. "Yes."

"I'm not coming back to MMT as the CEO. Not now, not ever."

"What?"

"I know it's a lot, but hear me out." He pressed the heels of his palms against his eyes. "I already knew that I didn't want to go back to the company. After everything that's happened, the last thing I wanted was to be in the middle of all those boardroom politics. But I needed to understand how things stood before I made a final decision. I spent the whole of last week listening to Constantine and Bastien and Ben. Eight years later, nothing's changed in terms of their working dynamic. Except me. I don't want to spend the next twenty or thirty years constantly trying to get them to behave. I want to make a difference. I want to figure out how to make more impact on the world—a meaningful impact. The kind that Jai always wanted us to."

Her eyes filled up, as they always did, when Jai's name was mentioned. "I don't know what to say."

"Just say you'll support me in this decision. That you'll

continue as the CEO. Unless you absolutely loathe it as much as I do, of course."

"I love it. I love running the company. I love telling crusty old men what they're allowed and not allowed to do with the company resources. I like being powerful because I can change things, from the inside."

"That's what I was hoping to hear." When she'd have protested, he pressed a finger to her mouth. The sensation of her soft lips against his fingers felt like heaven. "Listen to me. If there's one thing that stood out from every single report, it's that you've really come into your own. You've made MMT stand for connecting communities everywhere. You've forced it to live up to the initial vision Jai had for it. So if you want to continue keeping those greedy jackals in line, you have my full support."

She looked so taken aback—in a good way—that Christian smiled.

"But what will you do?" she asked eventually. "Not that I'm saying you have to do anything. The returns on your investments alone will keep you in luxury for years to come."

"I'm working on a few things—a couple of apps and systems that focus on bringing resources to places and people that have been denied them for too long. Like the one Jai and I planned before he…" He ran a hand through his hair, feeling the twin prickles of grief and guilt as he always did whenever he thought of his best friend. God, so much had changed in eight years. But not that. Never that. "Beyond being here for you and Jayden, I don't care much about anything else right now." He forced a smile into his voice when she continued to stare at him steadily. "Unless you don't like the idea of a bum husband?" he added with a wink.

She came to him then and Christian wondered if

he'd ever get used to it. The small, simple pleasure he'd dreamed of for so long. Of having this woman he'd respected and admired and wanted for so long smile and look at him with such joy in her eyes.

"Thank you, Christian," she said, pressing a soft kiss to his cheek. "For having so much faith in me."

"You're an amazing CEO who's dealt with my stubborn goat of a grandfather and nauseating snakes like Bastien for eight years. You don't need my approval."

"I do need it. Because there were so many moments when I lost faith in myself. When I wondered what the hell I was doing."

She clasped his cheek and he closed his eyes, reveling in her touch. He felt almost shaky with relief. Relief that at least he'd gotten this right.

When she looked at him, however, there was a shadow of fear again. "Christian? Will you give me an honest answer if I ask you something?"

"I'll try," he said, loving the feel of her in his arms.

She sighed. "You're not doing this because you're…because you're cutting all ties, are you? Because you think you…might not want this life at all? Because you're preparing for something…bad to happen?"

He tipped her chin up, humbled as always by how perceptive she was. "Preparing for the eventuality that I might lose my memories again… It's never far from my mind. But this decision hasn't been driven by fear, Pree. It's simply because I'm a different man now, with different priorities."

She studied him for a few seconds and then nodded. "So I have an idea," she said, her breath drifting over his mouth and chin.

He kept his eyes closed, enjoying the amplification of every other sense in identifying her. She smelled like heaven and lust and fire and woman. His hand drifted to her hip and he held her loosely. Her breath hitched instantly. "I'm waiting," he growled, tension tightening every muscle.

"The bed in the back of the jet, you and me. Now."

His eyes flicked open to find her smiling at him. He gestured toward the other bed and then back at their son, still lost to the world, fast asleep. "What if he wakes up?" he asked, both hands cupping her hips now. His thumb and forefinger drifted toward the steep dip of her waist.

She hid her face in his chest, but he caught the twist of her smile. One palm landed on his heart, which was thudding away. "He's not going to be up for at least five hours, I promise you. Not until we land. And if he does, we're right there."

"Even so, I don't want to traumatize my son. Especially because once I get you under me, I'm not budging for hours. Unless it's to get you on top of me."

He felt her quick breath, the shift and slide of her breasts against him sending a fierce stab of lust through him. But she didn't push him away or slide closer. As if she'd never wanted more than to be simply held by him.

Cheek pressed against his chest, she set those large eyes on him. Humor and desire shone through, underpinned by something else that pierced him. "I meant we should have more like a nap date."

He was laughing as he thrust her away from him. "What the hell's that?"

She shrugged, not the least bit dismayed by his reaction. "We find a bed and we nap together. Like wedged up all against each other."

"That sounds like something an eighty-year-old couple would do," he said with a mock shudder. "Not that I won't be up for that when we're that age and nothing else can go up, you know."

She scrunched her nose at his teasing.

Though his shudder wasn't completely fake. The idea of lying next to her, holding her, touching her without kissing her, without losing himself in her, without being inside her was…nothing less than torture. "What do you get out of it?"

The sneaky minx didn't answer. At least not immediately.

She shrugged off the cream jacket she'd been wearing and neatly hung it up in the small wardrobe. A thin blouse in sheer cream silk hugged her breasts. Her nipples pebbled plump and tight against the fabric. His mouth watered at the sight. Swallowing, he watched her greedily, taking in her every move and step, every dip and flare in that sensually curved body. The simple V-necked tee he was wearing felt too warm. Every muscle in his body curled tight and hot, his erection twitching.

She gathered the silky mass of her hair and tied it in a loose knot. Gaze never breaking away from him, she slowly pulled the blouse out of her black trousers. A sliver of brown skin flashed at him and he let out a low growl. Like an actual, animalistic growl, as if he was no better than instinct and desire around her. No, not as if. He'd always been like that when it came to her.

"Pree…" he whispered, unable to say anything else.

"Give me a minute, Christian."

The black trousers slithered down her long legs with a hiss that sent desire pinging over his skin. "I really hate napping in my work clothes. And I didn't have time to change before." She was wearing panties in the same beige color as her tank top. Her thighs rippled with long muscles as she pulled her legs out of the trousers.

He could see the effort it cost her, too. The pulse at her neck was flickering away, like a caged bird flapping its wings to get out. And then she was moving toward him again and he thought this could be the moment his heart might burst right out of his chest.

"What I get out of it is...intimacy. A sense of security that I haven't known for so long. I gave birth to our son alone. I fed him alone for endless nights. I woke up numerous times dreaming of you, only to find that damned vast bed empty. And cold. I want to sleep, at least for a couple of hours, with you holding me tight. I want to feel the warmth of you at my back and the solid strength of your arms around me. For once, I want to wake up feeling as if I'm tethered to someone else, and not just flying alone."

She put her hand on his chest again and kissed his cheek. "I know you don't want me to see you struggling to sleep. But please don't deny me this, Christian."

Tugging her gaze away, she got into the bed and pulled the duvet over her. Her back was stiff, her shoulders tight as she settled on her side. He saw the curve of her bottom, the long length of her legs before the duvet hid her from his eyes.

His hands were shaking as he lifted the duvet up again. Cursing and muttering like an old fisherman who used to rant about his wife on the Caribbean island they were flying to, Christian got into bed.

"You're not taking your shirt and trousers off?" came Priya's muffled voice. He could hear laughter and pleasure coiled together in her voice, just as arousing as the taut length of her.

"Don't push your luck," he muttered, lying completely still on his back. Still, he couldn't help but feel her bottom wedged firmly against his thigh. The scent of her—that

damned rose scent that always made him think of her—
filled his nostrils.

"You're supposed to spoon me," she said more loudly
this time. "That's the entire point of a nap date."

Christian wondered if this was a punishment for all
the times he'd dumped a woman because she wasn't
Priya. He'd never been cruel, but he'd always known
his heart had never been in it to begin with. "You're
making this up."

"You've been gone for eight years. You don't know
what's trending in the world. Pardon me for remembering you as the guy who's usually up for any kind of adventure."

"This is not an adventure. This is…" She scooted back,
still on her side, and Christian felt his breath jump out
of him as he was being thrown here and there by lash-
ing waves of frustrated desire. "…torture," he whispered
on a groan.

"You used to be so much fun, Christian. Now you're
mostly grumpy and grouchy. No, you became like this
even before the plane crash. Those few months when we
were married… You became someone else."

He laughed rather bitterly at that. "That's what happens when life gives you the very thing you want, despite knowing you shouldn't want it. And at a price you
could never pay."

She stilled against him. As if she didn't even dare take
a breath. Moments tumbled into minutes, and still she said
nothing. And the longer the silence stretched on with her
non-reply, the more it felt like a rejection. Not of him.
But of his truth.

He'd had no intention of saying that and yet… Now that
it was out, he wanted her acknowledgment. He wanted
her to accept it.

His first impulse was to get off the bed and run away, far and fast. Given that they were on a private jet right now, that wasn't too far. Fighting the urge to stomp away because he wasn't getting what he wanted—he had to act better than his son, after all—he decided to defuse the sudden tension by saying, "I'm not really into spooning. I'm more of a forking guy myself."

"I have no idea what that means," she said, breathlessly.

"Shall I show you?"

And then he heard it. Her laughter, muffled by the duvet.

He couldn't have resisted turning if his very last breath depended on staying still. Placing his arm around her, he scooped Priya closer until she was plastered to his front. Her legs somehow crisscrossed between his and her ass was tucked up directly into his groin.

A ragged groan left his mouth as his erection twitched for room, and neatly snuggled into the curve of her bottom. She stiffened for a second and then she settled into him, notching herself even more snugly against him.

"God, Pree, what did I ever do to you to deserve this torture?"

Her head tucked into the crook of his folded arm, she sent him a sideways glance that went straight to his heart. Her full-body shudder rocked him to his core when she said a little brokenly, "You left me, Christian. After making all those promises...and after saving me from myself, you suddenly left me."

"Shh...baby," he said, softly crooning. "I'm not going anywhere this time. Not ever again."

And then he pulled her impossibly closer again, until his forearm rested between her breasts. They were locked so tight against each other that it was a miracle they could even breathe. He pressed his lips to her temple and whispered sweet nothings in her ear.

Her breathing settled into a slower pace and his followed. Like the softest down duvet, Christian felt a peace that had been missing from his life for a long time finally settle over his skin. Every inch of his body, every muscle felt lax, loose. His heart resumed a soft rhythm, trying to match hers. He heard the soft exhale of her breaths, the rise and fall of her chest against his arms. She was asleep.

In a matter of minutes, he felt a deep weariness pull him under and for the first time in eight years, Christian sank into sleep, without worrying about which nightmare would drag him out of it.

CHAPTER TEN

PRIYA WOKE UP SUDDENLY, hurtling out of some dream she couldn't hold on to. She reached out to find an empty space next to her. For a few seconds, pure panic filled her. Panic that it all had been a dream again. That Christian hadn't truly returned to them.

To her.

Soft sunlight filtered through the windows and two voices—trying to whisper and failing miserably—drifted in through the open bedroom door. She smiled, the panic receding at the sight of the vast expanse of the ocean through the French doors on the other side of the room.

She grabbed the pillow next to hers and buried her face in it. That musky, purely male scent of Christian's had her gulping in deep breaths. They'd been at the island for ten days now and the best part—her favorite part—was that he hadn't gone back to a different room or a different bed again after their nap on the jet, although he still struggled to sleep each night.

The door closed softly and she looked up.

Christian stood against the door, his sweatpants hanging dangerously low on those lean, tapered hips and wearing a loose T-shirt. "You okay?" he asked, his gaze taking in everything about her face. Neither did he miss that she was clutching his pillow.

"I thought I dreamed your return again," she whispered, her mouth dry, her skin far too tight. "I hate that dream. It's tortured me for years."

"Go back to sleep," he urged, taking a step into the room.

"Is Jayden okay?"

"He was hungry. He had a banana, I told him a story and he's sleeping again. That good?"

"That's perfect."

This was pure luxury—being looked after like this. Not having to worry about Jayden. Being able to take a moment to simply catch her breath. Having Christian here to share all the small things with. She hadn't realized how much she needed this break until Christian had forced the issue. "What story did you tell him?"

"He finally asked me again about why I fought with Bastien."

She nodded, knowing how important it had been to Christian that Jayden come to him about that. While he'd forgotten his hurt the next morning and behaved normally, he'd not been receptive when they'd tried to mention it. And it had tormented Christian ever since—the very idea that his son might have retreated a little from him.

"I told him I was wrong to have hit Bastien, that I understand that things are confusing for him because of me suddenly showing up. That you and I are trying so hard to figure out how to be a family, too."

Priya thought her heart might be melting in her chest right then.

A family—that's what she wanted. That's what she'd wanted for eight years. And she wanted it with Christian, no one else. The realization slammed into her, shaking her.

His blue eyes were like a beautiful abyss—taunting her, inviting her, hiding what she might find at the bottom.

But she'd already jumped. She'd jumped from the moment he'd reappeared. Her heart had already made the choice. Only her mind hadn't caught up.

No fear coated her breaths. For the first time in her life, she didn't care where she'd end up in all of this. Where she'd end up with him. She just wanted this intimacy with him so much that it left all her previous fear in ashes. She wanted this marriage. And she wanted this life with him, whatever label it fell under.

That simple yet groundbreaking truth had never been never clearer.

"I told him that Bastien and I had always been like that since we were kids. Always far too competitive, trying to outdo each other. I also tried to reassure him that I'd never force him to choose sides. That being a dad meant I'd have to earn his love. Not just demand it."

"That was smart," she murmured.

"I know it's natural because he's my son, but Jayden makes it easy to love him."

Just like his dad, she wanted to say. *Just like you, Christian.*

Even when he'd been nothing more than an acquaintance who'd pushed her and needled her, when he'd been a protector who'd shared her grief with her, when he'd been a friend who'd dragged her back to life, when he'd been a lover who'd given her so much she couldn't even verbalize it—she realized it had always been easy to love Christian.

"He does," she said, clearing her throat, hoping he'd put her husky voice down to sleep. "But let's give credit where it's due. You're good at this, Christian."

"At what?"

"At being a father. At being a friend to a seven-year-old boy." And at being a partner, a husband, even, she wanted to say. But she had a feeling he wasn't ready for that truth yet.

He stood there, his thighs just touching the high bed, watching her, studying her.

Something niggled at the back of her mind. It had been there last night, too. A missed appointment? An important meeting? Reaching for her watch on the nightstand, she stared at its bold face. Her heart thudded in her chest. "Christian?"

"Yes?"

"Did you notice the date?"

"Yes."

She saw his lashes flick down, hiding his expression from her. A thread of hurt wound itself around her heart. "It's the day we got married."

His gaze met hers, the blue vivid and all-consuming. "I know."

"Then why aren't you in this bed with me, celebrating the day as we should, screwing like those pet rabbits Jayden wants?"

He suddenly looked wary. "I thought we both agreed a long time ago that this wasn't going to be a real marriage."

"To begin with, yes. But…things change. Or rather people change."

His head jerked up.

Pushing the duvet away, Priya sat up. Resolve was like steel in her spine. She'd wanted this day to be different for so many years. And today, she could finally have that. She had him within reach. "We need to talk about that weekend in the Alps."

"No."

"Yes, we do," she said stubbornly. "Today, of all days, I need to say all the things I've wanted to for eight years. The things I whispered to myself while you were gone."

He walked to the opposite edge of the bed, his features haunted. As if this was a punishment.

"Before you asked me to marry you…all those months I stayed with you, I… I was crazy about you."

He flinched. "Pree, don't—"

"If you say I'm making this up, I'll punch you right in that pretty mouth."

He leaned back, his jaw still clenched.

"I was struggling with it, because it had barely been a year since Jai died. How could I feel so much for you when it had been barely an year since we lost him? I thought it was escape. I called it lingering grief over Jai. I called it anger at life. I gave it every name except what it was, Christian.

"I just wanted you. And not just simple lust either, though it felt safe to call it that. I could understand lust. I… I was jealous of every soccer star and actress you dated. I wanted you to look at me the way you looked at them. I wanted to flirt with you, and kiss you. I wanted to laugh with you. I wanted to be the one who danced with you.

"And then, in the blink of an eye, I was your wife. But instead of bringing us close, it only pushed you further away from me. But I was okay because it was safe. I didn't know how to get your attention. I didn't even know what I'd do if I had it.

"It became clear how much of an inconvenience I was but you wouldn't ask me to leave. Instead, you stayed out more and more before we went on that trip to the Alps. You made every excuse you could to avoid coming home to the apartment—your apartment. And to me…" The sound that ripped from her throat was a mixture of anger and disgust. "The more I wanted you, the more I was determined to hide it. The more lies I told myself. I acted like a victim and a coward. God, I was such a self-righteous fool. And then, we took that trip. We got stranded at the cabin in the snow, and it looked like we'd be stuck for a few days."

Christian leaped out of the chair, as if he couldn't bear to be still. "Pree, we don't have to go over this right now."

"Yes, we do. I know what we did that weekend bothers you. The next morning you looked at me as if I was the worst mistake you'd ever made. You wouldn't even make eye contact with me, and I see that in your eyes even now."

Finally, after what felt like an eternity, he turned toward her. "I didn't, for a single second, regret what happened that weekend."

But it wasn't the entire truth; Priya knew that now. There was more. It ate through her…this need to know. This need to understand all his truths. All of him.

"I thought I'd let you down." He groaned. "I'd promised you I wouldn't let anything mess with our relationship and I…"

"One night with me messed up our relationship?" she asked curiously.

"Didn't it?"

"You spent three weeks away after that and then your plane crashed. I'd like to think, given enough time, I'd have been brave enough to tell you outright that I wanted you."

He stood there, stock-still, as if the truth had skewered him.

Drawing her knees up, she wrapped her arms around them. It didn't matter if he didn't like it. Or if he didn't want to see it. She was done hiding the truth from him. "I'll never be that foolish girl again, Christian. I'll not wait another eight years for what I want when it's within touching distance. I'll never again live my life safely. Because that's no life at all."

Her fingers bunched in his shirt, her eyes searching his. He didn't pull away, and that in itself felt like a victory. "What do you want from me, Pree?" he asked quietly.

"I want you in my bed, Christian. I want you to make love to me because we both want it this time. Because we see each other. Because I can't breathe for wanting you."

His eyes were like twin blue flames, so many questions and demands still swirling in them. With one smooth move—which was a miracle in itself given how much she was shaking—she peeled off her pajama top. She didn't let herself think or hesitate. Or pause. Because if she did, if she let the voluble silence get to her, she might stop.

The cool breeze from the ocean hit her bare breasts at once. A soft gasp loosed from her mouth and her dark brown nipples instantly puckered. Christian stared at her, only the granite tightness of his jaw betraying his reaction.

"Your shirt," Priya demanded.

He grunted and she wondered for a second if that was a no. But then with an intensely masculine gesture, he held the top edge and plucked off his T-shirt in one movement. She was so lost in his nakedness that it escaped her for a second that it seemed he was agreeing. To all her demands.

The sparse hair on his chest shimmered almost golden in the orange light that filled the room. His chest was tight with definition, his belly rock hard.

All the boyish charm was gone. So much of his twenties just vanished in a puff of smoke. So many years they could have spent together. No, she couldn't think like that. She couldn't go down that rabbit hole again. Not when he was here now. With her. Watching her with such intensity that she felt claimed before he even touched her.

And she couldn't act as if he'd lost some essential part of himself.

No, he was a better man now, even though she wouldn't

have thought that possible. Where there had been a brash, almost ruthless charm and will, now there was compassion and depth. Ambition had been tempered by a fierce fire to make each day hold more meaning than the last. It was as if the eight years he'd been gone had distilled the very best part of him into something stronger, more wonderful.

Her mouth dry, Priya licked at her lips.

"At some point, you'll have to take over the wheel because I've used up all my courage," she said with a shaky pout.

His gaze moved over every inch of her bared flesh. Her breasts felt heavy, her nipples aching for his mouth. One dark brow rose in a silken question as he signaled at her shorts with his chin.

Priya pushed them off. She had nothing on but light brown skin-colored panties. Her fingers played with the waistband of the flimsy fabric, her entire being pulled taut and thin. Just one breath, one touch from him would break her. Or would it set her free?

That weekend at the cabin, she'd resolutely stayed underneath the sheets. And she'd kept him there, too. She frowned. Something about the last ten nights they'd spent sleeping together in the same bed clicked into place.

"What?" Christian demanded.

"You hate being swallowed up by sheets." She looked around her, heat swarming her face. "I don't know if you've noticed but our bed is quite the battlefield every night. I pull the duvet up and you push it away. If not for the fact that you continuously give out enough warmth to fuel a village, I'd be cold."

He grunted.

"That weekend at the cabin… I probably half choked you."

He rubbed a brow, a grin tugging at those gorgeous lips. "I do have a vague memory of being out of breath. It was the most singular sex I'd ever had. I remember wondering if you were into pain-play and breath-play and just didn't know it."

Her gasp of outrage made him laugh. That deep, infectious sound that burrowed into the center of her, becoming a part of her.

She lifted her leg to kick him, stopping her foot an inch from his chest. Fingers wrapped around her ankle and pulled her forward until her foot sat flush against his chest. Even that simple contact lit her up from the inside. "But I wanted you so badly that I'd have rolled around in the snow, half freezing to death if you'd said that's where you wanted to—"

Her toe touched his mouth, cutting off his words. When he'd have bitten her, she scampered away. But not far. Not tonight. Or ever again.

"You ask questions, Starling. But you don't really want the answers."

"I'm not running anymore, Christian. I just don't want this to become a talking session instead of a doing-all-kinds-of-wickedly-delicious-things-with-my-husband session. A husband I've desperately missed."

Heat flared in his eyes. And she realized it was because she'd called him her husband. As if she'd triggered it by saying it, something indefinable shimmered into existence between them.

Priya traced his throat, his pecs, his hard abdomen with her foot and then she brought it down, down, down, slowly, gently to his crotch. His erection pressed into the arch of her foot, and the solid length of him made her lower belly clench and release in agonizing emptiness.

She applied just a little more pressure and felt his immediate reaction. The faint thrust of his hips following her foot when she pulled back made her gasp. "Now, please, Christian."

She watched as he shed his sweatpants. Took in his body. The hair that dusted his corded thighs gleamed copper. He prowled onto the bed, the very breadth of his shoulders her entire field of vision. His shaft nudged up toward his belly, hard and long.

"I want to return the favor now," she said, scooting closer, pushing his chest back with her hand. His fingers touched her immediately, playing with the ends of her hair where it fell on her breasts. "Start getting my practice in. It's going to be at least a decade before I get really good at it. In case you didn't know this about me, I'm very stubborn."

Now his hands were on her hips, nudging her closer and closer. "You're the most stubborn woman I've ever met. But what does that have to do with giving me head?"

"I wouldn't want to be found wanting. Or to find you thinking of someone else—"

One long finger pressed against her mouth to quiet her, his blue eyes full of that wildfire she hadn't seen in so long. He drew a line down her body, from her mouth to her throat to her chest and down...watching her with hooded eyes. "I'll gladly take whatever you give me, Pree. In this or anything else."

"Yeah?" she said, arching her back into his touch, some wild thing inside her responding to the quiet declaration.

"Yes, Starling." His mouth went to her shoulders. His teeth grazed her pulse, his rough hands continuously roaming, stroking, touching and cupping every inch of her. Hands on her hips, he lifted her. Priya let out a cry when his mouth opened and sucked in her taut nipple.

On and on, he continued the caress, switching between her breasts, sometimes ravenous, sometimes so agonizingly gentle that she thought she might explode simply from that. His hands and lips and tongue, they played her, stroking her higher and higher, until release hovered just there... But he didn't push her over the edge. Instead, he brought her down and then pushed her back up, again and again, until she was damp all over, sobbing, begging for release.

"I'm selfish," he whispered against her shoulders.

"How?" Priya asked on a broken breath.

"I don't want you to come until I'm inside you. I want to feel you all around me."

"Please, then come inside me now, Christian. I've waited so long for you."

Now he was gently spreading her legs apart until she was straddling him, and then his erection was caught between his belly and hers and Priya instantly arched her spine, wanting more, needing to be closer.

His thumb found its way in between their bodies. Down, down, down, until it reached her sensitized clit and began its magic all over again. Teasing and taunting, readying her.

His hands were everywhere; his legs caged her, his chest held her. She felt enveloped by him, his warmth, his heat, his desire. Their hearts thudded in unison.

His open mouth pressed against her temple and he dragged it down to her cheek, to her jaw, to her neck, to her shoulder and then back up again. Priya moaned when his mouth found hers. The kiss was so gentle, so tender that a sob built in her chest again.

"Pree?"

"Hmm?" she said, her own hands spanning his broad back, tracing the line of his spine, to the divot above his hard buttocks. She could spend an entire lifetime doing this with him. And not just the sex. But this intimacy, this give-and-take, this joy, this pleasure, this pure feeling of being gloriously alive.

Putty in his hands, Priya felt him lift her up. His mouth searched for hers just as he notched his shaft at her entrance, and he whispered, "Happy anniversary, Starling."

All the while watching her. His blue eyes devoured her, noting every soft gasp and moan, every arch and ripple that swept through her, his mouth nibbling away at hers.

That first thrust in was like hanging on the edge of heaven. Her belly contracted, her thighs clenched as he fed himself into her, inch by inch. His shoulders were so tense under her fingers.

Impatience swirled over her skin. She'd been empty, so empty for so long. In her heart and soul and in her body. Gripping his shoulders tight, her nails pricking his skin, Priya thrust herself down. And then he was home. All the way home.

She jerked at the alien, almost painful feeling of him. At how big and hard and tight he felt inside her—almost uncomfortably so. How he filled her every inhale and exhale, how she could feel him in her very heart...

His curse boomeranged around them, the pleasure in his voice clearly contrary to his disapproval at what she'd just done.

Only then did Priya look down at him. Their bodies were damp and locked tight against each other, their hearts thundering away in unison. And she knew why he'd chosen this position. Because he wanted to see her face when he took her.

If only he'd let himself have her, if only he would see what was in her eyes...

"Christian?" His name on her lips came out like a little sob, a request. For what, she had no idea. She didn't know why or how she could feel so tightly wound up and also loose in a way she'd never felt before. How intimate and soul baring this was.

He looked at her then, and his blue eyes were aglow with an emotion Priya never remembered seeing before. His fingers pushed away a sweaty tendril of hair from her temple. A soft buss at that spot made tears swell up in her throat. It had nothing to do with passion and want, but everything to do with what she didn't want to say. What she was terrified to give voice to. What she needed from him but was afraid would never be on offer.

"Is it okay like this? Am I hurting you? Do you want me to pull out?" he asked with concern.

"I'll kill you if you do," she said, and he laughed with relief. "No, this is good. This is…better than good. This is heaven, Christian."

His head leaned back against the headboard, and his Adam's apple bobbed as he swallowed. Tilting her head, Priya kissed the hollow at his throat. "Tell me please. Tell me…how it feels to you."

His eyes flicked open and he was smiling. But she didn't miss the shadow there. That in a matter of seconds, he'd swallowed his instinctive response. "It feels so good that every muscle in me is begging me to move, Starling. Shall we?"

Teeth digging into her lips, Priya nodded. She wouldn't deny him his pleasure now when he'd waited so long. The very last thing she'd ever do was to force him to give her anything he wasn't ready for.

Might never be ready for.

And she'd have to live with that. Would have to live with the uncertainty of never knowing what might change inside his head.

But she was okay with it. She was strong enough. She'd

love him for the rest of their lives, be whatever he needed her to be. "Yes, now."

He laughed again and the motion caused their bodies to slide and thrust and they both groaned loudly at the flicker of pleasure that arched so fast and just as quickly disappeared.

He took her mouth in a savage kiss, his tongue diving in and out of her mouth in a vivid mockery of what she wanted below. "I love this version of you, Starling."

"Yeah?" she said, nibbling his lower lip. Knowing that it was heady sexual desire that prompted those words. "I like this version of me, too. And you know what, Christian? You had a hand in the making of it."

Astonishment flickered over his features. "Don't say that, Priya."

"It's the truth," she insisted. "Now are you going to give me what I want or what?"

He smiled, taking the lifeline she'd thrown him.

And then he was moving, and her breasts were rubbing against his hard chest, and Priya thought she would die from the pleasure. It wasn't long before they understood each other's rhythms, with their voracious hunger guiding them.

She was already close when Christian suddenly tipped her onto her back. Hands cupping her bottom, pulling her up against him, he thrust slow and deep, hitting that spot inside her with every slide in. When his finger reached between them, flicking her most sensitive place, she fell apart and his thrusts quickened until he, too, was groaning and shuddering in her arms.

And Priya never wanted to let him go.

CHAPTER ELEVEN

"DAD, I'M HUNGRY. Can we go back now?"

Christian turned toward Jayden, still feeling that same jolt in his chest every time his son called him Dad. And how easily those brown eyes reminded him of his mother's.

He ruffled Jayden's light brown hair and made a face at the sand stuck in it in wet clumps. "Did you check the picnic basket?"

Jayden inserted his hand into the basket and came up empty. "We ate everything. Like everything...including the pretzels and the kebabs. Only your beer's left. Mama says I'm going to eat her into bankruptcy."

Laughing, Christian packed up everything they'd scattered on the strip of the private beach. He'd always been a boisterous boy himself, but Jayden seemed to have the energy of ten boys. Dusk painted the sky glorious shades of pink and orange. "Okay, let's go."

He picked up the picnic basket and Jayden tucked his small hand into his large one as they made their way toward the villa.

Today, the turquoise blue of the waters and the white sands had become more an escape, and less of a welcoming haven. Not that he begrudged spending one-on-one time with Jayden. In the four weeks they'd been here, he'd made it a point to spend as much time as possible with him every single day. Without Priya providing some kind of bridge.

The even-tempered boy that he was, Jayden made it easy to while away hours and hours with him. Already, it felt like his son had come to know and trust him. So Christian was happy he'd insisted that they get away— from the company, from their interfering family members. And from real life.

"Does your head hurt, Papa?"

"Hmm?"

"You're frowning. Are you having bad dreams again?"

The frown clearing from his brow, Christian smiled down at his all-too-observant son. "No. There's no headache at the moment, champ. I've been sleeping a little better since we got here." He almost brushed away Jayden's concerns but then decided not to. "I do still have some bad dreams but they're not as bad as they used to be."

Jayden nodded in that solemn way of his.

Nightfall came swiftly while they were halfway back to the house. Noticing that Jayden was leaning heavily against his thigh, Christian bent his knees and picked him up with his free arm. Arms tight around his neck, his son let his slender body sink into Christian's.

Christian felt an overwhelming rush of love for the little guy—love like he'd never felt for anyone else.

God, he was so selfish. Priya had told him that Jayden would tire and might even get cranky after two to three hours of play. But because he was a coward escaping not only his wife but also the familiar grief and guilt that always came attached to this particular day, he'd kept him at the beach through the evening.

He had an excuse for forgetting the day they'd lost Jai

for the last eight years. But there was no excuse for forgetting it today. Shame had chased him away, out of the villa.

The last four weeks with just Priya and Jayden and him doing nothing but lazing around, playing on the beach, cooking and baking in the kitchen had been sheer paradise. The location had very little to do with it. In the afternoons, Jayden napped and Priya, the workaholic that she'd become, would check to see if there were any company fires to put out and he... He'd attended online therapy sessions thrice a week.

The other two weekdays, he'd sit in the wide-open office space across from her, familiarizing himself with all the tech that had bloomed in his absence. He liked looking up and seeing her scrunched-up face, or solving problems in the smooth, calm tones she used.

Eight years was a long time to be absent from a groundbreaking field like his, but once he'd opened his system, programming had come back to him with all the ease of swimming or cycling. He was building something now that he believed would have quite an impact when he was done tinkering with it.

And at night, all three of them sat outside, sometimes in the hammocks, listening to the sounds of the ocean, watching the starry sky. The arrival of the telescope he'd ordered the very evening they'd arrived had been quite the surprise for Jayden. That first evening, they'd spent hours talking while Christian set it up.

Now, every night Jayden and he studied the stars while Priya curled up nearby, listening to music. Once even Jayden's inexhaustible supply of energy was drained, Christian carried him to his bedroom.

By the time he'd showered and arrived in their own room, Priya would already be under the covers, sometimes more than half-asleep. The thought of her buried under the covers in buttoned-up pajamas that very first night made him smile now.

After eight years of dreading it, the inky blackness of night was something he finally looked forward to. He loved gathering her up against him and nodding off to sleep. But whether he woke up with a nightmare or just hungry for her, she was always there next to him.

And she matched him in his appetite. The number of times she'd woken him up with her mouth at his ear, teasing him, telling him she'd read about a position she wanted to try... A shiver went down his spine, heat gathered in his pelvis. It was as if she was determined not to lose a moment with him. As if she was determined to make up for every moment they'd lost in the eight years.

As if she'd never get enough of him.

But the strangest thing was that with Priya, sex became an adventure, often filled with laughter. It was so much more than just sating their mutual desire.

She gave everything to this, to them. Just as she had back then to Jai. Just as she did to being a mom. Just as she did for the company and its people. Just as she always would to this...marriage of theirs.

And he knew she always would. It had taken him this long to truly see it, to believe it. This long to understand why she'd said it was important to untangle the past from the present.

He felt so incredibly guilty that he'd forgotten that today marked the day they'd both lost Jai. He hadn't remembered even when he'd woken up with sunlight slanting over his face and stretched out an arm to find the space next to him empty.

Only when he'd walked into the open lounge to find Priya on a call, speaking to Jai's parents, did the significance of the date hit him. And when it did, it was like a punch to the gut. In its wake came a massive surge of grief and guilt. He'd felt the same way about Jai's death right up until he'd lost his memory, but it was so much more powerful today because he'd realized he had everything that should have been Jai's.

Priya and a son and the second chance to get it right.

So, instead of offering the little comfort that she might have needed today, he'd fled to the beach with his son in tow. He couldn't face himself in the mirror, much less bear witness to Priya's grief. Knowing that he was running away when she needed him the most.

And thinking of his lost best friend meant facing what he'd been hiding from the first moment he'd seen her. From the moment Jayden had turned those solemn brown eyes at him.

Facing that he'd needed to first tell Priya the truth. First, he had to give her the complete truth. Only then he could think of the future. Because if he didn't tell her now and if he lost himself again, she would never know.

And she deserved to know.

Once she knew about the past, then he'd be free to address the future. Because, as much as it terrified him, he had to try. He had to be the best man he could be for her. He had to address the possibility that he might have another episode, address how it would ripple through Priya and Jayden's lives, how much it could hurt them. He had to face his worst fear because he owed it to his son.

He owed it to his wife, the fierce woman who had kissed him, cajoled him, challenged him and pushed him to embrace who he was now, to embrace the life they had—so determined to see the best of him even when he wasn't.

He owed it to himself because that's the Christian he saw reflected in her eyes.

The Christian that deserved to find a measure of peace after all this time.

The Christian that Priya deserved to have as a husband.

Between him and Priya, who'd been waiting anxiously for their return, they managed to get the sand out of Jayden's hair in a quick bath. How both of them ended up wetter than their son was a mystery Christian didn't even try to solve. While Christian showered, Priya helped Jayden finish his soup and get into his bed.

He found her in the main lounge, her bare legs tucked under her, her face illuminated by the glare from the muted giant flat-screen TV on the wall. Pillow tucked under one elbow, she was staring off into the distance while strains of the sitar filled the air. A jolt went through him as he realized the overlarge sweater she was wearing was his. The washed-out yellow made her brown skin glow.

A pink bra strap winked at him from the dipped neckline. He swallowed and looked away. A hundred years and he wondered if he'd ever be used to looking at her and thinking he shouldn't want her. If he'd ever see her as his, completely.

She scrunched into herself with a sudden shiver. With a curse, he walked across the room and closed the French doors.

The image of her sitting on that couch like that, forlorn and lost to the world around her, reminded him painfully of the months he'd spent cajoling her out of this very pose after Jai had died. But the shadows in her eyes now... They weren't because of a love that had been lost a long time ago.

This wasn't about how she'd once loved Jai—an excuse he'd been hiding behind. This was about him, his moods, his...head.

She uncoiled from her cozy position slowly, reminding Christian of a lazy cat. A line appeared between her brows. "Is everything okay?" she said, taking in his face.

He ran a hand through his wet hair, uncomfortable with how easily she could read him. "No." Her face twisted into instant concern. "Nothing's wrong with my head. I meant that I've been thinking a lot and it... It's left me antsy."

She pushed off from the couch. The neckline of the sweatshirt didn't simply dip. It hung off to her elbow on one side, revealing acres of silky, smooth brown flesh he wanted to bury his face in. "Okay." She covered the distance between them and Christian breathed her in like a junkie. "Is there anything I can do?" She looked wary all of a sudden. "Do you need space? Was Jayden too much today?"

"No, of course not."

She cocked her head curiously, like the precious bird he called her. "While you figure out how to say what you want to, can I have a turn?"

He grimaced and nodded.

She came at him like a hurricane. One moment, it was stiflingly tense and quiet in the lounge and the next, her arms were around his neck and she was plastered to him and her mouth was at his ear. For a few seconds, Christian couldn't hear what she kept whispering. Because his damned heart was lodged in his ears. And his throat.

She was soft and curvy and warm, and he couldn't resist wrapping his arms around her any more than he could stop breathing. This was the part he couldn't still believe—this easy affection she showed him.

"It's the best gift I've ever received. Today of all days..." The sound of her stifled sob had him squeezing her tighter. Their mutual love of music had been something she and Jai had shared—a private thing that had left

Christian in complete awe whenever they played together. He couldn't take away her ache and loss—the very same that burned through him today—but they weren't alone with it. That was Jai's legacy to them—this bond that he'd begun to forge between them, this ability to love that he'd taught them both.

"The sitar arrived, then?" he said softly, overcome by a cocktail of needs.

She nodded, a tremulous smile curving her lips. "You're spoiling me."

"I haven't heard you play since I returned. Your mother said your instrument's still at their house, so I thought maybe you should just begin again with a new one." He ran his thumb over her jaw, unable to stop touching her. Unable to stop this avalanche of feeling inside his chest now that he'd admitted it to himself. "Why did you stop playing?"

A lone tear crested her cheek and he caught it with his thumb. "I just…didn't feel the music inside me anymore. Not after I lost you, too." She took a deep breath and set those beautiful eyes on him. "I tuned it up and played for a while." She scrunched her nose. "But to be honest, I was pretty bad. Not playing for eight years will do that to you. Give me a few weeks and I'll do a private concert. Just for my boys." She flicked the tip of his nose and his heart clenched. "And swear you'll tell me I'm amazing even if I suck."

"I will," he said with a smile. "But I'm not sure my son can manage that much deceit."

She mock punched him in the gut and he caught her hand. On his next breath, her arms came around him again. A shuddering exhale left him as he gave in to the inevitable. One hand on her shoulder, he pressed a kiss to her temple, batting away at the desire that flooded his body.

She had no such reservations, no such restrictions she placed on herself.

Long fingers fisting in his shirt, she took his mouth in a passionate kiss. No, she claimed him as she'd never done before. There was ownership in the sure way she slanted her lips this way and that against his. There was power in how she nipped and licked and teased him.

This was not obligation or friendship or companionship that she was seeking when her tongue pushed for entry. This was affection and love pouring over into physical need, demanding release.

Her moan reverberated in his mouth, through him when he let her in. She tangled her tongue with his with a boldness, a purpose, and that was nothing but pure pleasure.

Her pleasure. Their pleasure.

Deep and devouring, she dipped and dived and tasted every inch of him, her breasts flattened against his chest. Her fingers held him, for her convenience, with a tight clasp at the nape of his neck. It was the kiss Christian had always wanted from her. A kiss, sometimes it seemed, he'd been waiting for from the very moment he'd seen her stroll into his house, arm in arm with Jai. It was the kiss he'd imagined a thousand times and it nearly broke him that it had come now, at the end of everything.

She rubbed the pad of her finger against his stinging lip and pressed it inside. He licked at the pad, and then suckled it softly, all the while reading her desire in her eyes, completely hers. Then she took his palm and placed it over her neck. Her eyes were brown pools of need. "Touch me. Everywhere. Anywhere."

Acting on pure instinct, he curled his fingers around her throat. He felt her Adam's apple move against his palm. Then she wrapped those fingers around his wrist and dragged his palm down. Between her breasts. Down to her rib cage. Then to her belly, which had the barest hint of roundness to it from carrying Jayden.

She pushed their clasped fingers past the seam of her shorts. She directed his hand and Christian went where she took him. And then his palm was there, covering her mound. She was warm against his skin, her panties already damp, and his erection twitched painfully in his jeans. Her hips nudged into his hand greedily, and her flush deepened.

"Oh, God," she groaned. Her knees shook and Christian wrapped his arm around her waist until she was leaning against him. He moved his fingers gently, over the thin silk of her panties, tracing the shape of her, searching for her clit. He pressed down with the mound of his palm while he continued caressing her. And for every downward press of his palm, she thrust her hips into his hand and her breath came in fast, shallow gasps.

His mouth ran dry, his heart pounding in his ears. Every drop of blood in his body fled south. Her leanly muscled thigh pressed against his front, providing tantalizing friction for his already rock-hard shaft.

Her mouth opened against his throat.

An explosion of need swept through him, devouring him. Her cheeks were a fiery dark pink, her nipples tight against the sweatshirt, his sweatshirt. And yet in her eyes... He saw vulnerability and boldness and desire and plain need. All his plans to talk to her disintegrated. "I want to be inside you. Can't wait. Please," he whispered.

Fingers clasped around his neck, she murmured her answer into his mouth. "Yes. Now."

"Wrap your legs around me," he said, and she complied eagerly.

Breath like bellows, he carried them into their bedroom and shut the door with his foot. "Against the wall?" he asked, dipping down to claim her mouth again.

Now that he knew what he was going to do, now that he knew his course, his control was threadbare. There was that cavernous hunger inside him again—desperate, yawning, for everything she could give.

"You know I'm ready," she said.

He did know. She was already wet and warm and ready for him.

"This is going to be rough," he said in warning. "I need it fast and hard."

She clasped his cheek, something wicked and joyous shining in the depths of her eyes. "I want whatever you want. I want you to have whatever you want, however you want it."

Christian leaned his forehead against hers, even as desire and the need to claim her beat at him. "I don't deserve you," he whispered, drowning in the love in her eyes. God, how was he going to walk away from this? How was he going to leave her, not knowing what waited for them on the other side?

She bit his lower lip, a sort of punishment he realized when she said, "No, Christian, you deserve me. And I deserve you. We both deserve this happiness." Tears gathered in her eyes and she rubbed her nose against his. "And I deserve the fabulous climax that my wicked husband always delivers."

He laughed and kissed her.

He put her down on her feet for the moment it took to pull her shorts and panties down. Another moment—one too long—had his sweatpants down. He lifted her, placed his left hand between the wall and her back, and without another word, he thrust into her waiting warmth.

He groaned and she moaned out a filthy curse and he did it again.

Even with his hand buffering her, her head went thud against the wall every time he withdrew and thrust again. With each stroke, he went deeper and faster. He bent and licked the shell of her ear, pleasure already pooling low in his spine. "Touch yourself, Starling. Come for me. I don't want to go over without you."

Her eyes wide, she stared at him for a second. Then she grinned and it was the most beautiful thing Christian had ever seen. And he knew, in that moment, that even if he lost his memories again, he would always remember her exactly in this moment.

Her hand snuck down to between where they were joined and the sight of one long finger rubbing at the plump bundle at the apex of her thighs had Christian cursing. Bending, he took one taut nipple in his mouth. And then he withdrew again. Thrust in again.

He rolled his hips, holding her against the wall, holding his release back by the skin of his teeth. And when she made that sound deep in her throat, when she fractured around him, drenching him in the waves of her release, Christian let go of the last thread of his control. He pounded into her, until her tight sheath, her moans, her hands, her breath was all he knew and soon, he was splintering, pleasure suffusing the ache of his decision.

But only for a second.

Because loving Priya and walking away from her was going to tear him apart, all over again.

CHAPTER TWELVE

THE SKY WAS a shimmering dark blanket when Priya walked out into the covered patio at the back of the villa an hour later. All Christian had said was that they needed to talk and would she join him outside.

There had been such a serious note to his voice that she'd nodded. Her knees still shaking when he released her, she'd told him she wanted to change into something warm before she met him outside.

"Wear that sweatshirt," he'd whispered, pressing a fast, fierce kiss to her upturned lips. "I like seeing you in my clothes."

So here she was, wearing his sweatshirt.

A cacophony of sounds welcomed her—the shush of the ocean waves, songbirds calling out and the soft melody of the sitar record that was playing.

She hadn't missed the fact that it was their last night on the island. Was he worried about returning to real life? Did he think she'd balk if he didn't want to return? Did he still not realize that her home, her heart was wherever he was? If he wanted to live on this island forever—give up the company, the mansion, the lifestyle, the parties— she'd do it in a heartbeat.

He was home for her, wherever he was.

The last two and a half weeks of their month's stay had

moved at warp speed. Maybe because she and Christian had spent every night tangled up in each other. And not just to help him sleep. Which she could tell he was struggling with, as much as ever.

As he was with his frequent headaches. If it wasn't the first two, it was his therapy sessions that left him close to breakdown. And while it hurt her—like a thorny knot to see him in pain, in confusion—Priya didn't indulge it even for a second.

She'd never let him down that way. Never. The only relief he had from them was that he was coding again, all the hours he spent with Jayden and her, and the nights they spent exploring each other to their hearts' content.

Doing all the wicked, wanton things she could come up with.

Something had been unleashed in her that night when he'd finally made love to her.

And not just their respective, long-suppressed libidos, she thought now with a faint smile. It also wasn't discovering that the chemistry they'd shared that one weekend eight years ago was even more combustible now. Not just that their bodies had learned each other's wants and rhythms so well that every kiss felt like a conflagration.

Every touch made tension bubble up in the air around them. Every caress felt like a new beginning. And when he was inside her, when he moved inside her in that mind-blowing way that he did... Words shimmered behind her lips, begging to be spoken, to be released.

But she didn't dare. Because she still wasn't sure if he was ready for them.

He...hadn't exactly withdrawn from her in the last few days, but it felt as if he'd made some kind of decision today. Even if her instincts about that were wrong, there was the matter of all the hours he'd spent in the last week on phone calls. She'd been desperate to know what they were, but he'd said it wasn't anything to do with the company. Yet it was definitely something important to him. Which meant it was important to her.

She didn't know how long she stood there, warming her hands around a cup of tea.

"You look very serious," said Christian from the blanket he'd spread on the ground.

"Do you have eyes in the back of your head, then?"

"No. I turned around and looked and you were so deep in thought that you didn't notice me."

The blanket looked inviting and she waited for him to pat the space next to him in invitation. To demand she do her conjugal duty as she'd demanded of him one night. She was a little sore between her legs, but she had no doubt he'd go gentle on her. He'd take it slow this time, seduce her with that wicked mouth and that clever tongue until she was unraveling again. Until she was begging for him to come inside her, despite her sore muscles.

Seconds piled into minutes and she felt that strange rushing again. As if time was determined to cut short their last night.

She took a deep breath and wandered over. But instead of joining him on the blanket, she sat down on the chair Jayden had dragged around earlier.

"We're leaving tomorrow," she said lamely. "Is that what has you so tense?"

He shook his head. His dark blond hair gleamed in the moonlight. She was used to his silences and his sudden changes of mood, but this wasn't that. "I don't want to talk about this. But I think I have to. You were right. We're never ready for the future without facing the past. Without facing the shadow of the man we both loved."

She searched his face, something in the tone of his

words escaping her comprehension. It was always there these days when their discussions drifted toward the topic of Jai. Even Christian's initial reaction on learning what she'd named their son... "Is this about why you avoided me when...we were first married? Why you went away after we slept together?"

He dipped his head in a nod. "Ask me."

Priya took the time to arrange her thoughts into some kind of order. But there was no neat way to do this. The past was still a tangle between them. Though she thought she'd figured it out recently for herself. He'd given her enough pieces of the puzzle over the last few weeks. She'd just been too blind to see them clearly enough to put them together. "Did you avoid me because you... you wanted me?"

His answer was a long time coming. When he spoke, he addressed it to the sky or the stars or the quiet, beautiful world around them. As if he was finally releasing it to the universe. "Yes. As much as I do now. As much as I ever did. I hated myself for it, but I've never stopped wanting you. Not since the first day Jai brought you to our lab and introduced you as his girlfriend. Not since your smile turned from full and wide to reticent and wary when you looked at me."

She swallowed, feeling what? She couldn't name one thing. Each piece fell into the bigger puzzle, and her breath hitched. His memory of her on that day they'd met had been perfect in his words.

"But I never planned for that weekend at the Alps to happen the way it did. I didn't..." He thrust a hand through his hair roughly. "It's important to me that you know that."

Priya frowned, feeling her way through the minefield that suddenly lay between them. "It's important that I not think you used some nefarious wiles and your sexy charm to seduce me into bed? Is that it?"

"I know it sounds ridiculous put like that. But—"

"It is exactly that. Ridiculous." She sighed. He was hers now. The past didn't matter. It couldn't. "It happened because we were both consenting adults who couldn't keep their hands off each other, and for no other reason."

She saw his throat move and then he nodded.

"You had a thing for me when Jai was alive."

Long lashes shielded his expression before he raised his gaze and let her see him. "Yes. But it wasn't just a thing."

Her heart was in her throat now, thudding away. Her knees shook again. Her entire body, it felt as if she was standing outside reality. Outside herself.

He looked away then. "I was in love with you. I had everything—looks, fortune, brains, a girlfriend... And all I wanted was you, my best friend's fiancée. And being near you and not having you was... What do they call it? Character-building." A harsh laugh. "But I couldn't stay away from you, either."

The silence between them grew and grew... And Priya didn't know how to break it. She looked down at her palms as if she could find appropriate words written there. There was no chance of laughing it off because his every word rang with truth. She'd seen the anguish she heard in his words now, in his eyes. "Loving someone is never a bad thing, Christian."

The words felt trite, like a sop to his conscience.

And yet, she believed the truth in them, too. What she'd seen as friendship or obligation on his part had been love in its most unconditional form. No expectations, no demands, nothing but pure acceptance and love. The knowledge moved through her like a rush of river on parched land, soaking her, changing her.

He'd loved her and so he'd stood by her. He'd dragged her out of grief and pain. He'd dragged her back to life. And she'd fallen in love with him—not because he'd looked after her.

But because losing Jai had changed her. Because it had taught her that she couldn't spend it standing on the sidelines of life, forever afraid of her own shadow. By the time she'd realized the truth of that, Christian had been gone.

"Isn't it?" he said, not mocking her. Not teasing anymore. In a soft whisper that was ravaged by guilt and grief and by the weight of carrying it silently for years.

"No, it's never a bad thing," she said, her voice rising with conviction. "Jai taught us that, both of us. He loved us so easily, so openly, without reserve, without judgment. And that love, it changed us both. And your feelings for me—" she swallowed the gathering tears "—have only ever made me feel cherished. Have only made the world a wonderful place for me. How can I even begin to think it was a bad thing?"

"I loved you and I hated myself. Sometimes, I'd sit there, right across from him, and strategize how I would steal you away from him. I spent hours in meetings while we laughed and joked and worked together, and I'd wonder what you saw in him. What he had that I didn't." Something like an anguished growl fell from his mouth. "Of course, he was the better man. The best. And the damned thing is I'm certain he knew how I felt about you." His groan was guttural, wrenched from the depths of his soul. "God, he knew."

"He never mentioned it to me," Priya offered softly, shock buffeting her this way and that. "If he knew, that is."

"Oh, he knew. But Jai being Jai, he let it be. He trusted me, you see. And of course he didn't say anything to you. He wouldn't want how you saw me changed."

A strong breeze ruffled in, making Priya shiver. She wished it would carry away all the bitterness in his voice. Would cleanse away the confusion and grief and guilt and leave them both with blank slates. But that wasn't how any of this worked.

"And then—" his grief was a stringent note in his tone now "—he was gone. From one blink to the next. Just gone."

Priya blinked back tears. She'd made her peace with her own grief, but this was Christian's grief... And eight years ago, she'd never helped him process this. Never asked him what he needed. Never realized how much it had ripped him apart. And because she'd had the emotional range of a teaspoon back then, their relationship, in his mind, was always going to be tangled around this guilt and this grief that was still so raw.

This was what those eight years had cost him. Was costing them even now. If they didn't move on from this, if Christian couldn't move on, he would never allow himself to love her completely.

"That weekend at the cabin—" his blue eyes pinned her "—it was heaven. It was what I'd desperately craved for years. And it was also hell. Because it felt like he'd gone and I'd simply slipped into his place, taken everything that was his. As if all the horrible thoughts I'd had had become real."

"Christian..." Priya ventured, not really sure what she could say. Horrified by how hardened his guilt was.

"I told myself I was just an escape for you. That it was a one-off thing. That you were scratching an itch. That you were simply using me to escape your grief. I didn't mind being used by you." He laughed but there was nothing of his usual humor in his tone. "But then that made it all so much worse because I wanted you to want me. Just for me. I wanted to be the man you reached for because you couldn't stay away. Because you needed me as desperately as I did you. It made me angry, rash. I was like a wounded animal, angry with myself, angry with the world. I should never have piloted the jet that day. I wasn't there a hundred percent. Not in my head. And my actions hurt not just me, but you and Jayden."

The realization shook her. She'd simply put his actions that day down to his usual recklessness.

He looked at her then. And she couldn't let him be so far away from her. Not anymore.

She reached him on trembling knees. When she clasped his cheek, he didn't push her away, but he didn't turn to her, either. "Christian, you've got to let that guilt go. Otherwise it will destroy you. You never, ever made one inappropriate move toward me. That weekend happened because we were in a relationship, Christian, whether we admitted it to ourselves or not. We were married, and we had already begun to see each other for who we were, not just as Jai's best friend and Jai's fiancée.

"But as two people who were struggling to move on.

"Losing Jai changed us both.

"And I was confused about feeling so much for you so soon, yes, I admit it." She tugged and his eyes finally met hers. "But how can anything that gave us that sweet little boy be wrong? You've got to let it go because Jayden needs you. *I* need you."

And then she kissed him. She poured everything into that kiss, did her best to take all the guilt and grief from him. "I was so foolish for not seeing it then, Christian. But never again."

"Don't, Priya." He never called her *Priya* in that tone.

"No. Look at me, Christian. Even if he knew, he loved you. To his last breath." Something in her tone kept his gaze on her. "I loved Jai with all the naiveté of a sheltered girl. Of a girl who hadn't experienced life at all. Of a girl who'd always been so afraid of everything. But after he died, I became someone else. Someone completely new."

Cradling his cheeks, Priya continued. "Forget what was right or wrong eight years ago. Forget everything we were even two months ago. Now…" She took his hand and kissed it, tears falling down her cheeks. "…today…" She pressed his palm to her heart. "…the woman I am—"

Christian pressed his hand to her mouth, cutting off her words. "Pree… Don't make this harder than it needs to be."

Priya reeled back, searching his eyes. "What do you mean?" She bunched her fists in his shirt, fear beating a drum in her head.

"Listen to me, Pree. I have to do this, okay?"

"Do what, Christian?"

"I'm not returning with you. Not going home."

She fell back on her haunches, fear stifling her breath. And when she was afraid, she got angry. All those years spent in hospitals, she'd spent either being angry or learning to code. "Where the hell would you go if not back with us?"

"I've decided to see a neurologist. At a Swiss clinic. He's…a memory loss expert. It will be at least three months of in-house testing and treatment to help with the nightmares and the headaches."

Priya stared, shock traveling through her every cell, every breath.

Moonlight limned the strong planes of his face. That high forehead, those sharp cheekbones, the bridge of his nose…but his eyes, those eyes that could laugh or turn darker with passion or warm with affection…the eyes that had always showed her what she could be…were haunted.

He was leaving and he didn't plan on coming back to her. That's why he'd taken her with such rough need, such urgency just now. That's why he'd unraveled the past one last time between them.

He was saying goodbye. He was doing it properly this time. He was readying her for every eventuality.

"Okay," she said, on a shuddering exhale. "Okay. I'm glad you're going. We'll be waiting for you. I'm glad we spent this time together, Christian, before you left. I'm glad that we…"

But her strength lasted only so long and suddenly her calm practicality flipped to furious despair. "Why didn't you talk this out with me first, Christian? Don't I have any say in this? This is all our lives you're making decisions for."

He had no answer for that. Something shuttered in his expression, shutting her out.

After what felt like an eternity, he said, "Because if I'd told you, you'd make me weak. You'd want me to stay. I want to be a better man, Pree, for you."

Priya reared back. But she couldn't get angry because he knew her well. So damn well. "I want you to get all the help you need. But not at the risk of losing you. I don't need a different Christian. Or God forbid somehow a better Christian."

"I have to try, Pree." His blue eyes, filled with tears, looked like the ocean behind her. "I have to at least try to get better. For Jayden, if nothing else." That he chose to leave her out skewered her.

"And if you don't? What then? What am I to tell him, Christian?"

"I will speak to him tomorrow. And I plan to tell him the truth, for the most part. That I'm going away to get better. I'll call him. Write to him, talk to him every day—

I'll do whatever's necessary to make sure he understands that I love him."

"And me? What about what I need?"

"You don't need me, Starling. You're the bravest, brightest thing I've ever known."

Priya stared at him, tears running down her cheeks, her heart shattering in her chest. "That's the cruelest thing you've ever said to me."

He clasped her cheek with an infinite tenderness even as he decided to leave her behind. "It's the truth. You are strong. It is only me that's making you weak. That…"

"How dare you decide this for me? How dare you!"

"Aren't you the one who suggested I should have my head looked at? That I should be doing everything I can to help myself? To fix this so that I'm not constantly living on the edge of uncertainty?"

"Yes but before I understood what it might mean. But not at the risk of losing you. Never at the risk of losing what we have now…" She placed her hands on his chest and dipped down. Wrapping his fingers around his neck, she kissed him. He tasted like her tears and goodbye and such overflowing love that she gasped and pulled away.

But he didn't let her go. His grip had never been tighter on her arm, his body never so rigid. "Tell me the words I want to hear. Tell me, Pree. Please. I have waited an eon to hear them from your lips. I need them now."

"No," she said, falling apart completely. "No," she said again, denying him her words. "No," she repeated, angry now. She stood up, squaring her shoulders, holding back her words. Words she wanted to scream for the entire world to hear.

Because if she did, Priya didn't think she could make it a day without him.

And she had a son to be strong for.

CHAPTER THIRTEEN

THE CABIN IN the Alps was just as Christian remembered it from eight and a half years ago. From the outside at least. Except for the shiny electronic keypad near the door handle.

He pulled the piece of paper he'd written the key code on and jabbed the pad with fingers that were cold and clumsy.

Taking his shoes off in the foyer—it had become a habit long ago with how much he'd visited Jai's house first and then Priya's—he wondered at the warm burst of air that greeted him. He'd asked for the key code through William Constantine, too ashamed and too cowardly to call Priya for it.

Especially when she'd refused to speak to him even once in two months. There was nothing but a crisp polite hello when he called for Jayden and an equally terse goodbye when he was done. But never a single question. Not even to ask how he was doing.

He rubbed a hand over his unkempt face, knowing he deserved her cold silence. Two months of sleep trials and new medication and therapy sessions had changed him for the better and helped him put a lot of his fears about his health and his guilt into perspective. But it had also provided him with hours and hours of silence and thousands of thoughts swirling through his head to ponder all the ways he'd messed up with her.

God, in his exhaustion and despair, he'd pushed her away instead of telling her properly that he loved her, that he utterly adored this new version of her even more than he had the Priya from all those years ago. Like a schoolboy, he'd hoped she might still tell him how she felt about him.

His heart thumped painfully in his chest when he finally spotted the pair of calf boots next to the entry bench.

The fireplace in the sitting lounge was ablaze and now that he'd pulled his head out of the ever-constant spiral of regret and self-recriminations, he smelled roasted coffee. It could be Ben, he told himself. Or any of the friends who'd asked to borrow the cabin at the same time.

But he knew it wasn't.

It was her.

His throat felt so thick he wondered if it was possible to choke because of shock. His limbs felt mechanical, his body suddenly beset with shivers. Somehow, he managed to venture farther into the living room and there she was.

Lying on the huge sectional that seemed to swallow her slender body whole. Dark shadows cradling closed eyes. Even in repose, he saw the lines of tension bracketing her mouth.

How long had she been here? Why had no one told him she'd be there? What did she want?

He looked around, as if some inanimate object somewhere could give him a clue. There was such a deafening roar inside his ears that it was a miracle he was still standing. Slowly, he went and sat down at her feet. Lifting them, he plopped them onto his lap and settled into the deep reach of the sofa.

And then, with his fingers on her ankles, he laid his head back down and promptly fell asleep.

When he came to, he found her sitting on the other side of the giant sectional, her arms tucked around her knees. Her eyes were wide in her face, devouring him. Just as he was sure his were doing to her.

"Why are you here?" he asked, his heart in his mouth.

"Good. No niceties, then." She reached behind her to pull one of those huge handbags he'd seen her carry. Digging through it, she found a sheaf of papers that sent his soul into the coldest place he'd ever known.

Not even when his mind had been blank and empty had he felt that kind of chill.

"I came to bring you these. To give you an ultimatum," she said curtly, throwing the papers on the oak coffee table.

Christian eyed them as if they were a snake that could bite his head off. "Pree…"

"All you need to do is sign them, Christian, and I'll be out of your way. You can go back to your life of solitude and self-sacrifice without ever having to see me again."

He was shaking his head even before she finished talking. "I'm not touching them. Much less signing anything."

"Don't worry, Christian. I'm not ripping you off. In fact, I want nothing of yours."

"Jayden's mine, too," he said, getting defensive and angry now. Feeling like a cornered animal. Damn it, he'd left it too late to throw himself on her mercy and beg for forgiveness. He'd pushed her too far.

She lifted her chin in that stubborn move that had once felled him to his knees. That threatened to knock him over even now. "You can see as much or as little as you want of Jayden. I won't come between the two of you. But as for me... I'm done waiting for you.

"Do you realize I'm still only thirty-one years old? Thirty-one, Christian. I have an entire lifetime to live without being bogged down by an inconsiderate, cowardly, bastard of a husband who thinks he can waltz in and out of my life as he pleases." Tears filled her eyes but she didn't let them fall.

"I'm done with this—" she waved her hand between them "—whatever it was. This marriage was never real, so please let's just kill it dead so that I can change my status to single instead of separated on my social media profiles. You know, I've decided to give myself over into Mama's hands after all. She'll find me a prince or at least a lowly royal member from some far-flung country and I'm going to..."

Christian went to his knees in front of her and tugged her head down and took her mouth in a feral kiss. His heart threatened to burst out of his chest but he kissed her anyway. She tasted sweet and pure, like sunshine and frost and love and joy, and he just kept drinking her in. Her hands on his chest, she sank into the kiss with a guttural groan. She melted for him. She opened for him. She let him breathe her in.

For a few moments. A few measly moments only, though.

And then she was fighting him, beating his chest with her hands, tugging at his beard, until he filled his hands with her hips and toppled them both down and she was screaming in his face and pushing him onto his back and straddling him...

And then they were kissing wildly again.

Only this time, the kiss turned to tears and she was sobbing piteously against his chest and Christian thought his heart might break all over again.

He plunged his hands into her hair and pushed it back off her temple. "Don't, Pree. Don't cry over me. Don't divorce me. Don't leave me... You're right. I was inconsiderate. I was cowardly, I was...a stupid bastard who wanted to be a better man for the woman he loved but thought he couldn't be."

She thumped his chest with her fist again and he laughed and then coughed. "No. I don't believe you. If you loved me, you wouldn't have left. You wouldn't have..."

Christian tugged her face up, until her tears hit him in his beard. "It's messed up, I know, Pree. But it's true. I only left because I wanted to be whole for you. You deserve the very best any man could give you."

"No, I deserve to be loved, Christian. By you. In whatever way you can. The way you did before. That's all I asked you for. That's all I want."

Keeping her straddling him, Christian reached for the sheaf of papers, intent on throwing them into the roaring fire. But when he looked at them, he found them blank.

Shock pelting through him, he looked at her in horrified admiration. "You made me think you were going to divorce me? That's the most awful trick anyone's ever played on me."

She shrugged, as if she didn't give a damn. "Everything's fair in love and war. And this was both."

He tilted his hips and nudged her with his thighs until she scooted farther and slipped onto his chest. Their pelvises ground up against each other to such perfection that for a second, he forgot what he meant to say.

"I love you so much, Pree," he whispered, clasping her cheek. "These two months have been so helpful to me... They've given me a lot of techniques and strategies about how to manage my headaches and the insomnia. And the time away gave me the perspective I needed to finally see that I could absolutely be the man that you needed, the man Jai would approve of. I do have to warn you that this isn't—" he pointed to his head "—something that might ever get fixed a hundred percent."

Tears filled her eyes and she nodded. "I'm sorry if I wasn't ever—"

"You were exactly what I needed. You were the perfect friend, the perfect mother, the perfect lover, the perfect wife. I had everything I needed with you and Jayden. Will you…forgive me, Starling? I only wanted to be better for you. I…"

She nodded and then she was kissing him again. "Will you give me what I ask for?"

"Yes, baby, anything. The entire world is at your feet. I'm at your feet, Pree."

"I want to be your wife, Christian. I want a real marriage. And before that I want a grand wedding—with two different ceremonies. I want the entire world to know that you're mine. I want to celebrate us with all the grandeur I can manage. And if you agree, when we're ready, I want to have another baby. Two more, if it doesn't scare you. I want to have you by my side through it all this time. I want to build a life with you. I want to grow old with you, Christian. I want to make everything of this second chance we've got." She buried her face in his neck, her heart beating away rapidly.

He looked at her then, disbelief in his eyes. "Pree…"

"I'm so in love with you, Christian. I have loved you, it seems, for a long time. And I want to continue to love you, whatever happens in the future."

Christian nodded, no words coming to him. His heart was full to the brim.

"And you know something else that struck me when you were gone?"

"What?" he said, in a hoarse, husky voice.

She tapped his temple, a bittersweet smile curving her mouth. "Even if you did lose us again…" She took his hand and brought it to her chest. "…I have faith that you'll love me always, Christian.

"That you'll find your way back to loving me and our son whatever happens. You should have some faith, too."

And then she buried her face in his neck and sobbed her heart out.

Christian vowed this would be the last time his wife would ever cry over him. "I love you, Pree. I love you with everything I have in me. And I'll spend the rest of our lives proving that to you."

Priya knew, as she hid her damp face in his neck, as Christian ran his palm over her back soothingly, whispering filthy things and crooning to her, making her laugh, dizzy with laughter and pleasure and joy, that he'd finally returned to her.

Forever and always.

* * * * *

Enchanted by Returning for His Unknown Son?
Get lost in these other Tara Pammi stories!

A Deal to Carry the Italian's Heir
The Flaw in His Marriage Plan
Claiming His Bollywood Cinderella
The Surprise Bollywood Baby
The Playboy's "I Do" Deal

Available now!

PREGNANT BY THE WRONG PRINCE

JACKIE ASHENDEN

MILLS & BOON

This one's for Kevan and Dina.

CHAPTER ONE

'STOP.'

The voice came from behind, an avalanche of dark sound, crashing through the cathedral and silencing the bishop utterly.

Amalia De Vita, in the middle of the aisle, on her way to the altar, froze, her heart thudding in her ears.

He knows.

The thought was fleeting, icy, causing her hand that was resting on her father's arm to twitch, nearly going to her stomach in an instinctive protective movement. Luckily, she caught herself at the last moment.

It was impossible. He couldn't know. No one did. Not even Matias, her fiancé. She'd kept that precious secret all to herself and she was sure she hadn't let it slip.

At the altar Matias stood, tall and dark and dapper in his expertly tailored morning suit. He was frowning in her direction, presumably at the owner of that dark, terrible voice.

But Lia didn't turn. She knew who owned that voice already.

Fear crouched like a prey animal deep inside her.

You should have told him.

The silence in the cathedral was complete, every one

of the hundreds of people in attendance staring at the ornate oak doors.

'This wedding is cancelled,' the voice said, the weight of authority in his tone crushing everyone flat. 'The woman, if you please, De Vita.'

Beside her, Lia's father, the previous King's most trusted advisor, swung around, his whole body stiff with surprise. 'Your Excellency?'

'Rafael?' Matias said at the same time, taking a step forward from the altar. 'What is the meaning of this?'

There was no reply.

Footsteps came from behind her and someone took her arm in a gentle, but very firm grip. A royal guard.

No.

Lia trembled as denial coursed through her and she'd ripped her arm from the guard's hold before she could think better of it, her heart nearly beating its way out of her chest.

Her father was looking at her now and she could feel his shock. And no wonder. She was Amalia De Vita, the chosen bride of Matias Alighieri, heir to the throne of Santa Castelia. Why would the royal guard be coming for her?

'Lia?' There was confusion in her father's blue eyes as he looked at the guard and then at her.

Of course he'd be confused. But she hadn't been able to bring herself to tell him the truth. His disappointment in her would have been more than she could bear.

He'll find out anyway now.

Yes, he would.

Lia stayed silent, staring out through the fine gauze of her veil, tension crawling through her.

Perhaps if she didn't move this all might go away. *He* might go away.

Matias was drawing closer, anger written all over his handsome face. His groomsmen were standing at the altar, muttering among themselves while the bishop looked on disapprovingly.

Whispers, amplified by the magnificent acoustics of the cathedral, moved like a wind through the assembled aristocracy of Santa Castelia.

A scandal in the making. They'd think all their Christmases had come at once.

Then the whispers died, another profound silence falling.

A footstep echoed. Definite. Unhurried. As if whoever was coming towards her had all the time in the world. As if he didn't care one bit that the attention of the entire nation was centred on him as he interrupted the wedding of the century.

But then he wouldn't care, would he?

Matias might be the Prince and heir, but it was his older half-brother who ruled.

Rafael Navarro, the Spanish bastard. Prince Regent of Santa Castelia.

Don't turn around. Don't look at him.

She couldn't. She didn't dare. Because the minute she did, the second he saw her face and looked into her eyes, he'd know.

She'd never been able to hide anything from him.

Your father isn't the only one who's going to be disappointed.

A tremble shook her and she swallowed, trying not to give into her fear.

She was Santa Castelia's Crown Princess, the title

she'd been given when her betrothal to Matias had been
formalised.

She was pure and good. Well behaved. Respectable.
No hint of scandal touched her. No unseemly emotions
were evident.

She was above reproach in every way.

The footsteps behind her halted.

Lia still couldn't bring herself to turn. She concen-
trated instead on the stained-glass rose window above
the altar, all blue and red and green.

'Praying to God, Lia?' That voice was much closer
now, sounding like a night full of shadows and dark dangerous things waiting to rip her to shreds. 'I wouldn't.
I'm not sure he's listening. Not to you, at least.'

She said nothing, unable to hear anything over the
frantic beat of her heart.

'Your Excellency,' Gian repeated.

'Silence,' Rafael said casually, his tone bordering on
insulting.

Her father knew better than to argue and shut his
mouth.

Lia's heart ached and ached. But she still didn't turn.
She didn't have the courage. Not here, not now. Not with
her father present.

'I see,' Rafael continued. 'So it's to be like this, is it?'

Slowly, footsteps circled her and Lia was filled with
the insane urge to turn away and keep turning like a bal-
lerina in a music box, so she'd never have to see him.
Never have to look at his face. Never have that rapier-
sharp gaze meet hers, cutting everything away, uncov-
ering all her secrets, all her shame.

Not that he didn't know that shame already. There

was no other reason for him to stop a wedding that had been years in the planning.

Rafael Navarro might hate scenes and scandals, but it seemed that even he had a line. And she'd just pushed him over it.

What did you expect? That you could hide this from him?

Yes, that's exactly what she'd expected. How foolish of her.

She could sense him now, approaching from her right side, and soon he'd be in front of her. Soon he'd see her. Soon he'd know everything.

There was no hiding from Rafael, she knew that now.

Her only hope was to pray that she was wrong, that he had some other reason for stopping the marriage of the heir to the throne in full view of an entire nation. A reason that didn't have anything to do with her.

Keep telling yourself that...

She braced herself, clutching her bouquet in a death grip, and lifted her chin. At least the veil offered her some protection; she'd be grateful for small mercies.

Rafael stopped in front of her, blocking her view of the altar and Matias, so that all she could see was the wide expanse of his chest.

She swallowed, trying not to shake.

She'd forgotten how tall he was. How massive. How... immovable. He was a man built out of the most adamant of materials, granite and steel and iron. A man who could withstand any shock, any disaster. She'd been a teenager when he'd come to take his place as Regent and everyone had been terrified of him.

His background had been as a CEO of a multibillion-dollar company, but he'd never looked like a

CEO. He'd looked like a general, a warlord. A leader of armies. Dark, frightening, and dangerous, he made the palace guards seem like children merely playing at being soldiers.

He's not like that, though. Not really.

But that was her stupid heart doing the talking. The heart that had been somehow fascinated by the much older brother of the man she was supposed to marry. The heart that had nothing to do with the lovely, well-behaved daughter of Gian and Violetta De Vita, who'd been brought up and moulded to be the perfect queen. A heart that was dangerous, rebellious, passionate...

And stupid.

Lia stared at that chest, the dove-grey material of his morning suit stretched as it was over rock-hard muscle and bone.

Something quivered inside her.

She didn't want to look up, but if she didn't that would signal she had something to hide and he'd know. Then again, he already knew that passionate, dangerous side of her, so what did she have to lose?

You're a coward.

Yes, she'd been that, too. But maybe not today.

Lia took a breath and then lifted her gaze to his from behind her veil.

The air in her lungs froze solid.

He wasn't handsome, but then handsomeness was an irrelevant term when it came to the Regent of Santa Castelia. His black hair was cut short and close to his skull, his face all rough planes and hard angles that somehow came together in a way that was both utterly compelling, yet terrifying at the same time.

A man with charisma and an authority that made

people want to obey simply through the sheer force of his presence alone.

But it wasn't his face that struck the fear of God into her heart.

It was his eyes.

Deep-set below winged black eyebrows, they were a light, crystalline grey. Like silver. Like the edge of a sword or a scalpel, sharp enough to cut. To draw blood.

Impossibly beautiful eyes.

Eyes that saw the truth.

Lia couldn't breathe.

Rafael lifted his hands and grasped the fine silk of her veil, drawing it up and over her face, taking away that last barrier. So there was nothing between herself and the sharp edge of his gaze.

Nowhere to run.

Nowhere to hide.

The expression on his face was impossible to read. But his eyes…they blazed like molten mercury.

'Did you think you could get away with it?' His voice was quiet and somehow even more terrible than when it had been louder. 'Did you think I wouldn't notice?'

Lia couldn't have spoken if her life had depended on it. There was a roaring in her ears. All the air in the cathedral had vanished, as though she was standing in an airlock and someone had opened it straight into a hard vacuum.

There was nothing but darkness and ice, and that relentless silver gaze cutting into her.

'Rafael,' Matias said from behind Rafael's massive shoulders, clearly oblivious to his brother's frozen rage. 'What is happening? You were supposed to be here two hours ago.'

But Rafael didn't turn. He didn't acknowledge his brother in any way. He only looked at Lia as if he'd like to crush her where she stood.

'You will come with me,' he said in that same casually arrogant tone. 'And you will come without a fight.'

She swallowed, desperately trying to find her voice. 'But I—'

He leaned in slightly, looming over her, his mouth near her ear, that terrible voice dropping even lower, so she felt it in her chest. 'Unless, of course, you wish all of Santa Castelia to know that the baby you're carrying isn't my brother's.'

Lia nearly let go of her bouquet of white roses, a rush of the most intense heat flashing through her, closely followed by a wash of ice.

Did you really think you could keep it a secret for long?

No, not for long. Just until the wedding. Just until she could tell Matias, who would be surely understanding. Theirs wasn't a love match after all, but something arranged between her father and King Carlos, a long time ago when they were children.

But it was too late for that now.

She felt dizzy, sick. Her brain struggled through a morass of shock, trying to figure out how she'd let it slip, or whether the doctor she'd crossed the border into Italy to see had somehow told someone...

More whispers were rustling through the cathedral, people getting restless, wanting to know what was going on. Why had the Regent so abruptly called a halt to the wedding? And why was he talking to the bride? What terrible, delicious thing could it be?

You have no choice. You have to go with him. No one else can know your shame.

She could feel her father next to her, feel his shock and his confusion. He'd want to know what was happening, too, and what would he think when he found out? What about her mother? What would they say when they discovered how badly she'd let them down?

Her cheeks were burning and she wanted to cry, but somehow she found the strength to look into those terrible silver eyes.

She'd deny it. She'd tell him that he was wrong. She'd demand a test, get him to prove it—

'No.' The word was an anvil, crushing all her fight before she'd even had the chance to speak. 'There will be no denial. Just as there will be no escape. There is nowhere you can run to and there is nowhere for you to hide. Not from me, *princesa*.' He smiled and it turned her heart into a block of ice. 'I am inevitable.'

Rafael Navarro had never considered himself a good man. Good wasn't really in his nature. What was in his nature was a certain facility—some would say genius—with money, impeccable attention to detail, and the iron will required to run a tiny, mountainous nation sandwiched between Spain and Italy with relentless efficiency.

Oh, and he preferred to get his way in all things.

He was also a man who hated shocks, despised surprises and loathed plans that did not proceed in the direction he wished them to go, and right now he was furious, even though fury was not something he customarily allowed himself. Then again fury was the only logical response to the past two hours.

Two hours that had contained nothing but shocks, surprises and seemingly his entire life upended and very much not according to his plan, and all because of the woman standing in front of him.

A small, delicate woman wearing an eye-wateringly expensive confection of a bridal gown that he knew the price of down to the last euro, made of the finest white silk, hand-embroidered with silver thread and tiny crystals. He knew the price of her embroidered gossamer silk veil and the circlet of diamonds on her glossy black hair, the Alighieri ruby on her hand and the small hand-made silver slippers on her feet.

He knew the price of this entire wedding fiasco and the price of its cancellation, too.

Her fault.

It was she who'd upended his perfectly ordered life, she who'd ruined it, and he should have known from the minute he'd laid eyes on her that she would end up costing him.

And now he would make her pay for it.

It's not entirely *her fault.*

An inconvenient thought that he ignored, watching instead with some satisfaction the fear that glowed in her deep blue eyes.

She should be afraid. There would be a reckoning and it would be now.

Her face was white, the make-up that was supposed to highlight the serene perfection of her features unable to hide her sickly pallor. Even so, she was beautiful. Delicate, black arched brows and lush, silky black lashes. A sinful mouth tinted the prettiest shade of pink. A pointed chin that he knew from experience could be forceful and stubborn.

She was not the good, quiet, well-behaved girl she was reputed to be and he'd known that the night he'd caught her in her father's office, drinking his whisky and smoking one of his cigars.

He should have informed Gian then, but he hadn't.

Matias had been due to take the throne in six months and Amalia De Vita had spent her entire life in training to be his wife. There hadn't been another woman more suitable to be Santa Castelia's queen. The De Vita family was an ancient lineage, bringing nobility and pedigree to a throne sorely damaged by the antics of Rafael's father, King Carlos, and Rafael had agreed early on that no other woman would do.

This marriage was supposed to be his last gift to the country that had never warmed to him even as they'd begged him to rule after his father had died.

A lesser man would have used the opportunity to teach them a lesson in being grateful, but Rafael had never been a lesser man. He was above such petty concerns as revenge.

However...

Cold fury shifted inside him as he looked down into Amalia's deep blue eyes, even as it warred with a grudging respect.

She was afraid, yet that forceful little chin was lifted and set. 'There is no need for all the theatrics, Your Excellency,' she said in that low, well-modulated voice that he knew wasn't hers. 'If you want me to come with you, then I will. I just don't want to be dragged out of my own wedding by a palace guard.'

Gian De Vita's face was a mask of very real confusion. It was clear Lia hadn't told him anything, which was probably a small mercy. He'd never approved of Rafael, even if he'd been the one to beg Rafael to be Regent until Matias came of age, and this would not endear him to Gian any further.

Too bad.

He had nothing to lose. The wedding was in ruins now. He'd worked hard for the past six years of his regency to keep the peace in Santa Castelia, to make up for the decades of scandal and profligacy that had characterised his father's reign.

He'd wanted to set an example of restraint and decorum, and he had.

Only for it to end like this.

No, he had nothing to lose. The crown had never been his and it never would. And now he'd caused the kind of scandal he would have abhorred even a week ago.

But everything was different now.

The pure, good girl wasn't quite so pure after all and she'd been hiding a secret. A secret from him.

Well, she couldn't hide it any more.

He'd broken his own vow and he'd done so spectacularly by coming here. Might as well end it in the same way, in the time-honoured fashion.

'In that case,' Rafael said, 'if you don't wish to be dragged from the cathedral by a guard, you shall be dragged from the cathedral by me.' And before anyone could move or say a word, he picked her up, flung her over his shoulder and strode down the aisle to the doors, her veil drifting out behind them, leaving the entire cathedral in an uproar.

At the kerb, the limo that had brought him here was still waiting as instructed, the driver standing with the door open.

Anton didn't appear in the least bit fazed to see the

Regent striding down the cathedral steps with the bride over one shoulder. He simply waited until Rafael had deposited Lia inside and got in himself, then shut the door.

Rafael made a mental note to give his driver a substantial raise as the limo took off.

Lia sat on the seat opposite him in a drift of sparkling white tulle, her veil tangled, her diamond circlet hanging lopsidedly over one ear.

She wasn't pale any more and neither was she afraid.

Her cheeks were red with outrage and fury burned in her blue eyes.

Dios, she was beautiful when she lost the veneer of manners that her parents had drummed into her.

She said nothing. She only lifted her bouquet and threw it at him.

He caught it before it hit him in the face, the roses showering white petals all over his morning suit. If anyone looked through the windows of the limo now and didn't know who they were, they would have seen a beautiful bride and her new husband, perhaps having a fun game.

They were not having a fun game.

Rafael gently laid the bouquet down on the seat beside him. 'What were you saying about theatrics?'

'How dare you?' she burst out, that clear, well-modulated voice not so clear or so well-modulated any longer, but vibrating with a low, husky rage. 'In front of the entire country! In front of Matias and my father! How dare you even touch me!'

Rafael didn't reply. Sometimes saying nothing said more than a hot tirade, so he calmly picked rose petals from his suit and arranged them in a pattern beside the bouquet, letting her shout at him until she finally ran out of steam.

Then he lifted his head and met her furious blue gaze. 'Have you finished?'

'No!'

He ignored her. 'Good, now it's time we had a little talk.'

'A little talk? A little talk about what?'

'About your pregnancy,' he said. 'About the fact that you've been trying to hide it for months. Specifically about the fact that you've been trying to hide it from *me*.'

'You?' she demanded, her chin lifting. 'And why on earth would I try to hide it specifically from you?'

Rafael stared at her. She was trying to brazen it out, that much was clear.

'Why?' he echoed coldly. 'Because that baby is mine, Lia. Why else?'

CHAPTER TWO

LIA SAT VERY STILL, every part of her trembling inside with rage and fear. Rage that he'd picked her up in the middle of the cathedral in front of Matias, her father, the bishop, the entirety of Santa Castella's aristocracy, not to mention the rest of the country viewing the wedding via a live broadcast, and thrown her over his shoulder as if she weighed nothing. Then had carried her off like a…marauder.

Fear about what he would do now he knew what she'd been hiding from him for three months. What she'd felt she had no choice but to hide from him, because what else was she to do?

She'd made a terrible, *terrible* mistake and there had been consequences, and all of it was her fault. And even though her instinct was to keep denying it, tell him she had no idea her baby was his, she knew she couldn't.

He knew the truth about her, he always had.

It took a tremendous amount of effort to shove down both her rage and her fear, but she'd had years of practice at keeping her wilder emotions in check and so she managed. Throwing her bouquet at him had been a stupid loss of control and she couldn't afford another.

It didn't help that she could still feel the imprint of his

hard, muscular shoulder against her stomach, the heat of his body penetrating every layer of her bridal gown. Making her remember that night three months ago when there had been nothing between them but bare skin and raw, aching passion…

No, she couldn't think of that. Not now. Now with his icy silver gaze on her, fury burning coldly in the depths.

'What?' He went on in that insultingly casual way she so hated. 'Not going to deny it again? Perhaps you're going to tell me that you didn't know it was me in bed with you that night? Perhaps you thought it was a stranger, since that's clearly preferable to sleeping with me. Come, *princesa*, tell me. I'm all ears.'

Her voice wouldn't work. She wanted to wind down the window, get some of the snowy winter air into the car just so she could breathe. Because she felt as though she was choking while he just sat there and stared at her the way he'd always stared at her. As if he could see inside her, right down to her soul.

'I have a paternity test,' he continued when she didn't speak. 'If you'd like to see it.'

A paternity test. He'd done a paternity test.

'Why?' The word was hoarse, part of her irrationally furious at him for needing proof. Even though she hadn't even told him about the pregnancy. Even though she'd acted as though their night together had never happened. She'd had to. They'd both had to.

He didn't move, that terrible silver gaze glittering. 'Because I didn't know whether I was the only lucky recipient of your midnight visits. I had to be sure the child was mine.'

Lia had been brought up to be poised and graceful in all things. To be serene and ladylike. Well behaved and unfailingly polite. Yet in that instant the control that had been drummed into her every day of her life broke apart and shattered like delicate crystal.

All the fear and distress that had been her constant companion over the last three months, all her agony and rage suddenly rose up in a choking wave. She wanted to cry, but crying would solve nothing. And it wasn't really him she was angry at, but herself.

She should have told him the instant her pregnancy test had come back positive. She should have found the courage to face him, to take responsibility for the mistake she'd made. And to face the consequences.

Or better yet, she should never have allowed her anger to get the better of her and gone to what she thought was Matias's room in the first place.

But she hadn't…

Lia couldn't sleep. She'd been staring out of the window of her bedroom for hours, her heart nothing but a ball of barbed wire in her chest. It had been a couple of weeks since Rafael had stopped coming to those meetings in her father's study and she missed him. She missed him as if she was missing part of herself.

He was avoiding her and she didn't understand why. All she knew was that it hurt.

Behind her on the bed in a pool of deep blue silk was the gown she was supposed to wear tomorrow night to the ball where her engagement to Matias would be formally announced.

She couldn't even look at it. Every time she did, all she could see was her future laid out before her. Her future as the wife of a man who didn't love her and whom she didn't love. Her future as the virtuous Queen of Santa Castelia.

A future that felt like the bars of a cage closing slowly around her.

It was him. He was the problem. He was the reason she couldn't bear that future now and she didn't know what to do about it. Not that there was anything to be done.

She was the Crown Princess. She'd been promised to Matias since she was a child and her role was set in stone. Her father had always been very clear that after the excesses of King Carlos's rule Santa Castelia needed a firm and steady hand. Matias would be that hand and she his steadying influence.

Together they would steer Santa Castelia out of the storms of scandal and greed and corruption, and into calmer waters.

She was her parents' late-in-life child. Their IVF miracle. Much loved and much wanted, and she shouldn't complain, especially when some children never got to be loved at all.

But sometimes the weight of all that expectation was a burden. Miracles were supposed to do wondrous things and her parents had certainly expected wonders from her. She would be a queen because of the work her father had put into negotiating a betrothal with Matias, not to mention all the effort her mother had put into schooling her behaviour and moulding her into the perfect choice of a royal bride.

They expected all their hard work to pay off and she couldn't let them down.

Yet tonight was a night when she didn't feel like a miracle. Where she felt weighed down by all the expectations placed on her, crushed beneath them, and the ache in her heart, the longing that wouldn't leave her no matter how hard she tried to ignore it. The desperate and confusing desire for a man she could never, ever have, not when only one man was permitted to her.

She turned and stared at the gown, the anger she always tried so hard to keep control of licking up inside her.

Anger at her parents and what they expected of her.

Anger at herself for wanting what she couldn't have.

Anger at him because every night for the past two weeks she'd waited in her father's study the way she always did, expecting him to arrive. And he never did. And she didn't know why.

She should know better than to give in to her anger, but tonight it felt like too much. She wanted to do something, wanted to hurt him the way he was hurting her. Get rid of this terrible ache inside her somehow.

A sheltered girl, he'd called her at their last meeting, his silver eyes burning with an emotion she didn't understand. She'd been furious with him, wanting to deny it, but naturally she couldn't.

She was sheltered.

Was that why he hadn't come back? Because she was sheltered? Because she was too innocent? Too well bred? And if so, why did that matter to him?

Her anger tightened into a hard knot.

Well, perhaps she'd show him just how sheltered she really was.

The palace was quiet as she stepped out into the corridors, most people asleep. It was so very late and the corridors were dim. She hadn't been to the private wing where the royal family had their rooms very often, but she thought she knew the way.

The guards knew her and let her through, and so

she'd crept down yet more dark hallways until she found Matias's door.

There was no physical attraction between them. They were more friends than anything else, but tonight she would change that.

It was Matias she needed to be thinking about. Matias she should want. Matias, not Rafael. And there was only one way she could think of to get rid of these inappropriate desires.

She would forget Rafael in the arms of her husband-to-be.

The room beyond was in darkness, but she didn't turn on the light. She couldn't risk him sending her away. Instead, she found the bed, let her robe fall and slipped naked between the sheets.

The male figure in the bed stiffened in shock as she touched him, waking him up. She heard him take a breath to speak, but in the dark she found his mouth and laid a finger over it. It was soft beneath her touch.

'Don't talk,' she whispered, staring at the shape of the man next to her. 'It's only me. Please, I know it's wrong to be here, but... I need you.'

Matias didn't say anything, staying still for a long moment. Then he grabbed her and kissed her like a man possessed.

And as soon as his mouth covered hers, her brain finally caught up with what her body had already recognised.

The man she was kissing wasn't Matias.

It was Rafael.

Rafael, who generated so many confusing and tortured emotions inside her.

Rafael, who she desired so much it made her ache.

Rafael, who now seemed to assume that his wasn't the only bedroom she'd visited.

Normally when her feelings got the better of her, she went out for a walk in the palace gardens, but she couldn't do that now. She was trapped in a car with him. Trapped in the wild flood of her own emotions. All the unrequited passion and fear. All the choking rage that she had nowhere to direct but at him.

Lia lunged across the space between them before she could stop herself, no thought in her head but lash out at the most convenient target.

He seemed to be expecting it, however. Before she could land any kind of blow, he grabbed her wrists with insulting ease and hauled her on to his lap, her skirts bunched between them and flowing over the black leather seats of the limo.

Lia found herself staring into his eyes, the muscular heat of his body surrounding her, and abruptly she was trembling yet again, her body recognising his, her anger alchemising into something much hotter.

'I had to know, *princesa*,' Rafael said now in his hard, dark voice, his gaze blazing into hers, reading her mind as easily as if she was a book spread open before him. 'You cannot blame me for that. Especially when you didn't tell me.'

Lia shivered 'I... I thought it was Matias. I went to his room. I thought it was him in the bed...'

Rafael's gaze went molten as it raked over her. Then his expression twisted in what looked like a snarl and she found herself pushed hard away, deposited back firmly in the seat opposite him.

He pressed a button in the seat arm next to him and said something harsh and guttural in Spanish.

Lia's hands were cold and so were her toes. Shock, probably.

She didn't know what to do with herself. This morning when she'd woken up, she was the bride-to-be for Santa Castelia's Crown Prince and now...

You failed. You failed your fiancé. Your country. Your parents. And you failed him*, too.*

Her throat closed and she turned her head away from the fierce gaze of the man opposite, staring blindly out the window. The streets and buildings of Santa Castelia's capital were lost under a cloud of white. It was snowing and snowing hard, as if the snow was a living embodiment of Rafael's cold fury.

'I went to Matias's room, because I was trying to forget about you,' she said thickly, because she owed him an explanation and he had to know that it hadn't been— it had *never* been—Matias that she'd really wanted. 'I thought that being with him would...help me.' No point telling him that she'd been angry with him, too, not when that would possibly only inflame things.

'I see.' Rafael's voice was wiped clean of expression. 'And when did you realise you weren't, in fact, in Matias's room? Before or after your first orgasm?'

Anger licked up once again through the shame crowding in her throat, and she turned her head. 'Do you really think I wouldn't know who was touching me?'

He didn't look away. 'It was dark. And you clearly had no idea where Matias's rooms were. You could have walked into anyone's.'

'And I would have left the second I realised I was with just anyone,' she shot back. 'But I wasn't. I was with you.'

'Would you have stayed if it hadn't been? If it had been Matias in the bed instead of me?'

She shouldn't challenge him, not now, not here. Yet she couldn't help herself. Her emotions were all over the place, as they had been ever since she'd met him, and even more now she was pregnant. 'Do you really want to know the answer to that?'

Rafael's features were as uncompromising as his stare. 'I wouldn't have asked otherwise.'

She wanted to say 'yes, I would have stayed', because part of her wanted to hurt him. To get back at him for the situation she'd found herself in, for the months of mental anguish she'd gone through after finding out she was pregnant, for how he'd stopped coming to see her without explanation, for all the confusing emotions she felt whenever she was around him. Emotions she shouldn't be having about a man who'd never been hers and wasn't supposed to be.

But she *had* to control herself. Everything was too close to the surface already and Rafael had always been the spark to her dry tinder. He made her catch alight, made her burn. He got under her skin and she couldn't allow it.

The future she'd always thought she'd have might have been torn from her after today, but that was no excuse to let herself slip back into old patterns.

If the last three months had taught her anything, it was that she could *not* give in to her own wants and desires. That was selfish.

But why not? What does it matter? Who do you have to perform for now?

The thought whispered in the back of her mind, but she ignored it. Everything felt too precarious right now and at least the role of the Crown Princess was one she was familiar with. That, she could do.

'I don't know,' she said more carefully. 'It's a moot point now, anyway.'

Rafael's harsh features betrayed nothing, but she could feel the fury radiating from him all the same. A cold fury, though. So cold she was almost surprised it wasn't actually snowing inside the car.

'My turn then.' Ice threaded through his tone, his anger frozen over. 'I always knew it was you. Right from the moment you woke me.'

Lia swallowed, her throat closing. She'd kept herself rigidly locked down for the past three months, refusing to think about him or that night. Trying not to give in to her own fear and shame. But sometimes she'd find her thoughts straying to him, wondering what that night had meant to him. Whether he'd been as changed by it as she had or whether he viewed it as just another night.

Whether she'd been just another woman.

Her heart clenched tight. 'Rafael...'

'I should have stopped. I should have resisted. But you said "I need you". And then you kissed me as though you were drowning and I had all your air.'

She shut her eyes, the memory of that kiss burning in her mind like a brand. The moment his lips had touched hers, she'd gone up in flames.

'I didn't—'

'I thought you'd come to find *me*, Lia. I thought it was me you wanted.'

There was so much fury in his voice. It hurt. 'I told you, I was trying to forget you—'

'The next day,' he went on as if she hadn't spoken, 'you became officially engaged to my brother. And at that ball, you looked at me as if I was some dirt you found underneath your pretty little shoe.'

Oh, god. Was that what he'd thought?

Rafael was a tall, imposing figure in his black evening clothes, his only adornment the heavy gold ring of state—he'd drawn every eye in the ballroom. He was the still point about which the world turned and she hated it that, despite the intensity of the night before, her world still revolved around him.

She'd thought the night before, experiencing all that physical passion, would have changed things, would have made her want him less, but it hadn't. If anything, it had made her want him more.

Now she knew what she'd been missing, now she knew what they could have had together. So much pleasure that could have been hers if he hadn't been who he was and if she hadn't been engaged to his brother.

Being in his presence was difficult, yet she didn't have a choice. She couldn't not attend the ball thrown in her and Matias's honour, just as Rafael had to be there to give his blessing.

Normally his acknowledgement of her was cool and casual, but not tonight. Tonight, he stared at her, with so much intensity it nearly flattened her.

She'd been so terrified of giving herself away it was all she could do to curtsy and murmur, 'Your Excellency...' before excusing herself and fleeing.

Lia's heart twisted. 'I didn't—'

'I knew then it was for the best,' he interrupted once more, still coldly furious. 'To keep the night we'd shared as just a night. And it would never be spoken of again.

So, I put it from my mind. But a few weeks later I remembered that I hadn't used a condom. You hadn't contacted me, though, so I assumed it wasn't a problem.' He said it casually, as if none of this meant anything at all to him. 'Then I had reports you weren't well. That you were attending social engagements, but were pale and obviously hadn't been sleeping.'

She hadn't been. The morning sickness had been brutal and it had taken everything she had just to function normally. Her mother had been worried about her getting sick so close to the wedding, but she'd told her it was merely a stomach bug.

'So I made some enquiries.' Rafael's accent, lilting and melodic, had haunted her dreams for the past two years, but it did nothing to soften the hard edge in his voice. 'It seems you'd gone to a different doctor, not the one your family normally uses. That made me suspicious. From there it was relatively easy to discover the reason for it.'

The cold began creeping up her arms and up her legs. 'She wouldn't have told you.'

His expression was as unyielding as granite. 'She would. She did. Everyone has a price. Even doctors.'

'I don't—'

'It was simple to get a strand of your hair for DNA purposes. The paternity test was a match.'

'Rafael.'

'I found out today that I was going to be a father.' The words were heavy as iron, cutting her off cold. 'Only hours before you were going to marry my brother.'

'But I—'

'Silence.'

His anger filled the car, as icy as the blizzard outside,

making her shiver. If she let out a breath, she was sure she'd be able to see it.

'You have known for months and you *hid* it. You were going to marry my brother and pass *my* child off as his.' His hard mouth, that had felt so warm and soft beneath hers, that had given her so much pleasure, twisted in a sneer. 'Did you want him to be the father? Did you have doubts about me? Is that why didn't tell me you were pregnant?'

'No!' She curled her hands into fists to stop them from shaking. His assumption that she'd doubt him hurt, but she knew she had no one to blame for that but herself. 'I didn't tell you, because I was afraid. Because I was engaged to your brother and Santa Castelia needed the marriage.'

The fury in his eyes didn't change. 'How unfortunate for us both then that I discovered your little secret.' He leaned forward very slightly, his terrible gaze sharp as a scimitar, cutting right through her soul. 'But don't worry. Regardless of my feelings on the subject, it's not going to stay a secret much longer. Not when from now on you and the baby are mine.'

She'd gone white as a sheet and, deep inside him, Rafael felt something shift. But he ignored it. He was too angry with her to feel any kind of sympathy.

Not only had she hidden her pregnancy from him for months, if what she'd said was true then that night it hadn't even been him she'd been looking for.

She'd been looking for his brother.

For three months he'd watched the wedding preparations, fighting not only the jealousy that dogged him, but also the desire that burned in his blood whenever she was near. Consoling himself with the knowledge that, though she was marrying Matias, it had been him she'd come to that night.

It had been him she'd wanted.

But, no, apparently not.

The only thing she'd wanted was to forget him.

His anger was a bonfire, but he knew the dangers so he froze it solid, turning it to sharp ice. Anger could be a good fuel if used prudently and he was nothing if not prudent. His whole life had been built on it.

And while she might have turned that life upside down, he wasn't going to let her cause any more damage than she already had. Someone had to fix it and he was nothing if not good at fixing things.

He shouldn't have taken such a drastic course of action, but she'd forced him into it. By not telling him about her pregnancy, he'd only had a week or so to investigate and even then he'd only learned about the results of the paternity test a mere hour before the wedding.

That had left him with only one option. He had to stop her from marrying Matias any way he could. Unfortunately, his anger had got the better of him and he'd stopped the wedding in the most disruptive way possible.

Yet what else could he have done? Matias hadn't known about her pregnancy, Rafael was positive. And this was a mess that he'd made himself. He couldn't allow his brother to take responsibility for something that was none of his doing. He couldn't allow any doubt to be cast on the heir to the throne either, not after the scandals of their father's reign.

And apart from all that, Lia's baby was also his and he would not allow another man to claim it, even if that man was his brother.

He'd had no intention of having children, not after his own bleak upbringing, but now that decision had been taken out of his hands, he knew he couldn't let his own child grow up without someone to set them a good example. Not with the genes they'd no doubt inherited.

His own father, King Carlos, had been known for his baser appetites and profligate ways. Rafael, after all, had been a direct product of that appetite, his mother a hotel chambermaid. He'd been brought up in a one-roomed apartment in Barcelona and while he and his mother hadn't lived in dire poverty, they hadn't been far from it. Carlos had paid nothing for his upkeep and Rafael had had no contact with him, except every so often when his father would demand an exclusive audience at one of his residences.

His mother had always been very against him seeing Carlos, but his father had given neither of them a choice. He'd insisted on Rafael's presence, though always in secret since his father wouldn't acknowledge him openly. Awkward meetings where Carlos, depending on his mood, would either heap praise on him for doing well, or barely speak to him at all.

Once, when he'd been twelve, Rafael had asked him what the purpose of these visits was since it was clear that Carlos didn't have any feeling for him.

'Just because I don't acknowledge my mistakes doesn't mean I can't learn from them,' his father had responded coldly.

As if Rafael had needed more confirmation of his own status. He knew he was a mistake. His mother had been quite clear about that.

Regardless, he would never put any child of his through that. Never, *ever*.

Rafael had always prided himself on his control—he'd never be profligate with his affairs as Carlos had been—but controlled was the last thing he'd been when Lia had come to his bed.

He'd made a mistake, it was true. But unlike Carlos he owned that mistake. He took responsibility for it.

So he would claim his child. He would acknowledge them. They would be his and not a mistake to be buried and forgotten about. Or viewed whenever the mood took him. He would be a better father than his own had ever been.

Lia's blue eyes had darkened, her face still as white as her gown.

That thread of sympathy that he'd buried and frozen beneath the layer of his icy rage tugged harder.

So, she didn't come looking for you that night the way you thought, and she didn't tell you about the baby. Did you even bother to ask her why not? No. You dragged her from her wedding, locked her in this limo and shouted at her.

Unease twisted deep in his gut.

He'd never been a warm, empathetic man, but he was never cruel and especially not to a woman, let alone a pregnant one.

Then again, this was what always happened with Lia. She got to him in a way no other woman ever had and so he had to be on his guard.

He'd already made one catastrophic error of judgement and had only compounded it today. There was no need to make any more.

The snow was coming down even harder and the temperature of the car was a little chilly. That gown she wore wouldn't exactly be keeping her warm.

'Are you cold?' he asked, keeping his voice casual, which was his preferred method of modifying himself. 'I'll turn the heat up.' He didn't wait for her to respond, fiddling with the temperature controls until he was satisfied.

She ignored him. 'What do you mean I'm yours? What about Matias?'

The unease inside him twisted harder. So much for the example he'd been trying to set his brother. Moderation, control, cold focus. The country before all else. He'd modelled exactly none of those things.

Matias wouldn't be so much furious at Lia's loss as he would be at the loss of the future he'd planned. The bride he'd been promised. The upending of everything he'd thought set in stone.

He never appreciated her for who she was and you know it. He wanted a queen. He didn't want her.

Possessiveness wound through him, the angry, passionate thoughts that he'd tried so hard to keep buried. Because it was true. Matias liked Lia well enough, but he didn't know the heart of her. She had moderated herself so completely for him that Matias had commented once or twice to Rafael that he found her dull.

But Lia wasn't dull. She was the opposite. Fiery, intense, rebellious. A little impulsive, yet sharp as a knife.

He doesn't deserve her. But you do.

Rafael crushed that thought flat. Such entitlement. No one deserved anything. You had to work for it.

'Matias will survive,' he said, focusing on all the things that needed to be done instead of the things that seethed beneath the surface of the ice. 'Leave that to me.'

A new bride would have to be chosen and Lia's parents would have to be compensated. Gian would demand it and that would be expensive. Then again, the treasury was obscenely healthy these days, which was all thanks to him. Santa Castelia could afford it.

It was the finding of a new bride that would be difficult, but that didn't mean one couldn't be found. A bride more suited to Matias's personality than Lia ever was.

The political ramifications, though, would have to be dealt with and quickly. Lia didn't need to be a part of that. He'd take her to his private residence in the mountains and leave her there until he'd handled the fallout.

Then he'd marry her himself. There was no other option.

They'd both made a mistake that night, but the lack of contraception had been his error and his alone. An error that he would fix as soon as possible.

That's fine. Tell yourself you're marrying her because of all these other things and not because you want her for yourself.

It was not a particularly pleasant thought, mainly because it brought him face to face with his own baser urges. Urges that for the past fifteen years of his life he'd controlled without effort. Until he'd met her.

Yes, he did want her, he couldn't deny that, and a tiny part of him felt nothing but satisfied at this turn of events. Almost as if fate had delivered her into his hands, which was fanciful of him. Still, fanciful or not, he couldn't refuse that gift. He wouldn't.

'You didn't answer the question. What about me?' She'd modulated her voice into that low, pleasant tone that she used with everyone, clasped her hands in her lap. The Crown Princess back in control.

He wanted to tell her that there was no point in her princess façade now and definitely not with him, but the situation was already flammable and he didn't need to strike another match.

'You? You, I'll take to my residence in the mountains.' Rafael relaxed back against the seat, extending his arms along the top of it and stretching his legs out so that they nudged her skirts. 'Then I'll go to the palace and inform them of our intended marriage.'

'Our marriage?' Her modulated tone vibrated as she sat bolt upright, every part of her rigid. '*Our* marriage?'

He gave her a long, steady look. 'I'm a bastard, *princesa.* You can't think I'd let our child be born out of wedlock.'

'That's ridiculously medieval, even for you.' A spark glowed in her eyes, the white pallor of her cheeks vanishing under the faint blush of temper. 'It's the twenty-first century, Rafael, in case you'd forgotten. You can't make me marry you if I don't want to.'

Something stirred beneath the ice inside him, something hot and possessive. A recognition of the woman he'd spent so many illicit hours with in Gian's study. The woman she was beneath the gently bred façade of the Crown Princess.

A woman who'd given him the most intense pleasure he'd ever experienced that night in his bed.

Dios, he remembered every single second...

Rafael strode into the royal chambers and slammed the door shut after him. A bottle of the finest brandy and a glass of cut crystal waited for him on the table beside the overly ornate stone fireplace where a fire roared.

The day had been a nightmare. He'd spent it in meetings with his council, which wouldn't have been so bad if the rooms where the meetings had been held hadn't overlooked the gardens of the palace. And if those meetings hadn't coincided with Lia walking in those same gardens.

Rafael had had to spend hours trying to pay attention to his meetings, when all his awareness centred on the view through the windows of the lovely, lovely woman his brother was going to marry.

The woman he'd got to know over the course of months, meeting with her at night in her father's study. Nothing ever untoward had happened in those meetings. No lines had ever been crossed, but he'd known deep down that it was wrong. That he shouldn't be spending so much time with her alone at night.

Yet he'd kept going back, unable to help himself. Drawn by their discussions, by her wit and her intellect. Her fire and her passion, and by the way she looked at him.

That last time he'd nearly broken his vow to himself that he wouldn't touch her, and so had made the decision not to go back. And he hadn't.

Except he hadn't been able to drag his gaze away from that window, watching the last of the summer sun gloss her black hair as she'd wandered through the gardens...

Dios, this obsession with her had to end.

She would be marrying Matias and the sooner the better as far as he was concerned.

If only the last time they'd met, he hadn't got so close to her. If only he hadn't seen the hunger in her beautiful blue eyes and known that it was for him.

That though she might be promised to Matias, the golden boy, it was him she wanted. Him, the bastard Regent his own parents had felt nothing for.

And if only he'd looked away and pretended he hadn't seen it.

But he hadn't and he didn't, and for long seconds at a time they'd sat there, Gian's desk between them, frozen as their gazes had locked and held.

Rafael knocked his brandy back, then paced around. Tried to forget about her by throwing himself into some work. Then, when that failed, he went to bed.

Only to be woken in the dark by the familiar scent of a familiar woman and the soft touch of her finger, silencing him. 'Don't talk,' she'd whispered. 'It's only me. Please, I know it's wrong to be here, but... I need you.'

And when she reached for him, he didn't think about the last three months of agony. He didn't think about his brother. As soon as her hands touched him he didn't think at all, his much-vaunted self-control lost under a tide of need so acute all he could do was give in...

He shifted, his body responding to the memories so strongly it was all he could do not to reach across the space between them and haul her into his lap once again.

'And do you want to marry me?' he only asked in a mild tone.

The blue in her eyes glowed more intensely. 'What do you think? No, I do not.'

CHAPTER THREE

A STRANGER MIGHT think that Rafael's fury had subsided since his expression now betrayed nothing but mild interest.

Lia knew better. She could see that fury still in his gaze, an icy blizzard that made her breath catch.

The tension in the car had ratcheted up, making every muscle in her body go rigid. She was trying to control her own fury, because seriously, he couldn't think she would agree, could he? That he could kidnap her from her own wedding and then marry her himself, as if all of it was a foregone conclusion?

Except it was clear that he did.

Why not marry him? Wasn't this what you always secretly hoped for?

No, of course it wasn't and that was a traitorous thought. She'd never harboured any secret dreams of marriage to anyone, not when she'd always known that the man she would marry was Matias.

Except there was no hope of that now, was there? Matias was out of her reach.

'I see,' Rafael said, in that maddeningly mild tone. 'That is something we can discuss later then. Or would you prefer to argue with me now?'

Actually, she did want to argue with him now. But that would be a mistake with her control still so tenuous. There was too much tension in the air, too much of the past hanging over them, and the topic was too fraught.

Better to leave it until they'd both had a chance to calm down.

She decided not to speak, turning her head away, staring out at the falling snow instead.

The limo was starting to wind up one of the narrow roads that led into the mountains surrounding the capital, stark cliffs looming on either side. The world outside was all black and white and silence.

The temperature in the car had warmed and she felt less cold, though maybe she was imagining that, especially with the after-effects of shock still winding through her.

Certainly, thinking about what would happen between her and Rafael now was selfish, especially given how many other people had been affected by Rafael's actions.

Her parents and their hopes and dreams for her as Queen. Matias and his plans for her as his wife. Santa Castelia itself and the need for a steady, stable king and queen at the helm.

All of that gone.

The thought made her ache.

'My father,' she said at last into the silence. 'We will have to—'

'As I said, I will deal with that.' Rafael's voice was almost negligent. 'Your parents will be compensated.'

'I'm not a horse, Rafael.' She tried not to sound bitter. 'You think money will make up for everything they wanted for me?'

'Will it not?' He raised a black brow. 'Was it you they were thinking of when they promised you to Matias or was it themselves?'

A cold little pulse of yet more shock went through her. 'What are you talking about? Of course they were thinking of me.'

'Were they? You said you're not a horse and yet you were certainly bred like a brood mare for the role they'd decided on for you.'

Her anger was sitting far too close to the surface and she could feel it start to simmer in response. Because he was wrong. Her parents had spent years trying to conceive and when it had finally happened they'd been so happy. They'd wanted great things for her, because they loved her. She was their miracle.

'Don't be ridiculous.' Anger edged the words no matter how hard she tried not to let it. 'I was not "bred". They wanted a baby and spent years trying for one and when I was finally conceived, they wanted me to have the best life possible.'

'And the best life possible was you being married off to a man you felt nothing for and a role where you'd have to spend the next thirty years pretending to be something you're not.'

Lia felt as though he'd dumped a bucket of ice water over her head.

He just sat there, staring back at her the way he used to do during those nights they'd spent together, where he'd say something challenging, daring her to refute it. She'd loved it when he did that. It was such a change from the boring etiquette and protocol lessons her mother drilled into her.

Their arguments had never been personal, only intel-

lectual, and they'd made her feel alive somehow. Stimu-
lating in a way the endless lessons in finance and history,
deportment, and queenship had never been.

*Because you were bored and he was the only excit-
ing thing in your life.*

He might have been then, but she wasn't bored now
and this wasn't exciting. This was distressing.

'You're wrong,' she said flatly. 'Matias and I—'

'Matias and you would have had a perfectly dull marriage,' Rafael interrupted for the millionth time. 'And
you would have found being Queen—'

'Perfectly fine,' she snapped, deciding it was time
that she interrupted him for a change. 'This conversation is over.'

He lifted one massive shoulder. 'All I'm saying is
that your life is what you make it. No one was forcing
you to marry my brother. You could have chosen a different path.'

He had an answer for everything, didn't he?

'Easy for you to say. As the Regent of an entire nation.'

His silver eyes gleamed, his hard features not soft-
ening one iota. 'I'm a bastard, *princesa*. I grew up on
the edge of poverty in Barcelona. I expected nothing
and was given nothing. Everything I have, I made. And
everything I am, I created for myself. You think your
father and Santa Castelia would have come to me if I'd
still been that skinny boy grubbing in the gutter? No.
They came to me because of what I'd turned myself into.'

*And you turned yourself into their perfect daughter,
ready for the role they'd given you. With no thought in
your head as to what you wanted for yourself.*

No, that wasn't true. She'd wanted to be Matias's wife

and Santa Castelia's Queen. Her parents had so worked hard to give her that future, how could she refuse them? Especially after they'd gone through so much to even have her in the first place.

Plus, she loved her country and she knew she could do good for it. She could help Matias take a different path to that of his notorious father, put the scandals of the past behind them and forge a new future. One where the King and Queen served the country and not the other way around.

Except in the end you're no better than Carlos was. Falling prey to your own lusts. Putting your own desires ahead of everything else.

Lia ignored that, very conscious of Rafael's gaze on her and that she had no answer to what he'd just said. Because it was true. Everyone in the world knew Rafael Navarro's background; it had been one of the most talked-about stories of the last five years. How Gian, as the nation's first advisor, had gone begging to the bastard son of King Carlos after he'd died, desperate for someone to take over the disaster that had once been Santa Castelia. Inflation and unemployment had been sky-high, the treasury empty.

Matias had been too young to take over and there was provision for any illegitimate offspring to rule until the legitimate heir came of age.

So they'd come to Rafael, needing his financial genius to save the country and he had. Single-handedly.

But someone needed to ensure its future and Lia had always thought that person would be her, at Matias's side.

Not any more.

Her stomach dipped and hollowed, and she had to look away again, forcing down the riot of violent emotions that churned inside her, struggling to find her usual calm.

She didn't want to talk to Rafael or think about what he'd said, so she didn't, ignoring him as his phone rang a few moments later and he answered it, the dark, rough textures of his voice filling the car.

Twenty minutes later, they turned off the increasingly treacherous mountain road, drove through a pair of massive, wrought-iron gates and went up a winding, equally treacherous driveway. Snow-covered trees loomed on either side, making Lia feel claustrophobic and suffocated. As if she was a prisoner being transported from one prison to another, and this one smaller, darker...

The limo drew up outside what appeared to be a concrete bunker covered in snow. It was only after she'd blinked a few times and told herself not to be so stupid that she realised that it wasn't actually a concrete bunker, but an architectural house made of stone and built against the mountainside in a series of boxes, each on different levels, looking as though they'd been carved out of the mountain itself.

Snow blanketed what in summer would be lovely terraces, making a white carpet on the flat roofs. The house was heavy and monolithic, and, like its owner, looked as if it could withstand any kind of natural disaster thrown at it and then some.

Rafael got out of the car first and held the door open for her. Icy air made her shiver as she collected her skirts and followed him out. Instantly she was freezing, the silver satin slippers she wore ruined as they sank into the snow on the ground. The wind was biting, blowing her skirts and her veil around and making walking difficult. Snow fell everywhere, settling in her eyelashes and falling like white hot sparks on the exposed skin of her shoulders and arms.

Struggling to take a step, she slipped on the icy ground, only to feel a muscular arm slide around her waist, drawing her into the wicked heat of a hard, masculine body.

His scent hit her, warm and spicy and familiar. Unexpected, too, as it always was. In those first few days when he'd come to the palace and she'd been half-terrified, half-fascinated by him, she'd thought that he might smell of cordite or gunpowder, something sharp and dangerous and cold.

But he didn't. He smelled of sandalwood and cloves, making her think of warm nights in a desert, or spices in an exotic souk, fascinating, far-off places that she'd always wanted to visit and yet never had the opportunity.

Oh, God, the last time she'd been this close to him had been that night they'd spent together, his hands on her skin, that same, warm scent surrounding her, setting every nerve-ending she had ablaze with a sudden, insistent heat.

She'd known it was Rafael in that moment and her heart had swelled with happiness and relief. And the terrible knowledge that even if it had been Matias, she would never have been able to go through with her plan to sleep with him.

Because the only man she'd ever wanted was his half-brother.

Lia could feel her body melting into Rafael's heat now, into the strength and power of his hard, muscled torso, the cold that had gripped her fading, vanishing under a wild rush of pent-up physical desire.

Instantly, she tried to pull away, not wanting to give in to it, but his grip on her only tightened. Her skirts trailed in the snow, making it hard for her to take a step even with his help, and so the next minute she found herself swept up into his arms and being carried across the snowy ground to the big black metal front doors of his granite fortress-like house.

She wanted to struggle, to fight the terrible urge to melt against him, because it felt wrong, as though she was giving in somehow, but it was cold and she had to get inside and this was the quickest way.

She held herself rigid, though he didn't seem to notice, much to her irritation.

The door opened for them, a black-uniformed staff member murmuring something in Spanish. Rafael replied in a low tone, but Lia wasn't listening. Because despite how hard and cold the house appeared from the outside, inside it was beautifully warm.

The front entrance was flagged with dark stone, the walls a pale cream, the light warm and welcoming. Used to the clutter of decor in the palace, Lia couldn't help but notice that Rafael's house was comparatively bare and minimalist. There was art on the walls, but it was obvious that each piece had been chosen and placed there with some care. And each piece was beautiful, full of texture and colour: a beautiful landscape in oils, an antique woven tapestry, a rustic pot with a vivid red glaze, an evocative black and white photo.

Rafael turned and carried her down a short hallway and into a big living area where a crackling fire roared in a stark black fireplace. The floor was covered with a nearly black, thick charcoal carpet, the furniture low, comfortable-looking couches upholstered in heavily textured cream linen. The stark black and white decor was softened with jewel-bright rugs, more pieces of carefully chosen art, cushions and discreet lighting.

Rafael carried her over to the couch and deposited her on it—indeed, it was as comfortable as it looked. The staff member—an older woman with white-streaked black hair and dark eyes—had followed them to the door and Rafael spoke again in lilting Spanish.

The staff member nodded and disappeared. Rafael strode to one of the armchairs, picked up a soft throw of deep blue cashmere and carried it over to her, bending to methodically wrap her up in it.

She pulled away, his nearness suddenly too much for her.

His eyes narrowed. 'You're cold.'

'Yes, but believe it or not I can wrap up warmly myself.'

He ignored that, his gaze dropping to her bridal gown, the skirts of which were now wet and clinging unpleasantly to her skin. 'You will need clothing.'

'I'm fine.'

'You are not,' he said in that irritatingly certain way of his. 'You're shivering.'

Annoyingly, he was right.

Lia grimaced and pulled the soft, warm wool tighter around her shoulders. 'I'll be all right in a few minutes.'

His hands fell away and slowly he rose to his full height. He didn't say anything for a long moment, staring at her so intently she almost had to look away. 'How are you feeling? I had reports that you weren't well initially.'

'Morning sickness. It passed.' She felt suddenly very tired, the shock of the past hour starting to take its toll.

'Why didn't you come to me?' His voice was flat, yet

she could hear something vibrating beneath the words, a deeper emotion she couldn't place.

She met his gaze, but his expression gave nothing away. Well, there was no reason not to tell him. She was too tired to argue right now anyway.

'I told you. I was afraid. We shared one night together, Rafael. That's all. And like you, I tried not to think about it, but then I started feeling sick and...' She swallowed, remembering the fear that had gripped her, bone-deep and icy. 'When the test was positive, I didn't know what to do. I...couldn't tell you. You were the Regent, the scandal if anyone found out would have been terrible, and I knew you would have hated that, so I... I thought keeping it secret was better.'

His silver eyes flickered, the lines of his starkly masculine face hardening. 'And yet the secret came out anyway.' There was no compromise in his voice. 'You should have come to me. You could at least have told me that you were pregnant, given me the opportunity to help you.'

Her heart clenched tight in her chest. He was right, she should have. But she'd been too shocked, too upset and, fundamentally, too unsure of his reaction.

'I know I should,' she said. 'But I didn't. We never talked about anything personal those nights in Papa's study and I didn't know how you would feel about it.'

His expression was harsh. 'I would have thought that at least you knew you could trust me.'

Her heart constricted even tighter. 'How could I have known that? I didn't know how you felt about anything.' Unconsciously, her hand had dropped to her stomach in an instinctive, protective movement.

He noticed, the look on his face turning dark. 'You think I'd hurt you? That I'd hurt our son or daughter?'

Pain curled through her. 'No,' she said quickly, because Rafael Navarro was many things, hard and cold and pitiless to the rest of the world, but she knew he would never harm a woman or a child, still less his own. 'No, I know you wouldn't.'

He was silent a minute. 'Did you love him, Lia?' he asked suddenly. 'Did you want to be his wife so badly? Did you want to be his Queen?'

Everything in her ached. Because, no, she hadn't been in love with Matias. And she hadn't been in love with Matias because Rafael had appeared and thrown everything she knew about herself, everything she knew about her own feelings, into disarray.

She didn't want to tell him that, but he might as well know the basic facts.

'No,' she said. 'I didn't love him. But, yes, I wanted to be his wife and I wanted to be Queen. That's what I've spent my whole life training for and you know it. My parents worked so hard to give me that opportunity and I didn't want to let them down.'

He said nothing, simply staring at her, and what he was thinking she had no idea.

You didn't only let your parents down, but you let him *down, too. He thought you'd come to him and you hadn't...*

Lia swallowed and then went on, forcing out the painful truth. 'This baby is…my fault, Rafael. If I hadn't got so angry, I wouldn't have gone to find Matias. I wouldn't have come to you and so all of this wouldn't have happened. It's not your responsibility to fix this.'

Still he said nothing.

'You can't actually want to marry me, Rafael,' she said.

Something in his face shifted. 'You have no idea what I want.' He turned to the door. 'We will discuss this later.'

Then he strode out.

'I'm sorry, Your Excellency, but the road back into the capital is blocked. There is no way to get to the palace, not tonight.'

Rafael glowered at his driver, the anger he'd thought he'd firmly locked down threatening his usual cold focus. Though it wasn't Anton's fault the wretched weather had turned against him.

The Regent grabbing the bride and leaving for his own residence without a word wasn't going to be a great look. It was too much like his father's scandalous behaviour for Rafael's comfort, so he'd wanted at least to show up at the palace in person with an explanation.

However, it looked as though that wasn't going to be an option if the roads were impassable.

'By air?' he asked, even though he knew the answer.

Anton shook his head. 'No, Excellency. Not in this weather.'

Well, that was nothing he didn't already know. And there was one good thing about the weather—if he couldn't get to the palace then at least no one could get to him. Which meant now he had more than enough time to make sure Lia agreed to marry him.

He'd already decided that during the brief moment he'd had with her in the living area, before he'd had to leave to get control of the jealousy and anger he could feel seething under his skin: at her, at his brother, at himself.

He was sure of one thing, though. No matter what she'd said about this being her responsibility, it was his also and he had a duty both to her and his child. And, to him, that meant marriage.

Since he'd taken her from the cathedral in full view of everyone, their relationship would no doubt be in the process of being picked apart. People would put two and two together and come up with four.

Marriage was the only way to save them, to put a gloss of respectability over their illicit encounter and make sure neither she nor their child would be subject to gossip.

But it wasn't only her agreement to a marriage he wanted. He needed to know why she hadn't trusted him enough to come to him. Oh, she'd given him all sorts of reasons—fear, wanting to protect him from scandal, all kinds of things—but in the end it all boiled down to one thing: trust.

Why are you so surprised? Did you give her any reason to trust you?

Well, no. They'd been friends, though, or so he'd thought. Or, no, possibly friends wasn't quite the right way to think about it, since he had friends and the way he felt about them was *not* how he felt about Lia.

He'd wanted her, been desperate for her. Had been obsessed with her. He knew he shouldn't have kept wandering past her father's study every night, but somehow that's where his path had always seemed to take him no matter his intentions.

Those nights he'd spent sipping whisky and discussing everything under the sun with her, from politics to philosophy, science and the arts, social theory and everything in between.

Those nights where he'd realised he wanted her more than he'd wanted anyone or anything in his entire life and the fury he'd felt because she would *never* be his. She'd always been destined for Matias and for Santa Castelia.

She isn't now, though. Now, she can be yours.

The possessive heat he'd been trying to keep at bay for the past three months poured suddenly through him in a searing flood, as if a dam had broken.

Because it was true, wasn't it? He'd told her that she had to marry him, not fully thinking about what that would mean.

Her, in his bed. Her, whenever he wanted her.

He wouldn't have to constantly watch himself whenever he was around her in case he gave himself away. He wouldn't have to constantly fight his own intense desire for her or the jealousy that gripped him whenever he thought about her with Matias.

She would be his.

Possessiveness caught him by the throat, but he choked it down with an instinct he'd spent most of his life perfecting.

His emotions were too intense, too potent to allow free rein. Hadn't his mother told him often enough that he had to be careful? That he had to control himself if he didn't want to turn into his father? The only reason he hadn't yet done so was because he wouldn't permit himself off the leash.

Lia was a danger to that control, it was true, but marriage might help. It was likely she'd got under his skin so badly because of the forbidden element in their relationship and since that wasn't a problem any more, he'd likely obsess about her less.

Knowing he'd be a father, too, was its own leash.

His own father had been morally bankrupt and Rafael would *not* set that kind of example. No, the family he'd create would be different.

And Matias? Santa Castelia?

Yes, those two things were yet more reasons why marriage was the only answer. He had to set an example for his brother and for the country he ruled. He had to show them that taking responsibility for your mistakes was the only way forward.

Anton was still standing there, looking apologetic, so Rafael dismissed him.

Constanza, his housekeeper, appeared at the door, also looking apologetic. 'There have been calls, Excellency.' She paused, then added, 'Many calls.'

Naturally.

'From His Highness?' Rafael asked.

Constanza inclined her head. 'And from the First Advisor. Not to mention from Their Highnesses Prince Zeus and Prince Jahangir Hassan Umar Al Hayat, and His Royal Majesty the King of Arista.'

Rafael gritted his teeth. Naturally his three Oxford friends would know what he'd done and have something to say about it. The news media would no doubt be buzzing.

They could wait, though. Before he talked to anyone else, he had to get Lia's agreement to their marriage, because forcing it from her was a path he'd never go down.

You didn't find her agreement necessary when you kidnapped her from the cathedral.

Yes, and that was because he'd allowed his emotions to get the better of him. A good reminder of why he had to stay in control.

He was too dangerous otherwise.

'Tell anyone who calls that the Princess Amalia is well and that we will be releasing a statement shortly,' he ordered. 'Then see that the Mountain Suite is made ready. Also prepare some immediate refreshments suitable for a pregnant woman. We will also be dining in the formal dining room tonight. The food must be exquisite, understand?' He thought a moment. 'The Princess also needs a change of clothes. See what you can find for her.'

Constanza, who was very rarely flustered, inclined her head again. 'Certainly, Excellency.'

Rafael thought a little more. 'Are there any staff here ordained?'

She remained unflustered. 'No, Excellency. I am the only staff member here and unfortunately I cannot help you.'

Well, that would be an issue he'd deal with later if and when it arose.

Rafael dismissed the housekeeper, then turned and strode back down the hallway to the living area where he'd left Lia.

She was still sitting on the couch before the fire. Her face was pale and she looked...tired. Sympathy tightened in his chest and this time he let it.

His mother had been a maid at the five-star hotel in Barcelona that his father preferred whenever he visited Spain. She'd been beautiful and he smitten. He was a king, used to taking what he wanted and so he'd taken her. And Rafael was the consequence. He'd been her burden to bear, not his father's, and borne him she had, on her own.

He couldn't allow the same thing to happen to Lia.

He wouldn't leave her to do this alone. That was not the example he wanted to set.

She looked up as he entered, her eyes widening. 'I thought we were going to discuss this later?'

'We were.' He came to a stop in front of the fire, holding his hands out to the flames, letting them warm the chilled tips of his fingers. 'But it appears that the roads are blocked. No one can get in or out.'

'I see.' Her voice was very neutral.

He almost smiled. She always sounded like that when she disagreed with people—in public at least. In private, neutral was the last thing she was.

'Which means, *princesa*,' he said, 'that you and I will have our little discussion now.'

'Do we need to have a discussion? I'm not marrying you, Rafael.'

Of course, getting her agreement wasn't going to be simple. He couldn't say that he hadn't hoped, but this was Lia after all. She was a complicated woman.

He wasn't displeased with the notion of having to work for it, however. He'd always loved it when she argued with him, because so very few people did. Plus, she challenged him and he did so love a challenge.

Slowly, he turned from the fire and faced her.

She was composed, as if the woman who'd thrown her bouquet and tried to hit him had never existed. Her diamond circlet was now on straight, her veil draped decorously back from her hair, her long-fingered, elegant hands folded in her lap.

The picture-perfect Crown Princess.

Except for the wet fabric that clung to her ankles and the water stains that sprinkled the expensive white silk.

'Why not?' He kept his tone as neutral as hers, as if

they were having a discussion about what kind of food they'd like for dinner or what drink they preferred. 'You are pregnant with my child.'

'Believe it or not, I'm well aware of that.' Her inky lashes fell as she looked down at her hands. 'However, marrying me just because I'm pregnant is not the most compelling of proposals.'

'And what would constitute a compelling proposal? Is it money you're after? Power? You said you didn't want to let your parents down and, if so, perhaps they would be satisfied with you having a high-powered executive position in one of my companies?'

She shook her head. 'No. I just don't want to marry anyone who feels forced into marrying me.'

He stared at her, not understanding. 'How is that any different from marrying Matias? You've been betrothed since you were children.'

She kept her gaze on her hands and stayed silent.

His temper pulled at the leash, along with his hunger and that possessiveness he couldn't seem to lock away. 'You know what people call me. "The Spanish Bastard".' He said the words with a certain relish, watching her face. 'It is not a compliment, *princesa*. And let me be clear, I don't care. It doesn't bother me. But I will not leave my child open to such names or such contempt. And if you're expecting to be sent out of the country to live in exile somewhere with a nice stipend, you will be very disappointed.'

He put his hands in his pockets and took a leisurely step towards her. 'Some day, at some point, no matter how hard you hide it, someone will discover that I am the father of that child. And when they do, you will find the media camped on your doorstep. You will have no rest. They will hound you.' He took another step towards her. 'And they will hound our child, too. Your reputation will be called into question, because the press are always hard on women. Every aspect of your life will be picked over.' Another step. 'Matias will be made to look a fool. The crown will be embarrassed and everyone will say "Like father, like son". Santa Castelia will be the laughing stock of the entire world.'

She kept her gaze down, but her jaw became very set.

He stopped in front of her, the tips of his expensive, hand-made black leather shoes grazing the white spill of wet silk from her skirts. 'So, tell me, Lia. Is that a more compelling proposal?'

CHAPTER FOUR

RAFAEL STOOD IN front of her, the tips of his shoes brushing her gown, tall and dark, muscular. Towering over her.

She kept her attention on her hands, but she could feel him watching her. His barely contained sense of frustration was almost palpable.

He'd always hated it when people didn't give in to his wishes and he clearly thought she should. Then again, she'd had some time to think, sitting out here in front of the fire, and she'd come to a few decisions.

The future she'd always thought she was destined for had been ripped away from her and, yes, that had been her fault. Her parents were going to be so disappointed and so was Matias, not to mention Santa Castelia, but there was no hope of her regaining the position she'd once had.

That was gone, as Rafael had so clearly laid out just now.

Which meant that for the first time in her life, Lia was faced with a choice about what she wanted.

She didn't have to be Queen.

She didn't have to rule a nation.

She didn't have to marry a man she didn't love.

She didn't have to be the Crown Princess.

The only thing she had to be was a mother and, though providing heirs had always been another thing that was expected of her, she didn't have to raise them to be royal as she had been.

She could be the kind of mother *she* wanted to be. She could do the things *she* wanted to do.

And there was no one to disappoint, not when she'd disappointed everyone already.

She'd never had that before. She'd never even thought about it.

What this would mean for herself and her child she didn't know. But one thing she *was* sure of: Matias hadn't ever said anything to her openly, but she'd always had the impression that she wasn't his choice. That he was marrying her purely for duty's sake and not because he actually liked spending time with her.

She'd tried not to let that bother her, but it did. And since she was being given the choice, she didn't want that now.

For once in her life, she wanted to be someone who was chosen and not for what she could bring or for what she represented, but for herself.

But Rafael hadn't chosen her. He was only marrying her because her pregnancy had forced his hand. And she didn't want that.

She didn't want to be someone's duty or their fix, or their reluctant consequence. And she especially didn't want to be Rafael's.

So, no, she wasn't going to marry him, no matter how many reasons he gave her as to why she should.

Oh, they were good reasons, she understood that. But none of them necessitated actual marriage. Besides, she was tired of doing what everyone else wanted her to do. Why shouldn't she get what she wanted for a change?

'No,' she said flatly and at last lifted her gaze to his. 'That is not compelling in the slightest.'

It was hard to hold his intense stare, but she managed it. Giving him back as good as she got, the way she always had in the arguments they'd had with each other. Studying the harsh planes and angles of his face, so hard and uncompromising.

Her heart fluttered in her chest in the confusing way it always did whenever she was around him.

'Then what, *princesa?*' A muscle jumped in the side of his jaw. 'Shall I get down on one knee? Is that what you want?'

'No.' She had nothing but the truth to give him 'I want to be chosen, Rafael. I want someone to marry me because they want *me.* Not because they have no other choice or because our parents arranged it. I'm tired of being someone's duty and I don't want to be someone's obligation.'

His intense gaze narrowed. 'You're not an obligation.'

'Aren't I? You're only marrying me because I'm pregnant.'

'So? This wouldn't even be an option if you weren't, because you'd be marrying Matias.'

'Exactly. But I don't have to do that now.' She lifted her chin, held his hard stare. 'Which means I can choose for myself for a change.'

His expression didn't alter, but that muscle jumped in his jaw again, the sense of contained frustration gathering tighter in the room.

It was clear that he did *not* like this decision one bit.

'And what about our child?' His dark, harsh voice was gritty with temper. 'It's not just about you and your choices.'

Her own temper rose as it always did when matched

with his, the inevitable excitement she felt whenever she was around him rising, too.

She'd told herself she was going to be calm and measured, but she'd got to her feet before she could stop herself. 'Your whole life has been about what you want, Rafael. All the choices you've made have been for yourself. But mine haven't. Right from the moment I could walk I've been told what my future is, what role I have to take. No one ever asked me what I wanted. Everything was *always* chosen for me.'

Rafael's features hardened. 'Yes, and as I told you before, *you* could have chosen differently. No one was forcing you into marrying Matias.'

He's right and you know it.

Lia ignored the thought. 'Don't be ridiculous. I had to marry him. You think I could just go and tell him I'd changed my mind? That I could tell my parents that all the work they'd put organising the betrothal and all the training I was given—'

'All that work that no one asked them to do,' he snapped. 'It was what *they* wanted, Lia. You said yourself that no one ever asked you what you wanted. They didn't even think about you.' His gaze glittered. 'So why nail yourself to a cross you didn't even build?'

Her stomach hollowed, a cold feeling winding through her.

You told yourself all this time that they were doing this for you. But was that really the case?

Even as a little girl, no one had asked her what she wanted to be when she grew up. And no one asked because everyone knew exactly what Lia would be when she grew up.

Matias's wife. The Queen.

But it had never been a choice, no matter what he said. *Except what if you had said no?*

Lia shoved that thought away. She was tired and she didn't want to talk about this any more. 'We've had our discussion,' she said evenly, trying not to give in to her temper. 'I've told you why I don't want to marry you. I'm not sure why you're arguing with me about it, but I suppose it's because you hate it when people don't do exactly what you want.'

'That's not—'

'I'm tired, I'm cold and I don't want to continue this discussion.' She kept her tone firm. 'There's no more to be said.'

Rafael was silent a long moment, his relentless silver gaze boring into her.

She stared back, refusing to be cowed.

She was younger than he, less experienced than he and had no power to speak of, but none of that mattered.

Her will was as strong as his and they both knew it.

Tension gathered between them, drawing tighter and tighter.

Her breath caught, every part of her suddenly coming alive. Aware of him on the most basic level, of his height, his heat and his sheer masculine power.

He could make her do anything he wanted. He could use that power, that strength to bend her to his will. Yet he never had and she knew he never would—that was why she felt no fear as she faced into the storm force of his displeasure. She'd never been afraid of him even when everyone else had...

Lia stood beside some of the other palace staff on one of the balconies that overlooked the grand front stairs of the palace, all of them craning for a glimpse of the infamous new Regent.

Her father and Matias were among the delegation waiting on the steps, all attention on the long black limo that had pulled up in front. The door opened.

A man got out. He was so tall, taller than even the Prince, who towered over most. He was dressed in an expensive and perfectly tailored dark suit with a black shirt underneath and, the moment he straightened up, everyone fell silent. He wasn't handsome like some of her favourite actors, or pretty like her boy-band crushes, yet all the same he was the most compelling man Lia had ever seen in all her seventeen years.

There was something about him that drew her, that fascinated her. Something to do with the natural power and authority he radiated, a man in complete control of himself and the world he lived in. A man utterly unlike his father, King Carlos, who'd been unpredictable, wild and corrupt. No one wanted another king like that and everyone was afraid that the decision to bring in King Carlos's illegitimate son to rule until Matias was of age had been a bad one.

Lia could hear people whispering and knew they were afraid as they stared at the man they called the 'Spanish Bastard', a financial genius and CEO of one of the world's biggest finance companies.

It had been Lia's father's decision to ask Rafael Navarro to rule Santa Castelia as Prince Regent, in the hope that he would be able to restore a decimated treasury and guide the Prince on a better path than the one their father had walked.

Others had opposed the decision and, looking at the

man striding up the steps of the palace as if he owned it already, Lia could understand their fear.

But she knew—and how she knew she had no idea, she just did—that they had nothing to be afraid of. This man was not Carlos. In fact, Lia's almost bone-deep instinct was that he was the opposite. Strong where Carlos had been weak. Steady where Carlos had been unpredictable. Calm where Carlos had been wild and cool where Carlos had been hot.

This man would heal Santa Castelia, she just knew it.

At the top of the grand stairs, Rafael Navarro turned to address the assembled crowd. He had the most extraordinary eyes, a light grey that glittered like silver, in stark contrast to his black hair and brows.

He leisurely took in everyone that stood before him, as if acknowledging each and every one of them, even those on the balconies. And when that silver gaze came to her, she felt an answering pulse deep inside, as if part of her knew exactly what he would eventually come to mean to her...

'Well,' he said at last, his casual tone so at odds with that blazing silver gaze she knew so intimately, 'I can see that this might take some time. Then again, we do have the whole night.' He glanced down at the hideously expensive watch that circled one strong wrist. 'Constanza will have prepared the Mountain Suite for you and a change of clothes, so you can get warm at least. I've also ordered some refreshments to be brought. Perhaps some time to change and something to eat will help you feel better.'

'Feel better meaning change my mind?'

Strangely, something that looked like reluctant amusement rippled over his harsh features, gone so fast she wasn't sure she'd seen it at all. Reminding her that it hadn't all been fiery intellectual arguments and challenges. He had a very dry sense of humour that rarely showed itself, but when it did, when she'd managed to make him smile, she'd always felt as if she'd won a lottery.

That same rush of warmth sparked inside her now, lighting her up inside.

'You never know,' he murmured. 'What about if I added some whisky and cigars?'

The warmth expanded. Whisky and cigars, and Rafael's exciting, vital presence. The bright points in a life that had been far more curtailed than she ever let herself think too deeply about.

She'd missed him. She'd missed him so much.

'Sadly,' she said, 'I don't think the baby would like it.'

The lines around his hard mouth eased, that elusive spark of humour glowing briefly in his eyes. 'True enough.'

Their gazes met again and held. This time it wasn't the clash of their wills that held her still, but something else. Something aching and raw and painful.

The signs of humour in Rafael's face vanished, leaving behind it a familiar heat that stole all the breath from her body. Three months ago, when she'd still been the sheltered girl he'd accused her of being, she hadn't recognised that heat for what it was. But she did now. Oh, she did now.

Desire.

'Your gown is wet.' He didn't look away, the harsh gravel of his voice becoming suddenly rough velvet. 'Let me help you with it.'

Her mouth had gone dry, her heart beating hard and

fast in her ears. He was looking at her as though he wanted to eat her alive and, God help her, she wanted him to.

If anything could make her change her mind about marrying him, it wasn't money or power, or even warm clothes and good food.

It was him. It was his touch.

'I'm fine.' Her voice sounded almost as low as his.

'But you can't undo all those buttons yourself.'

Heat prickled everywhere, chasing away the cold, bringing with it a heady rush of excitement.

She couldn't drag her gaze from his, every part of her consumed with the sudden, intense need to close the distance between them. To end the nagging hunger they both felt.

It had always been this way with him. Whenever he was near, she'd been almost overtaken by this fierce craving for him. It had been an unfamiliar and alien feeling that before their night together she hadn't understood.

She did now, though. It was powerful sexual desire.

She wanted him to touch her, kiss her, be inside her.

She wanted him so badly she couldn't breathe.

But sex had created this problem, which meant that more sex was hardly the solution. She had to control herself and not give in. Put more distance between them not less.

'I'll manage,' she forced out.

The heat in his eyes nearly burned her alive, but he didn't move. Then his gaze shifted. 'Ah, Constanza. Please show the Crown Princess to the Mountain Suite. I assume you have found appropriate clothing for her to wear?'

Behind Lia, a woman said in low tones, 'Yes, Excellency.'

'Good.' His hard mouth curved slightly as his gaze shifted back to her, but there was no amusement in it this time. It was the half-feral smile of a starving tiger who'd just sighted prey. 'Turn around, *princesa*. You do not want to ruin that gown and you will if you're not careful. Constanza would help, but she has bad arthritis and those buttons are very small.'

Ah, God, this was a challenge wasn't it? And she'd never been able to resist the challenges he'd thrown at her...

Don't forget that the power isn't all with him. You have that same power, too.

Another thing she wouldn't have understood three months ago, if she hadn't been in his bed.

But she had and she knew that the same desire she felt for him, he also felt for her and that she could use it. She could tempt him every bit as much as he was tempting her.

It wasn't the wisest course of action right now, not when she'd already decided to maintain her distance from him, not get closer. But he'd kidnapped her from her own wedding. She was trapped in his house and he was trying to make her marry him and really, if she wanted to get brutal about it, he was also using their baby to manipulate her.

It was time to turn the tables.

Hunger gleamed in his eyes and a dizzying excitement caught at her. She'd never had the opportunity to flirt with him like this. To tease him, tempt him. She'd been too innocent before.

Yet she wasn't innocent now and there was nothing to stop them, so why not?

It didn't mean giving in. All it meant was giving him a taste of his own medicine.

'In that case,' she said huskily and turned around, presenting her back to him, 'you may deal with the buttons.'

The older woman she'd seen before stood in the doorway. Constanza, apparently. The woman inclined her head in response to some unspoken command and vanished back down the hall, leaving as silently as she came.

The only sound in the room was the crackle of the flames in the fireplace and the frantic beat of her pulse.

Rafael was standing close, but not too close. Enough to feel the intense heat of his body and smell his familiar scent.

Her chest tightened, her throat closing.

His fingers tugged gently on the first button, a delicious tension gathering deep inside her, along with a bone-deep longing.

It was the same tension she'd felt whenever Rafael strode in and sat in the chair on the other side of the desk. Whenever his silver gaze met hers.

Was he thinking about that right now? Had he felt that same tension? That same longing?

He'd never said anything openly, never mentioned the thick atmosphere that used to fill her father's study sometimes when he looked at her.

The first time she'd known that their attraction was mutual had been when he'd unleashed that storm of passion the night she'd spent in his arms.

He said nothing now as he began to undo all the buttons, his fingers deft and sure, the fabric parting, cool air drifting over her bared skin.

She remembered this. Remembered being naked with him, feeling the touch of his hands and the brush of his mouth, the heat of his hard, muscular body on hers. The strength of his arms, gathering her close...

Did he remember this, too? Did he long for it as she did?

Perhaps he didn't. Perhaps she was seeing things in his expression, in his gaze, that weren't there. Perhaps it was all in her head.

Whatever, this was a mistake. She had to stop letting her stupid emotions control her.

Lia swallowed, her throat bone dry, preparing to pull away.

Then he said quietly, 'Ah, yes. I remember this view.'

In the silence of the room, Rafael heard her breath catch.

She was warm and she smelled of the honeysuckle that grew on the stone walls in the older part of the palace. Light, sweet, delicious...

He shouldn't be doing this, not when she tested his control so completely, but she'd been adamant, refusing to listen to all good sense and logic about marrying him. Insisting on wanting to be chosen for herself and not because he'd been 'forced' into it.

He understood her protests, at least intellectually. She'd been chosen for Matias. Matias hadn't chosen her. He hadn't been passionate about her. He'd found her dull. She was a duty and if Rafael had taught him nothing else, it was that doing one's duty was imperative.

And it was true that she'd never been given the opportunity to choose for herself what she wanted out of life. Then again, she was an adult woman, full of fire and spirit, and she could have refused the path her parents had laid out for her. And he didn't understand why she hadn't.

He'd wanted to press her about that, but once Lia didn't want to talk about something, she didn't want to talk. She was stubborn like that.

Just as she was stubborn about refusing to marry him.

Using their chemistry to remind her that there would be some compensations to being his wife was perhaps manipulative, but when it came to the wellbeing of his child there was nothing he wouldn't do.

Anyway, if she wanted to be chosen, then he would choose her. Because while it was true that if she hadn't fallen pregnant, he would never have even contemplated marrying her, the fact that no other woman tempted him the way she did hadn't changed.

He'd never wanted to marry, but the more he thought about having Lia as his wife, the more attractive the idea became. Being married to her would certainly be no hardship and definitely not any kind of duty.

He just had to convince her of that.

The fabric of her gown had parted, revealing the elegant curve of her spine, all pale skin and softness.

Desire kicked hard inside him, stealing his breath.

'How could you remember?' She didn't ask him what he was talking about. She knew. 'It was dark.'

The fire crackled, painting her exposed back in shades of rose and gold, and he wanted to touch her, brush his fingers down her back, feel the warm satin of her skin.

'Not completely.' His heart was beating far too fast, the need to touch her almost uncontrollable. He curled his fingers into fists, dug his nails into his palms, trying to master himself. 'There was a gap in the curtains and the moon shone through it.'

The moon had made her look as though she was carved out of ice and snow that night. Yet she hadn't been a snow queen. No, she'd been made of fire...

Moonlight outlined the delectable curves of the woman lying in his arms, her back to his chest. She had her head turned away, her cheek pressed to the pillow and she was shivering with desire. His hand traced her side, the dip of her waist and the achingly beautiful curve of her hip. She was so warm, so soft.

He'd had so many illicit fantasies about her and she was everything those fantasies had promised. No, she was more. She was better...

This was wrong and he knew it, and continuing to do this with her when his instinct was screaming at him to stop was insanity. A betrayal of everything he'd told himself he was. Everything he'd worked for up to this point.

But the desire she'd unleashed in him was impossible to deny.

'Rafael,' she murmured, arching against him, his name a prayer and a plea.

And he was lost, his control in ashes.

She had come to him. *She had begged for* him. *She had risked everything to have one night with him and he would fight God himself if he tried to take her from him.*

She wanted him. *Not because he was the Regent, not for his power or his authority or the money in his bank account.* Him. *Not his brother, the heir, the Crown Prince.*

She wanted the Spanish bastard who'd grown up

in a rundown one-bedroom apartment in Barcelona.
Whom nobody had wanted, not his father and certainly
not his mother.

This night between them should never had happened,
but he was going to take it. No one would know. No one
would ever find out.

It would remain their secret.

He ran his hand down her side, her skin feeling like
warm satin, and she sighed, trembling with delight...

'You said you were angry when you came looking for
Matias that night,' he heard himself say, his hand half
lifting to brush the nape of her neck despite himself.
'What were you angry about?'

She was silent for a long moment and he thought
she wouldn't answer. Then she said, her voice husky,
'I was...angry with you for making me want you. And
angry with myself. I couldn't stop thinking about you, I
couldn't... I was supposed to be marrying your brother
and I wanted you out of my head.' She took a little breath.
'I thought Matias would help me forget you and I suppose there was a part of me that wanted to punish you.'

A hot, primitive sense of satisfaction gripped him, a
strange feeling, tangled as it was with anger and possessiveness and jealousy.

Satisfaction that she wanted him so much she hadn't
been able to stop thinking about him. Anger and possessiveness and jealousy that she'd wanted to punish
him with Matias.

'I didn't know what else to do,' she went on, as if once
she'd decided to talk, she couldn't stop. 'The betrothal
ball was the next day and you'd stopped turning up to
our meetings. And I didn't know why. And I—'

'You know why,' he interrupted. 'I stopped turning up because every night was a constant battle against the urge to touch you. And I was losing.'

She stood so very still, tense in every line. Her breathing was audible and fast, though he could also hear her trying to control it. 'You were losing?'

He stared at her straight back, at the soft vulnerability of her nape left bare by the ornate curls her black hair had been arranged in.

She had been so sheltered, so innocent. She'd had no idea about sexual chemistry or desire, and he hadn't wanted her to have to deal with his. What he'd felt for her was so wrong and the only thing he could do about it was to take himself out of her vicinity.

So that's what he'd done.

'Yes.' Telling her this was a mistake, but she'd given him a little piece of truth just before and it didn't seem fair not to reciprocate. 'I wanted you more than I'd wanted anything in my entire life. But you were meant for Matias and so I stopped coming. It was easier.'

There was complete silence in the room broken only by the crackle of the fire in the grate.

He wanted to touch her so badly his chest ached.

She turned, her pale face flushed, a blue flame burning in her eyes.

Dios, but she was beautiful when she wasn't the good, quiet, delicate Crown Princess that Matias had found so dull, when she was the hot, passionate woman. The woman who wanted him every bit as badly as he wanted her.

'I thought you'd stopped coming because you'd lost interest.' She searched his face as if he held all the answers to every question she'd ever had. 'I didn't think...'

She stopped, the flush in her cheeks deepening, the blue flame in her eyes glowing brighter.

You could take her now. Right here in front of the fire.

He could and she wouldn't resist him, he could see that right now. But the need inside him felt too big and too strong. Something that he should resist, not give in to. Especially when he knew himself and his desires. They were powerful and, if he wasn't careful, if he wasn't vigilant, he could fall prey to them like his father had.

His mother had been clear about the dangers when he'd been a child and he'd never forgotten those lessons. He couldn't afford to. And if he needed a reminder, he only had to look at the woman in front of him.

A woman he'd taken without any thought for her and her future. Who was now pregnant and alone, just as his mother had been.

No, he couldn't let himself be at the mercy of his own desires, not now, not when his control was so tenuous. He had lost so many battles since meeting her, but he would not lose this one.

He held her bright gaze, freezing every part of the fire that leapt inside him. 'Constanza will have prepared your suite by now,' he said, keeping his tone casual. 'Perhaps you would like to change your gown and refresh yourself.'

Lia took an impulsive step towards him. 'But I—'

'It was not a request, *princesa*.' He held himself still, ignoring the warmth of her that lapped around him, tugging at him. She needed to be out of his vicinity and quickly.

Uncurling his fingers with a certain deliberation,

he lifted his hand and instantly Constanza reappeared. 'Show the Lady Amalia to her suite, please.'

Lia stared at him a long moment, then abruptly her lashes lowered, veiling the glow in her eyes. 'Yes,' she said. 'Now that you mention it, perhaps that would be for the best.'

She didn't say anything more, turning and following Constanza, shoulders back, her chin held high, sweeping from the room in a cloud of silken skirts. It would have been dignified if her gown hadn't been almost fully open at the back and only on her shoulders because she was holding it there.

Rafael watched her leave, standing rigid until she'd gone, before turning back to the fire and getting a grip on his recalcitrant body.

If he wanted to try that tactic again, use their chemistry to get her to do what he wanted, then he was going to have to be very careful. That was a flame that could easily burn out of control if he let it.

His phone went off and he pulled it out of his jacket pocket, answering it absently, his head still full of Lia.

'What the hell are you doing?' a deep voice said in his ear.

Zeus. One of his three closest friends and the one least likely to judge Rafael's current behaviour. Which wasn't a point in his favour.

Why on earth had he answered his phone?

'Is there a point to this call, Zeus?' He kept his tone negligent as he stared into the flames. 'Because if not, my hands are rather full right now.'

'A point? Not at all. But I've had Vincenzo and Jag yelling in my ear for the past hour and I'm sick of it. Why aren't you answering our calls?'

'I would have thought that would be obvious.'

'You took your brother's bride right from under his nose,' Zeus said. 'You just threw her over your shoulder in full view of everyone. I have to say, I'm impressed. I didn't think you had it in you.'

Rafael gritted his teeth. He'd always been the most restrained of the four, while Zeus wouldn't know restraint if it punched him in the face. 'She's pregnant,' he growled. 'What was I supposed to do?'

'Pregnant?' Zeus sounded surprised this time. 'Rafael, did you—?'

'Yes,' he interrupted. 'The child is mine.' And then, because this was an old friend after all, he added, 'It's complicated.'

'Apparently.' Zeus's tone was dry as dust. 'So, what are you going to do now?'

'What do you think I'm going to do now? I'm going to marry her.'

'Oh, good.' This time Zeus did not sound in the least bit surprised. 'I'll get the jet ready.'

'No,' Rafael said. 'It's a white out. All the roads are blocked and no one can get in or out.'

'Well, that's disappointing. I was looking forward to marrying another of my friends. How is the prospective bride?'

'Very angry.'

Zeus laughed. 'I see. She wasn't happy with being thrown over your shoulder, I take it?'

'She wasn't.'

'She'd rather be with your brother then?'

'I wanted you... I couldn't stop thinking about you...'

'No.' Rafael was unable to keep the satisfaction from

his voice. 'She doesn't. She's angry because she doesn't like being told what to do.'

'I can relate.'

'But that child is my responsibility and so I'm taking it.'

'Indeed. Vincenzo and Jag will be relieved to hear it wasn't just you losing your mind.'

'Their concern is noted.'

'What about Matias and the rest of your country?'

Trust Zeus to ask the most uncomfortable question.

'What about them?' He didn't bother with any politeness, not that his old friend would expect it anyway.

Zeus paused, then said delicately, 'Considering she was supposed to be Matias's bride and Santa Castelia's Queen...'

Rafael's jaw clenched. 'I told you. She felt nothing for Matias and he felt nothing for her. And as for Santa Castelia, another queen can be found.'

'But wasn't she brought up specifically for the role?'

Another uncomfortable question. Rafael was tired of them. 'Did you have anything else you wanted to say?' he demanded.

'You didn't answer my—'

'Good.' Rafael hit the end button and got rid of the call. Then after a second's thought, he turned his phone off.

He didn't want any distractions and he most especially didn't want anyone questioning what he'd done in that cathedral. It made him think about all the lines he'd crossed, all the vows he'd broken.

Vows he'd made to Santa Castelia and to his brother.

Vows he'd made to himself.

He'd sworn the day he'd learned the truth about his father that he'd never let his anger rule him again. He'd never let *any* emotion rule him. And he would never allow another woman to go through what his mother had.

His birth had been a mistake and he had had to make up for that, channelling all the heat of his violent emotions into a cold, driving will that had taken him out of that one-roomed apartment in Barcelona and turned him into the man he was today.

The owner of a global company, ruler of an entire nation. Mentor to a king...

Matias had their father's height and his dark colouring, though his eyes weren't as dark as Carlos's had been. They looked at Rafael warily now as the last of the advisors filed out of the meeting room. Rafael had ordered them out for some privacy.

Matias, sixteen, yet looking even younger, didn't say a word. He stared at Rafael as if he was a rabid dog that might bite at any moment.

He was scared, Rafael got that loud and clear, and it made the low, sullen anger that burned constantly inside him leap. Carlos had not been kind to him, that was clear. If their father had hurt him...

Rafael gritted his teeth and forced his fury down, meeting his brother's gaze directly. 'First of all,' he said, 'I am not here to take your place. My duty is to get Santa Castelia into shape so that you actually have a country to rule and not a dictator's republic. Second, although I will make the ultimate decisions on how this country is run, I aim to involve you in all the decision-making processes. You need to be taught how to rule and, since our father neglected his duty and failed to teach you, I will do so.'

The boy remained quiet, still staring.

'*Third, you are the Crown Prince and I am here to protect your interests. Everything I do here, I do for you. Do you understand?*'

*Matias continued to stare for so long that Rafael wondered if the boy would ever talk. Then finally he said, '*Why? Why did you say yes?*'*

Rafael knew what he was asking and it was the same question he'd asked himself when Gian De Vita had called him out of the blue not long after the news of his father's death had broken, asking him if he would consider ruling Santa Castelia.

'*I said yes, because someone had to do it. Because I am not our father and I didn't want the crown. And because someone had to teach you the right way to be King.*'

*There was anger in Matias's gaze, though whether it was for him or something else, Rafael couldn't tell. '*Why not Gian? He could have been Regent.*'*

'*Santa Castelia needs money. And Gian doesn't have the financial understanding that I do.*' *He paused.* '*Are you angry with me?*'

*There was a silence, then Matias said suddenly, '*He always liked you better. He said I was weak.*'*

Rafael didn't need to ask who Matias meant. It was obvious.

'*Well,*' *he replied mildly, '*let's prove him wrong.*'

And they had. They both had. Matias had grown into his strength, gaining a quiet sort of confidence and authority that wasn't Rafael's hard edge, but had a power of its own.

And by taking Lia, you've undermined everything you

tried to build. And you thought you were nothing like your father...

Bitterness coiled inside him, but he shoved it down.

He *wasn't* anything like his father. At least Rafael acknowledged his own mistakes and took ownership of them.

Not that his child was a mistake. Never that.

'Your Excellency,' Constanza said from the doorway. 'Your Highness, your brother is calling. Do you wish to speak with him?'

'No,' Rafael said, staring down into the fire. 'Tell him I cannot be contacted.'

First, he would fix things with Lia.

Then, he would confront his brother.

CHAPTER FIVE

LIA KEPT HER back straight and her chin held high all
the way up the stairs that led to the second floor of the
house and all the way down a wide hallway with discreet recessed lighting and low ceilings. She didn't falter
as Constanza stopped outside a door of dark wood and
opened it, gesturing her inside. She simply inclined her
head in thanks and swept into the room.

It was only when the door had closed quietly behind
her and she was alone that she gave in to the trembling
that shook her entire body.

She was aware of every inch of her exposed back, of
how flimsy the hold of the fabric on her shoulders was
and how easily it could slip. Downstairs, all she'd had to
do was shrug slightly and her gown would have fallen
into a pool of silken tulle and lace at her feet.

She would have been naked but for her white silk
lacy underwear.

What would he have done then? Would he have
touched her? And if he had, what would she have done
in return?

'...every night was a constant battle against the urge
to touch you. And I was losing...'

She shut her eyes, feeling again the gentle tug on the

buttons of her gown and the warmth of him at her back. So close, so achingly close.

That's why he hadn't come to any more of their nightly meetings. *'I wanted you more than I'd wanted anything in my entire life.'*

She might have been sheltered, but she'd recognised his desire for her. She'd known. But to hear him say it out loud…

The stern, controlled Regent, so cold and so commanding, had wanted her, had burned for her…

'You're just like my father sometimes,' she snapped, unable to help herself. 'So damn patronising. Are you even listening to what I'm saying? Or is it because I'm a sheltered young woman you don't think I know anything?'

Rafael was in his customary pose, sitting back in the chair opposite the desk, his long, muscular body stretched out, ankles crossed. Ostensibly relaxed and yet tonight something was different. There was a tension about him that needled her, that stretched her own temper thin and she wasn't sure why.

Silver glittered in his eyes. He seemed cold tonight, the distance between them and their respective stations making the desk seem like an impossible gulf.

'No,' he said and she could hear anger in his voice. 'I do not think that.'

Her emotions had always moved liked quicksilver and her anger faded as quickly as it had come, because something was wrong, she could sense it.

She frowned. 'Is everything all right, Rafael?'

His gaze flickered. 'Yes. Why do you ask?'

'Because you're not usually this grumpy.'

He shifted in his chair, the tension around him gath-

ering tighter. 'There have been…some issues I have to deal with.'

'I'm sorry. Is there anything I can—?'

'You are a sheltered young woman,' he interrupted suddenly. 'And there are some things you don't know anything about.'

An intensity vibrated suddenly in his voice, a rough quality that made her go very still, her heart thudding hard in her head.

'What things?' she asked, staring at him, her breath catching.

He looked back and for a long time neither of them moved, the air in the study aromatic with the remains of her cigar and the warm scent of Rafael's aftershave drifting around her.

There was heat in his eyes, making her skin prickle everywhere.

Then abruptly he cursed, put down his tumbler of Scotch, pushed himself violently to his feet and walked out.

Lia swallowed, her head full of the look in his eyes as she'd turned to him downstairs. She'd wanted to see his face, wanted to see the truth and there it had been, that same look he'd given her that night months ago, his silver gaze full of desire. For her.

What if you weren't meant for Matias after all? What if you were meant for him?

Her heart was beating far too fast and she felt breathless.

Meant for him, for Rafael…

The idea made everything in her pull taut.

Ever since she'd first seen him on the balcony all those years ago, he'd generated such a strong response inside her. Back then she'd only been seventeen and sheltered, and hadn't known what it meant. He'd fascinated her, confused her, but even then part of her had known that the feelings she had for him were forbidden. That they should have been for Matias, not Rafael.

Her parents had ensured she spent time with Matias, organising decently chaperoned outings so the two of them could get to know one another. But he'd never seemed to display much interest in her. Their conversations had been stilted and awkward, both of them running out of things to say to each other.

She'd thought it would get easier between them, that they merely needed more time, but then those meetings with Rafael had happened and she'd become even more confused. Because conversation with Rafael had never been awkward or stilted. He'd never seemed bored by what she had to say and, unlike Matias, he was interested in her opinions.

She loved talking to him, loved spending time with him, and the more evenings she had with him, the more she wanted. She'd started resenting having to go on outings with Matias and on the days she did, all she could think about was that she didn't have these long silences with Rafael. And she didn't have to watch what she said with Rafael or be the perfect princess with Rafael.

She didn't feel the same heady combination of excited and afraid that she felt when she was with Rafael, that she *only* felt with Rafael...

It wasn't only physical desire you felt for him.

But her mind shied away from that thought. It felt too big, too dangerous. A teenage crush was far more manageable and really, that's exactly what it had been. A teenage crush she hadn't grown out of and a physical desire she hadn't managed to control.

Except she would control it now, because she had choices now and a future that hadn't been planned in meticulous detail for her by other people. She had decisions to make and she couldn't let those decisions be dictated by some emotion she didn't even have a name for.

She'd made that mistake three months ago and look what had happened.

Lia took a deep breath and moved over to the magnificent four-poster bed that stood against one wall. Opposite were windows that gave a view out over the mountains, the sharp, black shapes softened by the falling snow. Everything was white and silent.

The room itself was thickly carpeted in a dark charcoal, the walls a warm neutral white, nothing that would compete with the glory of the view. It might have felt cold if not for the rugs on the floor and the black fur thrown over the bed.

She paused beside the bed, looking down at the clothing that had also been thrown over it. A pair of cosy soft grey sweatpants and a dark blue hoodie. They looked huge.

Lia reached out and touched the fabric of the hoodie. It felt as soft as it looked.

These were his, weren't they?

Lia stood at the window of her bedroom that overlooked the famous gardens of the palace. It was early, but she'd woken up and hadn't been able to get back to sleep.

She'd looked out to see what kind of day it was supposed to be since her mother had told her that she was having riding lessons today; Matias liked to ride appar-

ently so she would have to learn. And she'd seen a dark figure running down one of the long paths.

It was cold, nearly winter, and the figure wore long, dark sweat pants and a dark hoodie. He was jogging, not fast, but not slow, and she could tell already by the presence of the guards that kept pace with him that it was the Regent.

Her heart beat faster.

She hadn't met him yet—she hadn't been important enough for an introduction—but she would. Once her father brought up the subject of her prospective engagement to Matias, of course.

Meanwhile, ever since he'd arrived at the palace, she'd been fascinated with him. She'd read everything published on the web about him, all the gossip columns and business pages.

The Spanish Bastard, the media had dubbed him. A shark, they said. A financial genius who'd built a global, multi-billion-dollar company from the seed of one small finance company in Barcelona, in just a few short years. A dangerous man, cold and calculating, who now ran Santa Castelia as efficiently as one of his own companies.

People were wary of him and with good reason. He was ruthless. And he was everything the media said about him, at least according to her father. But he also had a strong moral code, which was why Gian had brought him to Santa Castelia to rule. He'd included Matias in his decision making, teaching him about the business of ruling, and she'd once personally watched as the child of one of the palace staff had mistakenly run into him one day out in the grounds. Everyone had held their breath, waiting to see what he'd do, since if he'd been Carlos he would have punished both the child and the parent. But all he'd done was pick the child up, checked to see if he was okay, then set him on his feet, and had gone on with the meeting he was in the middle of as if nothing had happened.

A hard man, they said, and he was. But he wasn't cruel. He wasn't his father and that, if nothing else, proved it.

Lia watched him jog around and around the perimeter of the gardens, fascinated by the fluid way he moved. Easy and loose, with a long, loping stride.

Then finally when he stopped, right by her window, he tugged the hoodie off and over his head, revealing the hard, muscular lines of his torso, clearly outlined by the T-shirt he wore underneath.

Every time she'd seen him, he'd been in one of his meticulously tailored dark suits, but now he was in sweatpants and a T-shirt that clung to every line, showing off the carved musculature of his wide shoulders and powerful chest, the dips and hollows of his abs.

Her breath caught.

He wasn't built like a businessman. He was built like a warrior.

She'd only just turned eighteen and was sheltered. Her life revolving around her schooling and the lessons in queenship that her parents had insisted on. Men—boys—had never factored into anything she did. And why would they? She was promised to only one man and that man was Matias.

Except Matias wasn't a man, not yet. He was a boy and it had never been so obvious until this moment. Where she realised that Matias had never made her breath catch the way it did just now. She'd never wanted to look at him the way she wanted to look at Rafael Navarro. Never wanted to see what his chest looked like underneath the fabric of his T-shirt, never wanted to touch...

Lia shivered, memory tightening its grip. The first awakening of her sexuality and not for the man she should have wanted, but for a man so forbidden she shouldn't have been looking at him that way at all.

But she had.

She'd been naive, thinking that looking wasn't a crime. Not realising the power of her own obsession with him or understanding the feelings he'd awakened in her.

Her life was so curtailed, everything she did needing her parents' approval first. Her friendships were monitored, every activity needing to be signed off, and it had been dull. So dull. There had been no excitement in her life, nothing new.

He had been the first person she'd met who'd felt dangerous and exciting and she'd wanted more of him.

And now you have more and you're baulking.

Lia abruptly shrugged out of her wedding gown, gathering the soft, heavy folds and laying it carefully on the bed. Then she picked up the sweatpants and hoodie and went over to another door near the bed that led into an en-suite bathroom.

Tiled in pristine white, the room felt open and airy, the floor warm beneath her icy feet. She stood in front of the mirror and discarded her veil, the diamond circlet and all the pins holding her hair in place. Her makeup had run, her eyes looking shadowed and black, her cheeks pale.

Her mother would be appalled to see her like this.

She'd always hated Lia's wilder side, especially the adventures she'd had in the woods behind the palace gardens, climbing the trees and making forts, and playing illicit games of war with some of the other palace children.

Lia would come home with filthy, torn clothes and wild hair, and receive a lecture from her mother about how a future queen needed to be immaculate.

She was not immaculate now.

What kind of thanks is that for all your parents' hard work?

Something that felt like grief wound through her and she turned away from her reflection, forcing the thought from her head.

She didn't want to think about her parents, not yet.

Instead, she got rid of her underwear, then stepped under the shower, letting the stream of blissfully hot water warm her up and wash away the memories of the day.

As the water fell around her, she gently touched the slightly rounded curve of her stomach and a wave of protectiveness went through her. She had no idea what kind of mother she would be, but she certainly wasn't going to weigh her child down with a heavy load of expectations the way she had been.

She wasn't going to tell them how hard she had worked for them or how difficult it had been to conceive. How many tears had been shed and heartache endured simply for the privilege of having her.

She wouldn't lecture them about the sacrifices that had been made and how her happiness was dependent on theirs, and didn't they owe her that? Hadn't she been through enough for them?

So much for not thinking about your parents.

Her hand cupped her stomach as the grief turned into a sharp, painful kind of anger. Then from out of nowhere, Rafael's voice drifted through her head.

'That was what they *wanted, Lia. You said yourself that no one ever asked you what you wanted. They didn't even think about you... So why nail yourself to a cross you didn't even build?'*

She'd told herself for years that she was happy with the opportunities her parents had given her, because that's how they'd phrased the betrothal to Matias. An opportunity to prove her worth and make them proud, as her father had said. As if just existing wasn't enough and she had to do something more.

She hadn't questioned it. Her mother had talked a lot about how hard it had been to conceive and that by the time they'd gone through the IVF process, they were older parents. And that they didn't have the energy for a child as 'volatile and high maintenance' as she had been.

She loved her parents and so she'd tried to be good, to control the worst of her behaviours. To not have tantrums when she was angry or cry when she was upset, or shriek too loudly when she was having fun. To be well behaved and good, and to never give them a reason to regret having her.

She'd done that for years without question.

Until one night when she couldn't sleep, she'd been out walking the palace halls and had found the door to her father's office open. And she'd gone inside, because she was curious, poking around and finding a whisky bottle and a box of cigars.

Because it was midnight and no one was around, she'd taken a sip of that whisky. Then she'd tried one of those

cigars. She'd felt reckless and rebellious, all the things
she never allowed herself to feel during the day, and so
she'd kept doing it.

Then one night Rafael had caught her. She'd brazened
it out by offering him a glass of whisky, which he'd then
shocked her by taking. Then he'd sat down and they'd
talked and talked. She'd thought it had been a one-off,
but a couple of days later he'd come back and they'd resumed talking.

She'd realised then that he didn't care about her behaviour. That she didn't have to moderate herself with
him, that he *liked* her when she was 'volatile'.

Just as she'd liked him. And then more than liked.
She'd *wanted*...

*And you still do, so why not have a night with him?
Just one. And maybe it will vanquish this need for both
of you.*

Lia blinked through the water running down over
her face, the thought catching her unawares, making
her stomach swoop and dive.

As she'd already thought, she had the luxury of choice
now. While she didn't want to marry him, that didn't
mean she couldn't sleep with him.

Three months ago she'd chosen to go to Matias and
it had only been an accident that had led her to Rafael's
bed. But she could choose differently now.

Now she had the freedom to choose him because she
wanted him, not so she could forget him. And he was
hungry for her, too. She'd loved that. Loved how desired
he'd made her feel that night.

So why couldn't she have that again? Why couldn't
they both have it?

Lia turned off the water and got out. She dried herself

on a warm, fluffy white towel, then pulled her under-wear back on and dressed in the sweats that had been on the bed.

They were clean, smelling of laundry powder, but there was no doubt as to whose they were, because they swamped her. The pants weren't so bad because she had a little baby bump, plus they had a drawstring she could pull tight around her hips, but the hoodie was a differ-ent story. It swamped her, extending down to her knees and she had to roll the sleeves up hugely.

She was wearing his clothes. His. *Rafael's.*

Lia took a deep breath.

Yes, she would. She and Rafael were cut off, alone. No court to watch them, no parliament to answer to, no media to track their every move. What happened here no one would ever know about. There was no one to judge her, no one at all.

She didn't know what her future was going to look like and that was terrifying, but tonight was certain and he was here.

A rush of something went through her, excitement, anticipation, or something else, she couldn't tell what, but she grabbed on to it with both hands and held on tight.

What about marrying him? What about wanting to be chosen? What about giving in?

Sex didn't have to mean marriage and she wasn't giv-ing in. She was choosing for herself. And while he might not have wanted to marry her if she wasn't pregnant, he *did* want to sleep with her. He'd chosen her in that sense.

And your heart? What about that?

But Lia ignored that thought. Her heart had nothing to do with this. For the first time in her life she could do what *she* wanted to do, not what anyone else wanted her to do, and that's all that mattered.

Rafael kept tabs on the calls, social media notifications and emails that kept pouring in, while at the same time monitoring the state of the weather via the internet.

They'd be cut off from the outside world for some time since it was clear it wasn't going to stop snowing any time soon and all the mountain passes were blocked.

As he hadn't managed to get Lia's agreement on the marriage idea yet, he continued to maintain radio silence with the outside world. Which he wasn't sorry about in the slightest since it meant they would remain undisturbed.

Constanza delivered refreshments to the living room, small perfect sandwiches and delicate cut fruit. Some pastries as well as orange juice and a pot of coffee.

Rafael dismissed her and set out the food himself, arranging it just so on the coffee table in front of the fire.

The room was nicely warm now, the snow outside making it seem as though it was dark, even though night was still a few hours away.

It felt cosy, intimate, reminding him of Gian's study all those months ago, the first time he'd walked in...

Rafael paced along the echoing hallways of the palace. It was late and he couldn't sleep. He often couldn't, there was too much going on in his head, and so he roamed the palace at night, trying to solve the day's problems with some good old-fashioned pacing.

He'd been surprised to find out how much he en-

joyed being Regent—it was just the kind of challenge he liked—and he'd enjoyed being a big brother, too. More than he'd anticipated. Matias had got over his wariness after the first couple of months and had thrown himself into the business of learning how to be King. He'd proved to be a quick study and had blossomed over the past couple of years. He would be a good king for Santa Castelia, Rafael was sure.

His footsteps rang on the old stone floor as he strode down one of the narrower hallways.

He'd dismissed his guards for the night and it was good to be alone, since he hardly ever was. It gave him time to think.

One of the doors in the hall stood slightly open, light shining through.

Afterwards, he was never sure what had made him stop since an open doorway wasn't unusual, though it was late for someone to have a light on. Perhaps it was the faint, aromatic scent of cigar smoke drifting into the hallway that made him stop. Because that scent was familiar. Gian smoked cigars that smelled like that.

He took a quick look around, orienting himself, and realised he must be standing outside Gian's office. It seemed the first advisor was still working, even though it was late.

Rafael went to the door and pushed it open, wondering what was keeping the old man up till nearly midnight. But it wasn't Gian who sat at his desk.

The desk lamp was on, casting a warm glow in the small room. Bookshelves lined the walls, the shelves crammed not only with books but keepsakes, photos, bits of stationery, letters and all kinds of other things.

The desk itself was oak, large and heavy, the surface of the desktop scattered with pens and paper, a computer screen and an old keyboard, a blotter that had been doodled on, and old cups of coffee.

And a pair of pretty bare feet, complete with blue toenails.

Rafael blinked.

A woman sat back in Gian's chair with her feet on the desk. In one long-fingered hand she held a crystal tumbler full of an amber liquid that had to be alcohol of some kind and in the other a lit cigar.

It was Amalia, Gian's daughter. The same daughter who was promised to Matias.

Rafael had met her only once before, when Gian had shown him the agreement between Carlos and himself that Carlos's son would marry her. A match that Rafael had no issue with since the De Vita family was ancient aristocracy and very suitable.

He hadn't paid any particular attention to her. She was pretty, answering all his questions in a low, nearly inaudible voice. She didn't meet his gaze and was so self-effacing he'd almost forgotten she was there. He had tried to make conversation with her, but had eventually given up when all the conversational balls he'd lobbed in her direction were not lobbed back.

Matias had told him she was dull and it turned out he was right.

Except the woman sitting with her feet on the desk, sipping what looked like whisky and smoking a cigar, was the very antithesis of dull.

Her black hair was loose, a glossy, inky waterfall over her shoulders, and all she wore was a white night-

gown that would have been virginal if the fabric hadn't been so sheer he could see right through it. She was staring at him, her deep blue eyes gone very dark and very round, her luscious mouth in a perfect O of surprise. Her cheeks flooded with pink and for a second neither of them moved, both of them staring at each other in shock.

It hit him then, the sudden, hard kick of a desire he should never have felt.

But the feeling was so wrong that he crushed it before he'd even had the chance to feel it.

'What are you doing here?' he asked curtly.

Her mouth closed and something shifted in her eyes, though he couldn't tell what it was. Thick, silky sable lashes descended, veiling her gaze, and he thought she'd apologise, get to her feet, and move quietly out the door.

But she didn't.

'It's my father's study,' she said instead. 'I'm allowed to be here.'

He stilled. She sounded almost...challenging, which he hadn't expected.

Her lashes rose then, an irresistible glow in her eyes. 'Perhaps you'd like to join me for a drink, Your Excellency?'

He should never have gone in. Never have sat down in the armchair opposite her. Never have allowed his curiosity to get the better of him, wanting to know why she was in her father's study, smoking cigars and drinking his whisky.

He should never have started that first conversation,

that had led to all the others and eventually her in his bed as passion had exploded between them.

But he'd told himself it was only conversation, that he had to get to know his future sister-in-law, to make sure she really was as suitable for Matias as she appeared.

And she wasn't suitable for Matias, it turned out. Not suitable at all.

But she's perfect for you.

Rafael ignored that as a small figure appeared in the doorway, a small figure swamped by the far-too-big hoodie she wore.

Lia.

Her hair was damp and curling in waves down her back, the sleeves of the hoodie rolled up. She wore sweatpants and the hems of those, too, were rolled up nearly to her knees.

His clothes. But of course. He'd ordered Constanza to find her something to wear, yet he didn't have any women's clothes here. The only clothes available would be his.

The coiling possessiveness tightened once more, because he liked that. He liked that *very* much. It appealed to the territorial male inside him that the woman pregnant with his child was safe in his house, wearing his clothes. Protected by him.

His.

Careful. She's not yours.

No, but she would be. He'd decided. He'd make it happen.

She lifted her chin as their gazes met, as if daring him to comment.

He obliged. 'I see Constanza found you some clothing.'

'Yes. Yours, I assume?'

'Mine,' he agreed. 'It suits you.' And it did.

It wasn't that spectacular wedding gown, but somehow the oversized clothing drew attention to her femininity in a way that made him want to pick her up and hold her close.

'I'm not sure that's a compliment,' she said, then gave him a look that went through him like a quarrel from a crossbow, the same look she'd given him that night in her father's study. Her eyes had been so blue, glowing with a challenge he hadn't been able to resist...

'Perhaps you'd like to join me for a drink?' he murmured, in a very deliberate and conscious echo of her invitation that night.

Lia blinked, an expression he couldn't quite put his finger on flickering over her delicate features. Colour warmed her cheeks and then, like the sun coming out, she smiled.

His heart kicked hard inside his chest, his breath catching.

She'd been so generous with those smiles, making him feel as though he'd been given the most precious gift whenever she turned them on him. No one else smiled at him like that. No one else smiled at him at all.

He missed them.

'I'd love to,' she said, the warmth in her expression making him ache. 'But make it an orange juice.'

'And no cigars.' His voice sounded rough and he couldn't seem to smooth it over.

'What a pity.' Her smile faded, her gaze meeting his

with a directness that took his breath away. 'I miss those nights with you.'

His heart jerked again, the ache inside him spreading out.

'Prospective queens shouldn't be drinking whisky and smoking cigars,' he said, coming into the study and standing in front of Gian's desk.

'Perhaps someone should have told King Carlos that.' Her tone was dry, her blue eyes full of humour and something else, a very definite and most unexpected challenge.

'King Carlos was not a prospective queen,' he pointed out. 'He was a king.'

Amalia lifted her tumbler very pointedly and took a sip. 'Not a very good one.'

His interest, already caught, deepened. She was not at all the way she'd appeared to him the week before at their first meeting, with her gaze lowered and only speaking when she'd been spoken to.

How...interesting.

'Agreed.' Slowly, he sat down in the armchair before the desk and watched as she took her pretty feet off the desktop and began to rummage in one of the drawers. A second later, she'd pulled out another glass, produced the bottle of very good Scotch and poured him a measure.

'Does your father know who's drinking his best whisky?' he asked as she pushed the tumbler across the desktop to him.

'No.' She gave him a direct look. 'And you're not going to tell him.'

'Am I not? No one gives orders to the Regent, princesa.'

She pulled a face. 'I'm not a princess.'

He lifted the tumbler and took a sip. It was indeed very good Scotch. 'Then give me one good reason why I shouldn't tell your father right now that I caught you in his office, stealing his good alcohol and smoking his cigars.'

She capped the whisky, leaned back in her chair, picked up her cigar again and took a drag. Then blew a perfect smoke ring. 'Because I'll be sad if you do?'

Dull, Matias had said. Yes, the woman sitting at the desk was not dull, not in the slightest. It surprised him and he was so seldom surprised.

'That is not a convincing argument,' he said mildly, amused despite himself.

She gave him the sweetest smile. 'Well, other rebellions aren't permitted so I have to take mine where I find them. Also, I can hardly advise Matias on the dangers of drinking and smoking if I haven't tried them myself, can I?'

Women had always fallen into two camps for Rafael. They were either associated with work, in which case they were off limits, or they were prospective sexual partners. It wasn't a conscious choice on his part, that was just how it had happened. Mainly due to the fact that he never had a shortage of women throwing themselves at him, either for his sexual prowess or for a taste of his power.

But he felt something unfamiliar twist inside him as he looked into Lia's blue eyes.

She didn't seem afraid of him and she wasn't seeking his approval, or jockeying for his attention. And she looked at him as if he was a person, not the Regent. Not the CEO of a multinational company and not a powerful

man to seduce. Not the Spanish Bastard, the unwanted
mistake of an unpopular king.

But him. Rafael.

And he knew the feeling was dangerous, that he
should get up and walk away. Yet he didn't. He sat there
and he looked back at her and said, 'No, this is true.
What other rebellions have you tried?'

'There is no need to miss them, *princesa*,' he murmured,
the ache in his heart getting heavier at the memories.
'We can have them again, I promise.'

She lifted one black brow. 'But only if I marry you,
yes?'

'*Si.*'

Interestingly, this didn't seem to annoy her as much
as it had earlier, because she only nodded before sitting herself regally on the couch. 'The promised orange
juice, if you please.'

Despite the strange heaviness in his chest, amusement flickered through him. 'Do you expect me to wait
on you, Lia?'

She gave him a cool look, every inch of her queenly.
'Yes.'

It made him smile. She was ridiculously appealing
like this.

'Your wish. My command.' He moved over to the
coffee table and poured her a glass of orange juice, then
held it out to her. She took it and he made sure that their
fingertips didn't brush.

Judging from that feeling in his chest, his control was
suspect so it was best that he tried to limit temptation.

Lia took a sip of her orange juice, then leaned back on

the couch, her blue eyes lifting to his. 'Why marriage? Why is that so very important to you?'

He frowned, the question unexpected. 'I told you. I don't want our son or daughter having to—'

'No,' she interrupted calmly. 'I don't think that's the reason. Or at least not the real reason.'

Rafael tensed, though he wasn't sure why. 'What makes you say that?'

'There aren't many men who'd throw a woman over their shoulder and carry her off from the church on the day of their wedding, before absolutely *insisting* on marrying her themselves.' She took another sip, her gaze on his very steady. 'That's a drastic course of action simply to spare your child a couple of derogatory names. Especially for men who don't like scandal.'

He didn't like talking about his mother, but there was no reason not to tell Lia. 'My mother was a single parent,' he said shortly. 'My father got her pregnant, then left her alone in Barcelona with no means of support. It was a miserable existence for her and it left her very unhappy, and I will not do the same.'

'But there is financial support. You don't need—'

'Marriage also gives a degree of legal protection both to you and the child.' He still felt tense. 'I know you want to be chosen, Lia. In which case you should know that I have never proposed marriage to anyone before. You are the first and the only.'

She lifted a shoulder. 'Yes, but as I pointed out to you earlier, only because I'm pregnant. It would never have entered your head if I wasn't.'

Frustration wound through him. He didn't know what more she wanted from him. 'You were Matias's bride. Of course it never entered my head.'

'And if I hadn't been?'

He shoved his hands into his pockets. 'What exactly are you asking me, Lia?'

She looked back for a long moment, then abruptly put down her juice. Her blue gaze was suddenly very, very direct. 'If I hadn't been Matias's bride, would you have married me, Rafael?'

CHAPTER SIX

It was a dangerous question to ask and she knew it. But she couldn't help herself.

Rafael stood on the other side of the coffee table, the fire leaping behind him and outlining his tall, masculine figure. He'd discarded his jacket and waistcoat, wearing only the tastefully striped trousers in light and dark grey and a simple white shirt. It suited him, highlighting his olive skin and black hair, the clean lines of his broad shoulders and lean waist.

He stood casually, apparently relaxed with his hands in his pockets. Yet his silver eyes burned.

She'd come downstairs, intending to greet any more seduction attempts with a definitive yes, only to have him organise food, pour her orange juice, then try to push his marriage agenda on her, which was not what she wanted.

But then he'd reminded her of those nights together, of how they'd talked and discussed and argued. And a sudden realisation had gripped her—that though she might know how his brilliant mind worked, how science interested him and what he thought about the latest political situation in Europe, she had no idea about anything else.

There were facts about his life that she knew from

her internet research, but that's all they were. Just facts. And while she did know now what made him growl in the dark and what made him groan with pleasure, she'd didn't know his heart. She didn't know his hopes or his dreams or what he'd wanted to be when he grew up.

None of that should have mattered to her, not when she wasn't going to be marrying him no matter what he thought, so she wasn't sure why it felt so imperative now.

Yet the curiosity that gripped her felt more important than anything else. More important even than sex.

'No,' he said, his stare unwavering. 'I wouldn't have married you.'

A small, sharp pain shot through her. She ignored it. 'Why not?'

'Because a wife wasn't something I ever wanted.'

'So, what did you want then?'

His expression didn't change. 'To rule Santa Castelia to the best of my ability. Fill its treasury. Make sure the heir will be a decent king when he comes of age.'

'And then what?'

'What do you mean?'

'What did you want after that? Presumably, since you didn't want a wife or children, you had other plans. So, what were they?'

Something in his eyes flickered. 'It doesn't matter what they were. Nothing changes the situation we have to deal with now.'

'It does matter,' she disagreed. 'No one ever asked me what I wanted, Rafael, and I wonder if anyone had ever asked you the same. So now I'm asking. What do *you* want?'

A muscle flicked in his jaw. He was tense and she

didn't know why. It was clear something about her question bothered him.

'You,' he said roughly. 'I want you in my bed.'

A pulse of an answering heat went through her, but she pushed it aside. This was important. They'd never had the opportunity to talk about any of this and now they did. While she still hadn't changed her mind about marrying him, she wanted at least to understand him.

'That's not what I'm asking,' she said steadily. 'Did you want happiness? Success and a long life? More money? More power? Another country to rule?'

He was silent, the silver of his eyes blazing like liquid mercury. 'Why do you want to know these things? What purpose could knowing them possibly serve?'

'Isn't it obvious? I want to know you.'

That muscle flicked in his jaw again, his tall figure radiating tension. 'You know me already, Lia.'

'No, I don't. I know that you like whisky and Cuban cigars. And I know your thoughts on various political situations. I know you don't like the word "no".' She swallowed, a familiar, relentless ache unwinding inside her. The ache to get closer to him, to scratch the surface of him and find out what lay beneath. 'But those are all just parts of you. I don't know the whole. I know the Regent and bits and pieces of the man, but I want the rest, Rafael. If you want me to marry you, I *have* to know.'

Again, he stayed silent, merely staring at her.

'How long?' he demanded suddenly. 'How long have you wanted me?'

She didn't want to tell him because of what it would reveal, but then again, why not? Why shouldn't he know? She could hardly demand answers from him and then not give them herself.

'Ever since you arrived at the palace,' she said baldly.

'But you were only—'

'Seventeen, yes. Maybe I didn't quite know what it meant at the time, but over the years I worked it out, believe me.'

His gaze flared, though nothing else about him moved.

But she'd had months of those meetings in her father's study, of looking into his eyes, watching his face. Watching him.

She'd shocked him, hadn't she?

'Lia,' he said finally.

'What? I know you didn't feel the same way then, don't worry.'

Another long moment passed and then abruptly he turned and moved over to the fire, his back to her.

He was so tall, so broad. Outlined in flames he seemed somehow otherworldly. A demon or a dark angel, or even the Devil himself come to take her soul.

An eon passed and then he said, his voice roughened, 'Why? Why did you feel that way about me? I didn't even know you existed.'

She leaned forward and picked up her orange juice again, sipping at it, staring at his dark figure. He'd changed the subject, directing the topic away from himself, and now he'd turned away from her. Why? What was he trying to hide? Or did he not want to see her face?

Perhaps he needed honesty from her first before he shared anything with her and that was okay. She understood. Someone had to make the first move and it was clear that it wasn't going to be him. And there was probably a reason for that.

A thread of stubborn determination wound through her, tightening.

She'd hated all the expectations heaped on her—yes, she could admit that now—yet she'd done the same thing to him. Thinking she knew him when, really, she didn't.

She had to stop. She had to discover the man he actually was, not the man she'd always thought he was, and to do that she was going to have to give him the same honesty she demanded of him, earn his trust.

Why? When you've decided you're not marrying him?

Well, all those nights they'd spent talking together had formed a bond of friendship surely? So that made him her friend. And friends trusted each other.

It's not friendship you feel for him.

Her heartbeat speeded up, her breath catching, a knowledge she'd been avoiding shifting inside her, making her feel strangely vulnerable and uncertain.

He couldn't be more than a friend to her, that had never been allowed. Besides, hadn't she decided her feelings were of the teenage crush variety?

It is allowed now.

But something cold wound through and she shoved the thought away.

'I watched you arrive at the palace,' she said into the silence. 'I saw you get out of the limo. Everyone around me was scared of you, but the moment I saw you I knew there was nothing to be afraid of. You were strong and powerful, but…steady. Calm. In control. I knew you weren't going to be like Carlos. You were going to be different.'

He gave a rough laugh that held nothing but bitterness. '*Si*. So different that I got my brother's fiancée pregnant.'

So, he blamed himself. He thought that night together was his fault. His mistake and now, here he was, taking responsibility. Fixing it.

To hell with that.

'I wasn't his fiancée at the time,' she said. 'That didn't happen until after.'

'You were his intended. You've been intended for him since you were both three years old.'

'It wasn't just you in that bed, Rafael. It was me as well.'

'You were young. You were an innocent. You had no idea—'

'What I was doing?' Lia pushed herself to her feet, possessed by a sudden and intense need to take this burden from him or at least to share it.

He was always taking responsibility for things, always fixing things, and she understood that was his role, but he wasn't the Regent with her.

With her, he'd always been just Rafael.

'Yes, I was virgin and I let my feelings get the better of me,' she went on. 'I let my anger take control. But I could have got out of that bed at any time and I didn't.'

'You were inexperienced,' he said, ignoring her. 'Passion like that is so rare and once it takes hold of you—'

'Rafael, will you stop talking and listen to me!'

He turned from the fire suddenly and this time the expression on his face matched the fury in his eyes.

'I won't be thought of as a man who engages in casual affairs, sowing his seed far and wide,' he said harshly. 'I won't be a man who can't control himself. You will marry me and we'll tell the press some story of how it was some grand passion we both couldn't deny. That will reduce the scandal surrounding the throne at least and make Matias look less weak. And a marriage will be proof that it wasn't just a casual affair.'

She swallowed as a small shard of pain caught inside her, surprising her. Did he really think that? Because that night he'd been a force of nature, his unleashed passion sweeping her away. She'd hoped to forget Rafael in Matias's arms, but the opposite had happened.

She'd forgotten Matias instead and not only him, but her position as princess. She'd forgotten her parents and the weight of all those expectations.

She'd forgotten her country.

She'd forgotten her own name.

That night she'd been just a woman in the arms of a man she wanted and there had been nothing but the excitement of discovery and heat, and the heady blaze of a pleasure burned into her memory for ever.

The last thing it had ever been was casual.

'Is that how you view it, Rafael?' she asked, trying not to sound as if it mattered so very much when the opposite was true. 'Do you think that night we shared was just a casual affair?'

He said nothing, his expression closing down all of a sudden, as if all that fury had been doused.

And the feelings inside her tangled abruptly together in a tight, hard ball. Anger and pain and confusion, and a bright, hot need that surely felt too strong to be a mere teenage crush.

'It was never casual to me,' she said starkly, giving him the truth, unable to hold it back. *'Never.'*

He was very, very still. Every line of him radiated tension, as if there was something violent inside him struggling to get out and he couldn't let go of the leash, not for an instant.

'You want to know what it meant to me? You really want to know?' Those silver eyes of his blazed. 'Come here and I'll show you.'

Lia didn't hesitate, didn't second-guess. She'd already decided in the bedroom upstairs what she wanted and so she moved around the coffee table, coming closer. And he didn't look away, as if he couldn't take his eyes off her. And she was back again at that ball three months earlier...

The palace gardens had been lit beautifully for the gala, one of Santa Castelia's most anticipated social events, the last celebration of summer. It was always held outside and the weather had turned out perfectly, the intense heat of the day fading into a lovely soft warmth. Lights were strung in all the trees, more lights were wrapped around shrubs and statues and trellises. Fountains played and music drifted in the air. Palace staff moved among the crowd, carrying trays of drinks and food.

All of Santa Castelia's aristocracy were there, along with the nation's rich and famous. There were also more than a few international stars and captains of industry, because the late summer gala had a reputation for being a good party.

Lia stood next to Matias by one of the fountains, half listening to him talk with her father and a few government officials, half watching the crowds swirl around them.

Some of the women wore the most incredibly beautiful gowns, off the shoulder, plunging necklines, or some with a split up the thigh. Some glittered with se-

quins, while others looked like liquid satin, hugging every curve.

She envied the women who could wear gowns like that. She wasn't permitted anything that would show too much skin or be risqué, and her mother had advised her not to wear bold colours, that neutrals were more...decorous.

She hadn't been all that happy with Lia's choice of colour tonight—a bias-cut gown of deep, violet silk that gave a hint of her curves, but nothing too showy—but she'd let Lia wear it after she'd pleaded.

Just once she'd wanted to wear something that she felt pretty in, that didn't make her feel as if she was fading into the background, even though that was what was required of her, all the better to show off her future husband.

Matias hadn't commented on her gown and that was fine, it wasn't him she was wearing it for.

The crowd swirled and she watched, looking for a familiar, tall, broad figure, desperate to spot him. He hadn't joined her in her father's study for an entire week now and she wanted to know why. He hadn't told her anything. Just one night he hadn't turned up. She'd told herself it was a one-off, nothing serious, but then he hadn't come the next night either, or the one after that.

She wasn't able to talk to him, though she'd tried to surreptitiously ask for an audience since it was next to impossible trying to get time alone with him. Yet all her requests had been refused. She was starting to think that he was avoiding her and she didn't understand why.

Had she said something he hadn't liked? Done something, maybe? At their last meeting, their conversation had strayed into the personal a little, but surely that

wouldn't have made him stop coming? Maybe she'd of-
fended him...

Her heartbeat thudded and her palms felt sweaty. She
wanted to move, to walk around and see if she could spot
him, because standing here suddenly felt impossible.

Murmuring an excuse to Matias, she moved through
the crowds, trying to look as though she was going
somewhere, when in fact she was searching. Searching for him.

Then just when she thought that maybe he wasn't
here, she caught a glimpse of his tall figure. He was
standing in one of the arbours, surrounded by people,
since he inevitably was always surrounded by people.
A woman was talking to him, a beautiful blonde in a
red gown with a plunging neckline and he was looking
at her with that silver-eyed intensity that always made
Lia's breath catch.

It did now, though not in that way that sent a rush of
dizzying pleasure through her when they were alone.
This time it felt like a stab through the chest.

He wore formal evening clothes, all in black, even his
shirt, and with his massive height and warrior's build,
his innate authority, he was the most intensely charis-
matic man in the entire place.

Except she knew things about him that other people
didn't. Such as what he looked like when midnight struck
and he was relaxed and nursing a tumbler of Scotch.
When he was leaning back in his chair, no jacket or
tie, the top buttons of his shirt undone and his sleeves
rolled up. When their conversation was idle, on subjects
that weren't of any importance, such as the thriller he
was reading. Or the latest scientific advance he'd heard

about, since he liked science, particularly technology, and liked to keep abreast of what was happening.

When she made some silly joke and he smiled.

No one knew him when he was like that. No one knew him when he smiled.

No one but her.

She tried to tell herself that she had something of him the woman he was talking to didn't, hoping it would make her feel better. That she wasn't feeling jealous, not at all. She shouldn't be jealous anyway, because there was nothing to be jealous about. She was going to marry Matias and the Regent wasn't for her. He was older than she was, more experienced, more powerful, more...everything.

It didn't matter that the blonde was flirting with him.

He wasn't Lia's and he never would be.

She was just about to turn around and find her way back to Matias, when unexpectedly Rafael glanced at her over the woman's shoulder.

And his silver eyes met hers. And held.

And she knew that she'd let slip something she shouldn't and he'd seen what must have been in her gaze. Her whole soul.

He didn't look away, just stared at her.

Lia had no experience with men, none at all except for her interactions with Matias, which were friendly, but nothing more. She knew what sexual hunger and passion were, of course, but only intellectually.

Now though, she could feel both welling up inside her, a hot tide that felt as though it was choking her, a mirror of the same thing glowing in his eyes.

He felt it, too.

For a second they stared at each other, though it

felt like hours, days. Eons. Then, without any hurry, he turned his gaze back to the woman in front of him and carried on talking to her as if nothing had happened.

Lia's face felt hot and tears pricked her eyes. Her chest was tight and painful and she didn't even know why.

It wasn't as though he could suddenly stop talking to that woman and come over to talk to her, not when everyone was watching him. Not when she was a woman he was barely supposed to even know, let alone speak to.

Their friendship—what else could she call it?—was secret and had to remain so.

Left with nothing else to do, Lia swallowed the ache inside her, buried it deep and turned and went back to Matias.

But she didn't have to swallow that ache and she didn't have to turn away. Matias wasn't here and there was nothing between Rafael and her any longer.

So, she stood in front of him and looked into his burning gaze. 'Show me, then,' she said.

She was so close, looking at him the way she used to on those nights where they would argue about some philosophical topic or politics. Direct, fearless, challenging. They weren't talking about politics or philosophy, not now, yet the glow in her eyes was the same, a deep, aching blue with heat glowing at the centre, like fire in the dark heart of a sapphire.

But he was angry, he could feel it eating away at him, eating away at his control.

Angry at her for wanting him, for telling him that

night had meant something to her when it would be so much easier for them both if it hadn't.

Angry at the questions she kept throwing at him, picking away at him, trying to get under his skin.

'But those are all just parts of you. I don't know the whole...'

She couldn't know the whole, that was the problem. Parts of him were all he had to give. The parts he had control over, not the ones he didn't.

The violent, hot, primitive parts of himself that no one needed to even know about, let alone see.

He'd managed to derail her by turning her questions back on her, yet that had rebounded on him to a certain extent. He'd had no idea how long she'd wanted him, or that she'd felt so passionately about their night together.

You don't know her as well as you thought, do you?

Perhaps he didn't. Perhaps he was just as guilty as everyone else, treating her just like the innocent, pure Crown Princess rather than the sharp, intelligent, fiery woman she actually was. And she *was* a woman, not a girl. A woman with her own needs and desires, as passionate and intense as he was...

He was supposed to be in control of himself. He wasn't supposed to let his hunger off the chain, because that was dangerous.

He was dangerous.

But...she wanted to know him. She wanted to know what that night had meant to him, so maybe it was time to show her. Let her see the parts of himself that he kept hidden. Not everything, of course, because no one needed to see those. Just the ones that could be shared in the dark.

So, he reached for her, his hands lifting, his fingers

sliding through the black silk of her hair. Drawing her close so very slowly, because he had to be slow. He had to be careful otherwise the sheer weight of his hunger would crush them both.

She was breathing fast, too, looking at him as though he was the only thing in her entire world. Her hands lifted to his chest, her palms pressing lightly against him, sending bolts of white lightning through him.

The sweetness of her scent surrounded him, making him feel hungry and lost and desperate.

Careful. Be careful.

Oh, he would. He'd let himself off the leash, but only a little. Just enough for her to get a taste, but no more.

'Lia,' he breathed. '*Princesa...mi princesa...*'

Her hands slid up his chest and around his neck and she was coming up on her toes, her mouth finding his.

And he was lost.

His fingers closed into fists in her hair and he was kissing her hard and deep, as if the existence of the entire world depended on this kiss and that it would end if he stopped.

So he didn't stop, he pushed his tongue into her mouth, tasting her, desperate for the flavour he remembered from that night, a sweetness he couldn't place though he'd spent all night searching for it. Honey or brown sugar or cinnamon, or some kind of heady combination of all three. She was delicious, every kind of good thing he'd ever tasted, and he couldn't get enough.

She gave a soft moan, her body going pliant against his, her arms tightening around his neck. Her mouth was hungry on his, the sharp edge of her teeth against his lips.

Electricity shot through him.

The night they'd spent together she'd been an innocent, all sweetly hesitant and uncertain. And despite the need in him, he'd had to go carefully with her.

But there was nothing hesitant or uncertain about her now. She was as starved as he was and just as demanding, and it was obvious that careful wasn't what she wanted.

Something in him snapped as her hands clawed open the buttons of his shirt and he broke the kiss, dragging that wretched hoodie up and over her head. Then he shoved down the sweatpants, too, dragged her down on to the soft silken rug in front of the fire and got her beneath him.

Her black hair spilled over the jewel-bright colours of the rug, her cheeks flushed, her eyes black with desire as they looked up into his.

'Please, Rafael,' she whispered, reaching for him. 'Oh, please.'

She was pleading for him the way she had that night, holding nothing back, yet this time he could see it, her desire laid bare in her eyes.

It drove his own hunger to a sharp, bright point.

He had to be careful, so careful.

His hands shook as he pulled open his trousers before reaching down between her pale thighs, shoving aside the pretty lace of her knickers. Then, sliding his hands beneath the soft rounded curve of her bottom, he lifted her, positioning himself, before thrusting hard and deep, a groan escaping him as the intoxicating, slick heat of her sex gripped him tight.

She cried out, too, arching beneath him, her luscious mouth opening, red and swollen from his kiss. Her gaze was on his as he paused inside her, looking down at her, remembering that night, that moment when they were joined for the first time.

The memory swelled between them, filling the space, aching and hot and desperate.

Her face had been in darkness then, but he could see it now, lit by the fire, her skin rose and gold, flames reflected in her eyes. She looked at him as if he mattered, as if he was everything to her, and when she lifted her hand and touched his cheek, he felt something shift and turn inside him.

It was a feeling he couldn't name that pressed against his heart and it was familiar. He'd felt it then, too.

Careful, remember? You hurt people.

He remembered. But he wouldn't hurt her. He would *never* hurt her.

He reached for her hand, brought her fingers to his mouth and kissed the tips of them. Then the urge to move became too intense to ignore and he slid himself out, then back in again, a long, luxurious glide that made them both gasp.

Her hands touched him again, his face, his neck, his throat. Down through the halves of his open shirt to his chest. Touching him as if she couldn't get enough, as if she was starved for the feel of his skin.

He'd gone too long without a woman who wanted him like this.

He'd gone too long without *her*.

Three months of fighting it, of ignoring it. Of pretending the desire for her wasn't burning as hotly and as strongly as it had those nights in her father's study. Pretending that it hadn't grown, fed by that one long, hot night she'd been in his bed.

He'd pushed it aside, ignored it. Done the right thing

and acted as though it hadn't happened. But it had. He'd ached, he'd burned and now that he had her here beneath him, he knew he couldn't let her go.

That baby was his, but so was she.

He slid his hands beneath her, gathering her close, pushing deeper, harder, driving them on because this couldn't last. The pleasure was much too strong.

She twisted in his arms, as if she was desperate to get closer, so he found her mouth and took it. Kissing her hard so that they were joined here, too.

Her arms wound around his neck and she moved with him, the pleasure becoming so acute it was almost painful.

The orgasm built and built, then it was flooding through him, drowning him in pleasure, and he could feel it take her, too, her body convulsing around his, a cry of release vibrating in her throat.

For long moments he lay there with her in his arms, unable to move. Unable to even think as aftershock after aftershock pulsed through him. Her face was turned into his neck and he could feel her warm breath against his skin, hear the ragged sound of it in his ear.

That intense possessiveness moved through him and he responded without thought, lifting his head and looking down at her sprawled out on the rug beneath him.

She was all pale silken skin, naked and perfect, the curve of her stomach where their child lay making everything in him want to growl.

'You are mine, Lia,' he said roughly, forcefully. 'You will marry me.'

She didn't move, looking up at him. Deep in the shadowed blue of her eyes, passion still smouldered. 'Okay,' she said.

Surprise rippled through him. He'd expected another refusal. 'What do you mean, okay?'

She lifted her hand, one delicate finger stroking his cheekbone in a featherlight touch. 'I mean, yes, I will marry you.'

CHAPTER SEVEN

LIA HAD MADE the decision as she lay beneath him, staring up into his eyes and seeing his desperation and desire, all the blazing intensity that he hid from other people, but never from her.

He needed her, she understood, though what it was that he needed she didn't know. He probably didn't even realise it himself, but that didn't change the fact that he did.

Lots of people had expected things from her, but no one had ever *needed* her. Not the way she sensed Rafael did. And he didn't require her to be anything or to act a certain way. All he'd wanted was for her to say yes to his proposal and be his wife.

That need had made something inside her echo in response, the ache that she'd never been able to ignore or force away, that had lived in her heart growing deeper and stronger every time she saw him.

How could she let him bear sole responsibility for this and then deny him the means to fix it? If she said no, it would make everything harder and not only for herself and her child, but for him as well.

He was a bastard and he didn't want that for his child. What he wanted was to help her and, after what he'd said about his mother being a single parent, she could understand his motivation.

Denying him just because she wanted to be chosen for herself felt selfish, especially when all he was thinking of was what was best for their child.

So she wouldn't be selfish. And she wouldn't let him have to deal with this on his own.

She would marry him—after all, it wasn't exactly a life sentence. There would be considerable compensations.

His blazing stare narrowed. 'What? Just like that?'

'Yes.' She smiled at his suspicious expression. 'Just like that.'

He searched her face, though what he was looking for she had no idea. 'Why?' he demanded.

'Why?' Her finger brushed over his cheekbone again, loving the feel of his skin against hers. 'Because you're right, I have to think of our child and what's best for them, and I think being your wife will make things easier for all of us in the long run, especially when it comes to the press. And because I can't leave you to take sole responsibility for what happened.' She met his gaze squarely. 'I know I said I wanted to be chosen for myself, but that's making it all about me and I can't do that. Not when you'll suffer repercussions, too.'

The look in his eyes was full of something ferocious that she didn't understand, but it made her breath catch.

'Are you sure?' he asked roughly.

Lia stroked her finger across his cheekbone again, relishing the feel of him. Already she could feel that terrible, nagging ache inside her quieting, settling.

It was the right decision. She knew it in her bones.

'Yes,' she said. 'I'm sure.'

He said nothing, still staring at her intently, but she

was starting to get distracted by the burnished bronze of his olive skin glowing in the firelight between the open halves of his shirt and by the pulse at the base of his throat, the scattering of crisp black hair across his chest.

Oh, she wanted to see more. She wanted to see all of him. This wasn't enough to do him justice.

His body was pressing against hers, the weight of him reminding her of the intensity of the pleasure they'd just shared. She could feel the pulse of it still echoing inside her, could still feel *him* inside her.

Then suddenly Rafael bent and his mouth covered hers in a possessive, intense kiss, and there was nothing she could do but answer it. Kissing him back, desperate all at once to taste him, to drown their mutual hunger in passion.

There was nothing more to talk about now anyway. She'd agreed to be his wife and she was happy with her decision. Especially if would meant getting more of him, just like this.

She pushed at his chest so that they rolled over again, him on his back, her on top.

The flames from the fire were hot, illuminating his face. The ice had disappeared, there was nothing but that liquid mercury left and it swallowed her whole.

Fierce desire and a blazing satisfaction flooded through her, because finally he was hers. A man so full of intensity and heat that his soul must be a bonfire and he was, truly, all hers.

She hadn't realised how badly she'd wanted that until now.

Lia kissed him hungrily and then rained a trail of hot kisses over his hard jaw and the strong arch of his neck. She pressed her mouth against the beating pulse at the base of his throat, tasting the salty, musky flavour of his skin.

He didn't stop her, letting her follow the trail down over his chest and further, tracing the lines of his abs to the open zip of his trousers. She pushed her hand down inside and found him, smooth and hot and hard, pressing against her palm. She squeezed him and he made a harsh, masculine growling sound that excited her.

She had no experience of any of this, but that didn't bother her. She wanted to explore him, look at him in the firelight, discover all the power contained in his hard, muscular body. Unleash the passion she knew burned beneath his icy, controlled surface.

She didn't have to hold back any more and neither did he.

Trailing her lips further down over the hard lines of his abs, she went lower, gripping him, licking the hard length of his sex, then taking him into her mouth.

He growled again, his hips arching, and then he said her name in a hoarse, desperate voice.

It thrilled her, made her feel powerful. For so long she'd been nothing but a vessel for her parents' dreams. For Matias's vision of a perfect queen. For the expectations of an entire nation.

She was never herself, never had any power of her own.

But she did now. Here before the fire with Rafael beneath her, she was strong. She could make the infamously hard, cool Prince Regent of Santa Castelia lose his mind.

So, she did, giving him as much pleasure as she could with her mouth, her teeth and her tongue, relishing the rich, exotic flavour of him. Until he pulled her away with desperate hands, tugging her on top of him, guiding her until she was sitting astride his hips.

He was still half dressed, his shirt open, his skin like warm satin against hers, and he was magnificent. A god. She ran her fingers across the hard expanse of his chest, unable to get enough of him, but he cursed roughly in Spanish under his breath and abruptly sat up.

His mouth closed on hers, his hands on her hips, lifting her up and then bringing her down on him, impaling her.

Pleasure was like a lightning strike, bolting up her spine, expanding like a blast wave, tearing a gasp from her. His arms closed around her, holding her tight as he began to move.

He was everywhere, surrounding her with his heat and his strength and the warm scent that was intrinsically Rafael. The taste of him was in her mouth, the hard demand of his lips on hers, and she was lost to everything, the outside world falling away.

The man holding her wasn't the Regent, forbidden to her and as unreachable as the stars. He was just Rafael. The man she'd talked with and argued with, and laughed with at night in her father's study, over whisky and cigars.

The man who would be her husband.

Lia closed her eyes and gave herself up to him, letting him take her away from the outside world, surrounding her in heat and pleasure, and the promise of more to come.

Rafael held Lia in his arms for long moments, her warm body relaxed against his. She'd turned her face against his chest, her breath ghosting over his skin. It seemed as if she'd fallen asleep, which she probably needed after what had happened earlier in the day.

He should feel good, holding her like this, but he didn't. Something felt wrong, his chest was tight, as if he couldn't get enough air.

Trying to go carefully so he didn't wake her, he shifted her from his chest and on to the rug. Grabbing the throw from the couch, he wrapped it around her and put a cushion underneath her head. She made a sweet little sound, curling into the throw and snuggling against the cushion.

The constriction in his chest became acute, the need to move holding him tight in his grip, and he stepped out into the hallway, striding to the stairs and going up them with no thought to where he was going.

A couple of minutes later, he found himself in his office, a warm, comfortable room down at the back of the second floor. It had windows that showcased Santa Castelia's magnificent mountains and the green forest that carpeted the slopes. Everything was outlined in white and black, the lowering sky making the view seem oddly oppressive.

Or maybe that was just his mood.

The need for air hadn't lifted, his chest ached and he rubbed at it absently as he crossed over to the heavy, oak desk that dominated the room.

Now she'd agreed to marry him, there were things he had to do, things to organise, a nation to face and a brother to talk to.

And he didn't want to do any of them. He wanted to hold Lia in his arms, touch the soft roundness of her stomach, where his child lay.

She is doing this for you.

The iron band around his chest tightened still further and he found himself looking at the doorway, as if he could still see her lying fast asleep by the fire, curled around the baby she carried.

She had clung to him as he'd touched her, as he'd taken her, driven mad by the way she'd taken him in her mouth, tasted him. So innocent and yet full of passion, inexperienced and yet desperate.

The combination had been too much for him, he hadn't been able to bear it. He'd wanted to get as close to her as he possibly could, so he'd hauled her away from him and into his arms, holding her tight against his chest, kissing her deeply as he'd thrust inside her. And felt her welcome him...

Her arms had closed around him and he'd felt her relax, felt her give herself up to him...

Dios, he didn't understand it. He'd ruined her, taken her future away from her and yet she'd told him she couldn't let him take sole responsibility for fixing this, that she didn't want him suffering from repercussions, too, and had agreed to marry him. Then she'd held him as if she never wanted to let him go.

Why? When he'd done nothing for her but give her pain?

But isn't that what you always give people? Pain?

His jaw tightened and he turned back to the window, crossing to it and putting his hands on the glass. The surface was cool, but not cool enough. It felt as if he was suddenly burning up inside, as if there was a volcano inside him, heat building and building and if he wasn't careful he would explode.

That was dangerous, so dangerous. He had to cool himself down somehow.

There was a door that led to an outside terrace, so he pulled it open and stepped outside.

Snow fell on his burning skin, stinging like acid, the cold so intense it stole his breath. He ignored it, striding to the parapet that bound the stone terrace and then back again, working out this burning feeling inside him with movement.

Why the hell was he feeling like this anyway? The sex had been great and she'd agreed to his proposal. They would be married as soon as he could arrange it and, once all the media furore had died down, everything would be fine. They could then get on to thinking about their future together.

She's doing this for you and that's the problem.

Rafael took in a deep breath, the cold scouring the inside of his lungs.

He didn't want to think about that, but he couldn't help himself. If she was doing this for him, then it meant she cared about him. And he didn't like that thought, not one bit. Because why would she?

No one had ever cared about him all that much, not even his mother. And he sure as hell never had any kind of caring from his father, not that he'd wanted it anyway and definitely not from that old bastard.

Rafael put his hands on the stone of the parapet, ignoring the bite of ice against his palms, and leaned against it, trying to deal with the unease that gripped him.

Perhaps she didn't care that much about him. Perhaps she only thought she did. She was, after all, young and inexperienced, and their physical chemistry was intense. Maybe she'd mistaken passion for caring.

Anyway, it could have been worse. She could be in

love with him and that was something he could never accept. Not when love was so destructive and caused so much pain.

After all, what is there to love about you?

He crushed that thought. This wasn't about him, this was about Lia. This was about making sure that whatever she felt for him didn't become something more. Luckily, he had a solution.

Whatever she felt for him, he'd simply ignore it and then it would die.

What about if she gets bitter like your mother did?

Then he wouldn't give her cause for bitterness. He'd pay attention to her, take care of her, he'd make her happy.

Can you, though? Can you make anyone happy?

The ice in the air around him had somehow crawled into his veins and had begun to wind through him.

He ignored it. Of course he'd make her happy. He'd give her everything she could ever need. A beautiful home and a child. Support for whatever career she wanted to take on. Company when she needed someone to talk to. Great sex to keep her satisfied.

He'd be an exemplary husband since wasn't that what husbands did?

Rafael took a breath and shoved himself away from the icy parapet, conscious that no matter what he'd just told himself, the cold hadn't touched the strange heat inside him. It kept building, kept burning.

Perhaps if he did some work, that would help. That would keep him on track and stop his mind from going on this endless track, this second-guessing himself when he never, *ever* second-guessed himself.

He turned back to the door, only to see it opening and

a small figure standing in the doorway. She was wrapped up in that throw, her black hair spilling over her shoulders, her skin pale and bare and so very unprotected.

More heat flooded through him, along with an unfamiliar protectiveness.

'Rafael?' Lia wiped snow from her eyes. 'Are you okay? What are you doing out here?'

Instantly he was moving, striding through the falling snow to where she stood. 'Go inside,' he ordered. 'You'll catch your death.'

'But, what about—?'

'Inside.' He put his hands on her hips and gave her a gentle push so that she took a few steps back into the warmth of his office, then followed her in, closing the door.

She frowned, one hand clutching the throw around her, the other reaching to brush the snow from his shoulders. Then she went up on her tiptoes and brushed it out of his hair, too.

'Me?' she murmured as she did so. 'What about you? And what were you doing out on the terrace in the middle of a blizzard, idiot man?'

Something in her tone gripped him and held him tight. She sounded as if she was already his wife and had been for years, a warm tenderness in the words that he didn't know what to do with.

It made him feel off balance and he was *never* off balance.

He was always the one in charge, the one who made the decisions. He was the CEO, the Prince Regent. He was never in doubt, yet today this small woman had turned everything he thought about himself on its head.

Rafael took her wrist in a firm but gentle grip and

pulled her hand away from him. 'I needed some air. What are you doing here? I thought you were asleep.'

'I was, but I woke up and you weren't there.' She didn't pull out of his hold, merely standing there and looking up at him. 'Are you all right?'

'Of course. Why would I not be?'

The crease between her fine, silky black brows deepened. 'You looked upset.'

He didn't like that she'd seen the doubt inside him, the uncertainty that no matter how much he told himself he didn't feel, he did all the same.

'I am not upset.' He kept his tone casual, betraying nothing. 'Perhaps you would like a shower or a bath? You have some time. Dinner will be in a few hours.'

She was quiet a moment, just looking at him. 'You don't like talking about yourself, do you?'

The tight feeling in his chest that had driven him from the living room reminded him once more of its presence. 'No.' He gave her a smile that he knew held no amusement whatsoever. 'I find myself very dull.'

'I don't.' The expression on her face was searching. 'I'm going to be your wife, Rafael. Shouldn't a wife know a little more about her husband?'

He didn't want to talk about himself, not when there was nothing interesting about him or his past. Then again, he knew more about her than she knew about him and that didn't seem fair. And she was right; she would be his wife, so perhaps he could give her a little more?

'Fine,' he said. 'What do you want to know?'

Her mouth curved. 'Anything.'

'All right.' He stroked his thumb absently over the silky skin of her wrist. 'I could start with my father, though what to say about him that you don't already

know? He used to visit me when I was growing up in
Barcelona. Never at the apartment I shared with my
mother, only ever in his territory, which was the hotel
where he met my mother. I wasn't a son to him. I was
an object to gloat over, a reminder of his own prowess,
and really, it was pity that I was a mistake. I would have
made a much better king than his legitimate child.' He
couldn't hide the bitter edge in his voice, so he didn't
bother. 'My mother, on the other hand, was decent. She
didn't like me, but she cared for me all the same. She
fed and clothed me, taught me right from wrong. Saw
me as well educated as she could manage.'

She never loved you, though, and why would she?

He knew why. But that wasn't his truth to tell.

'She died when I was eighteen,' he went on, conscious of a certain tension gripping his muscles, an ache
he hadn't even been aware of until this moment. 'Is that
what you wanted to know?'

CHAPTER EIGHT

RAFAEL'S EXPRESSION WAS so neutral as he said the words, his tone so casual. As if none of the things he said had any real meaning. As if they didn't touch him in any way.

But she knew they did and the signs were there in the burning silver of his eyes. Anger, hot and deep.

It made sense though, that he was angry. Why wouldn't he be? Carlos was always going to be a terrible father and then losing his mother. A mother who hadn't liked him...

That felt personally painful to her, though she had no idea why.

He'd never mentioned a word of this in the nights they'd spent together, talking and arguing about everything under the sun except their personal lives.

'I'm so sorry,' she said thickly. 'I didn't know.'

'Why would you?' His expression betrayed nothing, his tone mild. 'I didn't tell you.'

She stared up into his face, searching. His childhood must have been painful and yet he sounded casual, the way he always did. 'That must have been awful.'

He lifted a shoulder. 'No more terrible than other people with bad parents. It was all so long ago anyway. It doesn't matter now.'

It did matter, though, she could sense it. And now that she looked past the careful, expressionless mask he always wore, she could see it in his eyes, too.

'If it doesn't matter now,' she said quietly, 'then why are you still angry?'

Rafael's gaze flickered and she knew she'd struck a nerve. 'I'm not angry.'

'Like you weren't upset just now?'

'Lia—'

'Why do you always do this?' she said before she could think better of it. 'Why do you always pretend that nothing's wrong? You start talking about painful things as if you're asking for milk in your tea.'

His expression hardened. 'If you don't like the way I talk about certain topics, then perhaps you shouldn't ask questions about them.'

Why are you pushing him now? It won't help anything and it'll only make him angry all over again. You'll have plenty of time to talk about this later.

That was true. And it seemed a pity to shatter the fragile sense of closeness they'd shared with an argument.

She already knew that they could argue with each other well enough, but what she really should be finding out was what they'd be like when they weren't arguing.

Lia pulled her hand out of his grip and laid it on his chest, feeling his warmth and firm strength. 'I'm sorry. If you don't want to talk about it, then we won't.'

His expression remained impassive, no hint of what he was feeling escaping, yet his gaze was so fierce. How could people not see how brightly he burned? They thought he was so cold and hard, but he wasn't.

He was a volcano in an ice field and lava gleamed beneath the snow.

Then unexpectedly, he put his hand over hers where it rested on his shirt, his palm warm. 'I shouldn't have snapped at you, *princesa*. The truth is…that is not an easy part of my life to think about. My mother did not want a child. My birth was not her choice. But she had me anyway and cared for me as well as she could. It was upsetting when she died.'

Shock rippled through her. Not so much for what he'd said, but for the fact that he'd said it at all. And prefaced it with an apology.

But this was a gift, wasn't it? He was giving her something of himself and this time she hadn't had to ask for it.

It left her with other questions, such as why a mother would make it obvious to her child—to her blameless little boy—that he hadn't been wanted.

Lia had never chosen for this pregnancy to happen, but she couldn't imagine not wanting her baby, let alone making it clear to them that they weren't a choice she wanted to make.

'I can imagine,' she said carefully, before pausing and thinking a moment. Then she went on a little hesitantly, because she wasn't sure if this was something he'd considered or not. 'Rafael, I…do want this baby. You know that, don't you?'

His thumb moved gently, stroking her hand where it lay beneath his. 'I assumed so, since you are still pregnant.'

'Well, it's true. My parents had difficulty conceiving and eventually they had to do it via IVF. And when I found out that I was pregnant, I…was upset. But I knew immediately that I would keep it, because it was yours.'

Her throat closed, realisation settling down inside her even as she said the words. 'This baby is a gift, Rafael. It's a gift for both of us.'

The look in his eyes shifted, some deep, powerful emotion rippling at last across his blunt, compelling features. He said nothing, letting go of her hand, but only to reach for her, drawing her in close, that hot, bright gaze on hers.

He didn't know what to say, she understood that. Or, no, perhaps it was because there was *too* much to say and he didn't know where to begin, or even that he didn't have the words for it.

But she knew one thing at least: what she'd said had meant something profound to him.

'It's all right,' she said softly, so that he didn't have to. 'You don't have to say anything. Just know I believe that with all my heart.'

His clothing was cool and damp where it pressed against her, the effects of his being out in the snow, but already she could feel the incredible heat of his body burning away the cold, burning into her.

Her only covering was the throw she'd wrapped around herself and she was still cold from her brief exposure to the outside air, but now he was warming her up. Making her feel hot and breathless and ready for him once again.

'This marriage of ours will work, Lia.' His voice was rough and demanding and full of an iron determination. 'I'll make sure of it. For the sake of our child's happiness.'

'Yes,' she said simply, because how could she argue against their child being happy? She couldn't and she didn't want to, even if some small part of her ached for reasons she couldn't articulate.

Rafael's expression changed, his brows drawing down. 'You're not convinced?'

Damn. How had he managed to pick up on that sliver of doubt? Especially when she hadn't said anything aloud?

'Of course I'm convinced.' She tried to sound firm. 'Did I say I wasn't?'

'No, but your expression would say otherwise.'

Lia cursed herself silently. She'd become very good at hiding her emotions, at locking them down, so good that even those closest to her hadn't known when she was in a temper or upset.

Well, everyone except Rafael. She didn't know how he did it, but he always knew.

She stared at her hands where they were pressed to the crisp cotton of his shirt, trying to figure out why she was reluctant to tell him. Because what did it matter if she did? Weren't husbands and wives supposed to be honest with each other?

'Oh,' she said on a long breath. 'I was simply hoping that there might be some happiness left over for us, too.'

His hold shifted on her, one long finger catching her beneath the chin and tilting her face up so his hot gaze met hers. 'Did you think I would leave you out of the equation? No, *princesa*. I know what it is to have a desperately unhappy mother and I wouldn't wish that on any child, still less our own. So all you need to do is tell me what you want and I'll give it to you.'

You want his heart.

The thought came out of nowhere and she shut it down hard. Because, no, she didn't want his heart. Her feelings for him were large and powerful, but it didn't involve hearts, not at all.

'What I want is for you to kiss me,' she said, instead, and it wasn't a lie. She did want that.

So, he bent, his mouth brushing over hers in a surprisingly delicate kiss. Her lips tingled from the slight pressure, the heat of him warming her straight through and making her hungry for him again.

She shouldn't have these doubts. They'd have all the time in the world to discuss them later and, anyway, it would be all right. This marriage between them *would* work. What with her stubborn determination and his cold focus, how could it not?

'You won't regret it,' Rafael said as he lifted his head, a fierce expression rippling over his face, as if the door to a furnace had been opened and the heat of the flames had licked out. 'I promise, Lia, that I will do all I can to make you happy.'

He meant it, she could see the resolve in his face, and it made her chest go tight. What more could she want?

You want love.

Lia ignored the thought, since it was wrong. She already had love from her parents and that was enough of a burden to bear, heavy as it was with expectations and pressures. She didn't need that same burden from Rafael.

Instead she rose on her tiptoes and lifted her chin, brushing her mouth over his. 'You'd better start now, then,' she murmured. 'Because I'm deeply regretting the fact that you're not kissing me.'

'Then I'd better remedy that, hadn't I?' he said, before sweeping her up in his arms and carrying her upstairs to his bed.

Rafael was feeling well satisfied about a great many things by the time they came back downstairs to the living area.

Lia had picked up his discarded shirt from the bedroom floor and had put it on as if it was hers, a possessive gesture that made him want to take her back to bed and teach her a few more new ways to pleasure each other. Except they were both ravenous and she, especially, needed something to eat.

He led her back out into the living area where the refreshments had been laid, making her sit on the couch while he brought her more food. Then he sat next to her and asked her questions as she ate, because he wanted to know how her pregnancy had been.

He'd promised her she'd never regret agreeing to be his wife and he wanted to start by making sure she was well physically.

Luckily, apart from some early morning sickness that had faded, things had gone fairly smoothly, though it was clear as she talked, that she'd found her situation distressing in the extreme.

He could understand that and he understood, too, why she'd thought marriage to Matias was the only answer. She'd wanted to protect her baby and that was the best way to do it.

Still, he was here and now he would take care of both of them.

He sat back on the couch and watched her as she sat cross-legged, the sleeves of his shirt rolled up, taking delicate bites of the sandwich she was in the process of eating.

She looked very young and very beautiful, reminding him once again of the young woman behind the desk in her father's study, challenging him with a lift of her pointed chin and a glint in her blue eyes. Making him have to defend his arguments and explain his thinking. Forcing him to think past his own natural arrogance and his tendency to reduce things to black and white.

He hadn't thought one young woman could have taught him so much about himself and the flaws in his thinking, yet she had.

'I know the treasury needs money,' Lia said, waving her cigar at him. *'But how do you balance that with what the people need?'*

'Do the people not need money?' He took a sip of his own whisky, irritated that he had to explain himself. *'Santa Castelia's treasury has been decimated by Carlos's rule. That's why I was brought in, Lia. To help fill the coffers so when Matias takes over, he can implement all the social programs he wants.'*

Lia shifted in the armchair, leaning forward to put her elbows on the desk, her blue eyes glowing with fervour. A strand of black hair fell over her face, but she made no move to push it back. She held his gaze without fear, as if he wasn't the ruler of her country and not given to taking kindly to people disagreeing with him.

'But people need some of that money now. Leaving it in the treasury won't help anyone.'

'Interest will be accruing—'

'The poor can't live off interest accruing.' She met his gaze head on. *'You need to implement some of those social programs now.'*

Rafael stared back, for a moment unable to think of a single thing to say because no one had ever interrupted him before, still less about fiscal policy. Oh, people did challenge him on occasion, but it was always very carefully done and often in the form of 'advice' rather than a command.

But not Lia. Out in the palace she might be shy and quiet, saying nothing, but in the privacy of Gian's *study, she wasn't like that at all. She was blunt with her opinions and passionate, with a strong sense of justice and fairness.*

She was...magnificent. And he found that he liked hearing her opinions. He liked arguing with her. He liked being challenged by her, even if it irritated him. It kept him on his toes, kept him sharp, and he hadn't realised how much he'd needed that until now.

'Social programs require money,' he pointed out. 'Which the treasury doesn't have.'

She waved that away as if it was nothing. 'But can't we do both? Can't we implement some for the most needy while keeping an eye on the bottom line?' Her cheeks had gone pink, passion glittering in her blue eyes. 'Why does everything have to be one or the other? The world isn't black and white, Rafael, so why do we have to do things as if it was?'

He was riveted, despite himself. 'So how would you suggest we go about it? Given how depleted the treasury is and how many loans the country has at the moment.'

Her gaze narrowed and she stared at him for a long moment, obviously thinking hard. Then she took a sip of her whisky, put the tumbler down. 'I don't know,' she said honestly. 'But if you give me a couple of days to think about how to do it, I'll bring you a plan.'

He couldn't refuse. He didn't want to. 'Do it,' he said. 'And if it looks like it could work, I'll implement it.'

The next night she'd come to him with a plan and—with a few tweaks—he'd been as good as his word and had implemented it. And it had been a success.

She'd encouraged him to think about more than just

numbers and figures. About the people his policies affected.

She is wasted on you...

No, he could use her. Put that clever mind of hers to work for him. Be his right-hand woman in the board-room as well as the bedroom.

She finished the sandwich and put her plate down, giving him a look from beneath her lashes. 'You're look-ing very pleased with yourself. What have you just been thinking about?'

'You and what an asset you are.' He leaned over to the table to pour some more orange juice into a glass for her. 'You probably haven't had time to think about what you might like to do with your future, but I wonder if you'd consider a role in my company.'

Surprise rippled over her lovely face. 'You mean work for you?'

'Yes. Why not? I can guarantee it would be challeng-ing and exciting. You'd enjoy it, I think.'

She blinked. 'Oh... And what about our child?'

'There are many options we can consider. A nanny or we can have the child at work with us.' He handed her the orange juice. 'I am the boss, after all, and I can arrange it to suit our needs whatever they are.'

She took the glass, sipping carefully, watching him over the rim, her expression thoughtful. 'And where would you consider us living?'

He shrugged. 'Anywhere you like. It would probably be polite not to live here after Matias becomes King. I'm not sure he'd like the former Regent looking over his shoulder.'

'Did you ever want to be King?' she asked. 'Or con-sider changing things so you could take the throne?'

He didn't even have to think about it. He wanted nothing of his father's, especially not his crown. 'No. Matias will be a good king when he gains a little confidence and I'm ready for other challenges.'

Lia tilted her head. 'Why did you agree to be Regent?'

It was a good question and one he saw no reason not to answer. 'Because someone needed to fill Santa Castelia's treasury and someone needed to guide Matias.'

'Yes, but why you?'

He raised a brow. 'You think I wasn't a suitable choice?'

'No, it's just… Well, it's clear you have no love for Carlos, so why bother with his crown?'

This was edging into uncomfortable territory, but again, there was no reason not to tell her. She'd been so honest with him after all and, besides, it was no secret.

'I wanted to set an example,' he said. 'To show Matias what a ruler should be. Steady and calm, and absolutely in control of both himself and the country.'

'Ah, yes, that's what you're doing with this marriage, too, aren't you?'

'Yes. People need to see that I am nothing like Carlos. And they need to see it in Matias as well.'

She gave him a slightly puzzled look. 'But it's obvious you're nothing like him, Rafael. Everyone can already see that.'

Can they, though? When even your own mother couldn't?

The unease inside him wound deeper, making the anger that had always burned sullenly in his heart flicker into life. He'd felt it out in his office, too, when he'd told her about his parents, about his father's egregious behaviour with him and his mother's dutiful care.

That Lia could see it had made him uncomfortable and he'd been glad when she hadn't pushed for more. So glad he'd given her another little tidbit just to show his appreciation. She'd been so sweet, too, putting her hand on his chest, pressing herself against him, her eyes full of sympathy.

He'd liked that. It had made the cold, icy part of him feel warm, which was perhaps a bad thing since his emotions had to remain frozen. Then again, channelling them into physical passion with a woman who wanted him, with his soon-to-be wife, wasn't wrong. And as long as he could keep doing that, everything would be fine.

What if she wants more?

Rafael pushed that thought aside, because really, what more could she want?

'That's because I work hard to make sure that's all they see,' he said casually. 'My father's genes aren't exactly easy to overcome.'

Lia blinked. 'Your father's genes?'

'He was a man very much driven by his not-inconsiderable hungers, *princesa*. Surely you remember? He was entitled, arrogant, selfish and had no self-control whatsoever.'

Her forehead creased. 'I don't remember much. I was young when he was King.'

Of course, she'd been a child.

So very unsuitable for the likes of you.

Rafael shifted on the couch, ignoring the thought. 'You didn't miss anything.'

She gave him an oddly searching look. 'Self-control is important to you, isn't it?'

'Naturally. It's the only thing that stops us from becoming animals like Carlos.' No, there was too much bitterness in his voice. He needed to change the subject. 'You must think it's important yourself,' he went on. 'Or did your father know that the Crown Princess regularly drank whisky and smoked cigars in his office after hours?'

Colour flickered through her face, her gaze dropping abruptly to her hands where they held her glass of juice. She did that a lot, he noticed, especially when she wanted to hide something from him.

'No,' she said. 'He didn't. I didn't tell him.'

There was a faint edge in her voice which was interesting.

You only think you know her, but you don't.

He shifted on the couch again. He'd thought that before, that he was guilty of treating her like everyone else, ignoring her like everyone else. She was so self-effacing, so uncomplaining, so biddable and good, yet she was none of those things and he knew it.

And suddenly he wanted to know why. Why she'd sneaked into her father's study. Why she drank whisky, smoked cigars, and argued with a man years older than she was. Why she pretended she was the queenly equivalent of wallpaper, when she was as far from wallpaper as it was possible to get.

He'd always thought she'd be an excellent queen, but now, abruptly, he'd changed his mind. She couldn't be a queen. It would kill her.

Queens had to be controlled and well behaved, and in Santa Castelia's case they had to give way to the King.

Lia was wasted in that role. She should have been the King, not the Queen.

'You're very worried what your parents think of you, aren't you?' he said. 'Why? You're your own woman, Lia.'

'Why?' She looked up and stared at him very directly. 'Because they tried so hard to have me. Years of tears and heartache. And then they finally conceived me and they had a plan for me, and they loved me. How could I not do what they wanted? After all they went through to have me?'

'Yes, I can see that. But don't forget, it was their choice to have you. And you're not their property. You are your own person, with your own thoughts and feelings. You don't owe them anything.'

She swallowed. 'But... I love them.'

Love. Love was always the problem, wasn't it?

'You can love them and still have a life of your own.'

'I know... I just... I just wish that that was enough for them. That I was enough for them.'

There was a raw feeling in his chest. 'You're enough for me,' he said before he could stop himself. 'You always have been.'

She said nothing, staring at him, her expression unchanging, her blue eyes full of something he didn't understand, but it was fierce.

Then a tear slid slowly down her cheek.

Rafael felt as though someone had stabbed him.

Mi princesa,' he said softly, hoarsely. 'Lia, did I hurt you?' He reached for her, unable to stand that look on her face, and drew her into his lap.

She was so small and delicate, yet she burned so hot.

His chest felt tight, his throat dry. He touched her cheek, felt the wetness of her tears. An ache spread out inside him, deep and intense. The same ache that had filled him when his mother had told him the truth about his father and what he'd done to her.

He didn't like it. He didn't want it, yet it filled him. Pain for another person, because they were hurt.

Because you care.

The cold he'd felt out on the terrace was back, winding through him, a chill that went bone deep. He didn't want to care. Caring hurt, caring made you vulnerable. If he had any kind of sense, he wouldn't be holding her like this. He'd be keeping his distance, changing the subject, making himself hard and cold.

Yet he couldn't let her go. She was in pain. She hurt and he wanted to know why.

'What is it?' he murmured. 'Did I say something I shouldn't?'

Mutely she shook her head. Then, before he could say anything else, she flung her arms around his neck and pressed her face to his throat.

For a minute he sat there, stunned. No one had ever put their arms around him like that. Not as if they wanted his comfort. As if he had something to give that was more than money or power, or an example to set.

His heart beat furiously, the ache pervading every part of him.

He wasn't sure what to do next, not when this was so outside of his experience.

Except, no, that was wrong. An instinct that he didn't even know he possessed told him that he knew exactly what to do. So, he obeyed it, wrapping his arms around her and gathering her close, holding her.

For long minutes they sat there like that, the softness of her gathered against his chest, close to his heart. And his chest was so tight he couldn't breathe, some immense emotion pressing against it. An emotion so strong, so vast, he couldn't fight it.

He let it pulse through him, hot and intense, because in this moment it didn't matter what he felt. She was the most important thing in his universe and he would never, *ever* hurt her.

Then she turned her wet cheek and her mouth burned against his skin.

And the flames took hold.

She was so sweet, so unbearably sweet.

He felt as if he was melting, frozen pieces of himself warming up and thawing, the feeling inside him escaping, permeating every part of him.

He slid his fingers into her hair and held on tight, devouring her mouth as one by one the checks he had on his control began to fall. And he let them go. He couldn't stop this need, couldn't fight it.

She was on her back on the couch, his shirt ripped from her body before he knew what was happening. And for a second, he found himself in the depths of winter again, frozen with a sudden terror that he'd done something she hadn't wanted, that he'd been so overcome with need he'd missed some cues.

But then she reached for him, her blue eyes glowing with heat, clearly unbothered by his intensity, the way she'd always been unbothered by it.

'I need to be careful with you,' he heard himself say in a voice that didn't sound like his. 'Lia, you must tell me if I'm too much.'

'You're never too much,' she murmured. 'Never.' Then she pulled him down.

And there was no stopping after that, no holding back either.

He'd somehow got rid of his clothes and then he was pushing inside her, feeling the slick heat of her hold him tight, melting the last cold parts of him.

Her arms were around him, her thighs closed tightly around his hips, and she was moving with him, her gaze on his a bright gas-flame-blue. There was so much pleasure, his whole body filled with delight, with heat and with passion.

'I want you,' she whispered and the fire that had been part of him, that he'd always denied, finally escaped, blazing bright between them.

And he let himself be consumed.

CHAPTER NINE

LIA LAY IN the huge bath and looked out the window at the snow outside. It had stopped falling, but the drifts were still huge, lying thick and deep against the sides of the trees, the house and the corners of the window.

There was something particularly delicious about lying in a warm bath while looking at an icy landscape and Lia took full advantage of it.

Rafael had suggested a bath before dinner and even though she'd already had a shower earlier, the thought of lying in some warm water was pleasant enough that she'd let Constanza run one for her.

Rafael himself had wanted to check any communications from the palace and the various media outlets to get an update on their situation with the outside world, so he'd disappeared into his office.

She rested her head against the black marble of the tub, staring at the window, her head full of him.

Rafael, sitting on the couch with her as she ate, handing her more food and pouring her orange juice. Rafael, telling her that she was enough.

Rafael, putting his arms around her.

Rafael, telling her that she was enough for him, as if

there was nothing attached to it, nothing she needed to do to earn it. As if it just was.

She hadn't meant to cry when he'd said that, but it had felt so painful and at the same time so unbearably sweet that she hadn't been able to stop herself. A strange and intense feeling had swept through her that she couldn't have articulated even if she'd wanted to.

And it was still there, lying heavy in her chest, that familiar nagging ache that had now become part of her.

It had been there for a long time, maybe even that first day she saw him getting out of the limo, but back then she hadn't recognised it. It had felt too big, too complex, too terrifying. She hadn't been ready, not when she was supposed to be marrying someone else.

Her eyes prickled and a tear slid down her cheek, joining the warm bathwater.

How ridiculous to cry about falling in love, because that's what this was, wasn't it? Not a teenage crush or mere physical desire.

It was love. She loved him. There was nothing else this deep, intense feeling inside her could be. And he'd showed her what it meant.

It meant being accepted for who she was, without expectation, without pressure. Without having sad stories of sacrifices made and heartbreak overcome just so she could exist.

Her hand slid over the gentle swell of her stomach.

It was the way she would love her child, too.

She sat there for long minutes, her tears falling slowly, but they weren't tears of sadness or despair. They were more for the intensity of the bittersweet joy inside her. Joy, because he made her happy. Bittersweet because she had no idea how he felt about her.

He wanted her, of course, and she thought he cared about her wellbeing, but did he feel this same ache that she did? And if he did, did he know what it meant? Probably not, considering his past.

Not that it mattered.

None of her previous concerns mattered. Being Queen, having a future, the press, being chosen. They were all petty problems that paled in comparison to what she felt for him.

She closed her eyes, remembering how he'd taken her on the couch with a fury and intensity that her whole soul had gloried in.

It amazed her how he could think he was in any way like his father and believe it, yet it was clear that he did believe it.

She wanted to know why. Had someone told him he was like Carlos? Was that the issue? And if so, who?

It made her furious, made her want to shout at whoever was responsible, because he wasn't like his father, not in any way. His self-control spoke of a very deep and intense desire to protect other people, which was a foreign concept to Carlos.

Perhaps what Rafael needed was simply someone to tell him, to show him what a good man he was. Strong and principled, and perhaps on the outside a little hard, but with a caring heart underneath that.

Well, she would be that someone.

Matias had needed a queen, but Rafael needed *her*. And while he might not ever say 'I love you' back, he needed her all the same and she knew the truth of that with every part of her.

Eventually the water cooled and she hauled herself out, drying herself off and going into the bedroom. He'd turned the heating up further, so she didn't need the sweat-pants and hoodie combo, but she had to put on something.

She was in his bedroom, a huge room with vast windows that looked out over the mountains. A massive bed was pushed up against the wall facing the windows, the frame heavy oak. A matching dresser, just as massive, stood against another wall, a door beyond it that must lead to an en-suite bathroom.

The decor was dark and luxurious, charcoal-greys and dark blues, and very masculine, and Lia liked it very much. Especially when she could smell the faint hint of his delicious aftershave in the air.

The shirt of his she'd been wearing before was presumably still on the floor of the living area downstairs, so she went over to the tall dresser of polished oak that stood near the bed.

After a brief investigation of the drawers, she found a soft T-shirt that looked comfortable, so she pulled it out. Then something caught her eye.

A photo frame had been tucked beneath a layer of neatly folded shirts.

Lia frowned and pushed aside the fabric.

It was a photo of a beautiful woman with black hair and the same grey eyes as the little boy she was crouched next to, her arms around him. Both the woman and the boy were smiling at the camera, the swings and slides of a children's playground behind them.

A little shock went through her as recognition dawned.

This was a picture of Rafael and his mother, wasn't it? The mother who'd never wanted a child and who'd never liked him, or so he'd said. The mother who was nevertheless holding him and smiling.

'What are you doing, Lia?'

Lia froze as Rafael's deep voice came from the doorway, her heart kicking in her chest. She felt oddly as if she'd been discovered doing something she shouldn't, which was ridiculous when she'd only been looking for something to wear.

She turned around to face him.

He'd taken a few steps into the room, his expression merely curious rather than angry.

'I was trying to find a T-shirt to wear,' she said. 'Sorry, I didn't mean to intrude on your privacy.'

He lifted one muscular shoulder. 'This will be your room, too. No apology is necessary. Did you find one?' His gaze fell to the still-open drawer and the photo in it, no longer buried by clothing. He went abruptly still.

Lia felt the temperature of the air plunging as if he'd opened the door to the outside and all the snow was blowing in.

She took a small breath. This photo meant something to him obviously, but nothing good, that was also clear.

He is hiding something from you.

Oh, she knew that already. And she'd pushed her instincts to ask him about it to one side, telling herself that there would be plenty of time later to discuss it. And she still could. She didn't have to push him now and what would it accomplish anyway?

But isn't this what you've been doing all your life? Doing what other people want. Doing what you're told. Doing what's expected of you. How does that help? What does it achieve?

A shiver of realisation went through her.

Nothing. It achieved nothing and it changed nothing. It didn't make anything worse, but it didn't make it better either.

*Is that what you want your marriage to be like? You
avoiding tackling painful subjects because you don't
want to rock the boat? What are you afraid of?*

Oh, but she knew the answer to that. It had been inside her this whole time if she'd only been brave enough
to look. Except she'd never been brave enough until now.
Until she'd fallen in love with Rafael Navarro.

Her fear was there, a cold kernel in her heart, of not
being the good, quiet girl her parents wanted her to be,
of not meeting their expectations. Of disappointing them
after they'd endured so much to have her.

The fear of not being good enough to love on her own.

So she'd tried to mould herself into what they wanted,
being good and quiet and biddable. Making them proud.

Except she wasn't like that with Rafael, she never had
been, and anyway, she didn't know how he felt about
her, so what did she have to lose?

She loved him and her fear didn't matter in the face
of that. The only thing that mattered was him and if she
wanted to help him, take away his pain, she was going
to have to push.

Determination settled down inside her.

'Is that a picture of you and your mother?' she asked.

His gaze had gone a dark, gunmetal grey, the door
to the furnace of his intensity firmly closed. 'Yes. Did
you find a T-shirt?'

It was very clear he was not going to talk about the
photo.

'I did,' she said. 'It's a lovely photo, Rafael. Why is
it at the bottom of your drawer?'

He pushed the drawer back in. 'Because that's where
I put it.' He turned toward the doorway. 'Constanza will
be serving dinner shortly. Shall we go down?'

It was clear that it was not a request.

Lia didn't move. 'The moment you saw it, I could feel the temperature of the room plunge about fifty degrees. Why is that?'

Again, he lifted a negligent shoulder. 'I'll tell you about it later.'

'No. You will tell me about it now.'

He was halfway to the door and he stopped. His back was rigid, every line of him stiff. 'I'm not sure I like you demanding answers from me.' That casual tone was back and she hadn't realised before how much she hated it.

'You're doing it again, making it sound like you don't care,' she said flatly. 'Except I know that you do. What is it with your mother, Rafael?'

He turned his head to the side, the muscles in his jaw tight. 'You'd prefer it if I shouted at you? Perhaps throw things like a child?'

But she could see past that reserve, could see beneath the ice field. She'd always seen the fire in him, no matter how deep he buried it beneath layers of ice.

'Being angry doesn't make you Carlos,' she said quietly. '*Nothing* you do will ever turn you into him.'

Something clicked into place inside her all of a sudden. His apparent coldness in stark contrast to the passion that burned inside him. The way he always sounded casual when there was something vital to be discussed. The quiet, frightening way he'd issue orders or warnings. He never lost his temper, not once. He was always in control.

Except with you.

'I think you're wrong,' Lia said flatly, staring straight into Rafael's silver eyes. She hadn't known where she'd got her courage from, whether from the whisky bottle

*in front of her or from the rush of adrenaline that had
filled her the moment she'd uttered the words.*

It was a challenge and they both knew it.

*'I'm wrong?' he echoed in that mild tone he always
used and yet that always sounded so menacing. 'Are
you sure?'*

*He was sitting sprawled in the chair opposite, the but-
tons of his shirt undone, his sleeves rolled up, relaxed
and so unbelievably attractive she could hardly breathe.*

*'Of course you're wrong.' She had to say it again, just
to see the silver in his eyes flare and because she liked
saying it. Like poking the tiger sitting across from her
with a stick. 'Money isn't the be all and end all.'*

*He tilted his head. 'Says the woman who's never been
hungry a day in her life.'*

*She flushed, because of course that was true. 'I'm
not saying money isn't useful and that it doesn't buy a
certain amount of happiness. But that happiness isn't
lasting.'*

*'But doesn't that depend on how much money you
have?'*

*'Fine.' She put her elbows on the desk and leaned
forward, bracing herself and looking into those fascinating eyes of his, feeling her heart begin to hammer in
her head at the risk she was taking. 'Then, given how
much money you have, are you happy, Your Excellency?'*

'Of course,' he said in that same tone.

*If she hadn't been gazing straight at him, she wouldn't
have noticed the flicker in his gaze, but she did notice.*

*'Really?' She didn't move. 'What makes you happy,
then?'*

'This is an irrelevant conversation.'

'No, it's not. Unless you're not telling me the truth.'

He looked away, stubbing out his cigar in the ashtray, then taking a last sip of his whisky. 'You'd better start talking about something interesting, princesa, *otherwise I have other things to be doing.'*

'You're not happy,' she said, watching his face and making a guess, amazed at her own audacity for questioning him. She shouldn't step outside the box of demure princess and she knew it, but she couldn't stop. 'And you don't want to talk about it.'

He pushed his chair back, rising to his feet. 'I think that's enough for one night.'

She didn't move, the need to keep pushing him, dig beneath the surface of him and find the fire that burned in his heart too intense. It was there, she knew it, she only had to keep digging. 'What are you afraid of?' She threw the question at him like a stone and then, because she somehow always went too far, she added, 'Rafael.'

He'd already turned to the door, ready to leave, but the sound of his name made him stop. And for a second she thought he'd stride out without a word.

But he didn't.

He turned back to her, so fast she barely had time to take a breath before he was right in front of her, leaning his hands on the desk, bare inches away, those silver eyes so close she could see the striations of charcoal running through them.

'No, princesa,*' he said, his voice not so casual now, but edged with a slight roughness. 'These kinds of topics are off limits, do you understand?'*

Her heart was beating so loudly she could hardly hear him. He was so close. All she needed to do was to lean forward slightly and her mouth would brush his. 'What topics?' she asked hoarsely, unable to look away.

'Anything to do with our private lives.'

'But what if I want to? What if I—?'

'Then I will not come to see you any more.'

He meant it, she could hear the flat note in his voice, the hint of steel.

'You don't mind me...arguing with you, though? Or disagreeing with you?'

Again, that flicker in his gaze and this time it was accompanied by a slight relaxing of that hard, implacable mouth. 'That, I do not mind. In fact...' He paused and for a second the whole world faded away, just simply ceased to exist. There was nothing else in it, but the burning intensity of his eyes. A molten, burning silver. 'I like it.'

A second later, he'd pushed himself away and was gone, leaving her sitting alone in the study, staring at the door he'd disappeared through, her heart fluttering around like a butterfly trapped in a net.

Everything felt darker and colder when he wasn't here. Everything dull and muted.

She was right, though, wasn't she? There was fire in him and it burned so bright. And now she'd seen it, she was going to make it her mission to make it blaze every single time....

And she had. He was never reserved and cold with her after that night and she couldn't let him be anyway. She'd flung challenge after challenge at him, letting him blaze and blazing along with him.

But he'd never shouted when he got passionate about an argument. He'd get up and pace and sometimes those silver eyes of his would get molten, but he was nothing like Carlos.

'I know I am not my father.' Again in that dangerously mild tone.

'Then why do you pretend that nothing touches you?'

'You think I'm pretending?'

She almost laughed. 'You think you're not?'

'Lia, I don't see—'

'What happened with your mother, Rafael?' She cut him off, suddenly knowing that if she didn't crack that icy exterior of his now she never would. That he'd be closed off to her for ever and she couldn't bear that, not for his sake and not for hers. 'And don't lie to me about how it doesn't matter. If it really didn't matter, you would have just answered the question.'

It was dark outside, the light in the bedroom dim. Yet he could see Lia's face and the determination written all over it with absolute crystal clarity.

She always looked that way when she was determined to challenge and push him, and most of the time he'd let her. Except there were some things he didn't want to discuss with her and that photo was one of those things.

It was a picture of one of the happiest times in his life. When for whatever reason, he was never sure, his mother had taken him to the playground. And for an hour or two it was as though she'd forgotten what he represented, as if he was simply her son and she loved him, not the constant reminder of the worst moment of her life.

He'd kept that photo because it was the only one he had of her smiling and it had felt important that he remember that smile, especially when he could count on one hand the number of times she'd smiled at him.

But he didn't want to tell Lia that.

He didn't want to discuss his mother with her at all.

'Fine,' he said casually, because all he had about this particular topic was casual. 'You're right, that's me and my mother. I keep the picture to remind me that she was happy once.'

Lia's expression turned suddenly soft, that almost tender look crossing her delicate face. The one that made his chest feel as if an iron band was crushing it. 'She looks very happy. She must have loved you a lot.'

'I think you're assuming she felt some motherly feelings towards me.' He bared his teeth in a facsimile of a smile. 'She did not.'

The soft expression on her face faded. 'What do you mean she did not?'

'I told you earlier. She looked after me because it was her duty, but there was too much of my father in me for her to care about me.'

Lia's blue gaze widened. 'She actually said that to you?'

'*Si*. And often.' So he'd tried to prove to her that he was nothing like Carlos. Endlessly. Trying hard not to lose his temper, trying hard to do what he was told and study hard, and treat his mother gently and kindly. To make up for the sin of being born.

Then she'd died and he didn't have to do it any more, but by that stage he'd realised that the easier way was just to cut those feelings out of his heart. To not feel them at all.

So, he hadn't.

'Oh, Rafael,' Lia murmured, crossing the distance between them. 'That's awful.' She put her hands on his chest, her palms warming his skin through his shirt. 'Why would she say that?'

He wanted to be angry, to hold on to the sullen, burning flame in his heart, but he couldn't. It felt as if the pressure of Lia's hands were stripping that anger away, leaving underneath the raw wound of the truth.

A truth he couldn't tell her, because it was his mother's and she was gone.

All he had left was the half-truth.

'Because she was angry that she had me. She had… plans for her future and I got in the way.' He brushed a strand of black hair back behind her ear, unable to stop the casual touch. 'She didn't like me making a fuss or throwing a tantrum or being difficult. She would tell me I had to be careful, that I had to be measured and considerate in my behaviour in case I turned into Carlos.'

The crease between her brows deepened. 'But…kids are like that. I was like that.'

'Not all kids. She set an example for me and I followed it.' He reached for her wrists, circling them with his fingers and pulling them gently away. 'Let's have dinner. It'll be on the table by now.'

But Lia's chin had a familiar stubborn slant to it. 'What kind of example? I mean, that's ridiculous. You don't have to practise not being like Carlos, Rafael. You just *aren't* him. Why on earth would you think that you are?'

The heat smouldering inside him flared. 'It wasn't my mother's fault. I was an angry child and that only got worse as I got older. I was wilful, stubborn and I had a temper, just like Carlos had a temper, and that frightened her.'

Lia was still frowning. 'But all children throw tantrums. And being wilful and stubborn aren't exactly unusual traits.'

The hot coals that sat in his gut glowed hotter, the iron band around his chest tightening yet again. Anger and pain, two things he'd cut out of his heart and never wanted to feel again.

Clearly it was time to end this conversation.

'Do you have a point, Lia?' He tried to keep his tone moderate the way he always did. 'Our dinner will get cold and Constanza will not be impressed.'

'I don't care about Constanza,' Lia said. 'I'm still trying to figure out why you think you're like your father.'

'What does it matter?' Impatience was creeping into his voice. 'Carlos is dead and so is my mother.'

'Yes, but you're not. So why are you acting as though they're still alive?'

His patience began to thin. 'I don't understand what you're talking about. I know they're not alive. Do you think I'm stupid?'

She paid no attention to his tone. 'No, of course not. But you do know what I'm talking about, Rafael. You're so cold, so detached. And that's not who you are.'

'I'm not detached. I'm simply in control of my emotions.'

'In control,' she echoed. 'Was that what kidnapping me from the cathedral was all about? You being in control of yourself?'

He could feel all his muscles tighten yet again, the tension excruciating. 'We have been over this. You're pregnant with my child and I had to do something—'

'You stopped a royal wedding. In the middle of the ceremony. And then you—'

'What is your point?' He'd taken a step toward her

before he knew what he was doing. Adrenaline coursed inside him, making him feel hot, making him feel the need to do something intensely physical just to get rid of it. 'You want a fight, *princesa?* Is that what you're trying to do?'

Lia took a step toward him, in no way cowed by him. Her eyes were glowing with that intense blue light that always filled them when they were challenging each other.

You're fiery and hot, the pair of you.

No, maybe she was, but he wasn't. He was the master of himself. He had to be.

'What I'm trying to do,' she said fiercely, 'is to get to know my husband. You told me months ago that you didn't want to discuss anything private or personal and I agreed. But things have changed.' She took another step. 'We're going to be married, Rafael, and you are going to be a father. I think the time for that embargo on private conversation is over.'

He could feel his temper fray, responding to the glint in her eyes and wanting to answer it. But he couldn't.

His mother, crouching down in the ruins of his bed-room, looking at him with fear in her eyes. Her grip on his shoulders was so hard it was painful. 'Rafael, do you really want to be like your father? Violent and hor-rible? Hurting people the way he hurt me? Is that who you're trying to be?'

His rage had burned out, leaving him hollow and empty, and he couldn't remember any longer what he'd even been angry about. Now all he felt was fear.

'No, Mama,' he said, his throat sore from shouting. 'I would never hurt you. I want to be a good boy.'

Her mouth was a hard line, her eyes full of a terrible ferocity he didn't understand. 'Then you have to control yourself. You must. You cannot get angry like this any more. Because one of these days you will hurt someone. You will hurt me.'

'I'm sorry, Mama,' he said, because at seven years old, all he wanted was not to hurt his mother. 'I'll try hard not to, I promise.'

She stared at him. 'You can't escape who you are, Rafael. You were born with your father's flaws, so you will have to do this all your life. Understand?'

Oh, he'd understood. At first control was his lord and master, but over the years, he'd mastered it. He would not let that temper get the better of him, especially not now, with this woman in his keeping.

A woman he'd promised to himself never to hurt.

'Please, Lia. Do not push me.' He put everything he had into keeping his tone level, to not letting the pressure of the heat inside, the hard, violent emotion he knew he couldn't let off the leash, not ever. 'We need to have this conversation at a later time. First, there is dinner—'

'Stop talking about dinner!' She was close to him now, all soft and warm in his T-shirt. She smelled like the bath oil she'd used, something sweet that set all his senses alight, no matter that he'd spent hours sating himself on her body already. 'I don't want this conversation at a later time. I want it now. Because if you can't have it now, you never will. And I'll never break through all the ice you're surrounding yourself with.'

His patience thinned to snapping point. 'You think you can order me around? Tell me to talk to you and I

will? Like a good little lapdog? Is that what you think?'
He closed the remaining distance between them, inches
away from her, burning up from the inside. 'Who gave
you the right to demand anything you want from me?'
He could hear the anger in his voice, the heat bleeding
through. 'Why do you think you deserve to know?'

She didn't look away from him, her own special brand
of ferocity burning in her eyes. 'Because I'm going to
be your wife, Rafael.' Her cheeks were pink, the blue
of her gaze as deep and dark as a midnight sky. 'And…
because I love you.'

It felt as though she'd slipped a knife between his ribs.
You can't have love. You don't deserve it.

'You don't love me,' he snapped, not acknowledging
it because if he did perhaps it would go away. 'You just
love the pleasure I give you.'

She went white. 'What do you mean by that?'

'You're a good girl, sheltered. Cosseted. You've
never known sexual pleasure until I gave it to you.'
The words spilled out of his mouth, harsh and sharp
and cutting. 'It's very common for virgins to confuse
love with passion and I'm sorry, but that's what happened to you.'

The fierce look in her eyes didn't change, she only
looked at him and he could hear his own words coming
back to him, tinny and cruel and wrong.

Then her hand came out unexpectedly and touched
his cheek and he felt that knife twist beneath his ribs,
pain radiating out. 'You want to believe that, don't you?
You want to believe that very badly. Why?'

He reached for her hand, pulling it away from his
face. 'This isn't about me.'

'Of course it's about you. I know what I feel, Rafael. I
know my own heart and I've loved you for years. Before
I even knew what love was. It's you that doesn't know,
I think.' Gently she pulled her hand out of his hold and
touched him again, just a brush of those cool fingers.
'Tell me, has anyone said that to you before? Has anyone told you that they loved you?'

His stomach dropped away, every part of him in
agony. 'Why would they?' he heard himself say. 'Why
would anyone?'

A terrible sympathy crossed her face. 'No one? Not
even your mother?'

'Let me tell you what I was to my mother,' he said,
the words coming out before he could stop himself, even
though it was a truth that wasn't his to give. 'I was the
living reminder of what my father did to her. Of how
he hurt her.'

Lia frowned. 'What do you mean?'

'She was a hotel chambermaid,' he said, because
now he'd started down this path he had no other option
but to keep going. 'My father regularly stayed at the
hotel where she worked and he decided he wanted her.
She was very strong willed, however, and she wouldn't
sleep with him, so he courted her. He couldn't marry
her, because he was a king, but my mother disapproved
of sex outside of marriage and so refused him. She
loved him and he told her that he loved her, but still
she refused.'

He bared his teeth. 'So, he got her drunk one night
and raped her. Afterwards he held her and told her she
was beautiful and that he loved her and that it would
all be okay. He manipulated her into thinking nothing

had happened. She thought it was all fine because she loved him and he loved her, but when she told him that she'd conceived, he gave her some money to make her go away. And that's when she realised she'd been used.'

Lia went pale, her expression horrified. 'Oh, Rafael...'

'So, no, no one ever told me that they loved me. Why would they? Why would anyone love a child that came from that?'

CHAPTER TEN

LIA STARED IN shock at him, that deep, vast emotion pressing against her heart, making it ache, making it hurt. Making her want to put her arms around him and hold him, keep him close.

'Oh, Rafael... Oh... I'm so sorry...'

The look on his face was terrible. 'I was the living reminder of what had happened to her, of why her life was ruined. She knew how I was conceived, could see the flaws in me, the same flaws my father had, and she taught me that I had to be better. That I had to learn how to control them otherwise I'd turn into him. And I tried. I did my best never to get angry, never to hurt her. She looked after me dutifully but I could understand why she never loved me. Why would she?'

There were tears in Lia's eyes, his tall figure wavering. Her chest felt as though it was full of barbed wire, the sharp points digging into her heart, pressing hard enough to draw blood.

No wonder he'd had no reaction to her telling him she loved him. And no wonder he'd told her that it was just physical passion.

He didn't believe in it because he'd never experienced it.

After what had happened to his mother, love for him was nothing but hurt.

Her throat felt tight and sore, but she forced the words out. 'You were a child, Rafael. You were blameless and your mother had been hurt very badly. It wasn't your fault.'

His mouth twisted. 'I ruined her life, Lia. Every day she looked at me, she could see my father. She could see what he did to her. And when she saw the same traits in me that he had, it terrified her. *I* terrified her.' His eyes had gone dark. 'I promised I would make our marriage work. I promised that I wouldn't give you a moment's regret, that I would make you happy, but… I've never made anyone happy. I don't know how.'

Her throat closed. She knew where he was going with this, she could sense it. 'You do,' she said forcefully. 'You *do* make me happy. You told me I was enough for you, that I was an asset. You accepted me as I was when even my own parents didn't.'

'It's not enough though, is it?' His voice was harsh. 'You love me, Lia. But I do not have the first idea of how to love you in return.'

'I don't need you to—'

'Yes,' he cut her off roughly. 'Yes, you do and you want it, too. Why do you think you did everything your father asked? Why do you think you went to the altar to be married? You want to be loved, *mi princesa,* and you deserve it. You deserve it so much. But I am not the man to give it to you.' He paused. 'I can't marry you, Lia. I'm sorry.'

The pressure in her chest became crushing. 'I don't understand,' she said, even though she had a horrible feeling that she did. 'I thought… I thought you wanted to marry me. I thought that I was yours.'

Slowly, he shook his head. 'I am poison. I hurt people the way I hurt my mother. I swore never to hurt you, but I will. One day I will and I cannot have that. This is the only way.'

Her throat had gone tight, her heart scraped raw. 'So, what? This is all about protecting me?'

His hands had curled into fists at his sides. 'You are so young. You have a life ahead of you and years to find someone else. I am flawed. Too flawed.' His eyes had darkened ever further, all that blazing silver doused. 'If I take you now, how am I any better than my father? Giving in to his emotions, giving in to his own lusts. Taking without asking and not giving anything in return. And you need that, *princesa*. You will suffocate without it.'

There were more tears, she could feel them sliding down her cheeks, her heart tearing itself to pieces as the future she'd only just started to imagine for them both slowly shattered into a million diamond-bright shards.

She wanted to be angry, to rage at him, tell him he was a fool and wrong. That she didn't care if he didn't love her. That being with him was all she wanted and he didn't need to give her anything.

But it was clear he wasn't going to listen. He preferred the ice he'd buried himself under and who was she to argue? Who was she to push?

She had no right to him or his feelings, and the only thing she had to give him was her love. And that wasn't enough.

'But what about the baby?' Her hand rested on her

stomach, grief tearing at her. 'Your son or daughter will need their father.'

The silver of his eyes had died completely, they were the colour of ash now. 'It would be better if my child never knew me. I am not an example they should be following. But don't worry, I won't leave you with nothing. You will be taken care of.'

'Rafael, no,' she said hoarsely. 'You can't.'

'I can.' A muscle leaped in his jaw. 'It is my final word.' He took a step back, away from her. 'You may stay here for as long as you wish. I'll deal with the outside world. You can leave that side of things to me.'

Lia nodded, barely hearing him. She felt cold all of a sudden, as if winter had come into the room, scattering snow and ice everywhere, the bitter chill making its way inside her and freezing the ragged pieces of her heart. She didn't know what to say. Not that she could have said anything anyway. It was clear his mind was made up and she couldn't change it.

He was the product of a terrible act, the way he saw himself set in stone right from a young age. And she couldn't blame his mother for that. She'd had a terrible experience and Lia could understand her grief and her fear. That she'd put it on her son was awful, but knowing that wouldn't change what had happened. Wouldn't change the past.

And it wouldn't help Rafael.

He wasn't poison. He was the antidote. He'd given her freedom within the cage she'd been trapped in and some of the purest moments of happiness she'd ever known.

She would do the same for him if only she knew how.

'You should eat,' he said at last. 'You'll be hungry.'

'No,' she said. 'I'm not. I think I need to go and lie down.'

Then she fled from the room before he could stop her.

It was late, midnight possibly, but Rafael didn't bother looking at the clock. He'd long since ceased to care. He sat in his office, staring at the bottle of good whisky on top of his desk, every part of him wanting to drink the entire thing, while his control told him no.

It felt important to resist. He *had* to. Because if he didn't, if he gave in, what was to stop him from going upstairs and dragging Lia from her bed and into his, and keeping her there all night?

Keeping her there for ever.

But he couldn't. Her tears had nearly killed him, the lost look in her eyes when he'd told her that he would never love her making him feel as if his heart was tearing itself apart in his chest. Yet it didn't matter how much pain he felt, he couldn't give in to that need.

He couldn't give in to the feeling inside him, the intensity, the ferocity. That feeling damaged people. That feeling hurt people. And it would hurt her if he wasn't careful.

'People do terrible things in the name of love,' his mother had said, when he was thirteen and in the grip of his first crush. 'You especially will have to be careful.' And then she'd told him the story of his conception. The reason why he was so very flawed, why she couldn't ever love him the way he always wished she could.

He'd been appalled. Shocked. Disgusted. And he'd sworn he'd never do what his father did. He would never give in to his own feelings, take what wasn't his.

And love especially he would avoid like the plague.

Nothing had changed since that day, no matter how Lia insisted. It hurt her, yes, but keeping her, knowing he could never give her the one thing she deserved above all else, would only hurt her more.

This was the right decision. The only decision.

His phone rang and he'd hit the answer button before he'd fully thought through the wisdom of it.

'So, Zeus told me what was happening,' Vincenzo said without any preamble. 'And I wanted to call you to tell you what a terrible idea—'

'I'm returning her to the palace,' Rafael snapped. 'As soon as the weather clears.'

Vincenzo was silent for a long moment, shock echoing down the phone line. 'You're returning her? But isn't she pregnant?'

'Yes. I can't marry her, though. And it was wrong of me to take her.'

Another long silence.

'I'm sorry, but I thought I heard you say that you were wrong.'

He gritted his teeth. 'I was.'

'Why?'

Rafael didn't want to have this discussion. Vincenzo had just married the woman he'd fallen in love with and probably wouldn't be here for his thoughts on the nature of love. 'Because she loves me.'

'Obviously a cardinal sin,' Vincenzo murmured dryly. 'And I suppose you're returning her now because she deserves better?'

Rafael glared at the desktop. 'She does.'

'Ah.' Vincenzo sounded as if he'd just discovered something very interesting. 'I see.'

'You see?' Rafael growled. 'What do you see?'

'You're in love with her.'

His heart froze, everything froze. 'No.'

'Yes, you fool. Of course you are.'

'What makes you—?'

'Because that's what I did with Eloise. You send them away, telling yourself you're protecting them, but it's not to protect them. You're protecting yourself, because you're in love and you're damn terrified.'

Rafael's heart felt like a block of ice in his chest. 'I can't,' he said roughly. 'Love makes people do terrible things. You know Carlos. You know what he was like. You know—'

'Oh, please,' Vincenzo said in some disgust. 'I wouldn't have thought you of all people would let that old bastard define who you are.'

'I'm not,' Rafael ground out.

'You are. Do you really think you're capable of hurting someone? That you would ever hurt her?'

'I'd rather kill myself than hurt her. That's why I had to send her away.'

'Dramatic, but that answers that question.' Vincenzo's voice was bone dry. 'You're afraid, Rafael. And you're using your father as an excuse. And that I understand. But it's not only you that you need to think about. Doesn't she deserve love?'

The block of ice around his heart began to soften, gradually, slowly.

Lia, sitting in that armchair with whisky and a cigar.

Lia, eyes glowing, arguing with him.

Lia, in his arms, passionate and loving.

Lia, looking at him. *I love you, Rafael.*

Who had ever loved him? Not his father. Not his mother.

Lia, looking at the photo of his mother with her arms around him. *'She must have loved you...'*

If you were all bad, why is she smiling?

'You were blameless, a child. And she was damaged...'

His heart shifted, shuddered.

'Yes,' he said hoarsely. 'She does.'

'Then stop putting yourself and your fears first and think about her.'

Was that what he was doing? Was that all this was? Just fear?

Fear that he was actually as bad as his father. Fear that he was poison. Fear that there was nothing but flaws inside him, that he wasn't worthy of anyone's love.

Except... Lia did love him. Lia had loved him for years.

She wasn't afraid of him. She never had been. Not of his anger or his passion or the ferocity inside him, the intensity. No, she'd simply matched it with her own. They were the same, weren't they?

Both passionate, both strong. And she wasn't poison, so... Why did he think he was?

You do love her.

He could feel it now, the fire of that love, heating him up, melting the ice. Warming his soul all the way through.

There was nothing toxic in it, nothing poisonous. It felt...clean.

He couldn't know that for sure, but...maybe if she wasn't afraid, then he didn't need to be either. Maybe, if he trusted in her strength and her bravery, he could trust himself, too.

'Rafael?' Vincenzo demanded. 'Are you still there?'

'I'll call you back,' Rafael growled down the phone. 'I have a wedding to organise.'

CHAPTER ELEVEN

LIA WOKE TO brilliant sunshine. The world outside was blindingly white, snow everywhere, but the blizzard had vanished.

Snow was piled high on the mountains, weighing heavily on the trees, and probably covering all the roads, but it was clear enough that a helicopter could get through, because she could hear the rhythmic sound of the rotors through the trees.

The outside world intruding.

Rafael, leaving.

Her eyes filled with tears and she wanted to turn over and bury her face in her pillow, the ache in her chest filling the whole world.

She would go on—she had to, especially now she was a mother—but something inside her had broken irretrievably and she knew that nothing was going to fix it.

It was her heart. And it would never be whole again.

At that moment the door to the bedroom opened and Constanza came in, her arms full of something white.

Lia blinked. 'What is that?'

The housekeeper laid the white thing down on a nearby chair. It appeared to be a white gown trimmed with silky white fur. 'For you,' she said. 'You have fifteen minutes.'

'Fifteen minutes?' Lia echoed blankly. 'For what?'

'No time to explain.' The housekeeper beckoned. 'Come on, I'll help you with the buttons.'

Lia didn't want to. Yet it was clear Constanza wasn't going anywhere, so reluctantly she dragged herself out of bed.

'You can have a shower,' the housekeeper said. 'But make it quick.'

Five minutes later, cleaner but no less mystified, Lia found herself being buttoned into the white gown. It was made of thick white silk, with voluminous skirts, and fitted her small bump to perfection. It was long sleeved, with a deep V at the neckline.

After Constanza had buttoned her into it, she folded a white fur cloak around Lia's shoulders and gave her a pair of white boots to put her feet into.

'Is this…?' Lia began to say and then faltered.

Constanza merely turned towards the door. 'Follow me.'

And Lia did, half in a daze, not understanding what was happening, though a part of her knew. A part of her had recognised that this was a gown and it was wedding white.

But she didn't want to think about it, didn't want to hope, so she followed Constanza down the stairs and into the living area, where the doors to the terrace outside were already open.

Chilly wind whipped through the open door, the terrace outside sparkling in the winter sunlight.

Shining on the man who stood by the parapet waiting for her.

He was dressed in black and he was staring at her, his grey eyes molten silver. He was alone.

'Rafael...' Her voice failed, her throat going thick.

'I'm sorry, Lia,' he said, his voice that rough velvet she loved so much. 'I am so sorry about last night. I kept things from you, hid things from you. What happened to my mother was her story and I didn't feel I could tell anyone, but... I felt you needed the truth. And here is another truth.' His eyes blazed. 'I love you, *princesa*. I have loved you for a long time, I think, but I didn't recognise it for what it was. I was afraid. Afraid that if I opened myself up to it, I'd lose control, become something terrible like Carlos. But it was you who showed me differently. You who made me see that love isn't something to be afraid of, that it isn't pain and suffering. That it is healing and warmth and strength.'

Lia's eyes were so full of tears, she could barely see his tall figure in front of her. 'Why? What changed?'

'A phone call from an old friend.' His expression softened just a touch. 'Yes, I have friends.'

She swallowed and then she was walking towards him, her feet crunching in the freshly fallen snow. 'You're not like Carlos, Rafael. You know that, don't you? You finally believe it?'

'*Sí.*' The fierce heat in his eyes had something else in it now, not just pain, but something more. Something that wasn't desperation, but a certain kind of peace. 'And because I am not my father, if you do not wish to marry me, you can walk away. Say the word and you'll never have to hear from me again. I'll leave you to make your own choices, to follow your own heart.'

Lia blinked hard through her tears, meeting his gaze.

'I've followed my heart already. That's why I'm standing here.'

A fierce expression crossed his face, part-possessive, part-protective, all love. 'Are you sure? You don't have to choose me if you don't want to.'

Even now, he was holding himself back.

Foolish, stubborn man.

Her throat was tight and sore, but there had never been any doubt about the feeling in her heart. That this man was worth the fight to have him.

And there would be more fights in the future, because no relationship was ever a simple bed of roses, but she knew in the deepest heart of her that she would battle to keep him with her last living breath, because he was worth it no matter the cost.

'I do want to,' she said simply. 'And I choose you, Rafael. I will always choose you.'

He lifted a hand, not taking his gaze from hers, and from out of the house came three men. All tall. All ridiculously handsome—one was even wearing a crown.

The dark-eyed man in the crown came to stand next to Rafael, while the other man, dark-haired and wearing sunglasses, came to stand on the other side.

The third man, again dark-haired and dark-eyed, with olive skin, who wore his immaculate suit with a certain careless insouciance, gave her a smile that if she hadn't been about to marry the man she loved would have knocked her socks off. 'Your bride, Rafael,' the man said, 'is exquisite.'

'Stop trying to charm her, Zeus, and marry us,' Rafael growled.

Lia coughed delicately. 'Rafael…'

'Mi princesa,' Rafael said, sliding an arm around her

waist and drawing her close. 'These are my friends, Vincenzo and Jag.' He indicated the man wearing the crown and the man in sunglasses. 'And my other disreputable friend Prince Zeus, who has been ordained and can marry us.'

'This is much better than the cathedral,' Lia said and leaned against her husband to be. 'Yes, please marry us, Prince Zeus.'

It was a very quick ceremony and afterwards there was champagne. Lia thought Rafael might want to spend time with his friends, but they didn't linger. Vincenzo had his own wife to get home to and Zeus and Jag had other 'adventures' to attend, according to Zeus.

Lia had her own adventure, too.

There were many things to organise, many issues that needed to be handled, but Rafael ignored all of them in favour of sweeping her up his arms and carrying her to his bedroom.

And they began their future together right then and there.

EPILOGUE

RAFAEL WOKE WITH a start to find the bed empty. He thought he might know where Lia was, so he got out of bed and went downstairs, and sure enough, his wife was sitting on the couch, their son and daughter in her arms.

The twins had obviously just finished a feed and, miracle of miracles, were lying there quietly.

He leaned in the doorway a moment, taking in the sight of his brand-new family. Twins had been unexpected, but he and Lia had coped and their birth had indeed been the gift she'd promised it would be.

As was she.

The fallout from his kidnapping her had been intense and people had talked of nothing else for a good month. It had helped that Matias had given his blessing almost immediately, telling Rafael that, actually, it had felt like a weight had lifted off his shoulders and that he had someone else he'd had his eye on for quite some time.

The transition of power had been smooth. Matias had become King and he'd promptly married the woman he'd loved since he was a boy, whom no one knew about.

Lia's parents had been disappointed, but not for long. Not once the twins had been born.

All in all, it had worked out very well.

Rafael moved into the room and went over to the couch. Lia looked up and smiled, the love shining in her eyes making him ache.

But it was a welcome pain, a sweet pain.

And when he took his daughter in one arm and curled his wife and son in the other, he let it flow through him.

He'd started out with winter in his soul and Lia had been the spring, thawing him out.

Now it was summer and he knew there would be sunshine to the end of his days.

Sunshine in his heart for ever.

* * * * *

MILLS & BOON

THE HEART OF ROMANCE

A ROMANCE FOR EVERY READER

MODERN

Prepare to be swept off your feet by sophisticated, sexy and seductive heroes, in some of the world's most glamourous and romantic locations, where power and passion collide.

HISTORICAL

Escape with historical heroes from time gone by. Whether your passion is for wicked Regency Rakes, muscled Vikings or rugged Highlanders, awaken the romance of the past.

MEDICAL

Set your pulse racing with dedicated, delectable doctors in the high-pressure world of medicine, where emotions run high and passion, comfort and love are the best medicine.

True Love

Celebrate true love with tender stories of heartfelt romance, from the rush of falling in love to the joy a new baby can bring, and a focus on the emotional heart of a relationship.

Desire

Indulge in secrets and scandal, intense drama and plenty of sizzling hot action with powerful and passionate heroes who have it all: wealth, status, good looks…everything but the right woman.

HEROES

Experience all the excitement of a gripping thriller, with an intense romance at its heart. Resourceful, true-to-life women and strong, fearless men face danger and desire - a killer combination!

To see which titles are coming soon, please visit

millsandboon.co.uk/nextmonth

MILLS & BOON

Coming next month

DESERT PRINCE'S DEFIANT BRIDE
Julieanne Howells

Lily watched as Khaled came closer, all smouldering masculine intent. Seconds ago she'd been in a snit. Now she couldn't remember why. By the time he reached her she was boneless and unresisting, letting him gather her hand and lift it to his lips.

'*Habiba*, you are beautiful,' he purred.

Beautiful? Her breath fluttered out. Dear Lord, she'd sighed. She'd actually just *sighed*.

He dipped his head. He was going to kiss her. She shivered as warm lips brushed the tender skin of her ear. A delicious, scintillating caress.

But not a kiss.

He was whispering to her.

'Something has come up. Follow my lead.' Louder, for the benefit of the others, he said, 'Mother, ladies, our apologies. An urgent matter needs our attention and we must go.'

Okay. It was part of the act.

'Can I leave you to gather everything Miss Marchant will need for her stay? You have her sizes?' The assistants nodded vigorously. 'And please send a selection of everything you think appropriate.' He turned to gaze adoringly at her. 'Don't stint.'

As if they would. They were staring at him as if he were a god come down to earth, imagining all their commission.

His long fingers curled through hers, warm, strong and wonderfully comforting—drat the man. And then he set off for the private lift they'd arrived in.

Focus, Lily.

He'd said something had come up. Perhaps there was news on Nate?

The lift doors closed. 'What's so...?' Where had that husky note come from? She tried again. 'What's so urgent that we needed to leave?'

'This.' He gathered her close and pressed his mouth to hers.

She should have pushed him away—there was no audience here—but his mouth slanted over hers in a kiss so tantalisingly gentle she leant in. He began a delicate exploration of her jaw, her throat, and found a tender spot beneath her ear, teasing it with a slow swirl of his tongue.

Her fingers sank into his biceps.

When he nudged a thigh between her legs she instinctively rubbed against it, seeking contact where she needed it most.

'Come,' he said.

Yes, oh, yes...

Wait...no. What?

He was walking. He meant her to go with him. He was leaving the lift.

She teetered in her new heels and he drew her protectively against his side. Together, eyes locked, they crossed the foyer and stepped outside into the now familiar intense heat and something else—something new.

With the dazzle of sunshine came camera flashes. A cacophony of voices. Crowding figures.

'Your Highness? Sir? When's the wedding?'

'Lily? Has he bought you a ring yet? When did you know it was love?'

She blinked as the lights exploded, over and over. With a jolt she realised he'd walked them into a press pack—and he knew enough about those for it not to be an accident.

Continue reading
DESERT PRINCE'S DEFIANT BRIDE
Julieanne Howells

Available next month
www.millsandboon.co.uk

LET'S TALK
Romance

For exclusive extracts, competitions
and special offers, find us online:

f facebook.com/millsandboon

🐦 @MillsandBoon

📷 @MillsandBoonUK

Get in touch on 01413 063232

For all the latest titles coming soon, visit
millsandboon.co.uk/nextmonth

MILLS & BOON
Desire

Indulge in secrets and scandal, intense drama and plenty of sizzling hot action with powerful and passionate heroes who have it all: wealth, status, good looks…everything but the right woman.